WHAT READERS ARE SAYING ABOUT KAREN KINGSBURY'S BOOKS

Karen's book *Oceans Apart* changed my life. She has an amazing gift of bringing a reader into her stories. I can only pray she never stops writing.

Susan L.

Everyone should have the opportunity to read or listen to a book by Karen Kingsbury. It should be in the *Bill of Rights*.

Rachel S.

I want to thank Karen Kingsbury for what she is doing with the power of her storytelling—touching hearts like mine and letting God use her to change the world for Him.

Brittney N.

Karen Kingsbury's books are filled with the unshakable, remarkable, miraculous fact that God's grace is greater than our suffering. There are no words for Ms. Kingsbury's writing.

Wendie K.

Because I loaned these books to my mother, she BECAME a Christian! Thank you for a richer life here and in heaven!

Jennifer E.

When I read my first Karen Kingsbury book, I couldn't stop.... I read thirteen more in one summer!

Jamie B.

I have never read anything so uplifting and entertaining. I'm shocked as I read each new release because it's always better than the last one.

Bonnie S.

I am unable to put your books down, and I plan to read many more of them. What a wonderful spiritual message I find in each one!

Rhonda T.

I love the way Karen Kingsbury writes, and the topics she chooses to write about! Thank you so much for sharing your talent with us, your readers!

Barbara S.

My husband is equally hooked on your books. It is a family affair for us now! Can't wait for the next one.

Angie

I can't even begin to tell you what your books mean to me.... Thank you for your wonderful books and the way they touch my life again and again.

Martje L.

Every time our school buys your next new book, everybody goes crazy trying to read it first!

Roxanne

Recently I made an effort to find GOOD Christian writers, and I've hit the jackpot with Karen Kingsbury!

Linda

When Karen Kingsbury calls her books "Life-Changing Fiction™," she's merely telling the unvarnished truth. I'm still sorting through the changes in my life that have come from reading just a few of her books!

Robert M.

I must admit that I wish I was a much slower reader ... or you were a much faster writer. Either way, I can't seem to get enough of Karen Kingsbury's books!

Jillian B.

I was offered $50 one time in the airport for the fourth book in the Redemption Series. The lady's husband just couldn't understand why I wasn't interested in selling it. Through sharing Karen's books with my friends, many have decided that contemporary Christian fiction is the next best thing to the Bible. Thank you so much, Karen. It is truly a God-thing that you write the way you do.

Sue Ellen H.

Karen Kingsbury's books have made me see things in ways that I had never thought about before. I have to force myself to put them down and come up for air!

Tabitha H.

I have read many of Karen's books and I cry with every one. I feel like I actually know the people in the story, and my heart goes out to all of them when something happens!

Kathy N.

Wow, what an amazing author Karen Kingsbury is! Her stories are so heart-wrenching ... I can't wait until the next book comes out.... Karen, please don't ever lay your pen down.

Nancy T.

Karen Kingsbury's words leap off the page.... I just finished a new series last night and once again she has touched me beyond compare!

Kendra S.

Other Life-Changing Fiction™ by Karen Kingsbury

9/11 Series
  One Tuesday Morning
  Beyond Tuesday Morning
  Every Now and Then

Lost Love Series
  Even Now
  Ever After

Above the Line Series
  Above the Line: Take One
  Above the Line: Take Two
  Above the Line: Take Three
  Above the Line: Take Four

Stand-Alone Titles
  Oceans Apart
  Between Sundays
  This Side of Heaven
  When Joy Came to Stay
  On Every Side
  Divine
  Like Dandelion Dust
  Where Yesterday Lives
  Shades of Blue
  Unlocked

Redemption Series
  Redemption
  Remember
  Return
  Rejoice
  Reunion

Firstborn Series
  Fame
  Forgiven
  Found
  Family
  Forever

Sunrise Series
  Sunrise
  Summer
  Someday
  Sunset

Red Glove Series
  Gideon's Gift
  Maggie's Miracle
  Sarah's Song
  Hannah's Hope

Forever Faithful Series
  Waiting for Morning
  Moment of Weakness
  Halfway to Forever

Women of Faith Fiction Series
  A Time to Dance
  A Time to Embrace

Cody Gunner Series
  A Thousand Tomorrows
  Just Beyond the Clouds
  This Side of Heaven

Children's Titles
  Let Me Hold You Longer
  Let's Go on a Mommy Date
  We Believe in Christmas
  Let's Have a Daddy Day
  The Princess and the Three Knights
  Go Ahead and Dream (Spring 2011)
  Far Flutterby (Fall 2011)

Miracle Collections
  A Treasury of Christmas Miracles
  A Treasury of Miracles for Women
  A Treasury of Miracles for Teens
  A Treasury of Miracles for Friends
  A Treasury of Adoption Miracles
  Miracles — a Devotional

Gift Books
  Stay Close Little Girl
  Be Safe Little Boy
  Forever Young: Ten Gifts of Faith
    for the Graduate

KAREN KINGSBURY

NEW YORK TIMES
BESTSELLING AUTHOR

Leaving

BAILEY FLANIGAN
SERIES

BOOK ONE

ZONDERVAN®

ZONDERVAN.com/
AUTHORTRACKER
follow your favorite authors

ZONDERVAN

Leaving
Copyright © 2011 by Karen Kingsbury

This title is also available as a Zondervan ebook.
Visit www.zondervan.com/ebooks.

This title is also available in a Zondervan audio edition.
Visit www.zondervan.fm.

Requests for information should be addressed to:

Zondervan, *Grand Rapids, Michigan* 49530

ISBN 978-0-310-26699-0

Published in association with the literary agency of Alive Communications, Inc., 7680 Goddard Street, Suite 200, Colorado Springs, CO 80920. www.alivecommunications.com

This novel is a work of fiction. Any references to real people, events, institutions or locales are intended only to give a sense of reality and authenticity, and are used fictitiously. All other names, characters and places, and all dialogue and incidents portrayed in this book, are the product of the author's imagination.

Cover photography: Bill Tucker Studios, iStockphoto®, Shutterstock®
Interior design: Beth Shagene

Printed in the United States of America

11 12 13 14 15 16 /DCI/ 21 20 19 18 17 16 15 14 13 12 11 10 9 8 7 6 5 4 3 2 1

DEDICATION

To Donald, my Prince Charming ...

I love that for now we can still see spring as the end of a school year. Summer lies ahead of us, and everything wonderful about the changing seasons is upon us. You and the boys are ready for the off-season, ready to work hard at football camp and dream about the fall ahead. The kids are itching for summer vacation, but here's the thing: We only have so many school years left, only so many years when summer vacation actually applies to our family. And how can that be, when just yesterday we were bringing Kelsey home? I remember the nurse asking if we knew how to buckle her seat belt into the backseat, and you and I looked at each other. It was sort of a "Yikes! Here we go!" look, because where was the manual? The Bible ... that was the only manual then, and it's the only one now. God walked us through the baby stage and the walking stage, He walked us through the off-to-school stage and now, somehow, He'll walk us through the years of letting go. The quiet days lie ahead, but for now, my love, hold my hand and let's run the journey together. You and our boys, making memories together. Isn't this what we always dreamed of? I love sitting back this time and letting you and God figure it out. Hard to believe that, as you read this, our twenty-third anniversary is almost upon us. I look at you and still see the blond, blue-eyed guy who would ride his bike to my house and read the Bible with me before a movie date. You stuck with me back then and you stand by me now — when I need you more than ever. I love you, my husband, my best friend, my Prince Charming. Stay with me, by my side, and let's watch our children take wing. Always and always ... the ride is breathtakingly beautiful. I pray it lasts far into our twilight years. Until then I'll enjoy not always knowing where I end and you begin. I love you always and forever.

To Kelsey, my precious daughter ...

How is it possible that you are twenty-one, my precious little girl? I still see you dancing in circles around your daddy, and carefully applying lipstick from a purse you got for Christmas when you were four. I remember listening to songs about letting kids grow up and watching them leave home and thinking, "Dear God, I'll never make it ..." But there was some comfort back then, because your childhood spread before us like one long endless summer of laughter and loving and days that seemed like they'd last forever. But this fall every line of every leaving song will come rushing back as we take you to college in Southern California. Sometimes when I think about the season ahead I struggle to draw a full breath. These times will redefine for me what missing someone really means. But you, sweet girl, were created to perform for Jesus. All through your childhood you would find a stage and hold your chin high, and you'd sing to whoever was listening. Well, sweetheart, more people are listening now. I'm so proud of you and all you've become ... all you stand for. Every prayer we prayed for you, God has answered. You have stood firm, holding tight to God's truth and His promises, and I know the answers will become more clear with each passing year. Remember that God walks every step of this life with us, and for those who love Him, the best is always yet to be. This fall we will watch you take wing, having worked hard to reach this point in your education. We believe in you, sweetheart, and we will be cheering for you every day. No matter where this year takes you, you'll never really leave our family. You'll always be our little girl, Kelsey. And you'll always be part of this family. Forever and ever. I'm so proud of the strength you've found. You are beautiful inside and out, and I am more convinced than ever that God has great, wonderful plans for you. Take your talents and go find your platform for Him! In the meantime you'll be in my heart every moment. And we'll leave the porch light on. I love you, sweetheart.

To Tyler, my lasting song . . .

My heart skips a beat when I think about you being a senior this year. I have thought about this time even as far back as you've been a part of our lives, and always it seemed so far away. Even last year, I couldn't really imagine you as a senior. But here we are, right? Graduation is just ten weeks away. This is where the Ferris wheel slows down; this is where you get off and make your way down the path, following God to the next season in your life. But here's the amazing part: We will always have a front-row seat! You have a single on the radio now. "Just Beyond the Clouds" is a favorite for many people, and there will be more to come. God is working, Ty, and the dreams you've had for the past couple years are coming true. I know God has a future in music for you, because I've seen your passion in singing and writing for Him. I love how the music is in you, Ty, and how you seem complete when you are caught up in the process of creating. I sometimes think about your Papa, and how proud he would be to watch the young man you've become. I still see him there in his favorite chair, the one by the fireplace, closest to the piano. He couldn't listen to you play and sing without getting tears in his eyes, and I can't either. So even though I'm sad your senior year is almost over, I'm excited too. Because this is the time of your life you've been waiting for. The world is your stage, Ty! Go stop the world for Jesus, and let your very bright light touch the lives of everyone who needs it. Thank you for the hours of joy you bring our family, and as you head into a year of lasts, I promise to stop and listen a little longer when I hear you singing. Your dad and I are proud of you, Ty. We're proud of your talent and your compassion for people and your place in our family. However your dreams unfold, we'll be in the front row to watch them happen. Hold on to Jesus, son. I love you.

To Sean, my happy sunshine ...

Some years don't turn out like we planned, and this year that was all too true for you, sweet Sean. A blown out knee the third game of the football season, which led to surgery and a time of healing and rehab. You never let me see you down, never complained. But my heart broke at the pain you went through ... and how you had to miss out on basketball season because your injury was that bad. But here's what God has taught me through this. Sometimes His greatest gift happens in the healing — when we are quiet enough to hear Him, quiet enough to listen to His leading. I have watched you spend hours shooting free throws, hours dribbling the basketball, and playing the drums so that when the school gathers for worship every Monday, you're keeping the beat. Who would have thought so much good could've come from something so painful? But then, isn't that the lesson of the cross? Jesus loves you, Sean. Even more than we do. He promises that with Him, all things work to the good. And somewhere down the road I believe you'll look back at this time and see it as a turning point. A time when God was very close to you, indeed. You still need to remind yourself of the truth. You can do everything through Christ who gives you strength. And you can, Sean. You proved that this year by suffering adversity and, in His strength, rising to the challenge. You remain a bright sunbeam, bringing warmth to everyone around you. And now you are an example of an all-star faith as well. I'm proud of you, Sean. I love you so much. I pray God will use your dependence on Him to always make a difference in the lives around you. You're a precious gift, son. Keep smiling and keep seeking God's best for your life.

To Josh, my tenderhearted perfectionist ...

You continue to amaze the opposition whatever sport you play, and for that I will always be proud of you, Josh. You train and play and lead with your whole heart. I don't know which records will fall or how many people will one day know of your feats on the field, but I do know this: It's so much more important that you have grown just as much in your faith. When God gives us talents, we must always remember where they come from. Who they come from. You have done this, dear son, and now you are ready to take on the world. Well, maybe not quite yet. But you're ready to take on the off-season, and give God the glory along the way. I remember when we first got word that your birthmother in Haiti had survived the terrible earthquake, after all. You only smiled and nodded. "I know," you said. "You do?" I was confused. None of us had known how she had fared for months after the quake. "I know she's okay — either way. In heaven or here. Because I prayed for her." Yes, Josh, you may laugh a lot and tease a lot, but we know your heart, and we are so proud of what we see. We have no doubt that someday we'll see your name in headlines and that — if God allows it — you'll play sports for a college team. You're that good, and everyone around you says so. Now flashback to that single moment in a broken-down Haitian orphanage. There I was meeting Sean and EJ for the first time when you walked up. You reached up with your small fingers, brushed back my bangs, and said, "Hi, Mommy. I love you." It might've taken six months of paperwork, but I knew as I heard those words that you belonged with us. The picture becomes clearer all the time. Keep being a leader on the field and off. One day people will say, "Hmmm. Karen Kingsbury? Isn't she Josh's mom?" I can't wait.

You have an unlimited future, son, and I'll forever be cheering on the sidelines. Keep God first in your life. I love you always.

To EJ, my chosen one ...

EJ, my jokester, you are finishing your first year in high school! I can't believe how fast time has flown for you and for us. The journey started a decade ago when we saw one little face on an internet photolisting of kids up for adoption. That face was yours, but the blessing of the journey has been ours. God has brought you so far, EJ, and now you stand on the brink of becoming everything He has planned for you to become. At our Christian school you have found friends, and a deeper faith and a fire for pursuing the talents God has given you. All the things we have prayed for you! As you start high school, you are one of our top students, and we couldn't be more proud of you, EJ. But even beyond your grades and your natural way of leading your peers in the right path, we are blessed to have you in our family for so many reasons. You are wonderful with our pets — always the first to feed them and pet them and look out for them — and you are a willing worker when it comes to chores. Besides all that you make us laugh — oftentimes right out loud. I've always believed that getting through life's little difficulties and challenges requires a lot of laughter, and I thank you for bringing that to our home. You're a wonderful boy, son. A child with such potential. I'm amazed because you're so talented in so many ways, but all of them pale in comparison to your desire to truly live for the Lord. I'm praying you'll have a strong passion to use your gifts for God as you enter high school in the fall. Because, EJ, God has great plans for you, and we want to be the first to congratulate you as you work to discover those. Thanks for your giving heart, EJ. I love you so.

To Austin, my miracle boy . . .

Seventh grade, and already you look like a tenth grader! I remember this past year when you would walk up to me on your tiptoes and look me in the eyes. "It happened, Mom! I'm taller than you!" You'd celebrate a little only to realize that I was in bare feet and you were in tennis shoes. "Not quite," I'd tell you. "You're still shorter than me." But now that is no longer true. You don't walk up on your tiptoes anymore because you don't have to. God has graced you with tremendous size and strength, Austin. I look at you and I see a young Timmy Tebow, a kid with an ocean of determination and leadership ability, a young man who is the first to thank his coach, the first to shake the hand of the ref, and the last one to leave the classroom because you're so busy cleaning up and expressing your gratitude to your teacher. Sure you still struggle in a few areas, and sometimes your competitive drive can get you in trouble with your brothers. But truly, Austin, there isn't a thing you can't do as long as you keep God first. I believe you have the chance to go all the way with your dream of playing sports, and I'm grateful to have a front row seat. Play hard, don't ever give up, and always remember where you came from. I know I do. I remember that hospital room when you were three weeks old and the surgeon was giving us a few minutes to say goodbye. Not every infant who goes in for emergency heart surgery comes back out again. But even then, through our tears, we were certain we'd see you somewhere — here or there. The fact that God has blessed us with the here and now is proof that He has amazing plans for you. How great that you are seizing them with everything inside you, with every breath. Keep on, precious son. We are here for you, praying for you, cheering for you. No one believes in you more than we do. I've said it before, and it's true. Heaven has windows, and I'm convinced Papa's still cheering for you, son. Especially this season. As you soar toward your teenage years, please don't forget that or him. You're my youngest, my last, Austin. I'm holding on to every moment, for sure. Thanks for giving me so many wonderful reasons to treasure today. I thank God for you, for the miracle of your life. I love you, Austin.

And to God Almighty, the Author of Life, who has — for now — blessed me with these.

ACKNOWLEDGMENTS

No book comes together without a great and talented team of people making it happen. For that reason, a special thanks to my friends at Zondervan who combined efforts with a number of people who were passionate about Life-Changing Fiction™ to make *Leaving* all it could be. A special thanks to Moe Girkins, whose commitment to excellence at Zondervan is unparalleled, and to Steve Sammons, who may be one of the only execs in publishing who actually gets the big picture of what we're doing for the Kingdom. Also, of course, a special thanks to my dedicated editor, Sue Brower, and to Don Gates and Alicia Mey, my marketing team. Thanks also to the creative staff and to the sales force at Zondervan who worked tirelessly to put this book in your hands.

Also, thanks to my amazing agent, Rick Christian, president of Alive Communications. Rick, you've always believed only the best for me. When we talk about the highest possible goals, you see them as doable, reachable. You are a brilliant manager of my career, and I thank God for you. But even with all you do for my ministry of writing, I am doubly grateful for your encouragement and prayers. Every time I finish a book, you send me a letter that deserves to be framed, and when something big happens, yours is the first call I receive. Thank you for that. But even more, the fact that you and Debbie are praying for me and my family keeps me confident every morning that God will continue to breathe life into the stories in my heart. Thank you for being so much more than a brilliant agent.

A special thank you to my husband, who puts up with me on deadline and doesn't mind driving through Taco Bell after a football game if I've been editing all day. This wild ride wouldn't be possible without you, Donald. Your love keeps me writing; your prayers keep me believing that God has a plan in this ministry of Life-Changing Fiction™. And thanks for the hours you put in working with the guestbook entries on my website. It's a full-time job, and I am grateful for your concern for my reader friends. I look forward to that time every day when you read through them, sharing them with me, and releasing them to the public, lifting up the prayer requests. Thank you, honey, and thanks to all my kids, who pull together, bring me iced green tea, and understand my sometimes crazy schedule. I love that you know you're still first, before any deadline.

Thank you also to my mom, Anne Kingsbury, and to my sisters, Tricia and Sue. Mom, you are amazing as my assistant — working day and night sorting through the mail from my readers. I appreciate you more than you'll ever know. Traveling with you these past years for Extraordinary Women and Women of Joy events has given us times together we will always treasure.

Tricia, you are the best executive assistant I could ever hope to have. I appreciate your loyalty and honesty, the way you include me in every decision and the daily exciting website changes. My site has been a different place since you stepped in, and the hits have grown a hundredfold. Along the way, the readers have so much more to help them in their faith, so much more than a story. Please know that I pray for God's blessings on you always, for your dedication to helping me in this season of writing, and for your wonderful son, Andrew. And aren't we having such a good time too? God works all things to the good!

Sue, I believe you should've been a counselor! From your home far from mine, you get batches of reader letters every day, and you diligently answer them using God's wisdom and His Word. When readers get a response from "Karen's sister Susan," I hope they know how carefully you've prayed for them and for the responses you give. Thank you for truly loving what you do, Sue. You're gifted with people, and I'm blessed to have you aboard.

And to Randy Graves, a very special thank you, as well. Randy, you and your family have been friends to our family for more than a decade, and now as my business manager and the executive director of my One Chance Foundation, you are an integral part of all we do. What a blessing to call you my friend and coworker. I pray that God always allows us to continue working together this way.

Thanks also to Olga Kalachik, my office assistant, who helps organize my supplies and storage areas, and who prepares our home for the marketing events and research gatherings that take place here on a regular basis. I appreciate all you're doing to make sure I have time to write. You're wonderful, Olga, and I pray God continues to bless you and your precious family.

I also want to thank my friends at Premier, Roy Morgan and the team, and my friends at Women of Joy and Extraordinary Women. Thanks also to the artists I sometimes tour with — Jeremy Camp, Mandisa, Britt Nicole, Newsong, Charles Billingsly, and Matthew West. Your music inspires not only me but my characters. How wonderful to be a part of what God is doing through all of you. Thank you for including me in your family on the road.

Thanks also to my forever friends and family, the ones who have been there and continue to be there. Your love has been a tangible source of comfort, pulling us through the tough times and making us know how very blessed we are to have you in our lives.

And the greatest thanks to God: You put a story in my heart, but you have a million other hearts in mind — something I could never do. I'm grateful to be a small part of what you're doing! The gift is yours. I pray I might use it for years to come in a way that will bring you honor and glory.

Forever in Fiction®

For a number of years now, I've had the privilege of offering Forever in Fiction®*as an auction item at fund-raisers across the country. So many of my more recent books have had Forever in Fiction characters that I hear from you reader friends how you look forward to this part of my novels, reading this section to see which characters in the coming pages are actually inspired by real-life people, and learning a little about their real stories. Then you enjoy looking for them in the coming pages, knowing with a smile how it must feel to their families, seeing their names Forever in Fiction.

In *Leaving* I bring you two very special Forever in Fiction characters. The first is Kassie Garman, a darling three-year-old who lost her battle with leukemia a few years back. Kassie was a precious sweetheart, loved by all who knew her — especially her grandparents, Ivan and Charmaine Garman — who won Forever in Fiction at the Lams Lititz Area Mennonite School auction.

During her brief life Kassie loved to play with her two older brothers, one of whom was a perfect match for a bone marrow transplant, which was performed five months before her death. She loved sucking her thumb and cuddling with her family and looking at picture books. Kassie lived with a mild form of Down Syndrome, so communication was usually done through her own form of sign language. But her favorite way to convey her feelings was simply with a smile. When Kassie smiled, everyone felt loved. She had that special sort of gift, a gift that today has made heaven a little brighter as a result.

*Forever in Fiction is a registered trademark owned by Karen Kingsbury.

I chose to keep Kassie's place in *Leaving* very much like her place in life. In the pages of this book, she plays the role of a sick girl who gives one of the main characters greater purpose in life. Because that's how Kassie was in real life, bringing purpose and meaning to the lives of everyone who loved her.

Ivan and Charmaine, it is my prayer that you will smile when you see Kassie honored in the pages of *Leaving* and that you will treasure this book, where she will live on, Forever in Fiction.

My second character Forever in Fiction is Roberta Johnson, a mother of five and a leukemia survivor. Roberta was placed Forever in Fiction by her friend, Jennifer Grieve, who won this chance at the St. Joseph's Catholic School auction. Roberta loves God and her family, and is known by her friends for her outgoing, positive attitude and her strong ability to live as an example for others around her.

Roberta is the mother of six children, including one she gave up for adoption when she was twenty-three. She loves reading and teaching the Bible, and has found ways to bring Scripture to life by doing mission work in Chimbote, Peru. Twice she has hosted exchange students from Mexico. She volunteers her time at homeless shelters and encourages her adult children to do the same.

I chose to make Roberta the neighbor of Jenny Flanigan, a friend who has said goodbye to young adult children, and who can understand the season of life Jenny is entering. Roberta, I pray that you feel honored by your placement in *Leaving*, and the way that your friend Jennifer chose to put you Forever in Fiction. Keep shining for Jesus!

In addition, here are the names of reader friends who helped raise money for a field campaign at King's Way Christian High School in Washington State. These winners each donated $100 for the privilege of having themselves or someone they love recognized here, Forever in Fiction:

Maggie Westover for Kylie Young
Terree Marvin for Karen Thommen
Tiffany Hargreaves for Irene Lenz
Liz McLean for Laurie Copelin
Rhonda Bradberry for Sherri Rash
Melissa Olson for Darin Olson
Monica Gere
Steve Tingwall for Virginia Tingwall
Carolyn Masek for Jaina Masek
Lamont Bourque for Haley June Bourque
Sheilah Hanes for Joyce Reneman
Sheilah Hanes
Marcia Ridenour for Bill Dillman
Rick Lin for Peggy Lin
Julie Sines
Jennifer Carlsen
Jennifer Carlsen for Debbie Carlsen
Jennifer Carlsen for Becky Boland
Jan Marie Newby
Edward Arrington, Jr., for Brenda E. Arrington
Susan S. Wolf
Susan Craver
Mindy Joy Goff
Barb Latt
Joel Young for LeahAnn Young
Lori Erickson for Kristi Erickson
Diane K. Weimer for Ferreter Weimer
Matasha Otte
Donna L. Wiles for Bear Wiles
Robin Tommerup
Melissa Jill Shields for Madison Allen

The winner of this auction is Marcia Ridenour, whose Forever in Fiction package will play out in one of the future Bailey Flanigan Series books.

For those of you who are not familiar with Forever in Fiction, it is my way of involving you, the readers, in my stories, while raising money for charities. The winning bidder of a Forever in Fiction package has the right to have his or her name or the name of a friend or family member written into one of my novels. In this way this person (or the loved one he or she chooses) will be Forever in Fiction. To date, Forever in Fiction has raised more than $200,000 at charity auctions. Obviously, I am only able to donate a limited number of these each year. For that reason I have set a fairly high minimum bid on this package so the maximum funds are raised for charities. All money goes to the charity events.

One

GOODBYES WERE ONE OF THE HARDEST THINGS ABOUT LIFE ... one way or another people were always leaving. Always moving on. That was the point the pastor was making, and Bailey Flanigan blinked back tears as she shifted in the pew beside her family. *Like Cody Coleman*, she told herself. *Always leaving.*

"Life changes. People come and go, and seasons never last." Pastor Mark Atteberry's voice rang with passionate emotion. "Nothing stays the same. We can count on that. Good times come and go ... finances are ever changing ... our health will eventually fail us. And through death or decision, everyone we know will someday leave us." He paused, his eyes searching the congregation. "All except for Jesus Christ. Jesus will never leave you nor forsake you. And because of that we have the strength to love with all our hearts ... even unaware of what tomorrow brings." He smiled. "That's what I want you to take away from today's service. Jesus stays."

Pastor Mark asked them to turn their Bibles to the book of Deuteronomy. Bailey did as she was told, but the rest of the sermon she struggled to stay focused. Cody hadn't talked to her since that day on her parents' porch, the day he tried to convince her it was finally and absolutely time to move on. Now, two months later, the pain and silence of the passing time was just about killing her.

When the hour was almost over, Bailey's mom, Jenny, turned

to her. "Powerful message." Her voice was barely a whisper, only loud enough for Bailey.

Bailey nodded and managed a slight smile. She'd tell her mom later how much her heart hurt, how Pastor Mark's talk about goodbyes stirred up all the missing she'd ever felt for Cody. Never mind the days when she seemed over him, when she didn't look for a text every hour or catch the phone ringing at night and hope it was him. Today, even with her mom and dad and five brothers seated along the pew beside her, there was no way around her feelings.

She missed Cody with every aching breath.

The service ended with a song Bailey loved — a Chris Tomlin song called "Our God" that always stirred her love for the Lord and her belief in His promises. She stood next to her mom and glanced down the row at her family. How great that they could be here together, worshipping and praising God, and sharing everything they believed. How amazing to celebrate Sundays with them always. She smiled, ignoring the sting of fresh tears in her eyes. Wasn't that the point Pastor Mark was making? This picture of the Flanigan family wouldn't last either. They were all growing up. And some Sunday not far down the road they'd be spread out to other churches, other places where they would begin their own lives.

Because only Jesus stayed.

But God in all His goodness still allowed moments like this, and no matter how far they might someday be from each other, they would hold tight to the memory of this: what it felt like to be a family who loved each other deeply and cared for the people around the dining room table like they were each other's best friends. The sort of family other people only dreamed about.

Bailey closed her eyes and let the music fill her soul. "Our God is greater ... our God is stronger ... God you are higher than any other ..."

The beauty of the moment mixed with the sweet sadness of losing Cody, of not knowing where he was or what he was doing. The idea seemed outrageous, really. He hadn't felt this far away when he was fighting in Iraq. Now he was only an hour away in Indianapolis, but it seemed like he'd fallen off the planet. At least that was where she assumed he was — the place he'd been the last time they saw each other.

Pastor Mark dismissed them, and Bailey felt her mother give her a side hug. "You were thinking about him." She pressed her cheek against Bailey's.

Bailey had nothing to hide where her mom was concerned. She looked straight at her. "How could I not?"

"We'll talk later."

"Okay." Bailey returned the hug and they moved into the aisle with the rest of the family. The knowing in her mother's eyes made Bailey grateful. Bailey kept no secrets from her mom and, because of that, they would always be close.

Anyway, the conversation would have to come later. Ashley Baxter Blake and her husband, Landon, had invited them over for dinner, which meant a house full of people. It was a Baxter family tradition, and at least once a month the Baxters invited Bailey's family too. The more people the better — that was Ashley's theory. She and Landon bought the old farmhouse from John Baxter, Ashley's father. Bailey was sure she saw a wistfulness in John's eyes whenever they gathered for dinner. A longing for days gone by maybe. Days that hadn't lasted any more than the ones now would last for the Flanigan family.

Bailey couldn't imagine raising a family for decades in a house and then coming back only as a visitor. But it was better than having strangers live in the place. Especially with all the memories that still lived between the walls and windows.

On the drive to the Baxter house, Bailey caught herself more aware than usual that even this — all eight of them traveling somewhere after church — wouldn't last. She was almost twenty-one, after all, in her third year at Indiana University. She leaned against the car door and listened to her brothers' conversations around her. Connor was seventeen and closest to Bailey in age. This was his junior year, and he was about to begin his final football season as starting quarterback — throwing for more than 200 yards a game, the way Cody had taught him.

Connor was class president and debating themes for the Spring Fling dance — an annual costume event at Clear Creek High. "I'm thinking 'Meant to Be.'" Connor glanced back at his brothers Shawn and Justin — both sophomores — and BJ, a freshman. "I mean, I kinda like it. What do you think? 'Meant to Be.'"

"Meant to be what?" Justin frowned.

In the seat beside Bailey, the youngest Flanigan boy — tow-headed twelve-year-old Ricky — giggled. "Like, you come as Batman, but you tell everyone you *meant to be* Robin?"

A round of laughter filled the Suburban. Bailey chuckled to herself and gave Connor a helpless look. The younger boys had a point.

Connor flashed a patient, crooked grin. "Not like that." He waited until he had their attention again. "Meant to be, like Batman and Cat Woman — two characters who were meant to be together."

"Or maybe just sort of 'Meant to *Bee*.'" Ricky let loose another few delightful bouts of laughter. "Like a bumblebee. Then everyone could dress in yellow and black."

"Yeah, or maybe Meant to *B*." Shawn's laugh was always louder than the others. "You know ... the letter *B*. That way everyone could dress as something that started with a *B*."

"Okay ... you're all comedians." Connor gave a mock surrender. "I'll ask the leadership class."

From the front passenger seat, their mom looked over her shoulder. "I like it." Her smile was kind, her eyes thoughtful. "A cowboy and a cowgirl ... a doctor and a nurse ... that sort of thing."

"Yeah, only if Justin goes with Kayla, he'll have to be the nurse." Shawn was working to keep his laughter down, but he was losing the battle. "Because she's a whiz kid at science. She wants to be a surgeon."

The conversation soothed the rough edges of Bailey's soul, helping her find perspective after an hour of being flooded with memories of Cody. This was her reality now. And though Pastor Mark was right — this season wouldn't last — for now it was exactly where she wanted to be.

"Have you heard from Brandon?" Her dad caught Bailey's attention in the rearview mirror. "Since they pulled the movie?"

"He texted me yesterday." The memory warmed her heart. "He's so different from the guy he used to be. His faith means everything to him."

"And the media knows it." He looked happy about the fact. "I'm proud of that young man. Very proud."

Bailey's mom angled herself so she could see Bailey. "His manager knows it, too. That's why they shelved the movie, I'm sure."

"Of course ... I agree, definitely."

The boys still chattered about the upcoming dance, but the family could easily hold more than one conversation at a time. Bailey slid forward so her parents could hear her. "Brandon knows that's the reason. Everyone loved us in *Unlocked*, but his manager doesn't want Brandon to seem soft to the Hollywood crowd."

"Casting him in a movie about a NASCAR driver will definitely keep that from happening." Her dad raised his brow. "And Brandon's doing his own stunts, is that true?"

"It is." Bailey wasn't happy about that part. "I'm still trying to talk him out of it."

"Next time you two chat, tell him we said hi." Her dad kept his eyes on the road. "I pray for him every day." He caught her eye one more time. "The same way I pray for Cody." He hesitated. "Which reminds me ... Matt Keagan asked about you the other day. He figured out you were my daughter about a week after the season ended. Every time he stops in the weight room he doesn't let up."

Bailey laughed under her breath. "That's nice dad." She shared a look with her mom. "Matt Keagan has a million girls in love with him. I'll pass."

"He is cute, though." Her mom's eyes twinkled — proof that she was only having fun.

"Of course he's cute." Bailey shook her head, enjoying the lighthearted silliness of the discussion. "He's the strongest Christian in sports, he wears a wristband with Philippians 4:13 on it, and he takes mission trips to Ethiopia whenever he has a spare weekend. He's perfect." She laughed, and the feeling lifted her heart. "I heard he's dating the daughter of a pastor in South Africa."

"Last week everyone on Facebook and Twitter said Matt's hanging out with a finalist from *Dancing with the Stars*."

"Exactly." Bailey laughed. An icon like Matt Keagan? The line of girls would be longer than ten football fields. "I'm not interested."

The three of them fell quiet again, leaving just the boys' conversation the rest of the way to the Baxter house. Bailey stared out the window. The countryside in Bloomington, Indiana, the rolling snow-covered hills, and the crisp, blue sky that spread out forever around them spoke peace to her soul. February brought a mix of weather, but always snow clung to the ground somewhere. This year more than most.

Bailey thought about her life and the guys God had brought across her path. The last year was so crazy amazing she almost felt like the whole thing had happened to someone else. Brandon Paul — the nation's most popular young actor — had singled her out to star in his blockbuster movie *Unlocked*. The film was set to release in April, but it was still being edited. Bailey had never worked harder, and in the end she was satisfied with her performance.

But Bailey's was nothing to Brandon's. He played a teenager whose beautiful soul was locked in a prison of autism. She played his friend, the girl who believed she could draw him out and find a way for God to work a miracle in his life. She couldn't wait to see what critics would say about the movie, about Brandon's stunning portrayal of Holden Harris. The story was riveting — just like the bestselling novel by the same name.

Brandon had done the story justice, for sure. But, along the way, God had given him more than a key performance for his resume. During the shoot Bailey had talked to Brandon about the Lord, and the Bible, and God's plan for him. Last New Year's Eve Brandon came to the Flanigan house and had prayed to ask Jesus into his heart. Later that night, Bailey's dad even baptized Brandon in their Jacuzzi.

Never mind that Brandon had a crush on Bailey. She didn't see him that way — not with his past and the throngs of girls screaming his name. Brandon was a friend, nothing more. But in the wake of filming *Unlocked*, talk had immediately turned to the two of them starring in a love story.

"The chemistry between you is too strong to stop with *Unlocked*," the producer told them. He wanted to film this spring. But in late January the movie was shelved so Brandon could focus on a NASCAR story about a guy living fast and dangerously, a guy in conflict with his racecar driver father. The story was called *Chasing Sunsets*, and Brandon had already signed on to play the part.

Bailey had been offered roles in other films, but nothing she would take. Agents and producers in Hollywood didn't understand. She didn't want to move to LA and spend her days auditioning. She was two years from finishing her theater degree at IU. After that, she still dreamed about performing on Broadway in New York City. But no matter where she did or didn't act in the future her friendship with Brandon Paul would remain — she was sure of that.

She blinked, and lifted her eyes to the sky over Bloomington. The boys were talking about basketball, how Justin would be the fastest guard in the league.

"Cody Coleman was the fastest guy ever at Clear Creek High — football or hoops," Ricky made the pronouncement proudly. "But Justin, you never know ... maybe you'll be faster."

Cody Coleman. The boys' voices faded as Bailey pictured Cody and the way he'd looked the last time they saw each other. She had just wrapped up the shoot with Brandon, and Cody seemed distracted. Different. Maybe the movie had something to do with his distance. Or maybe he pulled away because of Bailey's closeness with Brandon Paul. A quiet sigh slipped from her throat.

Brandon could never be Cody Coleman.

She heard the slightest buzzing sound from her purse and realized she still had her phone on mute from church. She dug around, but by the time she found it the call was gone. She pressed a button at the top of the phone and a number flashed across the screen — one she didn't recognize. The area code was 212. New York City.

Strange, she thought. Tim Reed was the only person she knew living in New York. But she had his number programmed into her contacts, so unless he used a different phone, the call couldn't be from him. She was still staring at the number when her phone flashed that a voicemail had come in. At the same time, her dad pulled into the Baxters' driveway. The place looked beautiful, surrounded by snow and barren trees. A thin ribbon of smoke came from the chimney, and already six cars packed the area adjacent to the garage.

"I can smell the barbecue sauce from here." Ricky took a long whiff as they stepped out of the SUV. "Best barbecue in Bloomington." He grinned at the others, but then his expression changed sharply as he caught a teasing look from their mother. "Except for yours, of course. Second best. That's what I meant to say."

The air was cold against Bailey's cheeks as they walked across the cleared sidewalk and into the house. For the next two hours the warmth from the fire and the Baxters was enough to keep Bailey distracted. They heard about Ashley's paintings being discovered by a new gallery in New York City — one much larger than any gallery that had ever carried her work — and about how well the Baxter grandkids were doing in school and sports.

Bailey sat near her dad and keyed into a conversation between him and Ryan Taylor, the head football coach at Clear Creek High. Ryan was married to the oldest Baxter daughter, Kari. Until this school year, Cody had always been connected to Clear Creek High. Like Ricky said, he was the fastest football player there when he was a student and then, after returning from the war, he coached at Clear Creek.

Her dad and Ryan talked about how off-season training was going, and then Ryan set down his fork. "You hear much from Cody Coleman?"

A shadow fell over her father's expression. "No." He shook his head and wiped a napkin across his mouth. "Not for a couple months. I'm a little worried about him."

For a few seconds Ryan didn't say anything. "Rumor has it he's going for the assistant job at Lyle — that small Christian school outside Indianapolis."

Bailey felt her heart slide into a strange and unrecognizable rhythm. Cody was going for a job? Already? He still had another year of school left, two if he wanted a teaching credential. She looked at the food on her plate, but she wasn't hungry.

"Hmm. I didn't know." Her dad's expression remained flat, his tone even. "Maybe that's better for him."

"I'm not sure. Cody needs accountability." Ryan squinted, his concern obvious. "Your family has always meant so much to that kid." He hesitated. "I don't like that he hasn't called. We should pray ... that he isn't drinking again."

Bailey had to keep herself from blurting out that of course Cody wasn't drinking. He wouldn't go back to that, even if he never contacted them again. But she kept quiet.

It wasn't until later as they were headed home along the dark country roads, and the Suburban was quiet, that Bailey remembered her father's expression when Ryan Taylor brought up Cody's name. He almost looked angry, and suddenly in the silence of the ride she understood. Cody might be someone they all cared for, and he might have been a part of their family for many years. But now his silence hurt Bailey. It hurt all of them. And for that, her dad would only have so much patience.

Which explained the way her father teased about Matt Keagan. He was ready for Bailey to let go of Cody and get on with life. With someone more like her — someone like Matt.

Bailey stifled a quiet laugh. *Matt Keagan.* As if that were even a possibility ...

Not until they were home and she and her mom were in the kitchen making hot tea did Bailey remember the phone call from the 212 area code and the message she still hadn't heard. "Hey ..." She ran lightly to the other side of the kitchen bar where her purse hung on one of the stools. "I got a call from New York."

"New York?"

"Yeah." She dug around her purse again and after half a minute finally found her phone. "Listen." She pushed a few buttons and put the phone on speaker so they could both hear.

"Hello, this is Francesca Tilly, producer for the Broadway production of *Hairspray*. I was given your name by a friend of mine, a producer with the show *Wicked*." The woman's Italian accent was thick. She talked very fast and sounded quite serious. "We've lost members of our cast for various reasons, so we'll host a limited audition in three weeks. We know about your role in the Brandon Paul film, and we'd like you to attend." Another pause.

What in the world Bailey locked eyes with her mom. She covered her mouth with her hand and kept listening.

"I apologize for calling you on a Sunday, but our schedule is crazy tomorrow. If you're interested, contact me at my office number. You'll be given details then. Thank you for your time. I hope to hear from you."

The woman left her number twice, and the message came to an end. Bailey set her phone down and let out a brief scream. "Did you hear that?"

Her mom grinned big. "I knew it …" She laughed out loud and reached for Bailey's hands. "I knew someone would notice you after your last audition."

Bailey danced her way closer and took hold of her mom's fingers. "Can you believe it? *Hairspray*?" She screamed again. "That's my all-time favorite show! And they want me to audition!!"

"What's the commotion?" Her dad had been in the garage. He looked happy, but bewildered as he came closer. "Whatever it is, you're sure smiling big." He came to her and kissed the top of her head. "So I'm sure I'll like it too."

"I'm going back to New York!" Bailey's heart was still grasping the reality of the voicemail. "This producer wants me to audition for *Hairspray*! Isn't that the craziest thing?"

He smiled as he searched her eyes. "That surprises you?"

"Yes!" She squealed, dancing in place. "Of course it surprises me. I can't believe I'm still standing!"

They laughed and for the next half hour they talked about the songs Bailey could sing for the audition, and how she was more prepared now, and the fact that her dance lessons would definitely pay off because she was a better dancer than before.

Bailey thought about something Francesca Tilly had said on the message and for a moment her happiness dropped off. "You don't think they only want me because of my role in *Unlocked*, do you?"

"Of course not." Her mom's answer was quick, her tone convincing. "You have to be more than well known to survive on Broadway." She smiled. "They called you because of your skills, honey."

She nodded slowly. "I hope so." The last thing she would want was a role handed to her because of her visibility. On Broadway a person needed to earn their place — it was that simple. They talked more about the logistics of what lay ahead, and what the producers would look for during the upcoming audition. Bailey was exhausted in every possible way by the time she went to bed, and even then she wasn't sure she could ever find her way to sleep. She thought about Cody and how tomorrow was Valentine's Day. Not only would she go another February fourteenth alone, but he wasn't even part of her life to share in the excitement that had just happened. She rolled onto her side and stared at the moonlight splashed across the wall.

She was going back to New York for another audition! She'd asked God for this every day since her last one, when the producers of *Wicked* had cut her and offered her former boyfriend Tim Reed a part in the show. Now ... now it was finally her turn to show a different set of producers she had what it took to win a part.

She breathed out. *Calm down, Bailey ... you need sleep.* She smiled in the darkness but as she did, she remembered Pastor Mark's message from earlier. *Everyone says goodbye eventually ... people come and go ... nothing stays except for Jesus.* And suddenly amidst her very great joy came a flash of sadness. Grief, almost. Because if God allowed this, she might actually win a part on Broadway. All of which would mean one very certain thing. Despite everything she loved about Bloomington and her family and her classes at IU, this wouldn't be a time to think about Brandon Paul or to meet Matt Keagan or to wonder about Cody.

It would be her time to leave.

Two

CODY STEPPED INSIDE HIS APARTMENT, FLIPPED ON A LIGHT, AND stomped the ice off his boots. His first real job interview was in two hours. He peeled off his jacket, dropped it over the back of the sofa, and headed to his room. His roommate wasn't home, which was just as well. He had too much on his mind to talk about any of it. Life had become a snowy, busy blur of routine, and for the most part Cody was comfortable in it. Better not to think about the passing of time or how every day put another calendar square between him and Bailey Flanigan. He took a full load of classes and worked a few times each week on his forty-page senior project titled "The Effects of Motor Skill Improvement on a Student's Ability to Learn." Cody loved the research. So far the evidence was compelling — the more active a child, the better he or she performed on academic tests. Sort of obvious, really.

Everything took time, and then on weekends he visited his mom in prison. Her current sentence had three more years, at least. Drug dealing penalties got worse with each conviction. His mother could attest to that. They would talk and pray and she would hold his hands — really hold them — like she might not survive after he let go and left the room. But he always left. He had no choice.

To fill the empty spaces, a couple times a month Cody had dinner at the house of his old war buddy Art Collins. Art didn't make it home from Iraq, and for the last year Art's mother, Tara, had taken to hosting Sunday dinners for her son's Army buddies.

"I own me a special place in my heart for you, Cody Coleman," she told him whenever he stopped by. "God's got Himself good plans for you, young man. You got any doubts, we'll talk about it, you hear? I'll change your mind!"

Tara was long on conversation and hospitality — her food rich and warm and homemade. Creamy sauces, soft fresh bread, and any number of cuts of beef. The woman was African American, with a hearty laugh and a loud voice, and her small house smelled of spices and laundry detergent. But, even so, she reminded Cody of Bailey's mom, Jenny. Tara Collins filled a broken place in Cody's heart. She helped him walk through the weekends without breaking down and calling Bailey.

Once in a while Tara invited Cheyenne Williams — the pretty girl who had once been engaged to Art. Cody had no delusions about Tara's intentions where Cheyenne was concerned. Tara was trying to set them up. But Cody kept his distance. Other than an occasional text message, he didn't talk to Cheyenne outside Tara's house. He had no intention of doing so. Bailey had taken his heart a long time ago — no matter how he tried to convince himself otherwise.

Combined, his schedule left his heart little room for feeling or missing or wondering what might have been if he hadn't let stubborn pride stand in the way when he saw Bailey outside his mother's prison last New Year's Day. He'd watched her pull away without showing himself, without saying a word. Never mind that she was like a drug, an addiction he couldn't overcome. He saw her face in his dreams and heard her voice in a crowded room. Even when she might as well have been a million miles away, Bailey was there.

Always she was there.

He stopped on the way to his room. There on the wall was a photograph he couldn't just walk past, a picture he stopped and looked at every day without fail. In it, he was twenty, maybe

twenty-one, at Lake Monroe surrounded by the Flanigans. All
of them. Jenny and Jim, and their six kids. The five boys — Connor, Shawn, Justin, BJ, and Ricky. And there beside him, her eyes
bright from the light inside her, stood Bailey. The photo drew him
in, made him feel even for a minute that he was there again. The
Indiana sunshine on his shoulders, a football tucked under his
arm, the family he loved around him ... and Bailey.

Breathing the same air as him.

A draft from the nearby window sent a chill down his arms.
He blinked and the warmth of that summer day faded. The interview. He had to focus on the interview. He pulled off the thermal
he'd worn to class that morning and slipped into a white T-shirt.
A smile tugged at his lips. Okay, maybe not the biggest job interview ever. But the biggest interview he'd had so far. A school forty
minutes east of Indianapolis needed a PE teacher and an assistant
football coach. He had a pizza delivery job most nights and weekends, but it didn't pay much. The interview at Lyle High School
was at least a step in the right direction.

One of his professors at IU had told him about the position.
"They'll grant you an emergency credential," the man told him.
"It's a small school. But since this is your career field, I think you
should at least talk to the principal."

The professor made arrangements for the interview and
Cody stopped by the registrar's office early this morning. If he
was given the job, he could switch his two morning classes to the
evening, and since his others were already at night, he would be
free to take the job. He was set to graduate from IU this May, and
after that he would take an accelerated course of classes to earn
his master's degree in education. The fit was perfect.

Cody peered into his cramped closet. He owned two dress
shirts — a solid white and a pale blue. He chose the white one. It
was a little wrinkled and maybe a shade grayer than a year ago.
But it was the best he had, and it would do for today. He slipped

it on, buttoned it up, grabbed a blue tie, and perfectly knotted it in place. After living with the Flanigans, he would never struggle with a tie. Bailey's father, Jim, had seen to that.

Snow was forecast for later that day, but for now his old pickup could get him forty-five minutes east for the interview. Getting home might be another matter. He grabbed his portfolio — a few copies of his resume and some newspaper clippings from Clear Creek High football, the team he'd helped coach in Bloomington. He was meeting with the principal, and then the athletic director and football coach. Might as well bring everything he had to convince them.

The drive took longer than he thought. Or maybe it only seemed that way because every radio station was playing another love song. Halfway there the reason finally hit him: It was Valentine's Day. Of course they were playing love songs. He narrowed his eyes against the glare of the setting sun on the snow-covered fields. So what was he doing driving to an interview halfway to Ohio? Bailey loved him, right? That's what she had told him outside her parents' house the last time they talked, right. He exhaled hard. Why was he so stubborn?

He clenched his jaw and kept his attention on the road. The reason hadn't changed. Bailey Flanigan settling for a guy whose only family was a frail, sad woman doing time for dealing drugs? Risking the possibility that the paparazzi would figure out the details and drag both their names through the mud? And there were other reasons. For the last six months he'd lived with the threat from his mom's abusive drug supplier. The man said he'd kill Cody or anyone Cody was with if his mom turned him in — which she did. Until the guy was caught recently, Cody's life was like some crazy crime movie. Cody wouldn't expose Bailey to that no matter how he felt about her.

God, I can't mix my life with hers ... You know that. He tightened his grip on the wheel. *But I can't get her out of my heart, either. Help me move on. You can see how I am. I can't leave her behind without Your help.*

A response came then, brushing like a whisper against his soul: *Son ... I have loved you with an everlasting love ... commit your plans to me and they will succeed.*

Cody relaxed back into his seat. *Is that You, God?* He waited, but nothing ... no more whispers. The verse was something his mom had shared with him last weekend. She was in Bible studies just about every day. "It's the only way I stay sane," she told him. "After what I've done to you ... to my chances at ever being a real mom."

"You'll always be my mom." He took her hands in his. "We'll get through this."

She blinked back tears, but she agreed. And that's when she gave him a slip of paper. Scribbled on it was Proverbs 16:3. *Commit your plans to the Lord and they will succeed.* But why would God bring that to mind now? Was it about the plans he had for teaching at Lyle? Was that why the Spirit would whisper the verse to him here? That must be it. This was a big interview, after all. So maybe God didn't want him thinking about Bailey but about the task ahead of him: winning the job.

He switched the radio station. Sports talk. That's what he needed. Get his mind off Bailey. Focus on something left-brained: The Lakers or the Heat — which team was stronger heading into the NBA All-Star weekend. Pro baseball's spring training. Who was moving up in the ratings for April's NFL draft.

Anything but Bailey.

The trick worked, and for the next thirty minutes he listened to a host take callers either raving about or tearing apart LeBron James. Cody exited off the main highway and took a two-lane country road through ten miles of farmland. Barren corn and soybean fields and orchards of empty-armed apple trees. Endless ranches and herds of cattle as far as he could see. The longer he drove the more he figured he was lost. Maybe he missed a turn off. What sort of school could be this far out in the sticks? He was about to pull over and check his MapQuest directions, when up ahead he saw a cluster of homes and small buildings — the tallest, a red brick church with a white steeple that pierced the cloudy sky.

As he approached, a sign came into view: "Welcome to Lyle, Home of the Buckaroos." The next one made him smile: "25 M.P.H. Thank you kindly for observing our speed limit." Polite people. Cody liked that. He slowed his pickup and looked for signs of life. A weathered, oversized American flag fanned in the breeze from the corner of a low-slung nineteenth century trading post-type building — Al's Hardware, according to the sign. Two guys in overalls sat on a bench outside the front door. Waiting for customers, no doubt.

A gas station with rusted pumps, Ali's Coffee Can, Shirley's Curl and Cut ... Cody felt like he was driving through a movie set. Small-town America. Up ahead a slightly tattered banner stretched across Main Street: *World Famous Lyle Rodeo.* The rodeo was the only reason Cody had ever heard of the little town. Same as most anyone in Indiana. A few of Cody's buddies from Clear Creek High made a trek of it every year, last weekend in June. One of them even competed. Saddle broncs. Crazy stuff.

Suddenly an image flashed in his mind. An Iraqi interrogation room. A view through the bars of a four-foot cage. Shouting, and slamming doors, and the butt of a rifle ramming him into a corner. The face of an Iraqi soldier opening the cage and ...

Cody blinked and the images disappeared. He pulled over to the side of the road and hung his head. His heart pounded, and his breaths came in shaky short gasps. A layer of perspiration beaded up across his forehead and on his forearms. He hated this, the way images from war took over his mind without warning. Especially lately. *I can't do this, God. Make them go away. That time in my life is over. Please ... make it stop.*

Gradually, a peace that passed understanding put its arms around his shoulders and he felt his body relax, felt his breathing and heart rate return to normal. *Thank You ... thank You, Lord. I feel You here.* He drew a slow deep breath.

Okay, maybe riding broncs wasn't the craziest thing.

He wiped the back of his hand over his forehead. Twenty minutes until his interview, but he might as well get to the school. Three blocks east and another north and there it was. Square in the middle of another massive field, surrounded by maple trees —a two-story brick structure with an old-fashioned marquis out front announcing: *Cake Walk and Carnival, February 19.*

Cody drove around back and there was the football field: Barely a hundred yards of snow and grass with a few rickety wooden bleachers. Weeds poked their way up through the asphalt track that bordered the end zone. In the distance, against a darkening sky, an army green water tank boasted the obvious. *Lyle Buckaroos—Class of '11* painted in blue on one side.

Another survey of the field.

The stands would hold maybe a hundred people. This couldn't be where they played their varsity games, right? He checked his watch. Ten minutes until the interview. He drove around to the front of the school and pulled the folded piece of paper from his pocket, the one his mom had given him. *Commit your plans to the Lord and they will succeed.* He had long since memorized it, but somehow reading it in his mom's handwriting made him feel more normal. Like his mom was waiting at home making dinner, encouraging him. Cheering him on.

"Here goes," he whispered. Once more he folded the piece of paper and returned it to his pocket. He shut and locked the door, straightened his tie, and made his way inside the school.

Three women were talking over one computer when he walked in the room. They stopped and looked at him. "Hello." The youngest of the ladies took a step closer. "Can I help you?"

"Yes." He stood a little taller. "I'm Cody Coleman. I'm here to meet Ms. Baker."

The woman smiled. "That's me." She glanced at the clock on the wall. "You're early." Her eyes were kind as she shook his hand. "I like that." She motioned for him to follow her, and he did. They went through the workspace to a private office at the back corner. She left the door open, took the seat behind the desk, and offered him the one on the other side.

"You come highly recommended by your professor." Ms. Baker picked up a portfolio on her desk and thumbed through it. "I'm impressed, Mr. Coleman."

Mr. Coleman . . . so old-sounding. Cody swallowed his nerves. "Thank you, ma'am."

She leaned back, relaxed. No way she was a day over thirty. "Tell me about yourself. Why do you want to teach at Lyle?"

"I was an athlete in high school." He talked easily about his time at Clear Creek and his service in Iraq. Then he shifted in his seat and searched for the right words. "To be honest, I didn't know about the opening at Lyle until this week. I want to teach because . . . because the people who've made the most impact in my life have been teachers. Coaches." He paused, and he could hear Jim Flanigan's voice. *You can do anything, Cody . . . God has great plans for you. Never let anything stop you from your dreams . . .*

He looked at Ms. Baker. "I was nearly killed in Iraq, ma'am. With this second chance, I want to make a difference. The way a few teachers and coaches made a difference for me."

She nodded slowly. "I respect that." Another glance through the folder in her hands. "You're aware you would be taking this position on an emergency credential basis." Her eyes lifted to his. "It's a temporary position, Mr. Coleman. We couldn't offer you a full-time job until you complete the credentialing process — after you graduate."

"I understand."

The interview lasted another fifteen minutes while they talked about teaching styles and the importance of hard work and family and faith to the kids of Lyle. "It's a public school, yes. But this is a community that lives and dies by the success of the crops that surround us. The people of Lyle understand hard work and they're early to church every Sunday."

"Yes, ma'am." Cody felt the light in his eyes. "I can relate."

Ms. Baker's expression softened. "I thought so."

A few more minutes and the principal led Cody to the school's gym. Inside, a class of maybe thirty guys was counting off jumping jacks while the coach barked out orders. "Faster! Louder! Come on guys. This is February. Champions are made in the off-season!"

Cody wondered if he'd like the man. Some coaches could yell and still get their point across, still show love and concern for their players. Others were mostly a lot of hot air. They stepped inside, and Ms. Baker waited until the coach spotted her. He blew his whistle. "Take five. Get some water. We'll try it again after that." The man's scowl remained as he walked over. "Ms. Baker," he nodded, terse, serious.

"Coach Oliver, this is Cody Coleman. The candidate sent over by the university."

"Right." The man gave Cody a quick once-over. "The kid on the emergency credential."

A slight look of irritation came over Ms. Baker's face, but only for a moment. "I'm prepared to offer him the position if he'll take it." Her approval of Cody was clear. "But he'll be your assistant. I'd like the two of you to talk for a few minutes, and then include Mr. Coleman in your practice this afternoon. So he can know if he'd like to be a part of our program."

"Got it." Coach Oliver's surly attitude remained. "Thank you, Ms. Baker."

She nodded and smiled again at Cody. "Talk to me before you leave. I'll be in my office."

"Yes, ma'am." Cody wasn't sure what was going on, but clearly there was tension between the coach and principal. It was easy to pick sides.

Ms. Baker left and Coach Oliver stared at him. "Notice she didn't say, 'Winning program.'" He sneered. "I've been coaching here for two years, and we haven't won a game." He took a step closer. "Know why?"

"No, sir." Cody crossed his arms.

"Because of Coach John Brown."

Cody could imagine how baffled he must've looked. "I'm … sorry, coach. I don't know John Brown."

The man raised his eyebrows. "I thought you were from Bloomington."

"Yes, sir."

"Boy … everyone in the state knows John Brown. He's a legend. Won a state title with Lyle for the 1A division six years in a row." He tossed his hand. "Retired two years ago when the talent dried up." He lowered his voice and leaned closer. "Even John Brown couldn't make a winning season out of this sorry group a' kids."

Cody nodded. He glanced at the guys, huddled in clusters around the drinking fountain. A couple of them were big — six-four, six-five maybe. Nothing about the group looked especially inept.

"Sure." The coach shrugged. "I need an assistant. I need an offense and a defense, for that matter. You can at least help me coach. Give the parents someone else to be angry at."

Cody crossed his arms. If this was Coach Oliver's sales pitch for Lyle, it was falling flat. He nodded absently, not sure if he was supposed to respond.

Without warning, the man turned to the kids and blew his whistle. "Time's up. Back in formation."

Interview over, Cody thought. He could already picture himself telling Ms. Baker no thanks. He didn't want to drive out here every day, and he had no desire to take heat from parents because of the defeated mind-set of Coach Oliver. A few minutes later — when the coach was finished with calisthenics — he led the team outside to the bitter cold field. Cody didn't want to be rude, so he followed.

The temperature had dropped and the clouds were dark and building fast. Forget a light snowfall ... a blizzard was about to break loose. Cody anchored himself on the sidelines and watched. The outdoor practice was more of the same: Coach Oliver barking and snapping while the kids walked through a series of passing drills. By the time the coach blew the whistle for the last time, Cody was ready to chock up the entire afternoon to nothing more than experience. A lesson in what he didn't want to do and where he didn't want to work.

"There you go, kid." The coach shrugged again. "Take it or leave it. That's Lyle." He walked off with his clipboard and whistle before Cody could respond.

That's that, he thought. He was about to find Ms. Baker and decline the offer when he spotted a player headed toward the opposite end zone. The guy stopped at the forty-yard line — or what looked like roughly the forty. He froze in a receiver's ready position and sprinted across the field. Once he crossed into the end zone, he turned around, jogged to the other forty, and did the same sort of sprint across that part of the field.

A couple stragglers stopped and one of them shouted. "Smitty, you're crazy! Ain't no runnin' gonna help you catch the ball." The player was a short redhead. He laughed out loud. "You don't get it."

His buddy chuckled too, and then both of them walked to the

locker room. As they passed Cody, they gave him a curious look and a distant kind of nod. The kind players might give each other when they want to look tough.

"Gentlemen," Cody said. He made eye contact with the guys, but only for a moment. Then he turned his attention back to the kid on the field. The player was running another sixty-yard burst, and this time when he reached the end zone he dropped to one knee. He planted his elbow on the other and bowed his head.

Cody narrowed his eyes. Who was the kid, and why was he on the freezing wet ground? He watched as the guy stayed there for a minute, stood and jogged back toward the building, toward Cody. He was about to pass when he slowed up and squinted. "You the new assistant?"

"Uh ..." A strange guilt flooded Cody's heart. He hesitated. "I'm ... I'm thinking about it." A second or two passed, but Cody didn't want the kid to leave. Not yet. He nodded to the field. "You do that ... after every practice?"

"Yes, sir." The kid crossed his arms. He was black, maybe an inch shorter than Cody, with arms that proved time in the weight room. Something about him reminded Cody of himself, the way he might've been in high school if he'd had the grasp of faith he had now. The player stared at the end zone. "I'm dedicating the season to God. Every game ... every drive. Every play. Every practice. Trusting God for what's ahead."

Compassion for the kid came over Cody. He nodded slowly. "You were praying?"

"Yes, sir." He let loose a lighthearted laugh and gave a shake of his head. "I'm a junior. If you know anything about Lyle, we need a lot of prayer."

"I hear." Cody liked the kid. His leadership and determination. The way he didn't care about his teammates laughing at him. "What's your name?"

"DeMetri Smith." He smiled. "Guys call me Smitty."

"Coach Coleman." Cody reached out and shook DeMetri's hand. "Nice to meet you."

"You, too." DeMetri grinned, gave a quick wave and jogged off. He wasn't too far away when Cody called after him, "DeMetri."

The player stopped and turned. "Sir?"

"What were you praying for today?"

DeMetri's smile filled his face. "You're here because of the job, right?"

"Yes." Cody paused, but only briefly. "Yes, I am."

"Then that's easy." He started jogging again, his eyes still on Cody. "I was praying for you." One last grin and he turned and finished the trek to the locker room.

Cody stood there, unable to move. In a moment's time, he remembered a message from one of the Campus Crusade meetings. The group leader had talked about service to Christ and the purpose of life. The guy's voice rang in Cody's mind again: *God never said life would be easy. The purpose in living isn't about our personal happiness ... it's about serving God. When it comes to our relationship with the Creator, we should always ... always have our yes on the table. If God asks us to do something, we do it. Our yes is a given.*

If Cody had wondered whether God was calling him to Lyle High, he had no doubts now. None whatsoever. DeMetri Smith had given him all the answer he needed. He began the walk to Ms. Baker's office. Now he would give the principal the answer she needed. Cody would take the job.

His yes was on the table.

He signed papers and promised to start the following day teaching five PE classes and helping out with the Lyle football program. Twenty minutes later Cody was ten miles into the drive home when snow began to fall. It didn't flutter slowly or take its time deciding whether it meant business. The clouds simply opened up and dumped. Cody slowed and focused on the road.

His lights were on, but they did little to shed visibility on the road ahead.

He drove that way — not more than twenty miles an hour — until the storm let up. The whole way, he couldn't help but think of Bailey: what she was doing right now on Valentine's Day, what her family was doing, and whether she ever thought about him. The storm was a lot like his life. He could focus all his attention on the road, stare through the blizzard as intently as possible, but that didn't mean he could see what was ahead. No, the future was as much a whiteout as the afternoon. He — like DeMetri Smith — had to trust God for what lay ahead. With the drive home. With Lyle High. And with Bailey Flanigan.

With Bailey most of all.

Three

ASHLEY BAXTER BLAKE SPREAD PINK FROSTING OVER A COOLED batch of chocolate cupcakes and still managed to keep her attention on Cole, her twelve-year-old son. He was sharing his valentines from his sixth grade class, reading each one and explaining why that person was important and how he didn't necessarily like this girl or that one.

"This one's from Carrie," he gave a slight roll of his eyes, but he couldn't hide his grin. "She's the one who writes on my arm all the time, remember?"

"I do." Ashley picked up another cupcake, her eyes on Cole. "The cute one with the dark hair."

Cole shrugged, but his eyes sparkled. "I don't know how cute she is, but yeah ... she writes on my arm." He took the valentine from its envelope and held it up. "Hers have these ballerina Barbie girls all over them."

"Which one did she give you?"

"It says, 'Valentine, I'd leap across the stage for you.'" Again he gave a slight eye roll. "But she doesn't really mean it, Mom. Half the cards in the box probably say that."

Ashley laughed. "She might mean it."

"Anyway ..." Cole's cheeks were a little redder than before. He moved on to the next valentine.

Across the kitchen, five-year-old Devin was helping little Janessa Faith color a Valentine's Day card for Landon. "That's right, Nessa ... Daddy loves pink." He pointed to part of the paper.

He kept his voice low, because Cole was still going through his cards. "How 'bout drawing a circus tent on this part? Daddy loves circuses."

Ashley glanced at him, struck as she sometimes was by how much he sounded like Cole at that age, how much the two of them looked alike. And Devin definitely had Cole's imagination. Everything was all about circuses lately. Even, apparently, Janessa's valentine picture. Not that she could really draw much of anything at three years old. But she liked to try.

"And this one's from that mean kid, the one who always makes fun of the short girls."

"Collin?"

"Yes." Cole shook his head. "I told him to quit it, but he likes the attention. He thinks he's funny even when the teacher tells him to be quiet and he has to go sit in the back of the — "

From the front of the house came the sound of the door opening, and at the same time Ashley heard Landon cough. Not once, but three times. Hard enough that it made her heart skip a beat. She tried not to react, but she set the butter knife on the counter and held up her index finger in Cole's direction. "Dad's home. Hold on a minute."

She wiped her hands on a damp rag and hurried toward the foyer. Landon was setting down his gear, and as she rounded the corner he coughed again. "Landon . . ."

He straightened and caught her eye just before she reached him. "Hey," he smiled big. "Come here." His voice was hoarse, his cheeks smudged with dirt.

"A fire?" She wrapped her arms around him and pressed the side of her face to his navy button-up uniform shirt. The smell of smoke was all over him. "Oh, baby, not another fire."

"A warehouse." Landon turned slightly and coughed two more times. "It wasn't bad. We saved most of it."

"But listen to you." She closed her eyes, her face still up

against his chest. As if by pressing against him she might hear his lungs or help stop whatever was happening inside them. "Your cough's bad."

"Daddy!" Devin's voice rang through the house. He padded barefoot across the wooden floor and into the entry way. "Hi, Daddy! We're making you val'tine cards."

"Hey, Dad," Cole called from the other room. "Come here and see all my valentines." Cole's voice was happy, upbeat. He was oblivious to his father's cough. "We had our party today."

"Landon," Ashley whispered his name. She searched his eyes and wondered if he could see her anxiety. The dangers of fighting fires had been there from the beginning. It was after a fire nearly killed Landon years ago that Ashley finally faced the way she felt about him. The fact that she was in love with him. But he'd been coughing more lately — even when he hadn't been around a fire in weeks. Every time she had to wonder ... was his cough some side effect of his time at Ground Zero? Landon had spent more than two months volunteering at the pile, moving debris and looking for victims and breathing the worst possible air.

No wonder every cough made her frantic with the possibilities.

"Daddy, ... come see." Devin jumped around and grabbed Landon's hand. Janessa took up her position on the other side, her arms wrapped around his leg.

"Just a minute, Dev," he laughed, and stifled another cough. He kept his eyes on Ashley's, deep to the places where their love knew no limits. Where it never had. "It's okay, babe." He touched his fingers to her hair. "Fires always do this to me."

Ashley wanted to believe him, wanted to convince herself that if she stayed here lost in his eyes, what he said might be true. Either way, she could do nothing by worrying. Especially now, when they had a Valentine's Day family dinner planned. She tried to hand her fears to God, and what she kept for herself she stuffed

in the corner of her heart. "Happy Valentine's Day," A smile tugged at her lips, even as the kids bounced around at their feet.

"Happy Valentine's Day." He put his hand alongside her face and kissed her, tenderly, with a passion that told her there would be more later. When the kids were in bed. "I love you."

"I love you more." She felt her heart grow lighter. "Come on." She ran her fingers over Devin's blond hair. "The kids have been busy."

They returned to the kitchen, and Landon fussed and raved over the kids' handmade cards. He listened to Cole do a second round of explanations about his class party and the cards from his peers, but Ashley caught him taking a few spoonfuls of cough syrup. After that he let only a few coughs slip. Otherwise his lungs seemed to settle down.

Ashley felt the relief to her core. Maybe he was right — the coughing was because of the warehouse fire and not the months at Ground Zero. Never that.

Dinner was spaghetti and meatballs, because, as Devin said, "Busgetti is red, and red is a val'tine's color." Landon helped Ashley set the table, and Cole tossed the salad. "Thanks for the ranch, Mom. It's the best."

"Sorry it isn't pink or red." Ashley laughed, and the relief in her voice was genuine. Landon would be okay. Of course, he would be okay.

"Yeah, but mom it still works," Cole pointed out. "Red, pink, and white — they're all Valentine's colors." He nodded toward his bag from school. "At least if you look at all those cards."

When they were seated and holding hands, Landon prayed. "Father, we thank you for this food, for providing for us. And we thank you for our family, where every day is a celebration of love and where every moment is a gift. We love you, Jesus. In your name, we pray. Amen."

They opened their eyes, put their hands together at the middle of the table, and did something Cole had started this year after his flag football season. "One … two … three … team!"

Janessa looked a little bewildered, like she wasn't quite sure what the cheer was. But she liked it anyway, and she gave a happy bit of applause before they all started eating.

"I think we'll have busgetti at my circus, Daddy," Devin was in a chatty mood. "Busgetti is a good circus food, right?"

"Yes," Landon looked at Ashley, and the two shared a quiet smile. "I think spaghetti could be as good a circus food as any."

"Dad," Cole set his fork down. "At least tell him the truth." Cole leaned over the table and smiled at Devin the way a teacher smiles at a kindergartner. "Hot dogs and hamburgers, Devin. That's better circus food."

Ashley raised her eyes in Landon's direction. Cole and Devin were best friends, but when Cole played the older brother card, Devin sometimes resisted. Ashley had a feeling this was one of those times.

Devin frowned. "But I want busgetti for my circus," he turned to Landon. "Right, Daddy? I can have busgetti at my circus, right?"

"More 'getti, peease." Janessa's interruption came at the perfect moment.

"Yes, sweetie." Ashley stood and went to their daughter's highchair. While she served her, she smiled at their oldest son. "You're right. Hot dogs and hamburgers are a more traditional circus food." She turned to Devin and gave him a silly grin. "But spaghetti would make your circus more interesting."

Devin processed that for a few seconds and puffed out his chest. "Yeah, I'm in'eresting."

Cole looked like he might counter with something only a witty twelve-year-old might come up with, but he caught a look from Landon. He gave a quick shake of his head and laughed quietly instead.

"Okay, so here's the dinner talk for tonight." Landon always had a way of keeping things upbeat, just like Ashley's father had done when she and her siblings were young, when they were being raised in this very house. "Let's go around the room and say something we love about each person in our family."

"Me!" Devin shouted. "I'll go first!" He gave a quick look at the faces around him, and he started with Ashley. "Mommy, I love that you can paint pictures and cupcakes."

"Thank you," Ashley gave Devin a polite nod. "I try my best." She giggled in Cole's direction and felt the slight tension from earlier leave the table. Under Landon's careful, loving leadership they would finish dinner on a happy note.

"Daddy, I love that you have the strongest arms in the world." Devin couldn't say his R's just yet.

Cole sat beside Landon and gave his father's bicep a squeeze. "You're right about that, buddy,"

"And, Nessa," Devin patted his little sister on the hand and then wiped his fingers on his jeans, "I love that you have a high-chair, so we don't get that mess all over us."

Ashley tried, but she couldn't stifle her laugh.

"And, Coley." Devin narrowed his eyes at his big brother. "I love that you ... will cook the busgetti at my circus!"

Cole hesitated and glanced at Ashley, but only for a moment. "Yeah." Cole pumped his fist weakly in the air. "I love cooking spaghetti. Thanks, Devin."

"There." Devin sat back, satisfied. "That's everybody."

Cole went next. He loved that Janessa was learning to talk better, and that Devin was a good drawer like their mom, and that Ashley was the best mom in the world. "And I love you, Dad," he turned adoring eyes on Landon, "because you're my hero and my dad all in one."

The muscles in Ashley's throat tightened and her eyes grew watery. Cole had always been able to speak his mind, and tonight was no exception. It was her turn, and she swallowed, blinking back the unshed tears. "I have to agree with Cole," she smiled at her son and then at Landon. "I love Daddy because he's my hero. And because he taught me how to love."

"Really?" Devin cocked his head, curious. "He gave you lessons?"

Ashley and Landon and Cole all laughed, and Devin shrugged and joined in. After a few seconds, Janessa added her baby-girl giggles so that the whole family was laughing. They finished up with Ashley telling Cole that she loved his honesty and leadership, and Devin that she loved his imagination.

Landon took his time, making silly faces and causing the boys to erupt in more laughter. Finally, when they'd settled down, he looked at Cole and Devin both. "I love that you're my sons. That's what I love most."

Again Ashley's heart felt full. She had Cole long before she and Landon started dating. But from the beginning he had treated Cole like his own son. His words tonight were more meaningful than either of the boys could possibly know.

Landon turned to her. "And I love your mom ... because she has the most beautiful hair."

"Hmm." Cole nodded. "She does have pretty hair."

But by then Ashley and Landon were already giggling again. When she and Landon first started out, Ashley worked at an assisted living home for Alzheimer's patients. One woman named Irvel — Ashley's favorite patient — had a habit of constantly complimenting Ashley's hair. Landon had adopted the practice as a way to lighten certain moments. And always his timing was impeccable.

Even tonight when he knew exactly what she needed. In the wake of his coughing and her concern, she didn't need an emotional statement or something overly sentimental. She needed to laugh.

Only Landon would know that.

When dinner ended and the kids had pink frosting on their faces, Cole reminded them that tomorrow Landon was off work and school had a late-start day. "And then there's tryouts tomorrow."

"Tryouts for me too?" Devin's eyes got big and he spun fast in Landon's direction.

"No, buddy." Landon chuckled. "You'll play T-ball this season. You don't need a tryout."

"But I do." Cole's voice seemed to get deeper, and he lifted his chin some. "I'm in Nationals now. That's the highest we go for Little League around here. Right, Dad?"

"That's right." Landon winked at Cole. "I have a pretty good idea you'll make it. You were in All-Stars last year."

"Still . . ." Cole looked at Ashley. "Can we watch a family movie tonight? Like *Sandlot*? To get me in the mood for tryouts?"

The Sandlot was a family favorite. There were a few unnecessary scenes, but for the most part Ashley loved the story: the tale of neighborhood boys playing ball together and believing that somehow their time at the local sandlot would go on forever.

"You too tired?" She looked at Landon. He hadn't coughed since earlier, and it was only seven o'clock. But still, she didn't want him worn out. If he needed rest, he should get it. "Should we wait till the weekend?"

"Nah," Landon put his arm around Cole's shoulders. "I say we get the league's best catcher in the mood for a little baseball."

"Yay!" Devin jumped around. "*Sandlot! Sandlot!*"

Janessa had crawled up onto the couch and was already falling asleep. Ashley took a blanket from a wicker basket on the floor and spread it over her little daughter. In a matter of minutes they were snuggled together, all five of them beneath blankets with the lights dimmed. Ashley sat with Cole on one side and Landon on the other, and even before the movie started she caught herself realizing the importance of tomorrow.

Cole's very last tryouts for Little League.

Sure, he might go on to play baseball for an older league or someday for his high school. But Little League would be over. A few short months from now she would watch Cole take his last at-bat in Little League, watch him catch his last ball behind the plate. He would do his best at every practice, play every game with the gusto he was known for. Landon would coach him, and the afternoons would feel like they might last forever.

But they wouldn't. This was the final season.

It made Ashley feel like she was leaving something behind, Cole's childhood, maybe. Bloomington's Little League played on a large multi-field complex where the little guys started out at one end of the park and worked their way — year by year — through the T-ball, Coach Pitch, and a handful of other divisions before making their way to the Nationals field.

As the movie started, Ashley remembered she and Landon taking Cole to his first T-ball game. Sitting in the bleachers she had shaded her eyes and looked far across the complex to the big baseball diamonds, the place where the twelve-year-olds played. *Forever away,* she had told herself. Forever until Cole was throwing that hard and hitting balls out of the park. Before he was one of the big kids.

But now here they were. Just like that.

She blinked and tried to focus on the movie, but still she wondered where the years had gone. She could see him the way he was back then, all batting helmet and wide eyes, his bat nearly as big as him. How could they be more than halfway done raising that precious little guy?

The movie gave her time to savor the moment, memorize the feel of Landon and Cole warm against her sides, the sound of Janessa Faith's sleepy breathing and Devin's laughter at the funny scenes. A shudder passed over her, and she realized — as she had a thousand times — how easily she might have missed all this.

But for Landon's relentless pursuit of her, his undaunted love . . . it would be just Cole and her tonight.

She gathered the deep feelings of her heart and held them close. They were so blessed, all of them. Living here in the old Baxter house, sharing time like this together. *Thank You, God. Thank You for this.*

The entire movie was a flashback, a look from the vantage point of adulthood at a time when the narrator and his buddies were on the brink of becoming, a time when for a little while longer they were still young boys. As the movie neared the end there came what was, for Ashley, one of the saddest scenes in all of moviemaking. The boys from the sandlot played on the dusty ball field while the narrator, Scotty, talked about how they had all grown up, what had become of them. How one went on to be an architect, another a businessman, another a professional wrestler, and so on . . . . . . and how one guy was never heard from again.

As the narrator finished talking about each of his buddies, one at a time the twelve-year-old player would slowly disappear from the sandlot. There one minute, and gone the next. The way it was with life. And this season that would be Cole: playing his heart out in a Yankees Little League uniform one day and the next having no reason to ever step foot on the field again. Ashley dabbed at her eyes as the scene came to an end.

"Mommy, why are you crying?" Devin peered around Landon, concern on his face.

Landon rubbed Ashley's shoulder and put his arm more tightly around Devin's arm. "Mommy's just thinking about Cole. It's his last season of Little League."

"Yep," Cole's eyes were damp too. He gave his brother a wistful smile. "You have forever to play."

His words pierced Ashley's heart, because the sentiment wasn't true for Cole and wouldn't be for Devin either. They had this season, yes. But the years would fly by for Devin as they had for his older brother, and one day all too soon it would be his last season. Suddenly a painting came to mind: Cole in his Little League uniform — his last season … Landon working alongside him, coaching him. The images and colors and broad strokes were so clear Ashley could hardly wait to get started. Anything to hold on to the days at hand, before the moments slipped away and the season was over. When the sight of Cole, like every other little boy who ever played Little League, would fade forever from the field where he had grown up.

His very own personal sandlot.

Four

JENNY RAN LIGHTLY DOWN THE STAIRS OF HER FAMILY'S HOUSE, and tried to remember everything she had to do before tomorrow's trip to New York City. Already it was late Saturday afternoon, and their flight was before sun-up. She hadn't started packing, and from the sounds of it Bailey and Connor were at the piano singing.

With a hundred things left to do.

She started to call out to her daughter to get her moving in the right direction, but as she reached the main floor she saw her husband standing at the entrance to the living room, the place where the kids gathered whenever they sang together. He looked up and smiled, then he put his finger to his lips and motioned to her.

"Jim," she muttered, but went to him anyway. As she took the spot beside him, thoughts about their New York trip faded.

Bailey and Connor were singing a duet from one of the newer Broadway shows *In the Heights*. The song was called "When You're Home" and it told the story of a local girl coming home after a stint at college. Connor played the piano and still managed to harmonize perfectly with Bailey. Jenny leaned into her husband, glad the kids didn't seem to notice them. They had always done this, Bailey and Connor. Sang together and allowed their voices and personalities to blend perfectly.

Like two best friends.

Jenny studied them, her grown children. And suddenly she

saw them as they had been through the years. Bailey three years old and hovered over a newborn Connor as he lay on a blanket sprawled on the living room floor. "Hi, Connor. Hi, little baby. Hi ..." And Connor was kicking his feet, and Bailey was leaning close enough that Connor's baby foot hit her in the shoulder. And Bailey was falling dramatically backwards, laughing her little-girl laugh: "Connor, that's not sair, you kicked me, Connor!" She was giggling, and the fact that she couldn't say the word *fair* correctly only made the moment that much more memorable.

The scene changed, and Bailey was six and dolled up in her velvet Christmas dress, her long hair curled, softly framing her face. Connor was three, wearing dress pants and a shirt and vest, and Bailey was practicing a song she was singing for the Christmas concert at church, while he was doing his absolute best to keep up. "Who's this baby, in the manger ..." Connor didn't have the words, but he would mimic the hand motions, his adoring eyes never leaving his sister.

And they were twelve and nine, and singing to a karaoke machine Connor had gotten for his birthday, doing their best 'N Sync imitation and laughing when the lyrics got away from them. In another blink Bailey was fifteen and Connor was twelve, and they were performing on stage together — *The Adventures of Tom Sawyer*, their first Christian Kids Theater show. In a matter of days, the show's run was over and Jenny could remember — she could remember with everything in her heart — what it felt like watching Bailey and Connor help tear down the sets, taking apart Hannibal, Missouri, where Tom Sawyer had lived and breathed and sang and danced just hours earlier. The thought that went through her mind then was the exact same one going through her mind now:

God, let me hold onto this moment ...

She watched them, memorizing the sound of their voices and the looks on their faces ... the way they laughed together, even as they sang. She didn't move, didn't even notice herself breathing. Because after a lifetime of scenes like this one, a lifetime of summers and rehearsals and late nights when it felt like Bailey and Connor and the idyllic childhood they'd shared would go on forever, here they were at the end. She slipped her arm around Jim's waist and leaned a little further into his shoulder. Briefly she lifted her eyes to his and she could see he was feeling the same way.

The show run for Bailey and Connor was drawing to a close.

Jenny looked at her daughter, at the beautiful young woman she'd become. She was ready for whatever was next. She earned high marks in college, and she'd played a starring role in a major motion picture. Her poise and confidence, her ability to sing and dance, her love for God — all of it was stronger now than the first time they'd gone to New York. Jenny had seen the look of determination and desire in Bailey's eyes over the last few weeks when they talked about the audition.

"I'm not letting the chance slip away," she spoke the words in the kitchen yesterday, her eyes bright with intensity. Nothing could hide her passion. "I'll prove it to them." She grinned. "They need me."

Now here they were, hours before she and Bailey would board the plane, days before an opportunity in New York that could give Bailey her dreams and her wings. The audition that could take her from their family for months or years.

Maybe forever.

The song came to an end, and Connor slung his arm around his sister. He was taller than her now — by half a foot, easily. His shoulders had filled out, and he was both a strong athlete and a gifted singer and songwriter. But he still adored Bailey as much as he had when he was three years old. Time could separate them and take them in different directions, but it couldn't change that.

"Well," Bailey was breathless as she looked from Connor to Jenny and Jim. "How'd we sound?"

"You could've sold tickets." Jim clapped a few times, and gave a brief nod to both kids. "I couldn't move if I wanted to. Seriously. You guys were fantastic."

"Honey," Jenny held her arms out and Bailey came to her. They hugged for several seconds, and Jenny ran her hand along her daughter's long hair. "Sing like that on Monday and the part's yours."

"Really?" Bailey eased back and smiled, her eyes an unforgettable mix of innocence and determination. "I sounded good?"

"Amazing." Jenny kissed her daughter's forehead.

Connor came alongside them and grinned at his sister. "Of course, you might need your sidekick to sound *that* good."

They all laughed, and as the group headed through the dining room into the kitchen, Jenny remembered why she'd come downstairs. "Your clothes are in the dryer, which means you haven't finished packing."

Bailey laughed. "I haven't started."

"Me, either." Jenny cast a sheepish look at her husband. "Like mother, like daughter. What can I say?"

"Let's not say anything." Jim's smile kept the moment light, full of the excitement that lay ahead for Jenny and Bailey. "This might be a better time for action."

Connor opened a loaf of bread and pulled out two slices. The peanut butter sat open nearby. "Leave room in your suitcase for me, Mom. Don't forget."

"Right." Jenny headed upstairs with Bailey close behind her. "They'll never notice."

They reached the top and Bailey turned to her mom. "I opened a Twitter account this morning."

"Hmmm." Jenny's laugh was light and easy. "That could explain your room."

Bailey glanced at the clothes scattered across her floor. "I guess I could've cleaned first." Her shrug helped her look innocent. "It didn't take long. And it's what Dayne Matthews asked me to do."

"True." Jenny leaned against her daughter's door frame.

As the movie neared, the producers — one of them former actor Dayne Matthews — hoped Bailey would be involved in publicity, and that by posting on Twitter she would gather movie fans who wanted to know more about her life and her connection to Brandon Paul.

"I have one friend following me." Bailey grinned.

"Connor?"

"Exactly." She headed into her room and then stopped short. "I thought maybe ..." her eyes became softer, more pensive, "I don't know, maybe Cody will figure out I'm on Twitter and follow my updates. So he won't forget about me."

The reaction in Jenny's heart was sure and immediate. An ache that would always come when her daughter mentioned Cody. "Honey,... he won't ever forget you. No matter what he's going through right now."

Bailey was quiet, and for a long while she looked at her floor, at the mess around her, and then at the photo of her and Cody on the table near the window. "I miss him."

"I know." Jenny nodded. "We all do." Moments like this she was tempted to be angry at Cody for what he'd done to Bailey's heart, leaving without any logical reason. But she had stopped being angry a while ago. Whatever lay behind Cody's decision, he had to work through it.

A sad smile came over Bailey's face. "There's nothing I can do about it. I just wish I could call him or text him. Let him know about my audition. How God's working in my life. That sort of thing."

Jenny didn't have to tell Bailey not to act on those impulses. She merely allowed the wisdom of the years to shine from her eyes, her expression.

"I know." Bailey picked her empty suitcase off the floor and tossed it on her bed. "I won't do it. Next time he'll have to pursue me like a man pursuing water in a desert."

"Right." Jenny went to her and gave her a side hug. "That's it. That's what makes you one in a million, sweet girl." She held her close for a few seconds. "I'm proud of you, Bailey. If I haven't said so in a while."

"Thanks." She took a stack of jeans and sweaters and set them in the suitcase. "I'm good. I'm over him, really." She smiled, but it didn't hide the sadness in her eyes. "I tell myself that anyway. But you know me." She hesitated. "I still miss him."

"Let's talk about it later." Jenny backed up a few steps and nodded toward her own room down the hall. "After we pack."

"Deal." Bailey looked okay. The sadness over Cody was always there, beneath the surface.

They had practically grown up together. No matter who came and went from Bailey's life in the years ahead, no one would ever replace Cody. Not the way Jenny saw it. She headed down the hall to her room to pack. The funny thing was, she couldn't be sure anymore that Cody was the right guy for Bailey. Especially with the silence he'd kept between them lately. But whether they ever spoke again, Bailey would always miss him. Jenny was sure of that.

She thought about Bailey's efforts these past weeks. Jenny would find her in their family's dance room working out long after dinner, when the boys were already headed for bed. And several times a day she heard Bailey doing vocal warm-ups, taking the audition ahead as seriously as she'd taken anything in her life. Her daughter's intensity lately was one more reason Jenny felt the urgency of change, the reality that life wouldn't always stay the way it was today, with her kids under one roof. If this was her time to fly, the goodbye would be bittersweet. Desperately hard for Jenny and Jim, but so very right for Bailey. Even now Jenny could do nothing but smile over her daughter's enthusiasm. She might miss Cody. But nothing could dim her excitement over this New York audition.

Not even her broken heart.

Five

BAILEY FELT DIFFERENT ABOUT THIS TRIP TO NEW YORK FROM the moment she learned she was going. The first time around, she was nervous and unsure, aware that she didn't have the experience or the training to pull off a successful audition. Today she felt like the favorite in an Olympic race. God had given her the ability and the confidence, and she had worked harder than ever before — honing her dance skills and her voice — so that now she was ready. She could feel it all the way to her soul.

They were ten minutes from landing, and Bailey looked out the window at the city coming into view. The Sunday afternoon was cloudless, blue skies spanning over the Hudson River and all of Manhattan. "So many buildings." Bailey turned to her mom in the middle seat. "It always looks surreal, like it isn't possible for that many skyscrapers to be on one small piece of ground."

Her mom smiled and leaned closer, peering at the dozens of tall buildings that made up New York City. "First time I saw New York from the air, I was in middle school. I wondered how an island didn't sink under so many buildings."

"Exactly." Bailey narrowed her eyes, trying to see the tiny grid of streets that wound their way through the maze of cement and brick and rebar. "If I make it ... I wonder where I'll live." She sat back in her seat, her eyes on her hands. She'd thought about this every day. Every hour, really. But she hadn't wanted to talk about it before now. It was enough to focus on the audition, without imagining what might happen if she really won a part."

Her mom didn't say anything right away. Proof that this was something she'd thought about, too. That's how it was with the two of them. They could talk about anything at length. But when a conversation was more difficult, when the answers weren't easily at hand, they didn't say a word. Just a supportive silence that didn't need a rush of words and ideas. A minute or so passed before her mom reached over and squeezed her hand. "I know this much," her voice was low, her head angled toward Bailey's. "If God opens the doors for you to win a part on Broadway, then He'll show you where to live." She peered out the window at the city once more. "No matter how intimidating New York City might be from up here."

"From down there, too." Bailey giggled, and she could hear the nervousness in her voice. "I mean, I love New York, but it's a crazy place."

They let the conversation stall, and Bailey guessed her mom was as lost in thought as she was. Would she live in a tiny apartment blocks from the theater, or would she share a place with someone in the cast? Would the show let out sometime around ten o'clock each night only to send her walking through the dark streets alone? Or off to the subway and a place in Jersey or Queens? Bailey felt the beginning of knots in her stomach, and she smiled.

I know what You're telling me, God ... I can hear You.

She closed her eyes and let the Lord's words resonate in her heart: *Daughter, do not worry about tomorrow ... tomorrow will worry about itself. Each day has enough trouble of its own.*

She had been memorizing Bible verses lately and this was one she'd taken on a week ago, in light of her pending audition. *Don't worry about tomorrow.* How great God was to bring it to mind now — when she could hardly draw a breath for imagining how she'd go from living with her family to venturing into a city like New York by herself. *Okay, Father. I hear You. I won't worry.*

Besides, she was getting way ahead of herself. She hadn't had the audition yet, and there were bound to be a thousand girls going for the handful of roles. Confidence was one thing, but worrying about housing this far out was a little ridiculous. She blinked her eyes open as the plane shuddered, tossed about in a patch of turbulent air. The aircraft made a few solid thuds, and then the flight path seemed to smooth out. Once the plane was on the ground the thrill of all that lay ahead helped her stay in the moment. That and the Bible verse from earlier.

They caught a cab into the city, and Bailey held onto the back of the seat in front of them. Their driver was a happy guy from Zimbabwe with the crazy ability to accelerate to breathtaking speeds and then stop on a dime for a light or a pedestrian. "Gotta love the city pace," he called out as he drove, his eyes alternating between the road and the rearview mirror. "Fast, fast, fast."

Bailey and her mom shared a look. Fast, indeed. They reached the Marriott Marquis in no time, checked in, and hung up their clothes. On the way back down to the lobby, Bailey stood as close as she could to the curved glass wall of the high-speed elevator. Once, a long time ago, she and Cody had taken a walk behind her parents' house and they'd talked about skydiving. "I want to do it someday," he squinted at the sky. "Jump from a plane and soar down to earth."

The idea sounded terrifying at the time, but with Cody it at least seemed possible. The elevator sped smoothly twenty-three floors back down to the shiny glitz of the hotel lobby. Bailey felt the rush as the floor seemed to rise up to meet them. Just like skydiving. Without Cody it was as close as she was going to get — for now anyway. She tucked the thought away and smiled at her mom. "I have an idea."

"What?"

"Let's find a Yankees hat for Ricky. That's his new favorite team."

"Of course." Bailey laughed. "That's all he's talked about for weeks."

It was only two in the afternoon, so they had plenty of time. The air outside was crisp and cold in the shade, but the cool weather had done nothing to deter the people. Times Square was so crowded they had to work to stay together. They headed south on Broadway, staying with the flow of people. Along the way they passed a guy with a golden python draped around his shoulders and a sweet-souled old man playing "Amazing Grace" on a clarinet, a bucket of change at his feet. Bailey and her mom stopped and listened for a minute, pulling themselves out of the crowd long enough to pay attention.

Her life would be like this if she lived here: looking for moments amidst the insanity to hear God's voice and the message He might have for her. *Amazing grace ... how sweet the sound ...* Yes, the message was sweet — especially here in the middle of Times Square with humanism and vanity and quest for monetary success dominating the general order of the day. They all needed God's grace, but only every so often did one of the people in the passing crowd even look in the direction of the clarinet player. Bailey breathed in deeply and savored the sound of the man's song. *I once was lost, but now am found ... was blind but now I see.* God's grace alone had given her this second chance, this opportunity to shine for Him at a Broadway audition.

Bailey left a five dollar tip in the man's bucket, and he nodded at her as they walked off. "There's not a lot of that in New York City," her mom slipped an arm around her shoulder. "If you live here, you'll have to *look* for God."

"I know. I've been thinking about that." The worry from earlier tried to clutch at Bailey's heart, but she refused it. "I keep telling myself that He wouldn't lead me here without also providing. I believe that."

Her mom smiled. "I believe it too."

The afternoon flew by, and they found the hat for Ricky and a handful of T-shirts for the other boys. An early dinner at the Olive Garden gave them time to talk about tomorrow. They had barely been seated when Bailey felt her phone vibrate. She pulled it from her back jeans pocket and for half a second she wondered if it might be Cody. Maybe he'd heard about her audition and wanted to tell her he was praying for her, believing in her ...

But as the phone's screen came into view, she reminded herself that Cody hadn't been in touch with her for months. She smiled as she opened the text message. It was from her old friend Tim Reed.

Big audition tomorrow, right? Can we have breakfast in the morning? At your hotel maybe?

"Who is it?" Her mom took a sip of her ice water and settled back in the chair, looking as tired as Bailey felt. They hadn't walked more than a few miles, but the city had a way of wearing out a person. Just the pace of it.

"Tim." Bailey read the text out loud. "What do you think? Do we have time for breakfast?"

"Maybe." Jenny pulled an itinerary from her purse. "We need to be at the studio at nine ... so, yes, if Tim wants to meet us at the hotel restaurant at eight, that should work."

Bailey texted back the time and location.

Perfect.

Tim's response came almost immediately, and Bailey read the message out loud. "He says he'll bring his girlfriend. He's dying for us to meet her. I guess she knows Francesca Tilly, so she can give me pointers for tomorrow."

Her mom raised her brow slightly. "So he does have a girlfriend?"

"He's mentioned her a few times." Bailey didn't want to sound affected by the fact, but she was. "I guess they're official."

She glanced at her phone and once more she let her eyes run

over the word *girlfriend*. The girl was in *Wicked*, same as Tim. She was pretty and talented — an ensemble dancer with long legs and short blond hair. Bailey had seen her in the show when Brandon Paul had flown them to New York City toward the end of their *Unlocked* shoot.

"Does it bother you ... Tim having a girlfriend?" They were seated at a quiet table near the window, the chaos of the city blocked out for now.

"A little." She angled her head. "I mean, sort of, I guess. But maybe more because he's happy and in love and I'm ..." She shrugged, and a smile lifted the corners of her lips. "I'm alone."

There were a dozen things her mother could've said at that point, bits of wisdom they'd discussed a number of times before. She could've said this was a season for Bailey and God — that He was all she needed. Or she could've said that Bailey's future husband was out there somewhere, so maybe this was a good time to pray for him. She could've reminded Bailey that this was a time to pursue her dreams and not worry about a guy in her life, and she could've pointed out that God had great plans for her, like in Jeremiah 29:11. That sort of wisdom. All of that would've been good and true.

But in this moment her mom did something even better. She reached out and gave Bailey's hand a squeeze and said absolutely nothing for a long moment. "I'm sorry, sweetie." She sighed and her half smile touched Bailey to the core. "I know it's hard."

Bailey nodded. "It is." Her throat was suddenly too tight to say anything more. What was there to say? Cody had disappeared, Tim had moved on ... and there were no guys whatsoever pursuing her. She thought of her father's comments about Matt Keagan from last week. Matt didn't count. He was a Christian hero — not a guy she might think about dating.

The waitress came with their dinner, and Bailey's emotions settled back into place. They thanked God for the food, and then

Bailey looked at her mom. "I'm happy for Tim. Really." She ate a bite of broccoli. "He wasn't the right guy for me."

"No." Bailey's mom moved her fork through her chicken Caesar salad. "He didn't cherish you, honey. He could walk out of the room while you were singing." A dreamy look came over her face. "I sometimes picture the guy you'll marry. I mean, his face isn't clear, but I can picture him. And one thing I know ..." She looked straight at Bailey, her eyes shining. "When you sing, he won't be able to leave the room. He'll barely remember to breathe. Because your song will resonate in the depths of his soul."

Bailey could've cried. Wasn't that exactly what she was believing for ... praying for? That a guy would love her so completely someday that her song would resonate in the depths of his soul? She released a slow sigh, and willed herself to be patient. God knew all these things. He would help her through this time of singleness, of going after her dream to perform.

She held onto that truth as they finished dinner and headed back to their room for an early night. Bailey ran through her audition material several times before falling asleep. But as she did, she wondered what seeing Tim with his girlfriend would be like, whether she would have feelings for him or regrets over their breakup. The next morning at breakfast, the answer was as clear as the morning sky.

Tim and Adrienne arrived just as Bailey and her mom were being seated. The group exchanged hugs, and Bailey was careful to note how she felt—being in Tim's arms again, even for only a few seconds. The feeling brought great relief and allowed Bailey to focus on Adrienne and her wisdom as a Broadway professional.

Because her feelings for Tim Reed were absolutely nothing but friendship.

They settled in around the table, and Tim helped Adrienne with her chair and then introduced her to Bailey and her mom. He seemed attentive and charming around her, and no question that his eyes sparkled when he looked at her. The reality hurt, but Bailey kept her voice and expression upbeat and happy. Tim had never looked at her the way he now looked at Adrienne. One of the reasons they hadn't worked out was that he never seemed truly captivated by her. Like her mom had pointed out, he could leave the room when she was singing. Bailey had a feeling he stayed glued to his chair when Adrienne sang.

Oh well, she told herself. Further proof that Tim wasn't the one. And better to know that much now — while she was still young — rather than follow after a guy that was wrong for her and waste these years. They helped themselves to plates from the breakfast buffet, and then gathered back at the table. The waitress served coffee, and Bailey had a cup. But no cream. She wanted her voice clear, her tone right on this morning.

"Tell Bailey about Francesca." Tim turned his body so he faced his girlfriend. "The stuff you were telling me the other night. Before our date."

Adrienne grinned, and a slight blush colored her cheeks. She ran her hand over her hair and seemed to work to find her focus. Whatever the date had been, it must've meant a lot to both of them. Bailey tried to ignore the fact.

"Francesca is intense." Adrienne looked at Bailey and her smile fell off. "You have to come to the audition with thick skin, not worried about what she says. If she gives you direction it's because she likes you."

"You've worked with her?" Bailey focused her attention on the blond dancer. This information was priceless.

"I was in *Hairspray* before *Wicked*." She shot a quick grin at Tim, as if the best part of being in the cast of *Wicked* was her relationship with Tim Reed. Then she seemed to remember that she was in the middle of telling a story. "Francesca has no barriers, no reservations about what she'll say. She'll walk up in the middle of an audition or rehearsal and adjust your posture or tell you exactly what she thinks of your singing. Don't let it bother you. She demands excellence, and she gets it."

Gratitude spread through Bailey. This was crucial. The fact that Francesca was hard on everyone — especially dancers she felt were talented — could help Bailey push through the audition later this morning if she felt she was failing. The hour was over almost as soon as it began, and Bailey felt like she'd found a friend in Adrienne. Never mind about Tim. If Bailey ended up in New York City, she could see herself hanging out with his girlfriend, if not him. Tim had already explained that Adrienne shared his faith, so they'd have that much in common.

Bailey was dressed in a V-neck white T-shirt and black dance pants, and in her bag she had her character shoes and a folder with her headshot and resume — all that was required according to Francesca's message a few weeks ago. The audition was only eight blocks away, so they made the trip on foot. The warm-up would be good for her. They walked on the sunny side of the street and Bailey began to feel herself loosening up. She could hardly wait.

As she expected, there was a line of girls stretched out the door and halfway down the block in front of the studio hosting the audition. Bailey wasn't bothered by the numbers. After all, Francesca Tilly had called her personally. Certainly she'd be looking for Bailey today. And now that she'd worked so hard, she was bound to catch the director's eye sometime today.

Her mom caught a car back to the hotel. She was working on an article for a women's magazine, so the hours alone would be good for her. "Call me with any updates." The routine felt familiar, much like last time they were in New York City for an audition. But this was different. Bailey was on her own, without Tim, and she wasn't nervous — not at all. The information from Adrienne played in her head as she signed in and found a spot on the expansive studio dance floor to stretch.

Again the room was filled with dancers — all of them about the same age and build. She would have to shine very brightly to win a part today. *Father, You know this is my dream ... I feel You've created me for this, to shine for You. So please help me do my best. Help me sing and dance and act in a way that brings You glory. Thank You, God ...*

Francesca was bringing order to the room. Bailey guessed there were two hundred girls there — and maybe another two hundred still down at the street level waiting for the next round. Francesca was a petite woman, angular with wiry gray hair. She dressed much like the dancers — black tights, a black leotard, and a spandex skirt with bright orange and blue swirls. Her hair was wound tightly at the top of her head, and her quick pace and hurried movements made it clear she was on a mission to get the auditions over with.

"Line up," she snapped. "Everyone." She waved her hand like she was casting a spell, and immediately three assistants jumped into motion, organizing the girls in even rows. Bailey tried for the front, but she wasn't fast enough. She wound up in the third row instead — two from the end. Francesca planted herself front and center, her hands on her hips. When the girls were in place, she barked a single word at them. *"Hairspray!"*

For a long half a minute no one dared speak. Most of the dancers — including Bailey — resisted the urge to look around the room for some shared bit of empathy. Maybe they'd all heard what Bailey had heard. That Francesca Tilly was a little eccentric.

Finally Francesca drew a full breath and stared them down, as close to one at a time as she could. "You know this show — at least I'd like to hope you know it." She clapped her hands, fast and sharp. "It's energy, energy, energy." She stood on her tiptoes, shielded her eyes, and stared over the center of the formation. "That's who I'll cut first. Anyone without energy." She began to pace across the front of the room. "Show me your energy, girls, or you're done."

Bailey was ready for this. She'd been jumping rope and doing Zumba classes in her family's gym every morning and practicing dance each evening. She was in the best shape of her life and bursting with energy. She shook out her fingers, keeping herself loose.

"My choreographer Suzanne will teach you the Corny Collins dance, and you will learn it faster than you've ever learned any dance before. That's how I run things."

Suzanne took the floor and began teaching. The dance was fast and demanding, Francesca was right. But Bailey grasped it. When they did their first run through she was ready. By then Francesca was walking along the outer edge of the square staring down the dancers, doing just what Adrienne had said.

She walked up to one girl and forcefully adjusted her shoulders. "Dancers pay attention to their posture."

Bailey straightened more than before. Francesca was on the opposite side of the room, but still ... she didn't want to be next.

As Suzanne taught the dance, Francesca made her way up and down every row, studying the dancers, sizing them up. When she reached the girl next to Bailey, Francesca stopped. A puzzled look came over her face and she took a step back. For a long while she looked the girl up and down — clearly disapproving of something. Then she stepped up and raised the girl's headband higher onto her head, off her forehead. "There. Your face looks thinner."

Bailey stopped herself from looking shocked. Was the woman serious? She had no problem saying something like that to a girl she didn't know? In front of all these people? She focused on Suzanne at the front of the room. The choreographer was snapping her fingers. "Run through it! Ready ... five, six, seven, eight."

Francesca stared at Bailey as the dance began. *She's not standing there*, Bailey told herself. *Dance for the Lord ... shine for Jesus.*

She threw everything she had into the number, smiling big and making every movement sharp and crisp and full of the rhythm it deserved.

"You're Bailey Flanigan ... the actress from *Unlocked*, is that right?" Her words were pointed and loud. Too loud.

"Yes, ma'am." Bailey glanced at her and continued dancing. What if one of the other girls heard the director? They'd assume Bailey had an edge, right? She put the thought from her mind. Francesca didn't smile or acknowledge that the observation mattered whatsoever. And she didn't straighten her spine or adjust her clothing or order her to stay with the beat.

That had to be a good sign. But still Bailey didn't want to win the part because of her role in *Unlocked*. She wanted to be recognized for her skill, her hard work.

Half an hour into the audition, the teaching was finished. "This will be a quick audition. If you survive the dance segment, we'll ask twenty of you to stay and sing. If I tap you, that means we don't need you for now. If you aren't selected, please leave. This isn't your show ... it isn't your day. Before I make cuts, thank you for being here. Musical theater is an art, and it's not for everyone." She stopped pacing and smiled at the girls. It was the first time she'd done so since the audition began. Her smile dropped off. "Now let's take this seriously and see some dancing." She clapped her hands three sharp times. "Energy ... energy ... energy!"

Francesca nodded at Suzanne, and the choreographer hit the play button on the boom box perched on a chair behind her. Music for the Corny Collins song filled the room and Bailey felt her heart soar within her. Sure she was tired and sweaty, but she still had an ocean of energy. This was the show she loved most of all, and the dance was the original Broadway choreography. The number was too fun to waste it being nervous. Besides, God was with her. She could feel Him cheering her on.

Suzanne shouted above the music. "And five, six, seven, eight!"

With that Bailey lit into the dance with everything she had inside her. She wasn't sure if Francesca could even see her from where she walked along the front line, but she danced hard anyway. Out of the corner of her eyes she watched the director briefly survey three girls at a time, and then brutally tap all three. As she did, she shook her head, her expression colored with disgust. The next three girls met the same fate, and Bailey had a feeling Francesca's first walk-through was more important than she let on. At least with the first row of dancers, the director already seemed to have her mind made up. As the girls were tapped, they quietly excused themselves from the dance floor, gathered their things, and made a hasty exit.

The second row included two girls who were allowed to stay, and both kept dancing — not willing to accept the pass over as proof they were in. Francesca stepped up to the third row and gave the girls a critical onceover. The song had started again, and Bailey no longer had to concentrate to get the steps right. Instead she put everything into her performance, dancing as if her life depended on it.

Francesca stopped in front of her, and then Bailey saw something that made her practically shout for joy. In the slightest, most subtle possible way, Francesca smiled at her. She gave a firm nod with her head and moved on to the next girl. And like that Bailey had survived the first round, the dance portion of the audition. Like the other girls who were being allowed to stay, Bailey kept dancing until Suzanne had restarted the music five times, giving Francesca time to work her way through the entire group.

"That's all," the director shouted from the back of the room. "That's our first cut. Get something to drink, girls. We'll start again in ten minutes with vocal auditions."

The music stopped, and Bailey hugged the girl in front of

her — one of those from the second row who'd been allowed to stay. Adrienne's information had definitely helped this morning. Bailey wanted to be the best performer not only at this audition, but on all of Broadway. That meant she needed to work with the best director in the business, and if that meant dealing with Francesca's eccentricities, so be it. Bailey was up for the challenge.

She hurried to the side of the room, found her things, and downed a water bottle. Then she pulled her phone from a side pocket in her purse and texted her mom: *Where are you? I made it past the first round!!*

Bailey dabbed her face with a towel from her bag as her mom texted back. *That's great! Can you talk?*

Francesca was meeting with Suzanne at the far side of the room. All around Bailey girls were on their phones, talking quietly. The director hadn't said anything about not using their phones, so rather than text back, she hit the call button and waited until she heard her mom's voice. "Bailey?"

"I'm still in it!" She kept her voice low like the other girls, but there was no way to contain her enthusiasm. "There were so many great dancers, Mom. I think I'm in shock."

"Honey, that's wonderful. So what's next? Will you sing for them?"

"Exactly." Francesca looked their way and checked her watch. Bailey lowered her voice. "I have to run. I'll call when I'm done."

The voice auditions were handled differently. The girls were told that everyone would sing and then the directors would make a decision after they were done. Francesca sat on a panel with two other directors who had arrived during the break. Only once did Francesca blow up at one of the girls auditioning. The girl who riled the director sang the song, "On My Own" from *Les Miserables*. Whoever she was, she didn't have much confidence. She was maybe twenty-three, twenty-four — thin with long, wispy pale blond hair and a pretty, frail voice. The other girls who hadn't sung yet waited off to the side. Collectively they cringed as Francesca stood and marched to the girl. She took her by the arm and led her another twenty yards farther away from the audition area. "There." Francesca cupped her hands around her own mouth. "Do this."

The girl did as she was told.

Bailey bit her lip, her eyes wide. Truly if Adrienne hadn't told her about Francesca, this would seem like some sort of joke. All around her she could feel the other girls barely breathing.

Francesca left the girl standing there, her hands up around the sides of her mouth, then she stormed back to the director's table. "Now." She picked up her pen and hovered it over a pad of paper. "Sing with projection."

The girl tried, but Francesca waved her off after three bars. "Enough." She gestured to the door. "Be gone." She craned her neck and peered at the line of girls yet to sing. "Next. Hurry up, people. Next audition."

Bailey planned to sing a song from *Last Five Years* called, "I'm a Part of That." When it was her turn, she begged God for favor and then took her place. As she did, a sort of other-worldly peace came over her. She wasn't auditioning for Francesca Tilly or putting herself in front of a group of strangers to be judged. She was God's girl, and she was doing what she was born to do.

The song was part ballad, part high-energy — the perfect choice for *Hairspray*, Bailey had decided. The music began and she was in character immediately. Her song lasted just over a minute, and not until it was over did Bailey realize she'd been allowed to finish. Many of the girls had been cut off halfway through their songs.

One of the directors — a guy with sympathetic eyes — had told them that it didn't necessarily mean they were out of the running just because they were cut off. But it didn't take a mind reader to figure out what was going through Francesca's head when she waved her hand and stopped some of the girls mid-song.

Bailey grabbed her bag and moved into the hallway in time to see two girls leave in tears, comforting each other as they headed out the door. Bailey hurt for the girls, for whatever their stories were, whatever might have been riding on this audition today.

"You're Bailey Flanigan?" A girl with long red hair looked her over. "I heard Francesca ... you're in *Unlocked*, right? With Brandon Paul?"

"Yes." Bailey felt strangely ashamed of the fact. She wanted to tell the dancer her involvement in the movie didn't give her an edge here. But she wasn't completely sure.

"Why'd you bother to show up?" The girl tossed her bag over her shoulder. "You'll get a part for sure." She turned and left without another word to Bailey.

Heat filled Bailey's cheeks. It wasn't true. The part wasn't hers because of her role in *Unlocked*. She had to work hard at the audition — same as everyone else, right? A part of her wanted to run after the redhead and tell her she was wrong. No one was giving her any favors. But the shame she'd felt a moment ago still lingered and she remained in place.

She leaned against the wall and pulled out her cell phone, realizing something that was only now hitting her. She had a chance. She really had a chance. Not because of her acting resume, but because she'd made it this far on her own merit, her own hard work. *Thank You, God ... because of You I left nothing behind. Nothing.* She had no idea if she'd get a part, but she knew this much: She had done her best. No, better than that, she had done the best she could in God's strength.

Now she could hardly wait to tell her mom.

Six

CODY WALKED THROUGH THE LAST SET OF THE SECURITY DOORS at the Indiana Women's Prison and spotted his mother at a table by herself. For a moment he hesitated, taking in the sight of her. She was thinner than before, her face more lined — the consequences of the hard life she'd chosen the first time she dabbled in drugs as a teenager. He walked to her, and she spotted him. A smile found its way to her face, and her eyes softened.

She was sober for now, sweet and kind, the mother he'd always wanted. The one she could only bring herself to be when she was behind bars. Cody pulled out the chair opposite her and took her hands in his. "Hi."

"Hi." Her hands were cold, her voice shaky. "Thanks, Cody ... for coming. Every week I ... I wonder."

"You don't have to wonder." Cody wouldn't stop coming. This was why he'd moved from Bloomington to Indianapolis, after all. "I'll be here." He smiled, remembering to be compassionate. "I'll always be here."

She smiled, and tears welled in her eyes. "I ... I don't deserve you."

Cody felt the sting in his own eyes, and he blinked. He wouldn't spend the next hour caught in a weepy conversation. If this was the single conversation he'd have with his mother for the week, he wanted it to be at least somewhat normal. "Hey ... so I love the job at Lyle."

His mom's shoulders straightened some. Pride filled her

expression and eased the lines on her forehead. "I always thought you'd make a great teacher."

"It's weird." He released the hold he had on her hands and rocked back in his chair. "The kids are so young. I mean, it feels like a lifetime ago that I was in high school. But still they relate to me."

"Of course they do." She beamed at him. "Look at you ... so strong and handsome. They probably thought you were a student when you first stepped on campus."

Cody grinned and stared out the window for a few seconds. His mom was right. His first week that's exactly what had happened. On the morning of his third day a girl walked up to him in the hallway and asked if he wanted to go to the Tolo dance with her. "It's girls ask guys." She batted her eyes at him. "And since you're new ..."

"Sorry." He took a step back. Flattering as it was to be thought he was still in high school, he wanted to make the chasm between him and the girl students as wide as the Grand Canyon. "I'm Mr. Coleman. The new PE teacher."

The girl's face turned redder than Christmas. Her mouth hung open, as if she might say something but no words would come. Then she turned and ran off to catch up with her friends who were laughing ten yards away. Cody chuckled again remembering the scene. "You're right. They definitely thought I was one of them."

"That's why they'll look up to you. You're their age." His mom folded her hands in front of her. "How about the coaching?"

"It's spring league — just passing drills three days a week after school." He paused. "There's this one kid, DeMetri Smith. People call him Smitty." Cody liked this, talking to his mom about life, as if they were any other mother and son, and this were a normal meeting — and not an hour-long visit at a state prison. "Anyway, he comes from a broken home, but he's a Christian. Spends a lot of time praying."

"Hmmm." Sadness crept into her tone. "Like you ... once you found the Flanigans."

Cody hesitated. "I guess." He'd thought about the similarities. It was partly why he wanted to help the kid. In DeMetri, he could see something he saw when he looked in the mirror. The sheer determination to find a path different than the one he'd been raised with. Cody had worked at Lyle High for four weeks. Long enough to understand how things ran — the small town ways and the big-hearted people. But this was the first time he'd shared details with his mom. Again, he was struck by how good it felt, how normal. Usually this hour was about her. Her Bible study. Her remorse.

Her regrets.

"Speaking of the Flanigans," his mom brought nervous fingers to her cheeks, and finding no comfortable position she lowered her hand back to the table. "Have you ... have you talked to Bailey?"

"Mom." Cody kept his tone in check, but he'd been over this with her before. "We don't talk about her. I told you that."

"I wondered, that's all. She ... she was important to you. For a very long time."

"We've moved on." Every word, every syllable scraped like a knife against his heart. "There's nothing to talk about."

"I guess," she looked down at her hands, her fingers still restless. For a long while she stayed like that, but then her eyes lifted to his. "I sort of hoped you'd find your way back to her. Have a new start."

Cody wondered how much heartache a person could take. "You know what, Mom?" For a brief moment, his emotions raced ahead of him. "Why didn't you think about that before you hooked up with a drug dealer?" He hesitated. "Right? I mean, did you think about how it might affect me to have some … some psycho drug king making death threats against the girl I love?"

He was breathing hard, his voice louder than he intended. A quick glance around the room told him that he'd caught the attention of other people. He rested his forearms on the table between them and hung his head. Treating her this way would get them nowhere. He looked up. "I'm sorry. I shouldn't have raised my voice."

"It's okay." Tears welled in his mother's eyes. "You're right. It's my fault. You and Bailey … I caused all of this."

"Not all of it." He sighed. "But please, Mom. Don't ask me about her. What happened is in the past. It's over." This time he kept the anger from his voice, but he could do nothing about the defeat. It crept in and spoke louder than his words. The rest of their visit was tainted by the moment, and Cody couldn't find his way back to the lightheartedness of earlier in the hour.

When his time was up, he held his mother's frail hands and prayed with her, asking God to continue to work in her life and to surround her with people who loved the truth. "There are consequences for walking away from You, Lord, from Your Word … consequences for walking in the darkness." His tone held no judgment toward her. A long time ago he had been the one risking his life for a night of going against God. He had nearly died of alcohol poisoning before the Lord got his attention. A sad sigh slipped from deep in his lungs. "Please, Father, bring healing to my mom, to our relationship. And show us both what the future is supposed to look like. In Jesus' name, amen."

He stood and hugged his mom. She held on longer than him, same as always. He didn't mind. His days as a prisoner of war in Iraq had taught him what life was like in captivity. Of course his mother held on as long as she could. It was a long time between Sundays, when every day was a reminder of all that could've been, all that might've been.

As he made his way out of the prison, Cody felt like the walls were closing in on him. His mind filled with images of bars and cells and people screaming for a chance at freedom. He blinked, trying to shake the pictures. Not until he was in his truck, the doors shut and locked, did the vision hit him again. This time clearly the scenes in his head weren't from his mother's prison.

They were from his own.

Crouched in an Iraqi cell ... dust crusted in his hair and fingernails and eyelashes. Dirt choking the breath from his throat, the only sound his raspy breathing and the scratching skittering of rats on the floor outside his cell. What was this feeling, the tightness in his chest? His heart pounded like it was looking for a way out, and he couldn't get enough air, couldn't shake the suffocation that had come over him like a wet blanket.

Dear God, why is this happening? Is it the prison? He gripped the steering wheel and let his head fall back against the seat rest. *It's been years since Iraq ... so why the flashbacks, Father ... why now?*

There was no answer, and again the visions came at him, relentless and vivid. The voice of an Iraqi soldier bursting into the room, barking at him, shoving a rifle butt into the cramped cage and shouting at him in Arabic. Despite the cold air in his pickup, sweat beaded on his forehead and trickled down his temples. *Help me, God ... take away the pictures in my head. Please ...*

Again, no response.

Cody forced himself to focus. When this had happened before, the only way out was Scripture. He closed his eyes tight and remembered a Bible verse from Deuteronomy. *When you go to war against your enemies and see horses and chariots and armies bigger than yours, do not be afraid of them. The Lord your God who brought you up out of Egypt will be with you.*

As the verse took root in his heart, the slightest relief came. For the first time in fifteen minutes the pressure in his chest eased. *When you go to war against your enemies and see horses and chariots . . .*

Cody said the words again and again, letting the truth of God battle against the horror of his memories. It was true, of course. God had rescued him from the prison in Iraq once already. He would do so again now, and as often as Cody needed His help. That was the point of the Bible verse.

Another five minutes passed before Cody could breathe normally, before he felt ready to tackle the rest of his day. Before he could open his eyes without feeling the walls closing in around him. *Thank You, Father . . . You care about me. I know You do.*

For the first time in a long time, Cody thought about his own father, the one he'd never known. Where was he this Sunday afternoon and did he know that his son was struggling? Did he care? Cody dismissed the thought as quickly as it came. His mother had explained the situation a long time ago. His father wasn't ready to be a dad. That's why he hadn't been a part of Cody's life. But still, it was normal to wonder, to wish on a day like this that he could drive across town and have a family day with someone other than his mom. Someone not in prison.

He rolled down the window and breathed in deep. The cold air felt good against his face. How crazy to think about his dad after all these years. Nothing good could ever come from such thinking. Not now or ever. He turned the key and waited a minute while the engine warmed up. Then he headed back home. On the way he remembered a message he'd gotten yesterday from Tara Collins. He took his phone from the other seat and at the next light he tapped a few buttons and played her message again.

"Cody, listen here! It's been too long since you dragged yourself over to my house for dinner." Cody smiled. Even Tara's voice was larger than life, the way everything was about her. "I'm cooking up a pot roast tomorrow and I'm setting you a place. So figure it out and take care of all y'all's chores and tasks and whatnot, and get your hungry self over here." She paused, laughter in her voice. "All right then. See you tomorrow."

Tara Collins. Cody shook his head, missing the woman. She was the closest thing he had to family now that he wasn't a part of the Flanigans. At the thought of Bailey's family, Cody felt the sudden urge to turn his truck around, head west to Bloomington, and show up at her house for dinner or for a conversation on the porch. He would tell her that he was sorry about how things had ended and he'd make her understand his reasons for staying away. But his argument sounded weak, even to him. He had no idea how he would defend it to her.

The truth — the real truth — was that by now there had to be little danger posed by his mother's drug-dealer friend. The guy had been arrested so he had his own troubles to deal with. Cody certainly hadn't seen any signs of the man.

So maybe he should make the drive. What if his mother was right? Maybe he should find Bailey and tell her he was at fault, that he never should've let her go. Cody kept his eyes on the road. No, that was crazy. Bailey deserved someone like her father. Someone whole, with a pristine past.

My son ... you are forgiven and whole. I know the plans I have for you ... good plans ...

The words filled the space around him and inside him, and the impact of them was so great Cody nearly pulled off the road. Cornfields and wide open spaces surrounded the highway under a gray sky and there were almost no other cars on the road. Cody decided not to stop. But even so he had trouble focusing on the drive when God had clearly just spoken to him. The Lord often reminded him of Scriptures and words of wisdom from the godly people in his life. But this? As if God was riding shotgun in his pickup?

Adrenaline worked its way through his body, and he sat up straighter, his heart beating fast again. What had the voice said,

the one that resonated through his being? That he was forgiven and whole, that God had great plans for him. The words were a combination of Bible verses, and they lifted his heart and mood. Maybe not this weekend, but sometime in the next few weeks he would make a trip to Bloomington. He missed Bailey so much he sometimes wondered how he made it through an entire day without her.

Yes, he would take the trip sometime this month, once the snow melted a little more. Maybe he and Bailey could take a walk the way they used to, talk about what the last few months had been like for both of them. Again Cody felt himself relax. He couldn't be sure what would come of such a visit, but he would take the drive, make the trip to Bloomington. But for now he would have dinner at Tara's.

He stopped at a grocery store and picked up a gallon of vanilla ice cream, something to go with the hot dessert Tara would inevitably make. It was the least he could do. He arrived at her house just before five o'clock — early enough to help out. As far as he knew he was the only one sharing dinner with her tonight. Usually if she'd invited anyone else she would say so.

Tara met him at the screen door of her neatly manicured brick house before he reached the porch steps. "Cody!" Her voice was almost as big as her smile. She pushed the door open and held both arms out. "I knew you wouldn't let me have dinner alone again."

"Whatever you're cooking, it smells wonderful." He hugged her and followed her into the house. "What can I do?"

"See that potato peeler?" She pointed to a spot next to the sink. Then she grinned at a bowl of freshly washed potatoes. "Put it to work!"

Cody rolled up his sleeves and crossed the kitchen to the sink.

"You look real good, Cody." Tara was ripping lettuce leaves

on the other side of the counter, making a salad too large for two. "Taking care of yourself, right?"

"Yes, ma'am." Cody stifled a grin. Everything about being with Tara made him feel like he belonged. The way he had always felt when he was with the Flanigans. Having dinner here took the edge off his loneliness. He glanced over his shoulder at her. "I work out with the team most days. Jog a couple miles, lift some weights."

"Well, it shows." She waved her knife in the air. "Art was always lifting weights, and it showed on him too. Good for a young man. Keep you strong."

"Exactly." Cody was about to ask why they needed so many potatoes when the doorbell rang. He raised a single eyebrow at Tara. "Thought it was just you and me."

"Are you kidding?" Tara grabbed a dishtowel and flicked it at him as she walked past. "You don't have half the sense of a turnip. If I didn't invite that pretty little Cheyenne over here, you'd never see her." She stopped and shook her head, a mock look of disapproval on her face. "Wasted youth. I tell you what ..." She walked off still muttering about the fact that Cody hadn't called Cheyenne once all month.

A strange sense of nervousness came over Cody and he doubled his effort on the potato in his hand. The way Tara was trying to set him up with Cheyenne was beginning to feel awkward, as if maybe she would truly be upset with him if he didn't pursue the girl who was once engaged to Art. Then there was Cheyenne, and however she might feel about all this. She'd already lost so much when Art died. The last thing he wanted to do was hurt her.

The two of them returned to the kitchen, and Cody set the peeler down in the bowl and turned. It had been three weeks since he'd seen Cheyenne at Tara's house, and he was struck again by her eyes. Gorgeous brown eyes with lashes that went on forever. Something about her was alluring, intriguing. It wasn't her looks—though she was very pretty. It was more something in her soul, a quiet strength born out of loss and pain, and the ability to survive, ready to live again on the other side.

"Hi." She smiled and crossed her arms, surveying him. She wore a pale blue turtleneck and jeans, and she was breathless from the cold outside. "I see Tara's put you to work." She came closer and picked up one of his finished potatoes. The lines were smooth, and none of the brown peeling was left. "Hmmm. I'm impressed." She was so close he could smell her perfume. Something woodsy or spicy maybe? "Most guys can't peel a potato."

Cody thought about all the times he'd made dinner for himself because his mom was passed out on the couch, or because he had to fend for himself when she was in prison. Potatoes were cheap, and his mom always kept them in the house. The first time he peeled a potato he was probably only seven or eight. Plus he'd learned his way around a kitchen watching the Flanigans too. Even the youngest of Bailey's brothers knew how to cook basic food.

"Well ..." He set to work on the next potato and grinned at her. "I'm not most guys."

She looked at him and held his gaze. Held it for several seconds. "That much I know."

Suddenly Cody caught Tara's approving smile from across the room. She was chopping tomatoes, sprinkling them onto the salad. Again a sense of alarm crept in around Cody's happy mood. What was he doing? And how come he could so easily find chemistry with Cheyenne when his heart still longed for Bailey? He made an effort to be less flirty, and the rest of the evening conversation was easy between the three of them. Tara talked about winning a promotion at work, and how Cheyenne was working hard on her classes this semester. She wanted to be a nurse—something she hadn't been sure of the first time Cody met her.

"Art would be so proud, baby girl. So proud." Tara stood and gave Cheyenne a side hug right in the middle of dinner. "I always knew you had the gift of sweet mercies. You go after those *A*'s."

Cheyenne cast a slightly embarrassed look at Cody. She was clearly not comfortable in the spotlight. Her humility was another reason Cody sometimes felt drawn to her. He smiled and gave a light shrug, then he turned his attention back to the pot roast still on his plate. What was this connection between them, and why did he feel it more strongly tonight?

He and Cheyenne both helped with the cleanup, and afterwards Tara talked them into a game of Scrabble — which Cheyenne easily won.

"See there, Cody!" Tara threw her head back and laughed out loud. "Better not let that girl go. Right, Chey?"

"Mama." Cheyenne hadn't changed the familiar title. Art was gone, yes, but the love between Cheyenne and Tara would always remain. Cheyenne giggled some, keeping the tone of the conversation playful. She angled her head and shot a warning look at Tara. "Cody's my friend. Leave him alone."

"But you don't have to tell me how smart she is," Cody raised his brow at his dismal Scrabble score. "Pretty sure her game just told us that much."

With the game over, they shared dessert and Cody dished the ice cream. As they sat back down, Tara's easy laughter faded. "So, baby girl, how are you really? You put Art's things away yet?"

Cheyenne clearly wasn't expecting the conversation to go in this direction. She looked off toward a framed photo of Art on Tara's dining room wall. She set her spoon down and shook her head — almost apologetically. "I can't do it, Mama. I still . . . I still feel him all around me." Her voice caught and she struggled for the next words. "If I take everything down, it would be like . . . like I've moved on and then," she shook her head, "what would that say about me?"

The conversation made Cody feel uncomfortable . . . like he

shouldn't be there. But he had no choice, and in this moment more than any other he understood again his connection to Cheyenne. Her loss, her vulnerability. She had paid such a very great cost for letting Art go to war, for standing by while he paid the sacrifice for freedom. For the freedom they all shared. It made Cody want to take her in his arms and hold her until the pain in her heart was finally healed.

Tara covered Cheyenne's hand with her own. In a voice that was as loving as it was stern, she looked straight at Cheyenne. "It would say you're a healthy young woman and you still have a life ahead of you." She gave a firm nod. "You put his things away."

Her words seemed to touch some part of Cheyenne's soul. She nodded, and some of the sadness faded from her smile. "We can talk about it later. Okay, Mama?"

"Okay." Tara leaned closer and kissed Cheyenne's cheek. "My Art would want you to live, baby girl. You get his things boxed up."

The conversation grew light again, Tara detailing how she found a frog in her basement and chased it up the stairs and around the house before she shooed him out into the cold. "I mean, I like frogs same as the next country girl, but that's pushing the limits."

"I'm surprised you didn't invite him in for pot roast." Cody laughed and he and Cheyenne swapped another smile. "You'll take anyone in."

Finally, after nine o'clock — with the kitchen clean — Cody and Cheyenne hugged Tara and headed to their cars.

Like always, Tara stood on the top step and folded her arms, her cheeks sucked in. "I'm telling you, Cody Coleman. Don't make me set you up next time. *Call* the girl." She let out an exasperated cry. "Heaven have mercy if all young men moved as slow as you."

"Enough, Mama." Cheyenne laughed and held up her hand, waving the woman off. "Goodnight."

"Yes, goodnight." Cody grinned and waved the same way, making light especially of Tara's command. "Thanks for dinner."

They were still laughing, still shaking their heads as Cody walked Cheyenne to her car. Again Cody noticed the easiness between them, and for the first time he considered the possibility. No matter how much he cared for Bailey, they had never found a way to make things work. So maybe he should call Cheyenne, take her out for dinner. Something to break up the monotony of his weekends. Something to encourage her to box up Art's things.

As Cheyenne slipped into the driver's seat, he leaned in near her window. "Do you mind?"

"Mind?" She gave him a curious look. "Mind what?"

"If I call you ... ask you out for dinner some time." His stomach dropped to his knees. Was he really doing this? Asking Cheyenne on a date? "I mean, Tara's going to make me eat in the backyard with the frogs if I don't, right?"

"Never mind Tara." Cheyenne's eyes shone in the light from the street lamp. "She's harmless."

Cody let the silence settle in around them. A comfortable silence. "But maybe I want to, Chey. You know, just have dinner with you."

For a long time she didn't say anything. Her eyes found a spot on the road straight ahead and she looked like she might drive off without acknowledging his offer. But then she turned to him, her expression shyer than before. "Really?"

"Yeah ... really." He smiled, and for a moment he allowed himself to be lost in her eyes. "Are you that surprised?"

Cheyenne didn't know about Bailey. He hadn't allowed himself to get that close to her. But even so she must have gathered that he was closed off to the idea of dating her.

"Yeah." She nodded, teasing. "Very surprised."

"Hmmm." Cody mustered up his best sheepish look. "I haven't been very social, huh?"

She made a face like she couldn't exactly argue with the idea. "Not really ..."

He braced himself against her open window. A chuckle filled in the empty spaces, and he looked at the ground for a minute before finding her eyes again. "Okay, so, I've been busy. But maybe next Saturday?"

"Maybe." A flirty look came over her and she started her engine. "I'm pretty sure Tara would want you to call and ask me, proper-like."

Cody looked over his shoulder back at Tara's house. She was inside, but they could see her peering at them through the living room window. Cheyenne followed his gaze and they both laughed and waved once more in her direction. She shooed her hand at them and closed the curtains. As his laughter died down, Cody nodded. "You're right about what Tara would want. I want that too." He stood and took a step back. "Look for that call, okay?"

"Okay." Her smile lingered. "I'll do that." She put her car into gear and drove off.

Cody headed for his car, but he carried with him a handful of deeply conflicting emotions. He wanted to have dinner with Cheyenne — he really did. Especially after watching her talk about Art.

She wasn't ready for love.

But both of them could use a friend. So why not get together? As the thought became more comfortable, another one barged in. What if Bailey was doing the same thing back in Bloomington? Meeting people ... making dinner plans and calling it friendship.

The thought made him glad he was far away from the town where he'd grown up. He'd watched Bailey date Tim Reed and then be the constant companion of Hollywood heartthrob Brandon Paul. Whatever she was doing now, he didn't want to know. The longer he thought about Bailey, the more sure he was that she couldn't possibly be dating anyone — not even as friends. She wouldn't be ready this soon after what the two of them had found together last summer. By the time he pulled up in front of his apartment, he realized something else. He had spent the entire ride home thinking not of Cheyenne, but of Bailey. Which could only mean one thing.

He wasn't ready either.

Seven

ASHLEY STARTED HER PAINTING THE MORNING AFTER COLE'S
first Little League practice. She hadn't been this excited about a
piece of art for a long time — and already she could see the finished picture in her heart and mind, the way the colors would
blend just so, and how the sunlight would splash against Cole's
blond hair, and Landon's profile as he hovered over Cole — posi-
tioning Cole's bat, adjusting his swing.

She was set up in the room upstairs, the one she'd painted
in for years — even before she and Landon bought the Baxter
house. It was Tuesday morning and Cole was at school. Janessa
and Devin were downstairs with Landon, who was off today.
They had plans to feed the ducks at the pond just off the Indiana
University campus. Devin already had the bread ripped into little
pieces.

"Mommy!" She heard his little-boy voice and the sound of
heavy tennis shoes on the stairs. "You done paintin'?"

She smiled. Devin still thought her paintings took about as
long as his. "Not yet, baby." She set her paintbrush on the table
beside her and brushed her hands against her apron just as Devin
raced into the room.

"Daddy's going for a run." He was breathless, peanut butter
smeared on his cheek. "So can this be a break?"

"Of course." She stooped low and kissed his head. Then she
took his sticky hand in hers and they headed downstairs. "Is
Nessa having a snack, too?"

"Yeah, but you know." Devin made a disgusted face and shook his head. He released her hand and spread his arms open wide. "She has a mess all over the place." His brow raised, his tone more concerned. "Not sure if she got any inside her tummy."

Ashley laughed quietly. She could picture the scene — both kids covered in peanut butter and cracker crumbs. Perfect time for Landon to take a run. Before they reached the kitchen, Ashley was about to call to her husband, tell him he could get to his run, but she heard him cough. Once ... twice ... and again.

Alarm filled Devin's face as he looked straight up at her. "Is Daddy sick?"

"No, honey." Ashley had to work to keep her tone even. "I don't think so."

They rounded the corner into the kitchen and Landon was near the sink, downing a glass of water. He held up his finger in her direction and took another sip. As he swallowed it, he cleared his throat and shook his head. "I'm fine. Just a tickle."

"Landon ..." she didn't want to overreact. His cough had settled down in the days after the warehouse fire, so maybe it was just a tickle. But still ... She went to him and put her hand on his shoulder. "Maybe you shouldn't run."

"I'm fine." He set the glass down, put his hand alongside her face, and kissed her. The way his lips lingered against hers made her almost forget where they were, or that the kids were sitting at the dining room table.

She took a step back and laughed. "If that was proof, I guess I can't argue." Her eyes locked on his, and she looked as deeply as she could, searching for a sign that he was hiding something, or that he was more worried about his health than he let on. But his eyes only mirrored the desire his kiss had stirred in her. He shrugged and gave her an innocent grin. "Like I said ... I'm great."

Ashley studied him, not quite ready to give in. He wore navy running shorts and a long-sleeved white Under Armour shirt, which clung to his torso. He certainly looked healthy. She moved in closer and put her arms around his neck. This time she initiated the kiss, and it lasted longer than before.

"That's called sharing germs." Devin had been helping pick up cracker pieces from around Janessa's highchair. Now he came up and put one hand on Ashley's leg, the other on Landon's. "That's what my Sunday school teacher said."

Ashley rotated so that she was still in Landon's arms, but now they were both facing their middle child. She tried not to laugh as she shared a quick look with Landon, and then turned her eyes back to Devin. "Can I ask ... why your Sunday school teacher was talking about kissing and germs?"

"Cause ..." He grinned, and his resemblance to Landon was uncanny. "I asked Bella if I could kiss her, and she said no. So I said why not, and teacher said kissing shares germs."

"You asked Bella James if you could kiss her?" Landon's expression was a mix of shock and humor, like he didn't know whether to reprimand Devin or laugh out loud. He gave Ashley a look, as if to say this was what they deserved for all the kissing they did in front of the kids.

In her highchair, Janessa was drinking milk from her sippy cup, content to watch.

"Well ..." Devin shrugged, his expression more meek than before. "At least I asked first."

"Oh, boy," Ashley muttered quietly to herself. She put her hand to her face, trying to imagine the waters they would navigate in the years to come. Cole had always teased the girls, but Devin was the charmer. She lowered her hand and tried to find her kindest — but most stern — tone. "Devin, kissing is for mommies and daddies. Not for children. Do you understand?"

"Yes, Mommy." Devin hung his head a little, his eyes still on her. He blinked a few times and then looked at Landon. "Even if I'm gonna marry Bella?"

Bella was the daughter of the new associate pastor. She had long curly red hair and bright blue eyes. Devin talked about her every Sunday. This time, Landon let out a slight laugh, but he covered it up with another cough. "I think you have a little time before you have to decide." Landon tousled Devin's blond hair. "How 'bout you finish cleaning up with your sister."

"Okay." Devin grinned again, no doubt grateful that the moment of discipline was over. He hesitated. "Just kidding, Mommy." He threw his arms around her legs and hugged her tight. "I'm gonna marry you, okay?"

"Hey," Landon put his hands on his hips, pretending to be offended. "She's my wife."

"Mine!" Devin held on tighter, giggling out loud. This was a game he loved to play, and usually it ended in a wrestling and tickling session on the living room floor.

But this time Landon kissed Ashley's cheek. "I might have to give in just this once." He gave Devin a few playful pokes in the ribs. "But when I get back from running, we'll wrestle to see who's the winner. Okay, buddy?"

"Me!" This time Devin included Landon in the hug, and then he ran off to Nessa.

Ashley put her arms around Landon again and whispered against his handsome cheek. "See what we started?"

"Ahh, it's okay." He kissed her again, quicker than before. "Germs are good for married people." He rubbed his nose against hers. "At least our kids will know what love looks like."

"True." Ashley didn't want the moment to end. The kitchen was warm and smelled like cinnamon tea and fresh bread, which Landon was baking in the oven — something he liked to do with the kids once in a while. Outside, the morning was clear but chillier than usual for mid-March. There were still several piles of snow that hadn't fully melted. She nuzzled against his face. "Mmmm, I like this. Being with you."

"Me, too." He drew back enough to make eye contact with her again. "Maybe we take a nap when the kids do." He smiled, the two of them lost in the nearness of each other. "But first ... I have to run."

She sighed. "I know." Reluctantly she released her hold on him. "Don't push yourself, okay?"

Landon only smiled and gave a lighthearted salute as he headed for the front of the house. "Be back in half an hour." She heard him head outside, heard the door close behind him, and for a few seconds she held her breath. *Father, please ... watch over him. His cough makes me so worried, Lord.*

She didn't hear a response, but she didn't really expect one either. Janessa was shaking her highchair, giggling at her brother. "Devin's funny, Mommy! Look at Devin!" Her son was crawling around the floor pretending to be a puppy, picking up cracker pieces with his mouth.

Ashley tried to memorize the way they looked, Janessa still small enough for her highchair and Devin sniffing around the floor like a hungry puppy. "Devin, stop." She couldn't help but laugh along with Janessa. "You're the cutest doggie ever, but talk about getting germs!"

Devin lifted his head and wagged his backside, a cracker sticking out between his teeth. He crawled to Ashley and dropped the cracker into the palm of her hand. "Ruff! Ruff, ruff!"

"Yes, well ... Just make sure you eat your food at the table." She patted his head. "Like all good doggies."

"Doggy cleans the mess, Mommy!" Janessa banged her hands against her tray again.

"Time to get you cleaned up, little girl." She took Janessa from her chair and they moved to the nearest bathroom. Devin was still on all fours, his tongue hanging out, panting. "No like cleaning," he said — each syllable more of a barking sound than an actual word. "Ruff, ruff!"

Janessa laughed and leaned down toward her brother, so that finally Ashley had to set her on the floor or risk dropping her. "All right you two. Let's get you cleaned up." She patted Devin's head again. "Even you, Mr. Doggy."

Ashley found a pair of washcloths from the bathroom cupboard and soaped them up with warm water. The process of cleaning the kids' hands and faces — all while Devin continued to play out a dog's life — took longer than she thought. By the time they were ready for story time, Ashley guessed at least fifteen minutes had passed since Landon left.

She led them onto the sofa and found one of Janessa's favorite books in the oak magazine rack beside it. *The Princess and the Three Knights.* Never mind that her little daughter was only three years old, Janessa definitely believed she was a princess. She sat in Ashley's lap, mesmerized by the story while Devin sat beside them — holding a running commentary.

"That's like me, right mommy? The third knight." He looked at Janessa. "I already know the ending, so I'm the third knight."

"Right, baby." Ashley read the next page. But with every sentence, with every passing minute she had the strangest feeling about Landon. Hadn't it already been half an hour? She picked up her pace, so much that Devin noticed.

"Mommy," he looked at her, shattered. "You're racing the book. You can't race this story."

"I'm a princess, right Mommy?" Janessa looked up, her wispy pale blond hair falling softly against her smooth cheeks.

"I'm sorry. I'll read it again later, but Daddy's going to be home in a minute." She stole a look at her watch. What time had he left the house? And how come she hadn't checked when he ran out the door? Knots grew in her stomach. "And yes, baby, you're a princess. Definitely."

She didn't want another interruption, so she kept an even pace as she finished the story. When she read the part where the third knight refused to take the princess anywhere near the edge of the cliff, Devin threw both hands straight up in touchdown victory fashion. "That's me! I'm the third knight!" He pumped his fist a few times. "Yes! Nowhere near the cliff!"

Ashley closed the book, set it aside, and led the kids to the coat closet. "Let's go find Daddy, okay?"

"I'm the third — " Devin's celebration stopped mid-sentence. His arms fell to his sides. "Why do we have to find him? Did he get lost?"

"No." Ashley forced a laugh, but it sounded half desperate, even to her. She led them closer to the closet and opened the door. Devin's red jacket was on the floor just inside. She picked it up and handed it to him. "Here, sweetie. Put this on. Sometimes it's nice to meet Daddy outside when he comes home from a run."

Devin started working his arm into the jacket. No question he had picked up on Ashley's fears, even if he wasn't sure what could be wrong. "We never met him outside before."

"Well, then ... this will be the first time!" Ashley searched the length of the closet but Janessa's pink winter coat was nowhere. *Hurry,* she told herself. Her arms were beginning to tremble, and her hands shook as she thumbed once more through the jackets on the rack. Finally at the end she found it, half falling to the floor and wedged against the wall. She crouched down and slipped the coat on her daughter as quickly as she could. As she finished, Devin was dressed but struggling with his zipper. Ashley helped him and willed herself not to look terrified. It had to have been forty minutes at least, and still no Landon. "Come on, Devin. This'll be fun."

He lowered his brow, worried. "What if Daddy's really lost?"

"He's not." She led them both to the door, and then she swept Janessa into her arms. "Let's hurry, okay, buddy?" She couldn't carry them both, and she certainly couldn't leave either of them home. At the last moment, she grabbed her cell phone from the coffee table and the three of them left through the front door.

The Baxter house sat on ten acres, same as the other houses in the neighborhood. If something had happened to Landon at the far end of the street, she'd be better off getting into her car. But first she had to at least walk to the end of the driveway and call for him — check if maybe he was just cooling down or stretching on the front porch. Either way the kids would need their coats. *Breathe,* she let the warmth from her children's hands work through her. *Come on, Ashley. Don't panic. Dear God, please be with him ... please help me find him.*

They moved quickly down the driveway, but Devin was dragging. "Not so fast, Mommy. Please ..."

"Sorry, baby." She slowed down, shielding her eyes and trying to see beyond the end of the driveway. The air was colder than she thought. Bitter cold. What if his lungs couldn't take working in this weather? A few more steps and suddenly she saw him, stopped along the side of the road, bent over somewhere between their house and the neighbor's, on the right. "Landon!" She screamed his name, and he stood a little straighter. He wasn't coughing, but he wasn't moving his feet, either. "Devin, stay here with Janessa. Hold her hand and don't move."

"Yes, Mommy. Is Daddy hurt?"

"I'm not sure." She set her daughter down and looked straight at her. "Stay with your brother. Understand?"

Janessa nodded, her eyes wide.

Devin put his arm around his sister as Ashley turned and bolted toward Landon. *Please, God ... let him be okay. Please ...* At the end of the driveway she was close enough to see that his face was red and ...

"Can you breathe?" She kept running, faster ... closer to him. "Landon can you breathe?"

He made a move with his head, but she couldn't tell if he was

shaking it no or nodding yes. She reached for her phone in her coat pocket, but just as she was about to call for help, he waved his hand at her, the sort of waving that usually signaled a person was okay. Only Landon was definitely not okay.

Faster ... closer ...

"Landon ... I'm calling 9 – 1 – 1."

This time his response was clear. As she reached him, he lifted his eyes to her and shook his head. "No ... I'm ... okay."

"Landon ..." Ashley felt the blood leave her face. Until now it had been impossible to hear whether he was getting air, whether he was breathing at all. But now she could hear him and the sound was horrific — every breath marked by an intense wheezing. This was a full-blown asthma attack, Ashley was sure. Landon needed all his energy to get barely a breath. She took hold of his shoulder. "Let me call for help. Please ..."

He held up his index finger, telling her to give him a minute. The problem was, if the restriction in his airways grew worse, he might not have even that long. Ashley put her arm around his shoulders. Again Landon hung his head, and he seemed to force himself to relax, to breathe more slowly.

I can't do this, God ... give me wisdom ... how can I help him, please ... open his airways. Please, God ... Ashley glanced back at their kids in the driveway. They hadn't moved from where she'd left them. Ashley leaned in close to Landon, listening to him. *Please, God ... calm his breathing ... please ...*

Peace filled the air around them, a peace so other-worldly that Ashley felt God's presence like only a few times before in her life. Suddenly, the wheezing let up and Landon's struggle to breathe eased. One minute passed, and another ... and Landon was able to stand. *Thank You, God ... thank You! Only You can breathe life into a person.*

Landon's face was still red, his forehead and back drenched

in sweat. "Wow ... that's never happened." He was still breathing harder than normal, but he could take in air without a wheeze.

"That's asthma, Landon. You had an asthma attack."

"I know." Landon loved to tease, loved to find humor in almost any situation. But he wasn't smiling now. His expression was marked by a sobering reality. "It was bad. I ... I didn't have my phone." He drew a slow, deep breath. "I wasn't sure ..." he looked at her and his eyes grew teary. "I couldn't breathe, Ash." He pursed his lips and exhaled, pacing a few steps from her and then back again. "I mean I seriously couldn't breathe." He looked up, struggling with his composure before he met her eyes again. "I wasn't sure ... I thought it was over, that I — " He couldn't finish his sentence. His chin quivered and again he exhaled, fighting his emotions. "Ash ..."

"Dear God ..." Her heart slammed around in her chest, searching for normal. Hadn't she known he was in trouble? "I should've come sooner."

"No." He touched his hand to her cheek. "You couldn't have known."

"But I did ... I knew." She pulled him into her arms and rested her forehead on his chest, exhausted, sick from the adrenaline pumping through her veins. For a long moment she stayed that way, listening to his lungs fill with air again and again and again. They were past the danger for now, at least she thought so. But he needed a doctor. Sooner than later. She pulled herself away and checked on the kids again. Like before, they hadn't moved. Ashley could only imagine what kind thing Devin said to his sister to get her to stay so still. She turned to Landon again. "You need to be seen. Let's get in and I'll call my dad."

"Okay." He started slowly walking beside her, back to their driveway. He took hold of her hand and eased his fingers between hers. He stopped walking for just a moment and looked deep into

her soul. "I love you … if I don't tell you enough, I want you to know. I love you with all I am."

"I know." Fear stepped aside long enough that the reality of what almost happened actually hit. Her eyes blurred with unshed tears and she hugged him once more. "I love you too."

"Thank God …" Again his voice was too strained, his emotions too strong for him to finish.

But she understood. She nodded. "I have been." They finished their walk, and when they reached Devin and Janessa, both kids were crying. Ashley felt terrible, and clearly Landon did too. She swept Janessa onto her hip, and Devin practically jumped into Landon's arms.

"You scared us, Daddy. We … we thought you were hurt." Devin sucked in three quick sobs. "S-s-so, me and Nessa prayed. We asked Jesus to make you b-b-better."

Landon still looked shaken, but he kissed Devin's cheek. "Thank you, buddy. God heard your prayers."

Devin wiped his chubby fists beneath his eyes. "So … so you're better?"

"Yes." He looked at Ashley as the four of them walked to the house. "Much better."

Ashley could see by the expression on her husband's face that he was concerned. They would call her father as soon as they were inside. John Baxter was one of the best and most respected doctors in Bloomington. He would know who Landon should see or whether he should get to the hospital right away. He needed an inhaler, at least. Maybe other medication. But as terrifying as this attack had been, as they reached the front porch what made Ashley sick to her stomach wasn't the idea that Landon had asthma. Rather she worried about Landon's lungs. She was sure her father would recommend further testing. And then it wouldn't be a matter of merely surviving an asthma attack …

But surviving whatever had caused it.

Eight

BAILEY CLOSED HER BEDROOM DOOR BEHIND HER AND WORKED to catch her breath. The bike ride was a good idea. Six miles through her neighborhood into Clear Creek and back again, time enough to pray and think and wonder what in the world God's plans for her might be. And when she'd start seeing them take shape. It was the last Saturday in March and warmer than it had been all spring. She peeled off her lightweight jacket and tossed it on her bed. Her legs felt tight — the result of too little exercise over the winter. She bent at the waist and stretched, feeling the burn in her hamstrings and calf muscles.

She wasn't getting a callback from Francesca Tilly and the *Hairspray* production team. That much was obvious. Nearly three weeks had passed since the audition, and since they needed to fill spots right away, Bailey was sure they'd already chosen other dancers. The rejection hurt, she couldn't lie. She worked so hard, and no matter why they hadn't offered her a role, she couldn't have done any better. So much for the assumption by the red-headed dancer. Bailey wasn't being handed a role because of her role in *Unlocked*, which was a good thing. But she hadn't won a part, either.

Which meant ... what?

Bailey kicked one of her legs further behind her, deepening the stretch. The answer was clear. She could keep trying out, of course. But if her best wasn't good enough, then she had to con-

sider the other possibility: Performing on Broadway wasn't part of God's plans for her life.

"Throw it long!" Ricky's voice cut the silent spring air and wafted up through Bailey's open bedroom window. "Make it a thirty-yarder. I can catch it ... watch me!"

Bailey switched the stretch to her other leg. She remembered one time last summer playing catch with Ricky. He was barely thirteen, but already he was six feet tall and most of the time he didn't know his own strength. He had told her to go for a long pass but she'd turned around too soon, and the ball hit her square in the stomach. Ricky was at her side immediately, but Bailey felt the blow for days after.

The way she felt it now in light of the failed *Hairspray* audition.

She didn't talk about her disappointment with anyone but her mom, and even then she rarely brought it up. Every day of silence only screamed the answer louder. They didn't want her. She wasn't good enough or pretty enough or talented enough. Something. She straightened and took a slow breath. Her brothers had their spring scrimmage in a few hours, and she planned to go.

But lately she had to wonder. Was this her life? She'd finish college, maybe fly out for a handful of other auditions, but then wind up here in Bloomington? She loved the town she grew up in, and she certainly didn't want to live in LA and spend her life auditioning for movies. But she wanted to perform on a stage, dancing and singing. It was a passion that burned in her with every breath. Still ... maybe she'd never have what it took to make it.

Bailey walked to her window and stared out at her brothers, laughing and tossing the football on the front yard. They lived on enough acreage that they could run forever without reaching the road. For a few seconds, Bailey envied them — so young, and with so much growing up ahead of them. They didn't worry about their futures or what they wanted to be when they grew up. Not yet. Even Connor, who was a junior at Clear Creek High this year, didn't have to think too hard about it. He would go to college — to Indiana University, no doubt. He had plenty of time to think about a career.

But at twenty-one, and with college almost wrapped up, the situation was different for Bailey. Her dad asked her yesterday if she'd thought about teaching drama someday, and she was honest with him. She'd thought about it. About maybe running a Christian Kids Theater group, like the one here in town. But always, though, the idea paled in comparison to being on stage.

She caught a look at her reflection and suddenly she felt shamed by her own thoughts. How dare she complain about her situation? Her family, her faith, her future — and everything that had led her to this point. Her whole life had been golden. And she'd had a turn to act, right? She'd starred in a movie opposite Brandon Paul, after all. Complaining now would only be the worst possible display of ingratitude.

Bailey took a shower and dressed for the game. She was blow-drying her long hair when she remembered the movie again. *Unlocked* was a runaway bestseller on the New York Times list, and everyone everywhere was reading it. Brandon Paul, Hollywood's hottest young star, played Holden Harris, the autistic teenager whose beautiful soul was opened up by friendship and the miracle of song. Bailey played Ella, the friend who had helped change Holden's life.

A week had passed since Brandon had texted her, but then he was gearing up for his next film. Still, she'd see him at the premiere for *Unlocked*. Her whole family was flying to LA in two weeks for the big event. Bailey smiled at the idea of seeing Brandon again. He had given his life to the Lord during his time in Bloomington, the direct result of his time on location, getting to know Bailey's faith and the faith of her family. He teased her about wanting a relationship with her, but Bailey could never take him seriously. Besides, she couldn't live her life in front of a hundred paparazzi.

She turned off the blow dryer just as her cell phone went off. The song was "Mama, I'm a Big Girl Now" from *Hairspray*. Bailey made a mental note to change it after this call. The number wasn't one she recognized. She tapped *answer* as she checked the time on her phone. Fifteen minutes before they had to leave for the game. "Hello?"

Silence.

Bailey checked her phone, and already the call was gone. Strange, she thought. She brought up the number again and studied it. The area code was 317. Indianapolis. For a long moment she wondered if the call could've been from Cody. She had his cell phone programmed into her phone, of course, but ... he might have a new number. Or maybe he was calling from someone else's phone. The prison phone, maybe. Where his mother lived.

It was possible. Bailey lowered her phone and stared at the framed photograph of Cody and her on the dresser. If he had made the call, why would he hang up? And why had he walked away in the first place? He should be at the football field, getting ready for the scrimmage. Coaching the Clear Creek kids the way he did last year. Her heart felt heavy as she stood and tossed her phone back on her bed. She needed to finish getting ready, but thoughts of Cody made her want to do something crazy.

Like get in her car after her brothers' scrimmage and drive to Indianapolis. Find him at his apartment or wherever he was working and beg him to come to his senses. Why not go to him? Whatever mixed up reasoning he'd used to justify leaving, he was wrong. They still felt for each other, still longed for the way things used to be. That's what his eyes had told her when they were last together — outside the prison, standing face to face in the falling snow.

She put on a touch of makeup, and flicked her hair into a

ponytail. On her way out of her room she grabbed her jacket, and as she reached the kitchen below she found her mom making turkey sandwiches. "You look pretty."

"Thanks." She didn't want her tone to give her away, but she could never hide anything from her mom. She grabbed a knife from the top kitchen drawer and took the spot beside her. "How many are we making?"

"Thanks. A whole loaf, like always." Her mom looked at her, a knowing in her expression. "You're thinking about him."

"Who?" Bailey could never hide anything from her mom. She kept her eyes on the piece of bread in her hands, and worked to spread jelly across the face of it.

"You know who." She set her knife down on a nearby paper towel and turned to Bailey. "He hasn't called?"

"No." Bailey sighed. "Not once."

"Honey ... look at me." Her mother's tone was tender, but it held a hint of finality.

"A call came in a few minutes ago. Someone from Indianapolis and I thought ..." Bailey set the slice of bread down and faced her. "I thought it might've been him."

"Don't do this to yourself." She put her hands on Bailey's shoulders. "Please, honey ..."

"He'll call ... he will." She believed it with all her heart. "One day he'll figure it out."

"Maybe." Her mom ran her thumb along Bailey's cheek. "But honey, that boy has broken your heart too many times." She paused, and a fresh empathy filled her eyes. "We all love him ... but he can't keep doing this to you."

Bailey wanted to argue, but she couldn't. Her mother was right. She blinked back tears and managed a slight shrug. "I still love him." Her voice was tight, strained under the weight of her broken heart. "What am I supposed to do about that?"

"Let him go. Give him to God, so that God can heal both

of you." Her mom raised her brow. "Remember what we talked about ... The next time that boy pursues you, he better do it like a dying man looking for water in a desert. When it's the right guy, you'll know, Bailey ... because he'll cherish you."

She nodded, frustrated and convinced all at the same time. Her mother was right. She couldn't dream about driving to Indianapolis and finding Cody. He knew how to reach her. If he cared for her, he'd do just what her mom had said — search for her like a dying man looking for water in a desert. She hugged her mom. "It's so hard."

"I know." Her mom smiled, despite the sadness in her eyes. "Let's have a good day with the boys."

They were almost finished making the loaf of sandwiches when Bailey's dad bounded in from the garage. "The Colts are gonna be amazing, I tell you." He whistled long and low, his booming voice full of energy. "I mean, what a great morning practice!" He walked up, kissed Bailey on her forehead, and swung her mom around in a hug like something from the movies. "How are my two favorite girls?"

Bailey and her mother exchanged a look, but after a couple seconds they laughed out loud. Her dad would never understand how Bailey felt. Cody had been gone for months. They would figure she had moved on a long time ago, even if the whole family still missed Cody. "Hmm," her dad pounded back a glass of water and grinned at them. "I must've missed something."

"Just girl talk." Bailey's mom grinned at her. "Everything's fine."

She offered him one of the sandwiches, and he took it with an appreciative nod. "Thanks. I'm starving." He looked at the clock on the microwave. "Good. I have a couple minutes still."

Bailey and her mom laughed again. She loved when her dad was in this mood — nothing but happiness and enthusiasm. She leaned against the counter and smiled at him. "Okay, then ... why was practice so good?"

"Two words." He raised his sandwich in the air. "Matt Keagan." With that he took a celebratory bite and finished off nearly a third of it.

"Oh boy ... here we go." Bailey's mom laughed lightly as she put the remaining sandwiches back in the bread wrapper and twisted the metal tie around the top. "Matt's awfully young to put the entire team's success on him."

"Ah, but you and every other naysayer haven't seen what I've seen." A grin filled his face as he waved his sandwich in the air. "The kid is amazing. I don't care if he's passing or running or working special teams. He's a leader, Jenny. When he's on the field, the performance of everyone on the team rises."

Matt had drawn national attention last year at Ohio State University when he tweeted a different Bible verse before every game. He also wrote the verse with a Sharpie across the small white towel he used on the sidelines. His bold stance for faith was rivaled by only a few other players. When it came time for the draft, most people were surprised when the Colts took Matt Keagan in the third round. Since then, his public persona had grown with every product endorsement and every press conference. He even donated a million dollars of his signing bonus to a mission in India that provided women with sewing machines, training, and Bible study.

Matt Keagan was a modern-day hero of the faith larger than life, no question about that.

Bailey's dad had believed in the rookie then, and he clearly believed in him now. He wolfed down the rest of the sandwich. "The thing is, I could put him at linebacker and he'd lead the league in a couple years. I really believe that. He has that something ... that 'it' factor that other guys can't manufacture."

"So ... we're headed for the Super Bowl?" Jenny found an old

supermarket bag in a drawer and set the loaf of sandwiches inside. She cupped her hand around one side of her mouth. "Boys! Time to go!"

"Maybe..." Bailey's dad nodded, more serious than he'd been since he walked in the door. "I mean, not necessarily this year, but soon. Matt Keagan's that good. The rest of the league is going to understand why we wanted him so badly."

The boys' voices mingled together near the top of the stairs, and in a matter of seconds they ran down, gear bags slung over their shoulders. Only Ricky was too young to play for Clear Creek. Otherwise every Flanigan boy was dressed out and buzzing about the scrimmage.

The group packed into their Suburban, and they were backing out of the driveway when Bailey's dad looked in the rearview mirror and grinned. "Oh ... I invited one of the players over for dinner."

"Wow, really?" Ricky was sitting next to Bailey in the middle row. He strained forward as far as his seat belt would let him go. "Who, Dad? Tell me it's Matt Keagan?"

"Crazy kid." From the back row, Justin gave Ricky a light push in the shoulder. "Matt Keagan would need a dozen body guards to go anywhere anymore. It wouldn't be him. Right, Dad?"

Their dad hesitated just long enough that Bailey knew what was coming next. She held her breath, waiting. Her father had teased her about Matt Keagan wanting to meet her, but he wouldn't invite him over for dinner, would he? Before she could think any longer about the possibility, her dad stopped at the end of the driveway, punched his fist in the air, and smiled over his shoulder at Ricky. "That's exactly who. Matt Keagan." He turned his attention to the road again and pulled onto the quiet street in front of their house. "His family's in Ohio — and with our schedule he won't be making the six-hour drive very often. So I invited him."

"Are you kidding?" Ricky looked at his brothers behind him

and then at his dad. "Seriously, dad? Matt Keagan is coming for dinner?"

"Yes." Their dad laughed. "Don't worry, he's like any other guy."

"Yeah, except he's one of the most famous rookies in the NFL." Even BJ was impressed. He was a freshman this year and not as into football as the others. He'd rather play basketball or soccer any day. But he clearly thought Matt Keagan was a big deal.

Bailey stayed quiet, listening to her brothers talk over each other about the day ahead. Connor hoped Matt might want to throw the football around, especially since he'd be the starting quarterback for Clear Creek again this year. He was six-foot-three now, and still a little thin, but he had grown to love football almost as much as singing and performing. Shawn just wanted an autograph from the football star, and Ricky planned to ask him to move in with them.

"You know ... because he probably wants a family like ours where he can feel safe." Ricky's tone couldn't have been any more earnest. "That way he can be part of our family during the week, and still play for the Colts."

"He has like ten million dollars, buddy." Justin always put Ricky in his place. This time with a tender sort of fondness, but still he knew which buttons to push. "I'm pretty sure he has his own family."

"Yeah, but even ten million dollars can't buy a family like ours." Ricky stuck his chest out. "Isn't that right, Dad?"

Touché, Bailey thought. She smiled to herself. Her younger brother was so much like her in some ways. He was full of life and always glad for any time their family was together. It made her sad to think that one by one they would leave until only Ricky was left. He'd be a very lonely only child someday for sure.

Not until they were out of the car at the football field did her

mom walk alongside her and give her a look. "So … what do you think?"

"About what?" She acted nonplussed and, truthfully, she was. Matt was a celebrity as big as Brandon Paul in his own right. It didn't matter if it was football or films that made them famous; they drew a crowd wherever they went. It just wasn't a lifestyle Bailey was up for, and despite the fact that her father claimed Matt Keagan was interested in her, she was pretty sure he didn't know she existed.

"Come on." Her mom smiled, willing to play along. "You know."

"Matt?" Bailey gave a look she knew was noncommittal. "It'll be fun for the boys, I guess. I mean, of course. They can tell everyone at school they had dinner with Matt Keagan." ·

"Bailey …" Her mom had the sandwich bag and a few bottles of water. She shifted it onto her other shoulder as they neared the stadium. "What do *you* think about it?"

"Truthfully?" She lifted her face, letting the warm spring breeze brush against her cheeks. "I think Dad loves me very much. He's worried about me ever since the Cody thing … and this is his way to get my attention on something else."

Her mom angled her head, thoughtful. "Pretty close." She nodded, her eyes straight ahead at the team getting set up on the field. The other team — the one from across town in Bloomington — was already there in formation doing their warm-ups. "Any father would want to introduce their daughter to a guy like Matt Keagan."

"True." Bailey wasn't bothered. She understood what her dad was doing, and that his intentions were good. "But let's be real, Mom. He's a nationally known role model, and I'm the daughter of one of the assistant coaches."

"You're more than that, Bailey." Her mom was quick to come to her defense. "You're a talented young woman with a heart for God as pure as Matt's. The two of you are very similar, actually."

"Except I can leave my house without cameramen following me."

Her mom laughed. "I guess that's true. Of course," she waved her thumb toward the west, "if you lived in Hollywood you'd have paparazzi everywhere you went. Especially in a few weeks when your movie comes out."

"I don't know about that. Anyway, I doubt Matt Keagan even knows I'm alive." They walked through the stadium gates and into the familiar stands, the ones she'd sat in when she watched Cody play for her dad so many years back, before her father returned to the NFL and the position with the Indianapolis Colts. The field where Cody had returned after his time in Iraq, and where he'd coached her brothers for the last two years. A lifetime of memories surrounded her as she took her seat. She didn't care who was coming for dinner. She cared about this.

Her brothers' scrimmage.

Nine

THE GAME WENT QUICKLY, AND THOUGH BOTH TEAMS PLAYED evenly, Clear Creek managed to pull out the win in the end. Connor was amazing, throwing for more than two hundred yards, and sending touchdown passes into the waiting hands of Shawn and Justin at different times. BJ played linebacker and sacked the quarterback from Bloomington three times before the clock ran out.

"All in all, a very good game for Clear Creek," her dad proclaimed on the ride home. "And a great game for the Flanigan boys!"

Bailey was anxious as they headed home, and several times she asked herself why. She wasn't interested in Matt. Like she'd told her mother, he couldn't possibly have asked about her. But somewhere along the afternoon of thinking about him and wondering about this night, she'd begun to care. Even just a little. She helped her mom make an enchilada casserole for dinner, a recipe Ashley Baxter had given them a few years ago.

The house smelled like melted cheese and spices when the doorbell rang at six sharp. *Of course he's on time*, Bailey thought to herself. She wiped down the counter one last time and hurried up to her room. A little powder wouldn't hurt. Besides, her brothers had been peeking out the window, waiting for the chance to greet him for the past half hour.

Laughter and happy voices filled the house as Matt came in. Bailey couldn't make out who was saying what, but she could sense the excitement from upstairs in her bathroom. She ran her makeup brush over her cheeks and forehead. Not that she wanted to impress him, but she didn't need a shiny face — no matter who was coming for dinner.

She started to leave, and stopped herself. Without giving her actions much thought, she grabbed her favorite bottle of perfume and spritzed some behind each ear and on her wrists. One last look at herself and again she hesitated. She wore dark jeans and a long-sleeved red scoop-neck T-shirt. Her chestnut-colored hair fell in long waves, and the combination made her eyes stand out. Yes, this look would do.

Downstairs, she joined in the mix without a lot of fanfare. The guys were in the TV room looking at film from the scrimmage that afternoon. Bailey would've had to go out of her way to find them, so instead she went straight at the bottom of the stairs and found her mother's water pitchers in the pantry. Again, Ricky was the loudest in the room. "See that! Connor's got an arm, don't you think so, Matt?"

He laughed, and the sound was instantly recognizable from his TV interviews. A fluttering sensation filled her heart, and she felt more nervous than she had in a long time. *Get a grip, Bailey … this is ridiculous.*

"Bailey!" Her dad's voice rose above the others just as she had almost filled the second pitcher.

"Just a minute." *Be calm … come on, this is any other Saturday night. Any other dinner with a football player.* She set the pitchers on the counter next to the cooling casserole and dried her hands on her jeans as she walked into the family room, the place where the boys were gathered in front of the TV. "Sorry, just helping out."

Her dad gave her a bewildered look, like she maybe should've been a little more excited about meeting their guest. "Honey, I'd like you to meet one of our players, Matt Keagan." He turned to Matt, seated beside him on the sofa. "Matt, this is our daughter, Bailey."

She turned her eyes to him, and at almost the exact instant she knew two things for sure. First, Matt's presence, his personality, and gentle spirit were more magnified in person than on any TV spot or football game Bailey might've seen him in. And second, he knew who she was. No question about it. His eyes fixed on hers as he stood and shook her hand. "Bailey," he nodded. "Nice to meet you." He paused. "I've heard a lot about you."

"Thanks," she released his hand, but the feel of his fingers against hers lingered. "I've ... heard a lot about you, too."

Matt never took his eyes from hers. "You're a junior at Indiana , is that right?"

"Matt ... we still have a few more plays." Ricky was quick to try to get the conversation back on track.

"Actually, it's time to eat." Bailey's mom entered the room. She had already met Matt when he first arrived, because Bailey had heard her voice among the mix. Now she seemed as comfortable as if they'd all known Matt forever.

As the dinner got underway, Bailey couldn't deny that she felt the same. Matt was maybe the same height as Connor, but a lot more filled out. Probably in the shape of his life, based on the way her dad and his coaching staff ran practices with the Colts. On top of that he had hazel eyes and a light tan face. No wonder Nike was using him as one of its spokespersons this year.

But his looks weren't what drew Bailey to him again and again throughout the night. It was the easy way he had about him, the kindness and gentleness. She remembered a verse from Galatians that her parents had woven into their family life while they were growing up: *The fruit of the spirit is love, joy, peace, patience, kindness, goodness, thoughtfulness, gentleness, and self-control.* Watching Matt, Bailey couldn't get over it. He was like a walking billboard for every single fruit. He couldn't be perfect, of course, but right now it was hard to see a chink in his armor.

When they were done eating, they had blueberries and

whipped cream for dessert, and after that they played a round of Catch Phrase. Bailey did okay in the game, mostly because she wasn't seated right next to Matt. She wasn't sure how she would look into those eyes and try to say or act out anything. Throughout the night she kept wishing he'd make eye contact with her across the room. But he never did.

By the end of the night, Bailey wasn't sure what she felt. He had come for dinner, but that didn't mean he was interested in her. After their introductions he barely seemed to notice her. She needed time alone to process all that had happened in the last few hours, and to remind herself that he probably didn't mean anything personal by his avoidance. Matt was not only a celebrity, he was insanely busy. On top of his football schedule, he did volunteer work for ministries throughout Indianapolis, and he had weekly meetings with the companies he was endorsing products for. He might as well work three full-time jobs.

Somehow as he was leaving, she wound up walking him to the door. Bailey was pretty sure it was no coincidence their dad had given every boy a chore just as it was time for Matt to go. Whatever had happened, suddenly it was just the two of them headed down the hallway to the foyer. When they reached the front door, Bailey felt suddenly self-conscious. They hadn't had a single conversation apart from the group all night. What could she possibly say now, considering she didn't know him?

He turned and slipped his hands in his jeans pockets. "I had fun tonight." His grin warmed her heart. "Your family's amazing."

"Thanks." She allowed a light laugh. "Ricky was going to ask you to move in. So you'd have a family in Indiana."

"He asked." Matt raised one eyebrow. "I might have to think about it."

This time they both laughed and Matt opened the door. "Well, thanks for coming ... it was nice meeting you."

"Hey," Matt angled his head, his eyes more serious. "I'm sort of seeing a girl in Indianapolis. She's a law student at IU."

Bailey felt her heart sink, and she could almost see the blood rushing to her cheeks. Of course he was seeing someone. Why had she thought even for a moment that this was about her? She smiled, working hard to save face. "That's great. It's a good law school."

"Yeah," he hesitated, the silence between them slightly awkward. "Anyway, if things don't work out ... I'd love to get to know you better."

Bailey nodded, and crossed her arms in front of her. "Sure ... I'll be here." She smiled and waved once as Matt headed for the door. "See you later."

He said something about how nice it had been meeting her, but Bailey wasn't really listening. She wondered how different her thoughts and actions through the night might've been if she'd known he had a girlfriend.

"Ughh," she muttered out loud as she headed back down the hallway to the kitchen. "Nightmare."

Her family was waiting for her, but she smoothly evaded any questions and feigned a sudden need to check her clothes in the dryer upstairs. One thing was sure: Matt Keagan wasn't the guy God had for her. She flopped on her bed. Maybe there was no guy for her. Either way, as she heard Matt Keagan drive off she was haunted by a single thought.

Maybe she should've spent the day in Indianapolis.

Ten

CODY WASN'T SURE HOW MUCH MORE OF COACH OLIVER he could take. He had tried working with him every day this spring, but it was the last Monday before April and Cody wondered if his presence wasn't doing more harm than good with the football team. He slipped the navy Lyle sweat jacket over his T-shirt and stepped into the silky sweats. A donor with the booster club had sprung for new warm-ups for the team.

But that was the only sign of anything new Cody had seen since he started.

The locker room was empty except for DeMetri Smith. The kid had been hanging back, and Cody had a feeling he wanted to sneak in a quick conversation before training got underway. When his last teammate had left the building, DeMetri walked up, his steps hesitant. "Coach?"

"Yeah, buddy." Cody took the baseball cap from his locker and positioned it on his head as he turned to the player. "Everything okay?"

DeMetri hung his head and for a long time he didn't say anything. When he looked up, Cody saw more anger in the kid's eyes than he had ever seen before. "I'm tired of Coach Oliver." He clenched his jaw and gave a firm shake of his head. "We all are." His hands were clenched, and he tossed them, frustrated. "Can't you see it? We ain't never gonna be nothing with him in charge."

The right thing was to take Dennis Oliver's side, defend him, and stay united as a coaching staff. But Cody felt exactly the same

way. He folded his arms in front of him and waited until he had the right words. "You still praying for this team, Smitty?"

DeMetri exhaled hard through his nose. "Yes, sir. Not sure what good it's doing."

"Well," he patted the player on the back. "I've never seen a time when praying to God didn't work one way or another. God's in this situation — same as He is whenever His people are involved." Cody led the way out to the practice field and DeMetri fell in beside him. "Now we only have to wait and see what God's going to do." They stopped at the door of the locker room. "You understand, Smitty?"

"Yes, sir." The kid didn't look any more convinced than before. As he jogged out to the field, his shoulders were more slumped than usual. But what Cody had said was true. God was in this. He knew because DeMetri wasn't the only one from the Lyle football team praying for a breakthrough. Cody was praying too.

He checked his clipboard, reviewing in a hurry the drills for the day. It was still spring ball — only ninety minutes of training and conditioning. The real work didn't begin until mid-summer. But by then if players weren't in shape, they never would be. So every day they spent on the field now would result in wins and losses come fall. Cody knew that much from experience.

"Coleman! What are you doing?" Coach Oliver's face was purple. He waved his hand wildly at Cody. "Get out here! What sort of example is that if my coaches can't be on time!"

The man was always angry — worse than before. Cody jogged out to the field and thought about DeMetri's concerns. He could hardly tell the kid he was thinking about leaving himself. As long as he stayed, he had to believe a few of the guys were remaining in the program only because of him, and right now he wasn't sure he'd recommend that for anyone. Least of all kids like DeMetri, who cared so deeply.

Cody pulled up beside the coach. "Sorry. I had a few students stay late. This was the soonest I could get here."

"No excuses, Coleman." He snarled every word. Something about the man looked different, like maybe he was more pale than usual. His eyes were a little off too. "I won't tolerate that from my players, and I certainly won't tolerate it from you."

"Yes, sir." Cody wouldn't have responded any other way. He had been raised to be polite — by the Flanigan family and then by his sergeants in the Army. But Coach Oliver always pushed too far, too hard. He ordered the guys to get in a line. "We're doing forties till someone throws up," he shouted. He lifted his whistle to his lips and blew. "Go!"

The team took off as fast as they could toward the forty-yard line. They no sooner stopped and regrouped than Oliver was blowing his whistle again. The man seemed a little more slumped over than usual, but it didn't change his approach with the kids. "Go!"

Cody shifted in the damp grass beside the man. "Coach — "

"Not now!" He waited barely a few seconds this time after most of the guys reached the goal line. "Again!"

Cody felt sick. "Coach, about this ... running till someone throws up." He struggled for a few seconds. He was begging for another diatribe from the man, but he didn't care. Someone had to stand up for the players. "They can maybe do this six, seven times, but then they need a real break. These are sprints, sir, not jogs. No one can sustain that sort of — "

"Stop!" He seethed the word straight at Cody, inches from his face. "If I want your opinion on how to run this practice, I'll ask you." He hunched over a little more, and for a brief moment he clutched his stomach. Under his breath he rattled off a string of cuss words. "You might have to finish this practice." He snarled at himself. "Dratted stomach."

Whatever was wrong with the man, Cody could only hope

it would take him off the field. He waved off the players and motioned for them to come closer. "Hurry up! You look like a bunch of third-grade girls. Not a man among you, and I mean that. You're worthless. Worse than that." He stopped to grab a quick breath. Whatever was wrong with his stomach it was getting worse. He looked like he wouldn't make it another five minutes without needing a restroom.

Cody stared at the muddy grass, helpless to save the kids. When he glanced up, he took in the looks on the faces of the players. They were losers in record and losers on the field. If Coach Oliver had his way, they would be losers in life. Because every word he said was like a dagger to the confidence of the young men standing before them. Kids who had grown up in a small town, guys who weren't sure how they were supposed to compete in the business world or how to make a living or raise a family. Whatever hope they might've brought to the experience of Lyle football, whatever confidence, Oliver wouldn't be content until it was dead and buried.

"No one has to ask what sort of football players you are," he snarled at them. "The kind that make a coach wanna quit, that's what kind. You're losers!" He panted harder than before. "If you don't start putting a little effort into every run, every drill ... then you're going to stay losers." He was shouting now. "Do you hear me?"

The guys clustered together, and collectively they appeared a foot shorter than when practice began. DeMetri met Cody's eyes, but then he looked away. Cody felt terrible. He had just told him that God was in this, that something was going to happen to show an answer to the kid's prayers. But here they were, Coach Oliver decimating them once again.

Before Cody could utter a silent, desperate prayer for help, Coach Oliver clutched his stomach once more. Whatever was hurting him, he hated himself for the weakness. But the situation was too much even for a surly old man like Coach Oliver. He paused, struggling to stand straight. "Coach Coleman is going to finish up." He glared at Cody. "Make good use of your time, Coach. Opening day is right around the corner."

More like six months from now, but Cody didn't dare say so. He was grateful just to see the man leave. In the weeks since Cody started teaching and coaching at Lyle, he'd never seen Coach Oliver leave a practice. For sure the man must've been very sick. Probably the flu, which would account for his purple complexion. The man probably had a fever, but even still he was out here barking at his players.

All twenty-nine young men who had come out for spring training watched along with Cody as Coach Oliver hobbled off the field and to the locker room. Cody could almost feel the sense of relief that went up among the guys as the door shut behind the man. Cody felt a sudden sense of relief. This was what he'd been praying for, right? Not that Coach Oliver would get sick, but that he would leave or take a day off. Anything so that Cody could have time with the players, time to let them know that he was very different from the coach they were used to.

Cody turned to the guys and studied them. Some gave off a look of angry indifference, and others of them looked frustrated. Most were discouraged ... even defeated. DeMetri was among those. Cody drew a long breath. "Which of you would like to pray for Coach Oliver?" On a number of occasions Cody had been told that prayer was allowed at Lyle. No form of government could stop the local school from doing what they had always done. In this case, he had very little to lose by praying publicly. And since he couldn't say anything nice about the coach, this was the only transition he knew.

At first, none of the guys stepped forward. But then — as though there was a mountain on his shoulders — DeMetri raised his hand. "I'll pray." Some of the guys looked at him almost with

disgust, like he was a traitor for lifting to their holy God a man like Dennis Oliver. But DeMetri seemed to draw his strength from Cody, from the peace and strength Cody hoped he exuded. None of the guys wore helmets or hats, so there was nothing for DeMetri to do but hang his head. "Dear God, we ask ... that you be with Coach Oliver. Whatever's going on with him, we ask that you make things right. In Christ's name, amen."

A few of the guys added their voices to the amen, and then they were silent again, sizing up Cody, wondering if he was going to snap at them the same way Coach Oliver had. Cody looked at his stopwatch. "I'd say we've done enough sprints." He set his clipboard down. Today's drills were going to be his alone. "Let's pair up."

For the next hour the guys went through a series of warm-ups and strength-training exercises, all in pairs and small groups. The drills were intended to build unity and fun among the players. By the end of the practice the guys looked like a different team. They stood straight, and the weariness in their expressions had been replaced by laughter and an easiness Cody hadn't seen in them before. And something else — with each successive drill their effort increased until he barely recognized them. These were players he could work with, guys who could win games.

Cody studied them. He couldn't say they looked exactly confident, but then ... that would take time.

"Okay, men," Cody looked each of them in the eyes. "Good work today. You should be proud of yourselves." He motioned to them to come closer. "Let's huddle up."

There was a chant Jim Flanigan liked to use with his kids when they worked out as a family in the backyard. Jim would bring the guys in close, have them put their fists high in the center, and then he'd shout out, "Whose way?"

And in response the Flanigan boys would yell back, "His way."

"Whose way?"

"His way!"

Again, it wasn't something often heard in public schools, but Lyle was different. Cody figured the kids needed it so badly he had no choice. It was time for drastic measures. Besides, the community was deeply faithful, and pretty much everyone at the school believed in Jesus. Cody had learned that working in the classroom, and now he could see it was true with the players, too. He saw it in the way they prayed together earlier, the way they respected Cody for asking them to pray.

Now, as the guys gathered close, Cody put his arms around the shoulders of the guys nearest him — one of whom was DeMetri Smith. "Huddle up ... that's right, come on." In all the days he'd been working with Coach Oliver for these spring sessions, he'd never once seen the man lead them in a group huddle like this. How could he possibly expect to have a winning team when the guys didn't have even a hint of team unity? Cody gritted his teeth. He'd change that. If nothing else came from his time in charge today, it would be that much. They would be a team, and they would be God's team.

When they were as close as they could get, when the entire group formed a single nucleus, Cody let the passion ring in his voice. "Okay, listen up." He didn't have to ask twice. The guys had clearly never been through a practice like this. Not in two years anyway. "Whatever happens with Coach Oliver, whatever he might tell you from this day forward, we're a team. You are all very capable, very strong young men, and you have it in you to be winners. You know why?" His voice rang with a sincerity that reminded him of Jim Flanigan, the way Jim would talk to him when he needed to be convinced of his worth. "You're winners not because of your record, but because of whose you are. You are God's men, and because of that this year will be different. I promise you that."

"Amen." DeMetri's voice wasn't loud, but it was a start, a show

of enthusiasm. A few other players added their voices to the mix, and then the guys quieted, allowing Cody to continue.

"Let's do this, let's dedicate this season to God — no matter what happens after today." He could only imagine the way he might be fired for doing this somewhere else. But not here. Not with the heritage of Lyle, Indiana. "Father, God, we come to you broken. Shaken from the past in a lot of ways. But we come to you, Lord ... we dedicate this coming season to you." Something in his tone was more on fire, more filled with energy for Christ than Cody had ever been before. "Every young man here is a winner, Father, they are winners because they are yours. And so we ask that you would bring about a miracle for the Lyle football team. Show us that you are here among us, Father, and make these boys believe they are winners. And God, please ... let them know ... I couldn't be more proud of them. In Jesus' name, amen."

This time the team let up a loud amen, almost in unison. The improvement in morale was so great Cody felt chills along his arms, and he wondered if he was the only one. "Okay, bring it in." He raised his fist to the center of the huddle and the guys did the same thing. This was something that didn't have to be taught, even if Coach Oliver had never led the guys in a display of team bonding like this. It was time for the chant. "I'll ask you a question — 'Whose way?' and you ... you all will respond, 'His way!'" He drew a quick breath. "Whose way?"

"His way!" Only DeMetri's voice rose above the others.

"Again, men. Louder." Cody paused. "Whose way?"

"His way!" A few more guys joined in.

"Whose way?" Cody raised his voice — not in anger like Coach Oliver, but with an intensity that showed how much he believed in them.

"His way!" This time most of the guys responded.

Their fists were still in the air, but it was time to wrap it up. Cody finished with something he hoped would become a tradition. "One-two-three ... Believe!" He hadn't told the guys about that part, so none of them said it with him. But that would change.

Cody believed that with everything in him.

He dismissed the guys ten minutes earlier than Coach Oliver ever had, and he noticed something that had never marked the moments after a practice. As the guys walked off to the locker room they were talking, pairing up in groups of twos and threes and fours, and patting each other on the backs. *They feel good about themselves, God ... but what about tomorrow?* He remembered that he'd prayed for a miracle. *Trust You, right God? That's what You want me to do?*

Don't worry about tomorrow, my son ... every day has enough trouble of its own.

That's for sure. Cody smiled as he removed his hat and wiped his brow. The response was more of a reminder, the Bible verse Cody had written in his school planner this week. It was from Matthew 6:34 and he'd needed it a number of times already. Don't worry about tomorrow — tomorrow would worry about itself.

He was gathering his gear bag when he spotted something in the parking lot, a flash of yellow that caught his attention. As he turned, he felt his knees grow weak. Leaning against the fence and looking stunning was Cheyenne, her yellow Volkswagen bug parked a few feet away. She was smiling at him, he could tell that much from where he stood fifty yards away. Then, very slowly, she started clapping. And he could only surmise one very certain thing.

In his coaching career at Lyle High School, he had won his first fan.

Eleven

CODY REALIZED TWO THINGS AS HE WALKED TOWARD CHEY-
enne. First, he was exhausted. The coaching session had taken all
his mental and emotional energy — and of course it had. He had
been thrown into the role of psychological paramedic, counselor,
and coach all with only a minute's notice. But with God leading, he had accomplished more in an hour than he'd seen accomplished with the players all spring.

He walked closer, ignoring his weariness.

The second thing was this — he missed Cheyenne. Missed
her more than he might've wanted to admit before this moment.
He must have missed her, because seeing her now was one of the
brightest highlights of his day. That she would drive all the way
from Indianapolis to watch him coach was more than he could've
imagined. More than any other girl had done for him.

Even Bailey.

When he reached her, he set his gear bag down and hugged
her. Not a lingering hug, but one that let her know how grateful
he was that she had come. The fact that he needed no words until
now was further proof that something was happening between
them. He stepped back and smiled at her. "How long were you
here?"

She smiled. "The whole time." Her eyes sparkled, and the
admiration she had for him was certain. An admiration that
hadn't been there before today. "I wanted to watch you in action."

He raised his brow. "You picked the right day."

"I see that." She looked at the field and then back at Cody. "That man ... he's awful. Those kids can't be expected to tolerate that."

"I know." Cody sighed. He picked up his gear bag and motioned to his car — parked not far from hers. "Can I treat you to dinner? There's a burger joint a block down toward Main Street." He made a funny face. "Haven't tried any of the other local cuisine, but ... I can vouch for the burgers."

She laughed and nodded. "One condition."

Again the feeling between them was comfortable, and Cody couldn't help but be attracted to her. "If you'd drive all the way out here to watch me coach, I guess I can take a condition or two."

"There's a hospital halfway between here and Indianapolis. I volunteer there once a week and there's a little girl ... Kassie Garman ... I thought maybe, if you don't mind, we could stop and see her." Cheyenne grinned, and again her eyes shone with kindness and depth — like her soul was twice as old and wise as she was. "She loves visitors."

Cody felt his heart warm. "I'd love to. Really." He led the way to his car, struck by the turn his evening had taken. Hadn't Tara told him all along that Cheyenne was a wonderful girl? Cody hadn't wanted to find out, because of Bailey. But this was friendship, and certainly he could spend a few hours with her.

When they reached the diner, they found a table, and Cody searched Cheyenne's eyes for a long few seconds. "So ... you spend a day every week visiting sick kids?" He nodded, in awe of her kindness. "That's very nice of you."

"You're no different." She angled her head toward the high school. "Watching you out there with those young guys. Whatever they're paying you, it isn't enough."

He chuckled. "True. The position doesn't pay."

"See?" She pulled her ice water close and took a sip. "You'd spend a day with sick kids if you had time." She wrinkled her nose, her expression one of polite disgust. "I can't respect that other coach. The way he treats those kids."

"We're praying for a miracle."

"He needs to be fired." She was warming up to him, letting a sassier side of her personality shine through. "Who do I have to call?"

They laughed, and after their burgers had been served, Cody allowed a seriousness to creep into his eyes, his tone. "So ..." He set his burger down and wiped his mouth with his napkin. "Did you pack up Art's things?"

"Not yet." She looked down, shy again. A sad smile tugged at the corners of her lips and she lifted her eyes to him. "I can't do it, Cody. I tried one day after class, but ... I feel like I'm betraying him." She sat up and pushed her plate away from her, her burger only half eaten. "I made a decision though."

"You did." He enjoyed this, getting to know her, spending his dinner with someone other than himself or his college roommate. "Sounds important."

"It is." She folded her hands, official-like. "Once I get my nursing degree ... I want to move to Iraq. At least for a few years."

"Iraq?" He didn't want to discourage her idea, but the Middle East still wasn't safe. Just last week three dozen Christians were killed inside a church. Nurses would be fair game for the insurgents, even if they were there to help.

She must've recognized the doubt in his eyes, because she rushed ahead. "I know what you're thinking. I already called Tara, and she feels the same way. It's too dangerous, too much of a risk." Cheyenne smiled, and there wasn't a hint of fear in her eyes. "But what better use of my education, right? I can go there and help soldiers. Help them so that more of them make it home."

Cody's heart broke for her, the exotic looking angel-girl seated across from him. She and Art should be married by now, maybe welcoming the birth of a child. Instead she lived alone, struggling through her college education and a job at the Indianapolis hospital, with volunteer work at another hospital outside of town. Alone except for Art's pictures and things — still up around her apartment. "Chey ..." His voice was soft, quiet enough that he had to lean closer for her to hear him. "Going to Iraq won't bring back Art."

"I know." She nodded, as if she'd worked through this possibility already. "It's not about Art. Not really." She looked out the window at the dark parking lot on the other side of the glass. "It's about the next guy, the soldier who might make it home to his fiancée if only he has the right help."

There was nothing Cody could say to change her mind. Besides, this wasn't the time or place. Cheyenne had two years at least before she'd have her nursing degree. Cody might not even know her by the time she had to make a real decision about Iraq. The conversation shifted and they talked about Lyle and the way God was still honored there. "Teachers, administrators, coaches ... everyone prays at Lyle." He finished the last few french fries on his plate. "I'm not saying the kids don't get into trouble on Friday night. I'm sure they do. But loving God is a way of life ... it's expected."

"Hmmm." Cheyenne looked more relaxed again, as if it had done her good to get the details about her decision out in the open. "The way all of America used to be."

"Exactly." He told her about DeMetri, and asked her to pray for him. "I worry about that boy. I don't know anything about his background, but I have a feeling it hasn't been pretty. I've never seen his parents pick him up after practice. Never heard him talk about them."

They chatted for another five minutes about the socio-economic breakdown of the town. There was a computer plant not far away, so some of the kids came from affluent families. But most were the sons of farmers, rooted in families who had

depended on God for the rain and sunshine and crops year after year. When dinner was over, Cody paid the bill and he followed her down the long two-lane road and onto another and finally to the highway. Thirty minutes later they pulled into the hospital parking lot.

Cody peered at the complex of newer buildings, surprised. He didn't know about this hospital, or why it would be out here in the middle of cornfields twenty minutes outside Indianapolis. When they had parked and were walking inside, he asked Cheyenne about it. "Land's less expensive here," the sadness was back in her eyes. "Most of the floors specialize in cancer treatment. That's why Kassie's here. She has leukemia."

Suddenly Cody wasn't sure if he could hold up through the visit. It hadn't occurred to him before now that the girl Cheyenne wanted to visit must be very sick. Otherwise she wouldn't need regular visitors. They reached the elevator and took it to the fifth floor. *Pediatric Oncology*, the sign read as they stepped off the elevator. Cody hesitated, wanting a little more information before they headed into Kassie's room.

"Tell me about her ... what should I know?"

Cheyenne leaned against the hospital wall and searched Cody's eyes. "Thank you. For caring about her." She allowed a small smile. "Not that I'm surprised." She took a long breath. "Let's see ... Kassie is three years old and she has acute myelogenous leukemia — AML. It's very serious, but three months ago she had a bone marrow transplant from her brother. He was a perfect match."

Cody could already feel an ache starting in his chest. A three-year-old with cancer? It was the sort of thing that made him want to demand a cure — whatever it took. Children should never have to battle something as awful as cancer. He folded his arms, still listening.

His interest must've warmed Cheyenne's heart, because she

didn't seem to be in a hurry to move on. "Oh, and Kassie has a mild case of Down Syndrome. She can only communicate with her hands ... and her smile." Cheyenne's eyes grew watery, despite the joy in her face. "She can always talk with her smile. And she loves her grandparents more than anyone in the world."

"Her grandparents?"

"Especially her grandpa. He stays the night several days each week. She's his constant companion."

Cody could feel tears welling in his own eyes. He sniffed and blinked a few times. "Okay ... maybe I better just see her for myself."

She linked arms with him and led him down the hallway. "I love that you have a tender heart, Cody. Tough football player ... big, bad Army guy rescues a bunch of prisoners in Iraq." She slowed and they looked at each other for a moment. "But you care ... more than most guys."

He didn't know how to respond, so he said nothing. He wasn't sure if Cheyenne was comparing him to Art or to guys she had known in school over the years. But one thing was sure about the man she'd lost to war: he had a kind heart. Cody was honored that Cheyenne would think him the same as Art.

They reached her room and stepped inside. Sure enough, an older man sat in the chair beside Kassie's bed, and there — with wires running into her from a number of places — was little Kassie. She sucked her thumb, her sweet eyes turned toward the man who had to be her grandpa. Cheyenne took hold of Cody's hand and led him into the room. She stopped to use hand sanitizer, and Cody did the same thing.

In a flash, Cody tried to process the way he was feeling. Overwhelmed with sorrow for the darling girl in the hospital bed, and conflicted by the feelings stirring within him at the touch of Cheyenne's hand against his. She was only trying to make Kassie comfortable, he realized that. But still he had to catch his breath over the conflicting emotions hitting him.

Cheyenne kept her voice low, appropriate for a hospital setting — especially at night. "Ivan," she led Cody to the spot beside the older man. "This is my friend, Cody." She released his hand. "He wanted to visit Kassie tonight, too." She smiled at the little girl. "Is that okay, sweetie?"

Kassie gestured with her hands in a way that Cody was pretty sure meant he could stay. Then she turned pretty eyes toward him and smiled, smiled so big and bright that Cody understood what Cheyenne meant when she said that Kassie spoke with her smile. No question, the girl's heart could be seen in the way her whole being lit up.

"Hi, Kassie," Cody came up alongside her bed. He wanted to touch her hand, show her some sign that he cared. But he wasn't sure of the situation with germs. So instead he returned her smile. Then he walked to the other side of the bed and the man stood so they could shake hands.

"Ivan Garman," the man said. He had eyes that spoke of the painful journey he and his family had walked — much of it in this hospital room, if Cody had to guess. "Thank you for stopping in." He looked at his granddaughter. "She's my little angel. Visits my wife Charmaine and me as often as she can." He nodded, a catch in his voice. "She's getting better. Right, baby?"

Kassie nodded at her grandpa and slid her thumb back in her mouth.

"Where's everyone else?"

Ivan settled back in his chair. "Charmaine and the family are in the cafeteria — having coffee and dessert." He smiled, and some of the weariness faded. "You should've seen Kassie and her brother. They unhooked her and she and that boy tore around the room with that push toy Kassie loves." He nodded to the corner of the room where the toy now stood. His eyes found his granddaughter again. "I never heard you laugh so hard in all my life, Kassie girl."

She giggled and again her thumb came out. This time her smile stayed, and she moved her hands in a way that Cheyenne seemed to understand.

"Is it sign language?" Cody returned to his place on the other side of the bed, and so did Cheyenne. They took the two open chairs on that side and Cody watched while Kassie continued using her hands — this time to talk to her grandpa.

"Not really." Cheyenne shook her head. "But I've learned what she wants — and generally she figures out how to convey her needs." Cheyenne put her hand on the bedrail. "You want a story, right baby girl?"

Again Kassie nodded big, and Grandpa Ivan chuckled. "That girl has your number, for sure."

Cheyenne didn't have a book, so Cody wasn't sure how she was going to meet Kassie's request. But before he could offer to find one from the front desk or a hospital library somewhere, Cheyenne began telling a different sort of story. One she seemed to make up as she went along.

"Once upon a time," Cheyenne slid to the edge of her chair, her eyes focused on Kassie, "there was a beautiful fairy girl, and her name was Kassie."

Kassie clapped her hands and rolled slightly onto her side so she could see Cheyenne better. She gestured in a way that made it clear she wanted more. Again Grandpa Ivan chuckled. "She loves this."

"One day, Kassie was playing near the frog pond when the very biggest frog in all the land came hopping over and sat beside her..."

The story went on for ten minutes, and involved not only frogs but a small deer, a royal queen, and a handsome prince. In the end, through many plot twists and turns, the fairy girl Kassie was swept away on a white horse by the handsome prince and rescued. "And the handsome prince took Kassie back to her parents where she was safe and where she grew up healthy and strong ... the most beautiful girl in all the land."

Cody was glad he wasn't called upon to add a finishing thought to the story. He couldn't have talked if he wanted to. He stole a look at Grandpa Ivan, and caught the man wiping a tear off his cheek. Kassie, though, was smiling as sweetly as ever, captivated by the story. She made hand signs that Cody understood. She wanted another story.

But this time Cheyenne stood and gave the girl a sad smile. "We have to go, sweetie." She grinned at Grandpa Ivan. "Your grandpa here will tell you the next story."

"Oh, sure." He laughed. "Like I could follow that act."

Kassie turned to her grandpa and nodded, excited and certain — as if she definitely believed her grandpa was capable of a story at least that good. Cody joined Cheyenne and they bid both Kassie and her grandfather goodnight. Outside in the hallway, Cody took a few steps and then stopped. "She's so precious ..." He pinched the bridge of his nose, staving off the tears that stung at the corners of his eyes. "How did you find her?"

"I know about this place," she smiled. "There's not enough days in the week to visit all the kids that need to hear a story of hope."

They walked back to their cars, quieter than before. So many kids needed help. The guys on his Lyle football team and sick little girls like Kassie Garman. He had no idea where God might take the friendship he felt for Cheyenne, but he knew this much. Their passions were the same. And if nothing else, he had found a friend in Cheyenne. A friend he admired deeply, one he wanted to see more often.

Whether it was his time coaching or the half hour with Kassie, or simply the way Cheyenne made him feel, he wasn't sure. But that night for the first time in weeks, Cody didn't wake up once with nightmares of prison cells and Iraqi soldiers. He slept in perfect peace, and when he woke he could only think one thing about his wonderful evening with Cheyenne and his perfect night's sleep.

There had to be a connection.

Twelve

THE FLIGHT TO LOS ANGELES WENT SMOOTHLY, AND NOW JENNY watched from the backstage wings of the *Tonight Show* set as her husband hurried their boys into seats near the front of the audience section. The premiere for *Unlocked* was set for tomorrow night, but first Bailey would appear with Brandon Paul on the talk show — an opportunity that had only come up yesterday.

Ricky turned back to Jim and said something, probably about wanting to be near the aisle. Whatever the concern, Jim positioned himself in the middle of the boys and with a calm look and gentle mannerisms he put an end to the discussion and got everyone seated. Jim saved a seat for her, right next to him. She had promised Bailey she'd stay with her until the show was about to start — or at least until Brandon Paul arrived. They had fifteen minutes until show time, so Jenny hoped Brandon would hurry.

For now, Bailey was changing her clothes, getting into an outfit she had brought with her. Jenny studied the full auditorium and shook her head, amazed. *Dear Lord, You sure have given us a crazy life ... a life we love, of course. But still ... so crazy.* She thought about the times they'd spent watching Jim coach the Indianapolis Colts, and how often he'd been shown on a national TV screen. Then the thought that Bailey would be chosen to star opposite Brandon, and now this. *Please, Father, let her shine for You. And let people see You when she's on the* Tonight Show. *This isn't about her or about our family ...*

It was an opportunity to be a light to the world — that's what

Jenny and Jim talked about with Bailey on the flight here. But no question there was added interest when the producers of the *Tonight Show* figured out Bailey was the daughter of a successful NFL football coach. Talk show hosts liked that sort of thing.

Bailey came up behind her. "Okay ..." she sounded nervous. "How do I look?"

The vision Bailey made took Jenny's breath. "Honey,... you look stunning." Bailey wore a sea-blue dress with short sleeves and a modest skirt that came to her knees. The dress was cut close to her body, but not in a way that was suggestive.

"Really? You like it?" Her doubts made her sound younger than she was. "You're sure this is the right color? I brought another one ..."

"No." Jenny smiled and gave her daughter's hand a squeeze. "This is perfect. You've never looked more beautiful."

A woman in a black pencil skirt walked up and checked her notepad. "Bailey Flanigan?"

"Yes?" Bailey turned.

"Time for makeup." She smiled at Jenny. "You're Mom?"

"Yes." Jenny wasn't sure if they'd let her tag along. "Can I watch?"

"Certainly." Again she smiled. "We're pretty low key back here. As long as you make it out to your seat before the show starts."

Back in the makeup room, Jenny sat off to the side and watched. She could hardly believe this was her little girl — all grown up and ready to take on the world. Something about the combination of the dress and the way her hair fell around her face as the makeup artist curled it ... Bailey looked like a classic beauty, the sort of timeless superstar the world would love to elevate to cover-girl status. Jenny was grateful again that this wasn't the life Bailey wanted. No matter what sort of impression

she made tonight, no paparazzi would follow her back home to Bloomington.

A commotion sounded in the room behind her, and she heard the familiar voice of Brandon Paul. She turned just as he hurried into the makeup area. "Where is she? Where's my Bailey?"

The woman doing Bailey's hair had a thick hot curling iron near her face, so she didn't move. But she waved her hand. "Here … I'm in here."

Brandon saw Jenny first, and he jogged the last few steps to close the distance between them. "Jenny!" He hugged her for a long time. "I've missed you so much! I'm definitely coming back to Bloomington." He pulled back and searched her eyes in a hurry. "That's okay, right? I mean, you're my family away from the insanity of Hollywood."

"Of course, it's okay." Jenny loved the energy Brandon brought into a room. No wonder he was becoming even more of a household name. He had a way of lighting up the silver screen the same way he lit up a room. From what producers of his next picture said, his acting ability had gotten even stronger. Jenny figured that had something to do with the new depth she saw in his eyes, the result of his ever-increasing faith.

He moved to Bailey's side and waited until the makeup artist released the curl from the iron. Then she stood and the two of them hugged for a long time, so long that again Jenny didn't have to wonder what Brandon's feelings were for Bailey. He cared for her very much. Jenny had always believed Brandon might even be in love with Bailey. But nothing would ever come of it. Not as long as Brandon lived and worked in Los Angeles.

As they pulled apart, Brandon looked her up and down. "You are absolutely gorgeous, Bailey Flanigan. Wait till the public gets a look at you." He winked at her and took the makeup chair beside her. "They'll talk about how I'm your co-star. It'll be, 'Brandon who?'" He laughed, completely teasing her.

"You haven't changed." Bailey didn't look nervous. She never had been around Brandon. Maybe because they were such good friends with the Baxters — and the Baxters' oldest son was Dayne Matthews — one of the most famous actors to ever grace a movie screen. Or maybe because her father worked around famous athletes all the time. Whatever it was, Jenny loved her daughter's level-headedness. It was like Jim always said: There wouldn't be autograph lines in heaven. Might as well not get used to all the attention here on earth.

"The minute one of my guys starts believing all the adoration, he's done," Jim had said a number of times. "Fame destroys the people who believe it."

Bailey certainly didn't believe it. Even now Jenny knew her enough to know she was playing a role … the role of budding new actress, thrilled to be starring opposite Brandon Paul in the anticipated smash hit *Unlocked*. The truth was, she was a girl from Bloomington who loved God and her family and who saw Brandon Paul as a friend, not a celebrity. For that reason, she would be calm once she took the set of the *Tonight Show*, and she would shine for all the world to see.

Jenny had no doubt whatsoever.

HER SPOT ON THE *TONIGHT SHOW* was slated for fifteen minutes, and Bailey had no idea how she'd fill that much time on national television. The makeup session was over, and they were being set up with hidden microphones. Then one of the production staff led them to the wings, and they waited for the cue. The band played the intro music, and the host welcomed her and Brandon to the set.

Though they walked out together, they didn't hold hands — the way Brandon suggested. "We can't give the magazines any fuel," Bailey giggled with him backstage.

"Even if I want them to talk?" Brandon looked like a little boy asking for his favorite Christmas toy.

"Even then." Bailey wagged her finger at him, playfully.

Almost as soon as they sat down and made it through introductions, the host ran the trailer for their movie. Bailey had seen it twenty times, easily, but it still choked her up. The movie would bring hope and healing to a generation who needed it — and with God's help the message would cause people to be kinder to others. Something desperately important for their culture. When the trailer finished, the host bantered a little with Brandon, asking if there was anything to the rumors about him and Bailey.

For a second, Bailey worried that Brandon might tease that yes, there was something to it. But instead he allowed his smile to fall off a little, and he gave Bailey a longing look. "I wish I could say there was, Jay, but truthfully ... Bailey's my friend." He paused. "Her family introduced me to Jesus while I was on set in Bloomington."

The Jesus comment made the host nervous, and he made a lame joke about whether Jesus wanted his autograph when they met. But Bailey couldn't keep from beaming at her friend. Here on national television with all the world watching, as easily as he might've talked about surfing or hiking or any other new part of his life, Brandon Paul was talking about Jesus. She couldn't wait to hug him later.

The discussion of Brandon's faith turned the interview back to Bailey, and the fact that she was the daughter of Jim Flanigan, NFL coach. "Your father's always had a strong faith, he's always shared that with his players, wouldn't you say?"

"Definitely." Bailey felt more relaxed than she had all day. She smiled, and she could feel the way her eyes sparkled. "My mom and dad built our family on faith in God. It's the most important part of our lives." There. She'd done it. She'd found a way to work her faith into the conversation without sounding forced or preachy. It was exactly what she and her parents had prayed for.

After that, they discussed the film for a few minutes and talked about the powerful message of treating people with respect and stopping bullying. The host spent a few minutes asking Brandon what was next. He didn't turn the same question to Bailey, which didn't surprise her. She was the "no-name" in the interview. It was enough that she had a part in *Unlocked*. Besides, what answer could she give? That she had just recently lost out on a Broadway role?

The interview ended with the host giving a plug for everyone to get to a theater that weekend to see *Unlocked*. He cut to a commercial break and shook both their hands. "Stop in any time," he told them. "Brandon, you make sure to see us before your next film releases."

With the cameras still off and the commercial still playing, Brandon held Bailey's hand and led her off stage. She didn't fight him this time. No one but the studio audience was watching, and clearly they had established that their friendship was rooted in faith — deeper and stronger than most Hollywood friendships.

Backstage, Brandon picked her up in his arms and swung her around in a full circle. "You were amazing! Please, Bailey ... don't tell me you're done making movies. You do every aspect of it so well. The acting, the connecting with people on set ... your humility. All of it." He was talking fast, his words practically running together. "Bailey, please ... do another movie. One with me." He let his head fall back and he laughed out loud. "You were absolutely a pro out there. I was more nervous than you."

The excitement of what had just happened, the way they'd showed the world a fresh side of moviemaking and the way it could connect to Christ was still working its way through her heart. She buzzed with joy and the thrill of the moment. "What about you? Telling Jay how you met Jesus, like it was nothing unusual?" She laughed, thrilled. She never dreamed the interview would go this well.

There were still two segments to the show, but at the commercial break Bailey's family had been allowed to exit to the wings. She could hear her brothers in the green room, and she laughed. What a wild experience for all of them — being here at the *Tonight Show*. The boys would have quite a story when they got back to school after the weekend. Girls in their classes still asked for autographs from Brandon, and so far none of her brothers had complained about the attention.

They met up around the snack table, and a producer motioned for quiet on the set. After the show, the host came back and visited with all of them, even taking time to sign autographs for Bailey's brothers. The show had taped around five that evening, and by the time they all left out the back door, it was nearly eight o'clock and dark outside. Bailey had been looking forward to the quiet outside the studio after a full day of travel, her appearance on the *Today Show*, and the three-hour time difference. But they stepped from the backstage quiet to absolute chaos, because gathered out back were too many cameramen to count.

"This way," her dad motioned them toward a waiting limo. Clearly he had worked this plan out backstage with Brandon's bodyguards. The two guys wore suits and had builds big enough to be featured on her dad's offensive line. Together the bodyguards parted the crowd as they led the group to the waiting car.

"Brandon!" someone yelled.

"Over here, Brandon ..."

"Are you and Bailey Flanigan dating?"

Bailey chided herself for being caught unprepared. She hadn't spent an evening with Brandon in a long time, and never here in Los Angeles. As they walked through the mob, Bailey doubted she'd ever seen so many camera flashes in her life. This was twice the paparazzi at the red carpet event in Bloomington for *The Last*

Letter — the film Keith Ellison and Dayne Matthews had produced before *Unlocked*.

She appreciated how Brandon led the way, right behind his bodyguards and in front of her parents. Not one camera could've caught a photo of the two of them together — something he had clearly maneuvered out of respect for her. When they were safe in the stretch limo, everyone seemed too shocked to speak, breathless over the frenzy.

Justin squinted at Brandon in the dim lighting. "You deal with that madness all the time? Like ... everywhere you go?"

Brandon shrugged off the inconvenience. "Paparazzi are part of the territory." He sat back and stretched his legs. Now that they were out of sight he had taken the spot next to Bailey. "There are ways around them. But not after a live appearance like that. They all know the way out of the studio."

Gradually the boys started talking, admitting that they weren't sure they could handle the pressure of living under that sort of scrutiny. "What if I had something caught in my teeth?" BJ always had the most off-the-wall comments. "I'd be afraid to eat."

"Nah," Brandon laughed. He seemed completely at ease, even if Bailey and her family were still dazed by the onslaught. "If you think that's bad, wait till tomorrow night. An LA premiere is big enough on its own. But for a movie as talked about as *Unlocked* ... yeah, it'll be a circus for sure."

Bailey appreciated how Brandon didn't credit himself for being the cause of the media attention — even though that was the primary reason. He was definitely different than the guy she'd met the first day she auditioned opposite him for the role of Ella. God had softened his edges and given him a peace. Something he'd been missing before.

Only then did Bailey sit up straighter in the seat and realize the chaos behind them. The paparazzi hadn't given up, and at least eight or ten cars were dodging traffic, trying to keep up

with them. The limo driver must've been part of Brandon's staff, because he drove utterly unfazed. Her brothers didn't notice. They were quiet and like her, probably tired from the long day of travel and the time difference.

"You okay?" Brandon turned to her, his voice a whisper. "With the cameras and all?"

"Yes. Of course." She took his hand and squeezed it. But when she went to let go, he gently held on.

"I want this weekend to be perfect." He smiled at her, and the depth in his eyes was unmistakable. "Please ... if you're ever uncomfortable with the attention, just tell me. My driver can take us somewhere private with almost no notice."

"Okay." She giggled. At the other end of the limo, her parents looked happy, in a quiet conversation of their own. Her brothers were dozing off, lulled by the highway drive they were taking and still unaware of the paparazzi behind them. "Where are we going?"

"To my beach house. You're staying with me."

"We are?" Bailey had left the arrangements to her mom and now she turned in that direction. "Mom ... you knew about this?"

"It made the most sense." Her mother kept her voice low, so she wouldn't wake the boys. "Brandon's used to dealing with paparazzi. We aren't."

"Exactly." Brandon slipped his arm around her shoulders. "I have room for everyone. Don't worry." He grinned, but his tone wasn't flirty like usual. It was more adoring, like he really would do anything to make sure Bailey was comfortable this weekend. "Plus, this way we can spend more time together. If we had to worry about getting in and out of a hotel, we'd never see each other."

Bailey felt herself relax. Her mother was right — the idea made sense. "No wonder your driver isn't worried about the paparazzi behind us."

"What?" Brandon's voice reverted back to the familiar teasing. "You mean someone's following us?"

Bailey released his hand and gave him a playful shove. "Very funny." She crossed her arms so he wouldn't be tempted to take her fingers in his again. She couldn't lie. She liked how it felt, riding in Brandon's comfortable stretch limo and holding hands with him. She cared enough about him that somehow holding hands seemed okay. But still … she didn't want to give him the wrong idea. She yawned. "How much longer?"

He glanced outside and surveyed the part of the freeway they were driving on. "Fifteen minutes. Maybe twenty." He settled back against the leather seat and found her eyes again. In the quiet dark of the late night, the friendly intimacy that had been a part of their time on set was instantly back again. "So … where's the boyfriend?" He made a curious childlike look, and with great exaggeration he peered around their feet and in the shelving behind their headrests. "Nope. Still doesn't seem to be hanging around."

Bailey couldn't help but laugh at him. Brandon entertained her, even when she was tired. "Okay … wanna know the truth?"

"That would be nice." He leaned back, and this time shifted so he could see her better. "Sort of a general rule of thumb I have with all my friends. Tell the truth … as much as possible anyway."

"Okay, then …" Bailey had known this moment would come when she and Brandon got together. She wanted to believe she had let Cody Coleman go, that he couldn't break her heart again. But even thinking about saying the words that Cody wasn't in her life made her heart ache. "He's gone." She refused to let her heart feel the pain here, now … while she was celebrating with Brandon. "He's not in the picture."

Brandon could've made a joke, teased her that starting tomorrow in theaters everywhere he, Brandon, was definitely "in the picture" with her. But he refrained from saying anything of the sort. Instead he held out his hand and waited until she tucked hers inside it. "I'm sorry, Bailey. His name's Cody, right?"

"Yes." She remembered to smile. "It's okay. We haven't talked since January. Three months now."

"How's your heart with all this?" Again this was a side of Brandon she hadn't seen. The guy she'd worked with spouted quick one-liners, always able to laugh at any situation. But not now. Once more she had to believe this new maturity could only have come from his deepening faith.

"I'm okay." She nodded, her eyes still on his. "Moving on, I guess."

Only when it was obvious she wasn't going to break down, and that enough time had passed that this situation with Bailey wasn't a crisis, did Brandon let the hint of a sparkle start up in his eyes. "So …" he gave his best *Dumb and Dumber* smile, "you're saying there's a chance!"

Their eyes held for a moment, and they both burst out laughing, the sort of late night laugh attack that made Brandon eventually reach for a couple pillows — one for him and one for her — to stifle the noise. *Dumb and Dumber* was a movie they'd called up once on Brandon's iPad during a break on the set. They'd watched only the funny scenes, and that day they couldn't stop laughing either.

When they could finally breathe, the driver had already exited the freeway and was winding up a steep canyon road to an enormous house on a hill. Bailey looked the other direction. "Are we at the beach?"

"Yes." He yawned, put his arm around her again, and leaned his head against hers. "I moved here in February. You'll love the view when the sun comes up."

"Feels like that'll happen in a few hours." She could've fallen asleep right here, like her brothers. The laughter had tired her out, and every wonderful thing about her friendship with Brandon was back to the way it had been the last time they saw each other. All that, and she had no reason not to sit close to him or hold his hand. She was single, after all. If she wanted to date Brandon Paul she could.

Matt Keagan had a girlfriend and Cody couldn't care less. But tonight with Brandon she felt more at ease than before, more appreciative of the changes that had happened to him since he'd begun living for God. They bid each other goodnight at the bottom of the stairs that led to the guest wing of his house, and Brandon was a complete gentleman. No long hug or hints at anything inappropriate.

As she walked up the stairs, a chill ran down her arms. *Brandon Paul* ... Bailey smiled at the thought. And that night, as she fell asleep in the bed opposite the one two of her brothers shared, she allowed herself to think about the possibility.

Even for just this one night.

Thirteen

THE SUNRISE REFLECTED ON THE PACIFIC OCEAN WAS EVERY BIT as beautiful as Brandon had said. Bailey climbed out of bed and saw she was the only one awake. Her brothers — and probably the rest of the family — were still sleeping. She checked the clock on the nightstand. Just seven in the morning. The time change must've had her body confused.

She had slept in a pair of shorts and a T-shirt, plenty warm enough for the California night. The entire back wall of this part of his house was glass, the panoramic ocean view mesmerizing. Bailey walked to the balcony, slid the door open, and stepped outside. Back home the weather was still chilly, snow still piled up in most parking lot corners. But here in Malibu, the breeze off the water was warm and full and fresh against her face.

Bailey breathed in deep and leaned against the railing. No wonder the movie industry had settled here in Southern California. It was impossible not to dream and create and believe the impossible standing here on the edge of the ocean. Bailey lifted her eyes to the vast blue that hung like a canopy over the sea. *Dear God, this is the day ... the premiere ... please, Father, use this film to change our country ... to lead people to You.*

She hadn't given a lot of thought to the movie, really. For her and the other actors, the film had been behind them for many months. But for the public, today was a beginning. Goosebumps flashed on her arms and bare legs. The possibilities were endless, and suddenly she was glad for this moment, for a sliver of sanity and solitude at the beginning of what would inevitably be a frenzied day.

Brandon's beach house was situated so that the ocean was his backyard. No paparazzi could've gotten into the small grassy yard behind his house unless they scaled a steep cliffy embankment and found a way over his eight-foot brick wall. The front, of course — where they had entered the house through the garage last night — was fair game. Bailey bet there were cameramen already outside waiting. Especially since she and her family were staying here. One more reason for them to think they'd catch a glimpse of something newsworthy, like her and Brandon, or her family, leaving the house together. The Flanigans were new and different to the Hollywood crowd, and Brandon had warned her last night that all of them would be under scrutiny the entire weekend. She laughed to herself. BJ was right about his teeth — at least for the next forty-eight hours.

"Hey," Connor joined her on the balcony. He shielded his eyes and scanned the ocean view. "Is this amazing, or what?"

"It is." She motioned for him to join her, and he did, leaning on the railing beside her, their arms touching. Connor had been her best friend all her life growing up. Only lately — when he'd been busy with football and music and she'd been in college — had they allowed some distance between them. "Could you live here . . . in Los Angeles?"

"I was thinking about that." Connor turned toward the water.

"And . . . ?" Bailey loved her brother so much. He was strong and virtuous and he wanted so badly to glorify God with his life. This moment alone with him was one more amazing gift to start the day.

Connor nodded slowly. "I think I could." His eyes danced, and his seriousness cracked and became a laugh. He looked again at the deep blue Pacific. "I mean, come on, Bailey. You couldn't do this?"

"Remember, this isn't exactly real." She turned her face to the breeze again. A pair of seagulls swept by and squawked as they lighted on the damp, sandy shore. "Brandon might come home here, but he spends his days fighting LA traffic, finding his way through the maze of city cement and asphalt and stucco and steel. High-rise buildings and almost no trees or grass or ocean views."

"Really?" Connor gave her a pointed look. "This from the girl who dreams about living in New York City."

Bailey hesitated, but then she laughed. "Good point." She thought for a long moment, trying to put into words the difference. "New York's a city, but it's more like a village. You can get around on foot or by subway."

"Yeah," Connor looked at her. "LA's more of a concrete jungle, I guess."

"Exactly."

"But for me ... if I want to act or sing ... this," he spread his hand toward the vista, "all of this is where dreams come true."

This was something Bailey hadn't heard from Connor ... at least not with so much certainty. "You might want to act?"

"Yes." He grinned. "I mean, I want to try out for *American Idol* first, of course. And I'll always love singing ... but Broadway's not for me, Bailey. The culture would drive me crazy."

Bailey understood. It was a very artsy community ... Connor — the quarterback of the football team — might have a hard time finding his place in New York City. "So acting, huh?"

"Maybe." He turned his back to the view, his arms crossed. "We'll see. But I could do this — the LA thing. I liked how Brandon handled the paparazzi yesterday." He paused, thoughtful. "I think if a guy is living for God, the whole fame thing isn't impossible."

"Hmmm." Bailey smiled at her brother. "I miss this, you and me talking."

"Me, too." He opened the patio door. "Hey, Brandon's making

breakfast. He says we're eating in half an hour. Then he's taking us down to the beach for a walk. He has a secret path or something."

"Brandon's making breakfast?" Bailey contained a light-hearted giggle. "Really?"

"Okay, not Brandon. His staff." Connor gave her a look like this was normal, hanging out on the balcony of a beach house and having breakfast with Brandon Paul. "You know ... just living the life."

They both laughed, and Connor went to get ready. Bailey remained on the balcony for another few minutes. She could stay in her shorts and T-shirt if they were headed down to the beach. Put her hair in a ponytail, grab a baseball cap, and call it good until later when they needed to get ready for the night. For now, she wanted to soak in every moment of how it felt to be here. Just the big wide ocean, the Lord, and her.

She replayed in her mind the time with Brandon last night. He was as charming as ever, but this time he was so much more thoughtful, more aware of her as a person. She stared at the crashing waves and tried to imagine her life, if somehow she found a way to live in Los Angeles and keep trying out for movie roles.

If she actually dated Brandon Paul.

For a single instant Cody's face came to mind. What was he doing this weekend while she was here celebrating the premiere of her movie? Did he even know the film opened this weekend? Did he care? Bailey felt again the pain in her heart, the ache that would probably always be there when she thought about Cody. The more time that passed, the more she realized how right her mother was. Cody had broken her heart, and he had done so seemingly without regret. Never mind that he thought he wasn't good enough for her. That argument was old. Whatever had really caused him to move on, it shouldn't have mattered as much as her, as much as she should've meant to him. Especially after she had loved him all this time. The truth was, he didn't care, not that

much anyway. He couldn't have cared. Otherwise he'd be calling her and insisting they meet and talk about what happened. He wouldn't let her go if he loved her.

The reality was that simple.

Brandon's interest — no matter how lighthearted — eased the hurt in her heart. It even helped distract her from the disappointment of not winning the *Hairspray* role. She could hardly feel sad on a day like today — no matter what doors God might close in New York City. Again she stared at the crashing waves. A few guys on boogie boards ran into the water, laughing and splashing up foamy surf as they headed for the breakers. Bailey watched them paddle out and then wait ... one minute, two ... until finally the perfect wave appeared. They caught it and rode it all the way to shore.

Life was like that. A lot of work and training and preparing, all so that when the time was right a person might catch the perfect wave. One problem ... Bailey wasn't sure what to look for, whether that wave would take her onto a Broadway stage — something that seemed less likely than ever — or whether it might even lead her to Los Angeles.

Enough daydreaming, she told herself. *Dear God ... You're in charge. I won't worry about which wave is the right one. Instead, I'll trust You that when the time is right, the perfect wave will appear. Just help me be ready to ride it in, Lord.* She smiled, enjoying the analogy. *Thank You ... for the beauty of today.*

I have loved you with an everlasting love, Daughter ... I am with you always.

Bailey savored the sensation, the feeling that the Creator of the universe was communicating with her right here on Brandon Paul's balcony. It was the best thing about loving God: knowing that He would never leave her, never let her walk alone. With that in mind, she fixed her hair, found the baseball cap from her suitcase, and met her family and Brandon for breakfast.

The smorgasbord of eggs Benedict, fresh fruit, waffles, and homemade jams was certainly not something Brandon whipped up that morning. But he teased that he had a knack for cooking. He took the seat beside Bailey, and he looked better than ever. Fresh and full of light, his eyes bright with possibility.

Amazing, Bailey thought, *how much better a person could look with God in their lives.* When she first met Brandon, he had a drinking problem. His eyes were dark, no matter how much he teased and laughed and charmed his way through the days. But now ... now she caught herself watching him, thinking about him, listening to him more than usual.

When breakfast was over, he led them through a door in the gate at the back of his yard. "Everyone thinks this hillside can't be climbed. But the previous owner built a trail." He laughed. "It takes a while, but it's worth it."

Bailey stayed close to Brandon, with the rest of her family following behind. The path zigzagged from one side of the hill to the other, cut into the rocks and protected by a small railing system on the cliff side — otherwise the path couldn't possibly have been safe. Not when they were a good two hundred feet above the beach.

"Coach Taylor would love to get a hold of this hill." Connor was behind Bailey. He looked back at the other boys. "Can you see it? 'Okay, men, let's run the hill!'"

Shawn and Justin laughed, and their dad stopped, studying the steepness of the path. "Good idea. Maybe we'll run back up. Just so we can tell him you didn't miss a day of training."

"I'm up for it," Ricky was always first to believe he could compete with the other boys. "Maybe we should run it one at a time and see who's the fastest."

Ahead of her, Brandon laughed and shook his head. "My dad would've given anything for a son like Ricky. The kid's competitive from the minute he wakes up."

The statement reminded Bailey of a time when Brandon had confided in her about his past, how his father had mocked him for liking theater, wishing instead that Brandon would've played sports. Back then a hike like this — with half a team of football players — might've been tough on Brandon, a reminder of all he hadn't been as a kid. The ways he had let his father down, however cruel his dad had been.

She put her hand briefly on his shoulder as they headed down. "You were the perfect son, Brandon. You know that."

He looked back at her, and his smile was warmed by a contentment, a peace that certainly hadn't been there last year. "You're right. I know that now." His eyes took in the boys behind them. "I was born to act. But your brothers ... they were born to compete. God makes everyone to carry out different tasks." He looked forward again, navigating the trail. "I'm good with that. I think my dad's even good with that now."

The conversation made Bailey realize how much they had to catch up. She wanted to know about conversations Brandon must've had with his parents in the time since he'd become a Christian. But this wasn't the place to talk about it.

"Don't leave me behind!" The voice was her mother's from the back of the caravan. Laughter marked her words, but she was definitely falling back. "My ankles aren't as strong as all of yours."

Shawn was the first to stop. He let the others pass and waited for their mom to catch up. "Go ahead." He motioned the others to keep their pace. "I'll walk with her."

Bailey loved that about Shawn. Of the three boys her family had adopted from Haiti, Shawn had the most tender heart — and for good reason. He had been abandoned by his mother, abused and rejected. Now that he had a family who loved him, he was loyal and kind to the core. Bailey wouldn't be surprised if Shawn wound up in ministry somewhere. He had that sort of heart for people.

"Almost there!" Brandon peered back up the hill. "I love that the paparazzi hasn't figured out about this path. I've only come down here a handful of times, but still ... it makes me feel like a regular person."

"That's cool." Connor was close enough that he could hear Brandon. "I like how you handle the pressure. You make it look possible."

"Connor's thinking about acting." Bailey could feel the downhill climb in the back of her legs, and she loved it. She hadn't thought they'd have time for a workout today. "We talked about it this morning."

"Really?" Brandon looked back at him. "That's great, man. Let me know when you're ready. I can hook you up with an agent."

They reached the beach, and the expanse of sand was all but empty. "Is this ... is it private?"

"It's called Paradise Beach," Brandon scanned the distance, probably making sure there were no photographers lurking anywhere. "It's part of Malibu, and it's open to the public. But it's more private. Too hard to get to."

"I love it." Bailey kicked off her tennis shoes and worked her toes into the warm sand. "I'd be down here every day."

"Until the paparazzi figured it out." Brandon stared back up the hillside, waiting until everyone in Bailey's family was safely down the trail. "So far, so good."

They walked to the water and played in the surf and searched for sand dollars on the damp shore. The sun was warm, but here on the beach the water was colder than it looked. Way too cold to swim without a wetsuit. Bailey walked out to where the water was knee deep, and suddenly from behind her she heard someone run up and grab her by the arm.

"Come on, Miss Bailey ... let's get wet!"

Bailey made a sound that was part laugh, part scream. "No ... the water's freezing!"

"It's not that bad." Brandon tugged at her, leading her toward the frothy surf. Water splashed up onto her shorts, and in the distance she could see her family watching, laughing at the possibility that Bailey might get tossed into the ocean even for a few seconds. The water was so cold it burned against her legs, and she turned to Brandon, pleading with her eyes. "Please ... it's too cold!"

He looked into her eyes, and even here with everyone watching she could feel the connection, a connection that went straight to her soul. "Bailey ... I'm kidding." He stopped pulling her, but he still held on. With his other hand, he presented her with the most perfect sand dollar she'd ever seen. "This is for you."

She took it, walking slowly back to more shallow water. "Brandon ... thank you."

"I want you to remember this weekend," he kept his pace even with hers. The sunlight made it hard to see, but even squinting his eyes held hers. "So that maybe someday ... you'll come back and hang out with me again."

The sand dollar fit perfectly in the palm of her hand, and she knew that she'd keep it as long as she lived. She smiled at him. "I won't forget ... I promise."

Their time at the beach was over, and like their dad suggested, the boys all ran the path back to Brandon's house. Brandon and Bailey brought up the rear, walking slowly so that Bailey's mom wouldn't be left behind. She shivered a little, because her shirt was damp from the splash of the waves — and because of the nearness of Brandon and her changing feelings for him.

He must've noticed, because he put his arm casually around her and then gave her a helpless look. "I have to keep you warm, right?"

"Right." She wasn't going to argue with him. He had been very respectful, and now she couldn't help but enjoy how it felt to walk the path with Brandon beside her, his arm around her.

"You think I'm kidding, don't you?"

Their pace was slower than before ... like neither of them wanted to rush this moment. She looked at him, letting her gaze hang on his for a few seconds. "About what?"

He hesitated, clearly not willing to rush ahead, making sure the impact of what he was about to say wasn't lost on the ocean breeze. "About us ..."

She sighed. "Brandon ... you know how I feel."

"That was before." He tightened the hold he had on her, ever so slightly. "When you had a boyfriend."

His point was a good one. Back then she'd had a reason to resist his charm, to discourage him when he acted interested in her. But now ... She stared at the dusty, rocky path ... searching for the right words. "I guess ... I never think you're really serious." Her eyes lifted to his. "I mean ... you have a lot of girls, Brandon."

"No." He shook his head, and again she saw something very different in his expression, a wisdom and maturity that told her he was being utterly honest. "I haven't dated once since we finished filming. I figured I needed time with God, time to see what He wanted from me the next time I fell in love."

If he wanted to melt her heart, his words were right on. She allowed a soft laugh. "When did you become so amazing, Brandon Paul?" She angled her head, searching his heart, his soul. The path beneath her feet felt less solid than before — like she was walking on air.

"You want to know the truth, Bailey?" He stopped and faced her. He was just ahead of her, and as he looked down at her, the vulnerability in his eyes was both raw and real. The rest of her family was nearing the top of the path, so they were alone now — the two of them on a Malibu hillside, the ocean spread out below them. He brought his hand to her cheek, a show of tenderness more than anything else. "The truth is I've been looking forward to this ever since the last time we were together. Asking God ... if He'd make me into the sort of guy you could fall in love with."

Bailey's head began to spin, so much that she covered Brandon's hand with her own and steadied herself. Was she dreaming? Could this really be happening? She had come to Los Angeles for a premiere and some time with an old friend — nothing more. But now she could see that Brandon was serious. And for the first time since she'd met the young actor, she had to actually consider what he was saying. "Brandon, I ... I'm not sure what to say."

For a moment, he looked deep into her eyes. "I've never known a girl like you, Bailey." He glanced back at his house on the hillside and the ocean behind her. "My life's crazy and different and very public ... I know that. But what would it take ... I mean, really?" His voice mixed with the warm breeze and she couldn't tell what smelled better: his cologne or the honeysuckle on the mountainside. He smiled at her, warming every cold place left in her heart. "This weekend ... at least consider the possibility." He brought her hand to his lips and kissed it — gently, tenderly. "Okay, Bailey?"

She could barely draw a breath. This wasn't a dream, it was happening. And Brandon was waiting for an answer. "You really mean it," her voice was soft, spoken from her heart to his. "Don't you?"

Again he ran his hand along her hair, her cheek. "With everything I am."

For a moment, she wished he would kiss her. Because what could be more romantic than sharing a sweet, innocent kiss here with Brandon, a guy who had been her friend, and who now was admitting he had deeper feelings for her. But Brandon didn't try to kiss her, and deep inside Bailey was grateful. God might be leading her toward a relationship with Brandon — she wasn't sure. But He wouldn't want them to kiss just because to do so would feel wonderful and romantic and unforgettable. The closeness between them was enough for now.

He pulled her into a hug and held her for a long time. "Just think about it."

She waited, listening to his heartbeat as it kept time with the pounding surf below. "I will." She pulled back and found his eyes again. "I promise." Their hug lasted another half a minute, and then Brandon kissed the top of her head. "Let's get back up. We have about two hours to get ready for tonight."

Bailey nodded and they continued up the hillside. Brandon was right — they had a lunch scheduled with the team handling distribution — and a meet-and-greet with the studio staff and executives. After that there would be an early dinner with Brandon's agent, and interviews with a few key media representatives. Then it would be time to walk the red carpet, time to sit next to Brandon in a dark theater full of Hollywood's elite and watch the movie they'd made together.

Suddenly everything about the coming hours seemed more exciting than Bailey could've dreamed a few days ago. Because today there were possibilities that God had only just now begun to present … waves that were appearing on the horizon that had never been there before. And for all Bailey knew, this new twist, these new feelings might mean the one thing she'd prayed about earlier that morning was already happening.

The perfect wave might even now be taking shape.

Fourteen

Usually Ashley and Landon would have the Baxter family over for dinner on a Sunday. But tonight — in honor of her older brother Dayne's first premiere as a producer — they were meeting on Saturday. Attending the event were Dayne and his family, and Ashley's other brother Luke and his wife, Reagan — along with their three kids Tommy, Malin, and their adopted infant son, Jonathan. The group of them would have a blast, no doubt.

But for everyone else, it made more sense to stay in Bloomington and celebrate here. Cole had baseball games over the weekend, and Landon was still trying to adjust his asthma medication. Her sisters — Kari and Erin and Brooke — all had kids in sports or other school activities this weekend. Besides, they had planned an all-Baxter movie night next Friday here in town, once Luke and Dayne and their families returned to Indiana.

Ashley checked on the two deep dishes of chicken in the oven. She'd made her mother's favorite tonight: frozen chicken breasts covered in cream of mushroom and cream of chicken soups combined. Mixed with the chicken juices, the meal always came out perfectly. Brown rice was cooking in the rice maker, and broccoli simmered on the stove. Two pans of it.

In the other room, she could hear Landon reading to the kids, and she held onto the moment. The week had been full of times like this, when she would catch herself lost in a scene from her own life and hold onto it like never before. She understood what was behind her recent nostalgia. They'd met with Landon's doctor a few days ago, and the news was enough to paralyze Ashley with fear. Even here in the kitchen minutes before a family dinner, it was only by God's grace that she was able to carry on in light of the new possibilities.

She stood at the kitchen sink and stared out the window at her mother's rose garden. "I miss you, Mom ... if you were here, you could tell me that it's all going to be okay."

Her voice was a whisper, a wish. As if by speaking the words out loud she could somehow connect to the memory of her mother. But even if her mother were here she wouldn't have assured Ashley that everything was okay. Her mother wouldn't have died of cancer four years ago if that were true. This was the world ... and like her father had told them often, in the world they would have trouble.

Landon's asthma attack the day he went running — three weeks ago now — was nearly a fatal one. Certainly not normal for someone with his physical health and conditioning, someone who had never struggled with asthma in the past. For that reason, the day of the attack, her father had directed them to a pulmonary specialist. The doctor had prescribed an inhaler and oral steroids as a first line of defense. But he had also ordered tests, the results of which they'd gotten a few days ago.

The conversation in the doctor's office came to life again, and Ashley gripped the kitchen counter, her eyes closed. "I'm afraid what we're finding isn't good." The physician was from India, kind and serious with a slight accent. "Landon, you show initial signs of polymyositis."

He went on to explain that the lung disease was something being found in rescue workers who spent lengthy time at Ground Zero.

"Okay ... so, what do I do next? I mean, let's start treatment."

Landon remained upbeat, confident. Tackling this news the way he would any other obstacle.

Ashley watched him, amazed. Landon had always been this way — strong and stoic, certain about what he wanted, and how to get it, and which direction God was leading him. He had been in love with her since they were in high school, and even after he left Bloomington to work at Ground Zero he kept quiet about his feelings for her. But in the doctor's office this week — as the doctor confirmed her worst fears — Ashley could only think of one thing . . .

This was all her fault.

If she had come to her senses and fallen in love with Landon sooner, he never would've left. He wouldn't have pursued a position with the New York Fire Department, and he wouldn't have damaged his lungs with his time at Ground Zero. All if only she wouldn't have waited so long to love him.

The doctor hesitated for what felt like forever before he answered Landon, before he addressed the idea of a cure. He pinched his lips together and gave a slow shake of his head. "There's not a cure, really. I'm afraid to say that even with research done on this disease, only a few options remain."

Landon reached over and took her hand. He didn't waver or cry out or flinch. Like every other time in his life, all that mattered to him was her.

Everything had slipped in a strange slow motion from that point. Ashley opened her eyes and looked past the Baxter house to the roses outside. Roses that were just now, this second Saturday in April, starting to bud and grow again. Proof that life would go on — no matter what devastating news had come into their lives that week.

Ashley remembered the doctor saying something about oxygen tanks, and how the progress of the disease could sometimes be slowed dramatically with steroid use and artificial air support.

She tried to picture her healthy, strapping husband carting around an oxygen machine when the doctor got to the point.

"The only cure," his tone was grave, "is a lung transplant. Now ... we don't know for sure that we're dealing with polymyositis. But if we are ... that's what we're up against."

What they were up against? A lung transplant for Landon? At his young age? Otherwise, what? She didn't want to ask, and at that point Landon must not have wanted to ask either. Because none of them said much after that. They simply discussed the next round of tests — scheduled for a few weeks out — and listened while the doctor insisted Landon continue to take his medication and use his inhaler, whenever his airways showed signs of constricting.

They thanked the doctor and drove out of the parking lot, mostly in stunned silence. Halfway home Ashley would never forget the way Landon took her hand again and pulled the car to the side of the road. "I know what you're thinking." He drew her close, cradling the back of her head with his hand, his face close to hers. His tone was kind, but it was also passionately adamant. "Don't do it, Ash ... don't blame yourself."

Like every other time in her life, Landon knew what she was thinking, knew how to read her heart. He had watched her rebel after high school, and waited for her while she went to Paris and slept with a married man. When she came home alone and pregnant, he had been her friend ... and after Cole was born, he was determined to be a support to her — as much as she would allow. And here — in the face of what might be the worst news they had ever received — there was no telling where she stopped and he began. He knew her that well.

She hung her head and let the tears come. Streams of angry, terrified tears because how could this happen? Hadn't they been through enough? The death of her mother ... and the loss of their little Sarah to anencephaly a year after that? Could God really think they were up to still another challenge: a lung disease that had no cure short of a transplant?

But more than all that, Landon was right. She did blame herself. Her stubborn pride had allowed Landon to get away from her, to leave for the job in New York for one reason alone — because she had given him no hope that the love he felt for her might ever someday be returned.

They had hugged then, and Ashley had sobbed in his arms until she had nothing left inside her. Until all that mattered was the rise and fall of her husband's chest against hers. Later that day they'd gone to the ball field for one of Cole's baseball games, and Landon had looked every bit the picture of health. He laughed easily and ran with the players around the field and, from every appearance, he breathed without effort.

Then and now, Ashley reminded herself to enjoy the moment. Savor the times when Landon was coaching Cole through this, his final Little League season, or when he was in the next room the way he was now — playing with their kids. They knew this was Cole's last time to play Little League, but with Landon, only God knew the lasts now.

She checked the chicken again, just as the doorbell rang. Her family was here, the way they would always be here. It was why her dad had recently reminded her of the rest of the verse from John 16:33. Sure, in this world they would have trouble. But God didn't leave them with that depressing fact. Rather, he finished the Scripture with the everlasting promise ... words she could hear the Lord whispering to her soul this very instant.

My precious daughter, be of good cheer ... for I have overcome the world ...

The house filled up quickly, everyone excited about opening night for *Unlocked* and anxious for the live coverage of the red carpet event slated for a few hours from then. Her sisters and Elaine, her stepmother, joined her in the kitchen and the conversation was light and easy. None of them knew about Landon yet, no one except her father and Elaine. And they had promised not to say anything tonight.

"We don't know he has it for sure," Ashley had told her dad earlier that morning. "Let's keep it quiet for now."

Her dad agreed. "I'm praying every day, sweetheart." He hugged her close. "But I know how hard this is."

Of course he knew. He'd walked with Ashley's mother through two bouts of breast cancer. The first had been tough — when the Baxter kids were little — but at least their mother had survived. The second had been swift and deadly. Yes, her father knew what she was feeling.

Ashley focused on the voices around her, the news that Kari and Erin had teamed up with a local co-op to homeschool their kids. The larger group of moms and students meant the kids could participate in science experiments and field trips. Brooke was excited about the growth of her medical practice, and all of them agreed that life was good and whole and going way too fast.

Devin bounded into the kitchen, mud on his face and a grin stretched from ear to ear. "Mommy, I'm working on the 'zact spot where my circus will go."

"His circus?" Kari raised a sweetly curious eyebrow at her nephew. "You're building a circus, are you, Devin?"

"Yes, ma'am." He jumped a few times in place and turned back to Ashley. "It's the best spot, Mommy. Right by the fish pond."

"Perfect." Ashley took a paper towel and wiped the smudge of mud from his cheek. "There you go ... get back to your planning."

Dinner was ready, the table set, when Landon found her in the kitchen. He helped her fill a tray of paper cups with apple juice, and he laughed recounting a story Devin had told him earlier. "You know about his circus, right?"

"I do." Ashley didn't like the way she felt around Landon lately

— uneasy and out of sync. She kept her eyes on the paper cups. "He's building it in the backyard near the fish pond."

"Right." Landon positioned the cups so there was room on the tray for another row. They would need every spot at least. "But get this . . . tonight he's going to assign jobs. After dinner."

"Hmmm." Ashley smiled, but she felt herself holding back. "That should be interesting. Especially while we're watching the red carpet event."

Landon stopped and turned to her. For a long few seconds he watched her, his disappointment palpable. "Baby . . . please. You can't stop living."

"I'm not." She set the pitcher of juice down and slumped a little. "I mean, really, Landon . . . how can I laugh about Devin's circus when I'm trying to convince myself you'll still be here to see him reach first grade?"

"No." He pushed the tray further back on the counter and eased her into his arms. "That's what I mean, Ash . . . you can't do that." He leaned back just enough to search her eyes. "You ask me how can I laugh about Devin's circus? Baby, how can you not?" His eyes begged her to understand. "God, eternity, and this dinner . . . that's all the guarantee we'll ever have — even the healthiest of us."

He was right, and here in his arms she felt her anxiety fade. "I'm sorry." She breathed out, wishing that with every inhalation she might breathe healing into his lungs, that they might grow stronger on her love alone. She found a smile that wasn't forced. "Thank you . . . I can't go through this without you."

"God knows that." He kissed her, long enough that she nearly forgot their dinner in the next room. "See? I'm fine."

She laughed, and they joined the others. Dinner was the usual mix of passing food bowls and catching up on the latest. Her father looked great — proof that he and Elaine had been walking again. But every now and then he caught her eyes, and the two of them shared a knowing. Better to enjoy tonight, like Landon had said. None of them knew what tomorrow might hold.

After dinner, they still had thirty minutes before they could turn on the TV for the live coverage of the premiere. Devin must've realized this was his window, because he stood at the middle of the two tables and waved his hands. "Everybody ... I need your 'tention, please."

Gradually, the conversations quieted. Ashley loved this about her sisters and their husbands, the way the Baxter family listened to everyone, whoever had something to say. In this case, Devin realized quickly that the floor was his. "Okay ... I'm having a circus, and ..." He looked around the room at each person sitting at both tables, scrutinizing them the way an employer might look over a roomful of potential new-hires. "Yes. I want you all to be in my circus, okay?"

Ashley smothered a laugh as she leaned in closer to Landon. On the other side of him, Cole rolled his eyes, but not in a mean way. He was the first to raise his hand. "I'm in, buddy. Definitely."

The others around the room nodded and added their voices to the mix. Everyone was willing to play a part. Only Maddie stood, her expression knit together in mild concern. "Devin,... I want a job. But tell me I won't have to wear tights." Disgust sounded in her tone. "I hate tights."

Ashley smiled to herself. Her niece was only playing. Maddie was thirteen, a tomboy who loved playing soccer and running track. She was too old to take Devin's proposition seriously.

Brooke — Maddie's mother — shrugged in Devin's direction. "What can I say? The girl hates tights."

"That's fine." Devin looked very serious. He stroked his chin like a businessman considering a high-risk investment. "Hmmm. Okay, Maddie. You can sell the busgetti."

Cole sent a quick look to Landon, but Landon only put his

finger to his lips. "Shhh ..." He leaned closer to Cole, his voice a whisper. "Let him have spaghetti at his circus."

Maddie considered the job for a moment. "Okay. I can do that. As long as I don't have to wear tights."

Devin turned to his Uncle Peter, Maddie's father. "And you, Uncle Peetah, you'll be my policeman. So no bad guys try to break into the circus without paying their tickets."

"Very nice." Peter nodded, fully accepting his duties. He was a doctor by day, but clearly he embraced what would be a definite change of pace. "I think I'll like that."

"And you, Mommy," he didn't stick to an exact order, "you'll be the flying girl ..." Devin's diction made it sound like he had assigned her the position of "flying ghoul."

Ashley bit the inside of her cheek so she wouldn't crack a smile. "I like flying ... that's perfect for me."

"Right." Devin sized her up. "Hmmm ... You'll wear a red costume ... and blue ribbons in your hair ..." He paused. "And American flag tights." He swung his arms from one side to the other. "And you'll fly back and forth across the whole ... big, long circus." He didn't quite smile. The matter was very serious to him. "Can you live with that?"

Ashley swallowed another bit of laughter. "Definitely."

Beside her, Landon brushed his cheek against hers, his voice low. "I'd like a private showing of those American flag tights."

"Thank you." She grinned at him. "I'll be sure to set that up."

Devin continued for another ten minutes until everyone had a job. The cotton candy seller, a joke teller, someone to wave flags as they walked around the room. But, he saved his grandpa for last. "And Grandpa ... you're the lion tamer, okay?"

"Okay." Ashley's father puffed out his chest. "That's because I'm the strongest man in the circus. Right, buddy?"

"No." Devin didn't catch the teasing in his grandfather's tone. "That's Daddy!"

Landon grinned at Ashley's dad. "What can I say?"

Ashley wanted to freeze the moment, hold on forever to this time when everyone was healthy and happy and thinking about the role they'd play in Devin's circus ... when Devin believed Landon wasn't only the strongest man in the room but in the whole wide world.

Devin smiled sweetly at his grandpa. "You tame the lions 'cause you're the nicest, Grandpa." He spoke with the patience of a teacher. "And the only way to tame a lion is to be extra nice."

"Oh." Her dad sank a little, drawing easy laughter from the others. "You don't think it'll be too dangerous, then?"

"Hmmm." Devin stroked his chin again. "I know." His eyes lit up. "Uncle Ryan can take out the lions' teeth first." He nodded, convinced the plan was a good one. "Right, Uncle Ryan. That can be another job for you. Can you live with that?"

"I hope so." He made a concerned face. "Selling pop and taking out the lions' teeth." Ryan was Kari's husband and the football coach at Clear Creek High. He was tall and built like the college football player he had once been. But in this moment he looked very nervous. "I might have to contact my lawyer about that."

Devin hesitated, not sure if his uncle was playing it straight with him. But given the seriousness of his circus he nodded. "Okay. Do that first."

Everyone had a position, and Ashley was about to wrap up the discussion when Devin gasped loudly, "I 'most forgot!" He looked around the room, nearly frantic. "I need someone to run the 'magination machine."

Ashley squinted at her son. Of all the things he had talked about regarding his circus, this was something new. "The what?"

"The 'magination machine." He used his hands to illustrate a contraption that would be big as his arms could reach and possibly taller and bulkier. "It's this size, and it fits on a person's head like this." He struggled to lift the invisible creation onto his head.

"Buddy, what's it do?" Ashley's dad put his arm around Elaine, his eyes twinkling. "I might volunteer for this."

"Good." Devin talked as fast as he could, the ideas coming to him with lightning speed. "The 'magination machine sits on the person's head and taps into their brainwaves and it helps bring their 'magination back to life!"

"You mean their imagination?" Ashley knew this wasn't a joke to Devin. She treated the situation with respect.

"Right." A burst of joy spread across Devin's face. "The 'magination machine! People would come to the circus and pay five dollars, and someone has to put it on their head and then … *Bzzzz!*" He pretended to push a button. "Their 'magination comes back to life!"

Ashley sat back a little. She looked around the room and saw that she wasn't the only one touched by Devin's belief in the power of imagination. She blinked back tears but kept her smile intact. "I like it, Devin buddy. I think people would want to come to your circus just for that."

"I'd charge more than five dollars." Ryan cast a definite look at Ashley's father. "Keep that in mind if you run it."

Landon's smile had grown tender in this recent exchange. "Buddy, why do you think people need to have their imagination brought back to life?"

"Because." Devin held up his hands and let them fall to his sides again. His smile dropped off for the first time since he'd started talking about his circus, and his eyes held a sort of tragic sadness. "When people get older … their 'magination sometimes hides in a corner."

For a few seconds no one said anything, and Ashley understood why. Every adult in the room was considering the very real possibility. At one time they might've all dreamed of a circus with toothless lions and spaghetti for dinner. But now … maybe Devin was right. Maybe an imagination machine would help all of them. The idea had certainly lightened Ashley's mood.

Then — and even later as the red carpet event started and everyone gathered around the television to watch Dayne, and Luke, and their families, and the Flanigans, and Brandon Paul — Ashley still thought about Devin's comment. She made a plan to work on the painting of Cole and Landon tonight when everyone was asleep. If she wasn't careful, her fears could kill her creativity — and she'd be first in line for Devin's imagination machine. And she made another plan too. As she painted she would pray for her husband's health, and for Cole and Devin and Janessa. That they would have many more nights like this one.

And that not for a minute would their imaginations ever hide in the corner.

Fifteen

BRANDON WAS RIGHT ABOUT THE RED CARPET EVENT. THE paparazzi that lined up half a block in either direction of the pathway into the theater was far greater than the crowd that had waited for them outside the *Tonight Show*. Bailey had never imagined anything like this. As she and her family and Brandon Paul piled out of his private limo, she wondered for a brief instant if an explosion had gone off, if maybe some terrorist was wreaking havoc on their otherwise perfect day. But it was only the combined flash power of too many cameras to count.

Even so, only as she stood, as her ivory floor-length gown fell around her ankles and she smiled for the crowd, did she realize just what magnitude of attention Brandon Paul commanded. "Don't think about it," Brandon whispered near her cheek. "Just keep smiling."

She nodded, and a sense of peace came over her. With Brandon leading the way, she could do this. They all could. Ahead of them on the red carpet were Dayne Matthews and Luke Baxter and their families. Even the kids were dressed for the event, with miniature tuxedoes and pretty dresses.

Bailey felt like a princess at the biggest ball of the year, arriving with the prince every other girl wished was at their sides. She hesitated, smiling and waving at the crowd as she and Brandon moved aside and waited while her brothers, and finally her parents, stepped out of the limo. Her brothers wore new suits their mom found on sale. At the time, they had all complained that no one would expect them to be dressed up, and that they couldn't move in suit jackets.

But here, they quickly embraced the part.

"Wow!" Ricky said it as loud as he could, and even then the sound was drowned out by the cry of questions from reporters and the clicking of cameras. He waved and grinned, and the other brothers did the same thing. But as much fun as the attention was, none of them wanted to linger in this kind of limelight. They hurried down the red carpet and caught up to Luke and Dayne. Her parents walked fairly quickly also, careful to wave and smile. Her dad was well known in the media because of his coaching position. Brandon had told them he was pretty sure the magazines would run pictures of Bailey's parents.

Bailey and Brandon took their time.

After all, the press had gathered mostly for Brandon Paul, in celebration of his new movie, and out of curiosity for the change in faith he'd publicly declared, and to see proof of his new, conservative lifestyle — also, of course, to see if there was more than friendship between Brandon and his new leading lady. Before tonight, when Bailey pictured this moment, she imagined staying with her parents and letting Brandon walk the carpet alone. It was his starring role, really. His place to shine alone, without her taking any of the attention. Not only that, but she hadn't wanted the paparazzi guessing at what the two of them shared.

But ever since the walk up from the beach, Bailey had been dizzy with everything about Brandon. He handled himself with professionalism at the studio meet-and-greet, careful to shield her from scrutiny or direct questions about her future plans to act. She had no plans to audition for more films, and he knew that. But he had told her on the way into the studio to keep her options open. Just in case. So when the president of the studio asked if she'd be interested in more films, Brandon answered for her.

"Bailey promised me that if she's asked to do a love story, she'd

want me to co-star." He smiled fondly at her, clearly teasing and keeping the moment light, directing the attention off her answer. As if he would be second in billing to her anytime soon. "Right, Bailey?"

"Yes." She laughed. "What are friends for?"

He was a gentleman then, and as they were whisked on to their next meeting — the dinner with his agent — and then back at his house where a crew of makeup artists waited to help them get ready for tonight. Through it all, Brandon played perfectly the role of her doting friend, her protector, and confidant. She had long since become convinced that he was serious. What he'd told her earlier on the mountain path was exactly how he felt. Now it was only a matter of Bailey agreeing that maybe ... despite his crazy life in Hollywood, they might have a chance.

With all that in mind, when he asked her in the limo on the way to the red carpet event whether she wanted to walk alone or whether she would give him the honor of walking with him, she had only one answer. The one that was right, and the one that overflowed from her heart. "Yes, Brandon ... I'll walk with you."

And so here they were, the two of them taking the walk down a red carpet that felt a mile long. They turned one way and then the other, and Brandon alternated between having his arm around her and waving for the cameras. She felt lightheaded and breathless, grateful for Brandon's peace and strong presence beside her.

"Are you two dating? Tell us, Brandon!"

"Brandon ... over here!"

"Bailey ... give him a kiss ... show us that you're in love!"

She laughed in amazement at the audacity of some of the requests being shouted at them. Brandon maintained his smile, but he spoke in a voice loud enough for only her to hear. "Ignore them ... they're fishing ... just keep smiling, keep waving."

His words were like balm to her soul, the only thing that kept her calmly moving down the length of the carpet. After what felt like an hour of smiling and waving, they finally entered the theater. Inside there were more recognizable faces than Bailey had expected. Everyone who had starred in movies in the last five years seemed to be mingling and sharing appetizers and champagne.

Again, Bailey wasn't overly shaken by the celebrities in the room. She had hoped to see her former college roommate Andi here, but Andi's dad — Keith Ellison, who was one of the producers from *Unlocked* — had explained that she was at a weekend retreat. She was healing from the last few years, still finding her way after giving her infant son up for adoption, and definitely getting stronger in her faith. They would have to catch up some other time.

"You don't look nervous." Brandon seemed entirely focused on her, practically oblivious to the actors in the room.

"I'm not." She smiled at him, feeling composed and ready for the night. But for the first time she realized how great the mission field in Hollywood really was. Across from them were a couple who openly practiced Kaballah, and down a few groups was a female pop star who proudly bragged about making out with girls and guys — usually at the same parties.

"I bet I can read your mind," Brandon held her hand. He leaned in, his words barely louder than a whisper. In this space, they could stand closer together, be the sort of friends Bailey enjoyed being with him. No one in here would talk about them in the morning. They all had their own dramas to tend to.

"What?" Bailey took a glass of sparkling water from a waiter passing by, and Brandon did the same. She clinked glasses with his and batted her eyes, enjoying everything about the moment. "What am I thinking?"

"How godless Hollywood is." A sadness shaded his eyes, though his smile never left his face. "Right?"

"Sort of." The room was loud, people decked out and connecting with one another all around them. But the two of them might as well have been back on the hillside path headed up from the beach. He still had hold of her hand, and they were facing each other. So their conversation was private from others nearby. "I guess ... I was thinking how much work there is to do. How badly we need actors who love the Lord ... working here, practicing their faith." She smiled, proud of him. "So the movie industry might see what living for God looks like."

"Hmmm." He clinked her glass again. "Cheers to that." They took sips of their water and looked at each other, not necessarily needing words.

"It's my turn." She giggled, grateful for this time with him.

"Never." He gave her his familiar teasing smile. "No one reads my mind."

"Mmmm." She laughed. "I have to try." She waited, watching him, searching his soul. Had this really been just one day? It felt like she'd been here in Southern California with Brandon for a week or longer. Already they felt closer than at any time during the shooting of *Unlocked*. "You're thinking if Hollywood needs more Christian actors ... why won't I audition for another movie."

He didn't even pretend to laugh at the idea. Instead, his expression immediately filled with a longing that had been there a number of times that day. "You got me, Bailey Flanigan." He rubbed his thumb tenderly along the top of her hand. "That's exactly what I'm thinking."

Bailey had to admit, in that moment she wasn't sure of her answer. She had always wanted to perform — and always on Broadway. Until now she believed that God would lead her to a stage in New York City where she would sing and dance and shine for Him. But clearly God had closed that door ... since Francesca Tilly and her staff still hadn't called. So what did that mean? And why was her heart doing flip-flops with Brandon Paul standing close enough to kiss her?

The mingling wound down, but not before Brandon introduced her to a few dozen A-list actors. Each time he said the same thing. "I'd like you to meet my friend Bailey." Like he'd told her, no one in the room would talk about them to the press or gossip about them in the morning. The introduction was purely out of respect for her, and Bailey couldn't express in words how much the gesture meant.

By the time they made it across the room to where her parents and brothers, Luke and Dayne, and their families were hanging out, it was time to move into the theater. They did so with a sense of thrill and anticipation that created an almost electric feeling amidst the crowd. As they took their seats — Brandon on one side of Bailey and Connor on the other — Bailey felt the presence of God's Spirit in the room.

You're doing something new, aren't You, Lord? I can feel it ...

Yes, daughter... Look at the new thing I am going to do. It is already happening... don't you see it?

The verse was from Isaiah chapter 43, something Bailey had studied last semester in her Campus Crusade meetings. The fact that God brought it to mind now was further proof of what she already believed in her heart. That God was at work in Hollywood, and that He was about to use Brandon Paul and *Unlocked* in a very powerful way. So where did that leave her?

Bailey had no answers for herself, but for the next two hours she relished the feel of her hand in Brandon's and her family all around her. The movie was better than she remembered it, but Brandon had told her she'd feel that way. Halfway through the film he leaned over and whispered, "See ... nothing like watching it in a theater on opening night."

She nodded, grateful again for the experience and swept away by Brandon's performance as the autistic Holden Harris. "Brandon,... you're so good." She put her face close to his. "I mean ... you're unbelievable."

He winked at her. "I've been trying to tell you that."

A quiet ripple of laughter lightened the moment, and they fell quiet through the rest of the film. When it was over, the audience gave the movie a standing ovation and the party and celebration lasted until well after midnight. By the time they pulled into Brandon's garage, her brothers were asleep again, and they had only a few hours before the Flanigans had to catch a plane in the morning.

Brandon helped wake up the boys, and when everyone was in bed, he asked Bailey out onto the downstairs deck, the one that was larger and not attached to a bedroom. She was glad he wasn't too tired to talk. He'd been right about their private time. Even though they were side-by-side through the night, they'd had very little time to talk.

When they were outside, they leaned against the railing and Bailey was struck once more by how long the day had seemed. How long and yet how short. "It seems like only a moment ago I was standing on the bedroom balcony dreaming about this day." She turned to him. "Now it's over."

He took her hands, his eyes shining in the darkness. "It doesn't have to be."

"Brandon." She shook her head and looked out at the moon on the water. "You're in the middle of shooting a new movie, and I ..." she turned to him again, "I'm back in Bloomington." She liked the idea more than ever, but the practicalities seemed too great to overcome. "I mean ... explain yourself. How does this not have to end?"

"Don't you see?" He took a step closer, his sincerity so real and raw it took her breath. "You finish up your classes and move here. My agent would take you in a minute." He uttered a nervous laugh. "You heard him earlier today. He'd love the chance to work with you."

She turned back to the ocean, processing the possibility,

imagining the reality. The surf drowned out the sound of her pounding heart. Was she really considering this? Could she leave Bloomington and her dreams of Broadway? Could she finally walk away from Cody and leave everything about the past behind her? She breathed in deep, fighting to stand when everything in her trembled with fear for the adventure he was suggesting to her.

"You're thinking about it." He turned, facing the water, his arm close against hers. There was a thrill in his voice that hadn't been there before. "You're actually thinking about it."

"You asked me to." She smiled, trying to keep the moment from slipping somewhere too deep to return from, trying not to commit herself to someplace from which there would be no coming back. No matter how hard her heart pounded.

"Bailey,..." he faced her again and tenderly ran his hand along her arm. "You know how I feel ... I've been honest." He searched her eyes. "But you ... you haven't said ... if you feel any of what I'm feeling." Brandon's confidence was something that magnified his charm and appeal. But here, before her, he looked shaken, like it had taken all his bravery to ask the question. "Do you feel it, Bailey?"

The night was warm, same as the day, but even so Bailey felt herself begin to shiver. If she let herself fall for Brandon Paul, if she gave in to the feelings he'd stirred in her this weekend, she might forget who she'd been a week ago. Her dreams and goals, the way she still planned to find Cody and at least get an explanation from him. All of it wouldn't matter if she allowed herself to get lost in Brandon Paul's eyes, if she let her heart take up residence here, with him.

She put her hands on either side of his face and for a long time she said nothing, but just let the ocean breeze move around them while she looked into his eyes. Finally she said the only thing she could say, the truth that had risen to the surface these past two days. "I feel it. I do, Brandon." She laughed, nervous because she had actually allowed herself to say exactly what was on her heart. "Wow." She lowered her hands and took a few steps away from him. When she turned back, she brushed her hair from her face and her laughter faded. "Did I really say that?"

"You did." He wasn't going to let the moment pass. He walked to her and took her hands in his again. This time — for the first time — he slid his fingers between hers. Bailey felt her stomach fall, the way it did when she and her brothers rode the Viper at Six Flags in Chicago. "So, I finish up my movie ... and I come to Bloomington." His words were slow. They had a hypnotic effect over her, like everything about his presence slowed time, and made the world stand still.

"Brandon,..." She swallowed, desperate for the right words. "I feel it ... I do. I never thought ..." She looked up, grasping for a plan. "I figured you and I would always be friends. That your ... your life would never work with mine."

"It can. Bailey,... you have to believe that." Slowly, ever so slowly, he pulled her close and just when she thought he might kiss her, he brushed the side of his face against hers. "Please, Bailey,... give us a chance. You're the best friend I have." He eased back, searching her face, her eyes. "But I'm in love with you. Completely and fully."

Bailey had a million questions, logistics that simply didn't line up. Brandon would finish his shoot when? In six weeks? And then he'd come to Bloomington to do what? He would be recognized everywhere he went, which meant they could really only hang out at her parents' house. And even then eventually that would draw paparazzi. Bailey Flanigan in Bloomington might not be worth their time. But Brandon Paul staying at the Flanigan house? That would bring an army of them. And then what? She would finish her semester and move to Los Angeles? Fight her way through the maze of concrete high rises and never-ending freeways?

With all the unknowns crashing together in her mind, she

could think of just one that made sense. "Your life ... Brandon, you're busy." She could smell his cologne from earlier in the night, and he looked impossibly handsome. Something she hadn't really noticed working with him on the *Unlocked* shoot, or even yesterday on the *Tonight Show*. But now ... when she could see his heart for God and for her ... now her attraction was so strong it shook her.

He stepped back, clearly concerned. "Look at Dayne and Katy ... they made it work."

Katy and Dayne's relationship was something she'd tried not to think about this weekend. Because if she did, if she allowed herself to picture the way her dear friend and drama teacher, small-town girl Katy Hart, had worked things out with one of the country's hottest movie stars Dayne Matthews, then Bailey could come to no other conclusion than the obvious one: If Katy could find a way to make things work, she could too.

The hours were slipping away, and already it was nearly three in the morning. "Can we do this?" Bailey put her hand alongside Brandon's face again, lost in his eyes the way she wanted to stay. "Let's pray about what God wants ... whether this is His plan or just ..." she felt the sadness in her smile, "just a magical weekend where both of us were bound to get swept away."

He shook his head slowly, never breaking eye contact. "It's not that. I told you ... I've been thinking about this since the last time we were together. You're the only girl, Bailey, ... the only one I want." He thought for a quick moment. "I wasn't going to point this out, because I know it's hard for you. But, Bailey, think about it ..." He ran his hand along her arm again. "You auditioned for a Broadway show, and what happened?"

She hadn't wanted to tell him, but she should've known him better. Of course he remembered. She had told him about the audition the last time they talked. The disappointment rang through her again. "They didn't call. I ... didn't get the part."

"But see? That's how God answers prayers, Bailey, . . . it is." He hugged her again, moving ever so slowly, holding her like she was the most rare treasure. "A no to Broadway might just mean a yes to Hollywood. Maybe a bigger world needs you." He kissed the side of her face. "The way I need you, Bailey, . . . here with me."

His words hit their mark, making her feet feel ten feet off the ground one more time. If she didn't step back, create at least a little distance between them, she would lose herself in this moment, and they'd spend the next hour kissing and making promises she had no idea if either of them would be able to keep. With a self-discipline that could've only come from God, she drew back, breathless. "Brandon, . . ." she forced herself to find a voice of reason. "Can we pray . . . please?"

Their closeness had gotten to him, too; she could see the intense desire in his eyes, a desire that hadn't been there even a few minutes ago. He breathed in deep, searching for control. "Of course." He took her hands and, after nearly a minute, he began. "Dear Lord . . . You've brought Bailey and me together for a reason. I believe that . . . and we both feel it. I don't want . . . just any casual relationship with her, God. You've changed me forever. You've changed what I want."

Bailey again felt her heart melt at his words. She focused on God, on His place between them as they prayed.

"What I'm saying, Lord, is I want us to take our time and . . . and find Your plan. So please, God . . . make Your path clear. And as Bailey and her family leave in a few hours, let her know that she will take a piece of my heart with her. In Your name, amen."

"Amen."

He pulled her close, hugging her one last time. "I don't want you to leave."

"I don't want to go." Once more she was almost certain he was going to kiss her. Here in the moonlight, with the ocean in the background and Brandon's arms around her, Bailey couldn't imagine anything better. But instead Brandon released her and slipped his hands into the pockets of his dress pants. Another deep breath, and like before he seemed to struggle with his resolve. "We better get inside."

"Yes." Bailey almost suggested they forget about getting sleep, sit out here on his balcony and talk and dream and watch the sun come up. But that would only leave her more confused when she left in a few hours. Whatever happened, she knew this much. Her feelings for Brandon were real, and just because her night as Cinderella was over, that didn't mean she was going to disappear from his life. She had a very strong feeling he wouldn't let her even if she tried.

Back in the house he walked her to the foot of the stairs, where she faced him one last time. "Tonight ... this weekend. It was amazing, Brandon."

"I'm glad." He leaned close and very gently kissed her cheek. "I prayed that it would be."

"I'll call you. When I get back. And I'll pray about this ... about everything."

"I know." He smiled. "Go get some sleep. I'll ride with you and your family in the morning."

They hugged again, and Bailey was glad they were inside. The limits of her self-control were beyond tested. Before she could change her mind, she ran lightly up the stairs, brushed her teeth, and climbed into bed. She didn't sleep, because she wasn't the least bit tired. Not then, and not as they drove to the airport, and not as she and Brandon said goodbye.

Even on the plane she couldn't do anything but stare out the window and beg God for clarity. She missed Brandon already, but that didn't solve some of her bigger concerns. Like how she'd handle the public eye or when they'd find time to hang out together with hundreds of paparazzi trailing them and both of them most likely working on different movie sets — maybe even in different

countries. Nothing about that life sounded like something Bailey could embrace. It was entirely different than the life she'd once pictured with Cody. But, despite her reservations, she felt her heart dance when she turned on her phone as the plane landed and there was this simple text from Brandon:

Praying... believing... knowing God will show you the way.

She sighed and kept the text to herself. Her mother had asked about her night, but she hadn't wanted to go into detail yet. She and her mom would need an evening on the front porch for her to go over everything she and Brandon had talked about, everything she'd felt while she was in his arms last night on the balcony.

The family trudged into the house weary and dragging suitcases behind them. It was already three in the afternoon, and they all had much to do to get ready for the morning. Only by chance did Bailey wander into the kitchen and see the red light flashing on their home phone. *Strange,* she thought. Her dad had already passed this way. Usually he checked the messages.

She went to the machine and pressed the play button. There was only one message, and it was quick and to the point. "This is for Bailey Flanigan ... this is Francesca Tilly." Her voice was stern, clearly frustrated. "I'm not sure why we haven't heard from you. I can only assume you didn't get our first message. We didn't ask you in for a callback, because you clearly won the role. We have a part for you, but I'll need to hear from you on Monday." The director left her number and then hung up.

Bailey's hand shook as she returned the phone to the base. The last time she took a message from Francesca Tilly she'd felt completely different. She'd run around the kitchen screaming and celebrating. This time there was the familiar thrill, no doubt, and she couldn't wait to tell her mom and dad. But the call — like a sudden storm — came with very strong certainties. Soon ... in a matter of weeks ... she would move away — leaving everything she knew and loved about Bloomington and life here with her family. The producers would help her locate housing — they'd promised that at the audition — and Bailey would have to learn how to survive in the city. But there was more to her emotions than that.

Tears filled her eyes and for this moment she stood still, processing what had happened. Especially after the weekend with Brandon. She blinked, trying to rope in her crazy conflicting emotions. Why was she sad? This was her dream! She'd won a role on Broadway! A part in a real actual Broadway show, and not just any show but *Hairspray*. In almost every way she had never been more grateful, more excited in all her life. God had answered her prayers ... she *had* been good enough!

But at the same time she could still feel Brandon beside her, still smell his cologne as it mixed with the ocean air. The life they'd talked about, the relationship he wanted ... they had asked for God to show them, and now Bailey had no doubt whatsoever. This was the answer. Which was why her heart hurt, despite the celebration that lay ahead. Because if God was opening the door for her to live and work in New York City, that could only mean one thing.

He was closing the door on Brandon Paul.

Sixteen

THE MINUTE CODY REPORTED FOR WORK THAT FRIDAY HE GOT word that the principal wanted to see him. Since he'd started teaching and coaching at Lyle, he'd had nothing but glowing reports from the administration — especially the principal, Valerie Baker.

But now, as he walked to her office, he began to doubt himself. Maybe Coach Oliver had complained about him ... or possibly one of his students hadn't appreciated the way he'd handled a PE class. He couldn't think of any single situation, but there was no way to tell. He walked toward Ms. Baker's door and smiled at the ladies who made up the front office staff. "Good morning."

"Morning." The woman closest to him was younger than the other three. She always went out of her way to be friendly, but today her eyes danced and she seemed about to burst. Like she could barely contain a secret.

Cody hesitated, but only for half a second before he finished the walk to Ms. Baker's office. After a quick knock on the door, she welcomed him inside. As always, the woman was the picture of professionalism. Her desk — though a little scattered — was full of probably half a dozen projects she must've been working on. She motioned to the chair opposite her desk. "Have a seat, Mr. Coleman."

Whatever it was, she sounded serious. "Thank you." He sat and folded his hands, not sure if he should make small talk or just wait. He decided on the latter.

Once she was situated, she pulled a piece of paper from a file and studied it. "Coach Oliver won't be returning to Lyle." She lifted her eyes, the consummate professional. "I want to explain the reason." She paused. "This is a private matter, Mr. Coleman."

Cody wanted to quietly rejoice, but he needed to wait. He didn't wish ill on Coach Oliver or anyone. No matter how difficult the man had been to work with. He had to hand it to Ms. Baker. The coach had been nothing but rude to her, questioning her authority and talking behind her back — at least as far as Cody had seen. But here the woman refused to celebrate the man's departure from their staff. Instead she stayed matter-of-fact as she launched into the explanation.

"Coach Oliver is a Vietnam vet," Ms. Baker sighed. "Did you know that?"

"I didn't." Immediately Cody was seized with regret. If he'd been paying a little more attention he might've figured that out, right? The man had certain pins and insignias on his jacket, the one that hung in his office. But Cody had never been invited in, never spent more than a minute or two at the man's doorway. He'd never had the chance to ask about the jacket or whether the man had served their country.

"Yes." Ms. Baker studied the paper again. "I imagine ... at some point back in time, Coach Oliver and you would've had a lot in common." She sighed. "From what I know now, the war changed him. The strain — even after so many years — has gotten worse, apparently."

An uneasy feeling spread through Cody's chest. What was she saying? Could she possibly have known about the nightmares he suffered from, or the way he could, for no reason, suddenly smell the body odor of an Iraqi soldier the moment before he beat Cody? He swallowed, his eyes on his knees.

"Anyway, he's gone out on a stress disability. The memories of war ... the rejection ... all of it. I guess it weighs heavy on him."

There had been no way to tell any of this, and Cody was almost too surprised to respond. The coach had continued his verbal abuse right up until yesterday. Now — on a Friday midway through April — he was suddenly unable to come to work? What did that say about his performance and attitude, his treatment of the guys? Was it all part of his stress? If so, why hadn't he gone out on leave a year ago?

Another sigh slipped from Ms. Baker. "Mr. Coleman, I realize that Coach Oliver has been very difficult to work with. He left us no apology, no explanation for the way he treated students and staff. Truthfully, I should've fired him a long time ago." Her voice softened. "But I knew about his time in Vietnam. My father served with him."

It was another revelation, and Cody felt his expression change. "Did ... did they know each other?"

"Yes." There was no hiding the sorrow in her eyes. "They were friends. My father died saving Coach Oliver's life." She narrowed her eyes, as if she couldn't help but remember how the man used to be. "Back then ... he was a much ... much different man."

"I ... didn't know." Cody felt like someone had sucked the air from the room. So much of the past suddenly made sense. Ms. Baker's reason for keeping the coach on staff, the man's bitterness, his anger toward life. And in as much time as it took to exhale, all Cody could think about was himself. How would he be around people a year from now? Ten years or twenty? Would memories of the war haunt him forever, change him into someone even he wouldn't recognize?

"What I'm trying to say, is that the school board has given approval to offer you a full-time position at Lyle, Mr. Coleman. With the understanding that you will finish your teaching credential, of course. And ..." she smiled, "we'd like you to take over as the varsity football coach."

Cody should've seen it coming ... as soon as the principal

told him Coach Oliver wasn't returning, the obvious conclusion was that he might take over. But still the news hit him like a sudden wind, and for a few seconds he couldn't think of a thing to say. He was being offered his first full-time teaching and coaching position — the dream he'd spent years imagining and planning for. God had worked good out of all of it — his mother's time in prison, his decision to leave Bloomington, his transfer to the Indianapolis campus to finish his education. He never would've learned about this position otherwise.

"Mr. Coleman?" A slightly bewildered expression came over Ms. Baker. "Are you ... considering my offer?"

"No!" He spoke before he had time to think and then he laughed and shifted in his seat ... nervous, excited energy bursting through him. "I mean, yes! Yes, I'll accept the position. Of course." He laughed again, trying to get his mind around all that had just happened. Coach Oliver's situation was sad, and Cody wanted to talk to the man at some point, explain how much he could empathize with the man's time at war. But for now it meant the kids were free! Free to enjoy football and believe in themselves and begin an entirely new and positive season at Lyle High.

"Very well," she laughed, too. "I was beginning to wonder if this was something you'd be interested in."

"Beyond interested." He shook his head, still searching for the right words. "I've been praying for those kids ... for a miracle for them and the program." He wasn't sure how much he should say. "I'm sorry about Coach Oliver, but ... yes." He could feel his smile filling his face. "I'm beyond thankful." He stood to shake her hand. "You won't be sorry, Ms. Baker. I'll give those boys everything I have."

She smiled, her eyes warm. "I believe you."

He signed paperwork next, and then it was time to resume his place in the classroom — no longer a part-time teacher, but a full-fledged instructor at Lyle High. The students might not have noticed it, but Cody had no doubt he was standing taller, walking more confidently and believing in God's plans for his life more than ever before.

All through the day he couldn't shake his smile, not through five PE classes, and not as he dressed out for football practice and headed to the field. "Hey, Coach," DeMetri caught up with him as they walked to the nearest end zone. "What's up with you?"

"Smitty!" Cody couldn't have hidden his excitement if he wanted to. "Is it a great day to be a Buckaroo, or what?"

"Uh ... I guess." For a few steps DeMetri said nothing, just kept walking and casting strange glances at Cody. "Where's Coach Oliver?"

"We'll talk about that in a minute." From this day on Lyle football would be a different team, a different experience. He would care about these kids and invest in them, and he would teach them the game of football the way it had been taught to him — at the highest level, with intensity, hard work, and compassion. And with a sense of teamwork and camaraderie that would change this group of guys from a fledgling team to a family. Cody grinned and chuckled again. "I mean let me tell you, Smitty. It *is* a great day to be a Buckaroo."

They reached the field, where other players waited and still others were running in from the parking lot. Cody stopped and faced DeMetri, put his hands on the boy's shoulders, and looked straight at him. "I'll say this." He could feel his eyes shining with possibility. "God always hears us when we pray, isn't that right?"

DeMetri still looked baffled. "Yes, sir ... of course."

"And you, Smitty ... you never stopped praying, isn't that right?"

"That's right." DeMetri's mouth hung open a little and he blinked a few times. "Can I ... can I ask what's going on?"

"It's good, Smitty." He winked at the player. "God heard your prayers." Cody chuckled and turned to the group of players

gathering around him. Coach Oliver's troubles were a sad situa-
tion, and maybe one day Cody could help be part of the solution.
But for now all that mattered was the change in command here at
Lyle. "Alright, everyone. Bring it in. I've got an announcement!"

CODY PULLED UP IN FRONT OF TARA'S HOUSE and checked his
watch. Cheyenne was already here, and he was ten minutes late.
Not surprising, with how well practice had gone. They were in
such a groove, making such headway, and clicking so well that
they'd gone ten minutes over.

Not until he got in his truck and checked his phone did he see
the invitation from Tara for dinner that night.

"Cheyenne will be there ... so I'll just take that as a yes, Cody."
Her laughter filled the phone line with joy and life. "Besides ...
what else you got going on this Friday night?"

A few times in the past week Cody had talked to Cheyenne —
about little Kassie and how she was doing and about Cheyenne's
schooling and his. She was one of his only friends in this new
season of life, someone who had filled the empty places when he
might've talked to Bailey or her family. He wasn't anywhere near
as close to Cheyenne, of course, and he didn't have feelings for her
like he still did for Bailey. But she was kind and intelligent, and
he enjoyed the newness of her friendship more than he thought
he might.

Tara was at the door to greet him, talking a mile a minute
about work and the water heater bursting last week and how
Indianapolis was one of the last great cities because even a repair
man had the sense to use his manners and get his work done in
a timely manner.

It wasn't until they were seated at the table around meatloaf,
mashed potatoes, and gravy that Tara turned to him and cocked
her head. "Now, Cody, I've been doing all the talking ... but I

know sure as the roof over my head that something's up in that big ol' mind of yours." She kept her eyes on Cody, but poked an elbow in Cheyenne's direction. "You see it, Chey? You see what I'm talking about?"

"I do." Cheyenne giggled. Tara left neither of them any choice but to enjoy every minute with her. Chey turned her pretty eyes to Cody. "Football practice must've gone well, maybe?"

"Yes. Very well." Cody laughed and set down his fork. It felt good to have these two women know him so well, to sit around a dinner table with people he felt comfortable sharing with, and who could read his expression as easily as if he were family. He'd already told them both about the tough situation with Coach Oliver and the way the players seemed defeated and discouraged and the season was still six months off.

"Actually, yes ... something's up." He drew a long breath. "I was offered a full-time teaching position at Lyle today."

Tara slapped her hand on the table, pushed back, and stood. "You were not!" Her hands flew to her face and she turned one way, then the other, like she wanted to run a few laps in celebration, but given the size of the house, the idea wasn't possible. She lifted her hands toward heaven, talking fast and loud. "Merciful God, ... what a great answer!"

"I know." He laughed, enjoying Tara's reaction. "I can't believe it." He paused, letting the moment build. "And ... they made me the head football coach."

"Cody!" Cheyenne's eyes shone with pride. "That's amazing! What happened?"

"Yes," Tara muttered a few *Praise Jesus'* under her breath as she sat back down. "I've been praying for that school to come to their senses ever since I heard about all the troubles over there, so tell us ... what happened?"

Without getting too detailed, Cody explained that Coach Oliver needed a stress disability ... unresolved issues from decades ago during Vietnam. Even as he said it he felt a pang of fear. What if that's what people said about him decades from today? He pushed the thought from his mind once more. "I told the boys today at practice." He grinned, ignoring the way his hands suddenly shook. *Breathe, Cody ... you won't be like Coach Oliver. Not ever.*

"I'll bet they celebrated loud as little girls at a princess party." Tara clapped her hands a few times and nodded big. She had made it clear on a number of occasions that she thought there was a place in prison for anyone who berated kids. Especially young men. This time she pointed straight up. "That-a-way, God ... You always get the final word."

Cody felt himself relax again. This was a celebration, a happy moment. No reason to think about war or the ramifications his time in Iraq might have twenty or thirty years from now. He forced himself to focus. "They were happy ... but first thing we did was pray for Coach Oliver."

"Yes." Cheyenne's take was slightly more serious than Tara's. "The man needs our prayers."

"I'll tell you what that man needs ..." Tara's expression took on that of a mother bear about to settle a score. But she must've caught the earnestness in Cheyenne's tone, because she visibly relaxed and her wrinkled brow smoothed some. "Prayer." She cleared her throat and nodded, clearly working to convince herself. She folded her hands in an attempt at sweetness. "Prayer. That's exactly what he needs."

They all laughed, and Cody explained that he was careful not to let the practice become a discussion about Coach Oliver's shortcomings. "We put all our energy into the practice, and I'll tell you what ..." he shook his head and exhaled through pursed lips. "Best practice I've ever seen from those guys." He looked from Tara to Cheyenne. "I'm beyond excited for the season."

The conversation moved from Cody's new position, to good

news about Kassie, whose blood counts seemed to be better than ever. "She's not out of the woods, but she's getting there." Cheyenne glowed, obviously taken by the little girl. "We'll keep praying."

"That we will!" Tara punctuated the air with her fork. "Our God's a great God. He's working in that little girl's life, I have no doubt."

Dinner ended, and after dishes Cheyenne came to him and touched his arm. "Want to take a walk?"

Cody looked at Tara, but she was already waving her hand at him. "Cody Coleman, don't make me lead you outta this house by your hand." She waved at him again, making a brushing motion toward the door. "Take that girl for a walk! Don't make her ask you twice. And whatever you do, don't ask me to go along. I've got a boatload of email to answer." When they still hesitated, she brushed her hands in their direction again. "Git ... git! You hear me?"

Both Cheyenne and Cody were still laughing as they headed outside and down the steps. The mid-April night was warmer than it had been a week ago. Cody had a feeling spring would be beautiful, and for a split moment he remembered the flowers in the Flanigans' backyard. They would be beautiful this time of year.

"I ... I hope this is okay." Cheyenne slipped her hands in the back pockets of her blue jeans. She glanced at him, her pace slow and easy. "Taking a walk, I mean."

"Of course." He looked at the sky through the maple trees that lined Tara's street. The leaves weren't open yet, but the buds were close. Stars hung low in the sky overhead, and the night air was still. "I like walking — especially after dinner."

Quiet came over them for a little while. They walked side by side, their arms occasionally brushing against each other. "Beautiful night."

"It is." Again they were quiet, but Cody could sense a restlessness in her, like she wanted to talk about more than the weather but she wasn't quite sure where to begin. He slowed, and caught her eyes as they rounded the corner. "What's on your mind, Chey?"

She smiled. "I like that."

"What?" He felt entirely at ease.

"Just ... the way you call me 'Chey.'" The way she said it sounded like she was saying her name and describing her personality all at the same time. Her painful past made it easy to understand why she might be a little more shy, a bit more reserved. She gave him a pretty smile. "Chey's what my friends call me."

"And I'm your friend." They might not know each other all that well yet, but he could've told her anything. He trusted her.

"Exactly." She smiled, laughing a little, her eyes straight ahead again. "Now that we have that settled." Again she waited, and gradually her smile fell flat. She crossed her arms, as if a slight shiver had come over her. They were about to pass a small city park, and she pointed at a bench ahead in the darkness. She glanced his way. "Can we sit? For a few minutes?"

"Sure." Cody had no idea what was on her mind, but he wasn't worried. They reached the bench and sat ... a few inches between them. Here, with trees all around them, the night felt cooler than before. He angled himself so he could see her. "Is everything okay?"

"Yes. With me." She turned, pulling one knee up onto the bench. "It's just ... earlier when you talked about that coach ... his time at Vietnam and his stress disability." She narrowed her eyes, as if she were searching beyond his eyes to his soul. "I saw something change in you. For the first time since I've known you ... it was like you were afraid."

Her keen awareness made his heart beat faster, and after only a few seconds, he could no longer look into her eyes, no longer sit

here and let her see straight through him. He breathed in slowly through his nose and stared at a spot on the ground a few feet ahead. Should he tell her? Should she know about his nightmares and flashbacks? He was about to look up and tell her everything. How he could still smell the rancid Iraqi prison and how he could feel the sharp butt of the rifle against his ribs. How sometimes he still felt trapped in the same cage that had held him back then.

But just as he turned to her, just as he was about to speak, another image came to mind ... one as strong and powerful as any flashback he'd had about Iraq. The face of Bailey Flanigan. He raked his fingers through his short dark hair and released a sound that was as much nervous laugh as it was a groan. "Nah ... no fear, Chey." And in as much time as it took to feel her honest eyes on his, Cody stood. "I guess I feel a little sorry for the old coach." He held his hand out to her. "Come on ... we have to get back." His tone wasn't unkind, but it put a clear end to the moment.

"Cody,..." Regret filled her eyes as she took his hand and stood before him. "I didn't mean to push, I just ... I could be wrong, but I thought ..."

He made a conscious choice to release her hand as soon as she was on her feet. But even so, a part of him wanted to hug the kind-hearted girl before him and tell her exactly how right she had been. *Be careful, Cody ... don't hurt her ... you're not ready* ... Bailey's smile flashed in his mind again. He couldn't tell Cheyenne anything as personal as his struggles with memories from war. Opening up like that would only complicate things. Instead he hid his fear below the surface of his heart and found a careful smile. "Good idea ... taking a walk."

They picked up their pace some on the way back, and Cody kept the conversation light — the drills they'd run in practice, the antics between some of the kids in his third-period PE class, and his roommate's seeming inability to wash even a single dish.

When they returned to Tara's, they were laughing, the brief awkwardness from earlier gone.

But that night and the next morning he couldn't shake his thoughts of Bailey. Their separation was his fault, he was aware of that. And now that so much time had passed, she was probably no longer looking for texts or calls from him. No longer wishing he hadn't left. Still, with everything in him he wanted to see her, spend a few hours with her.

So after breakfast he cleaned his apartment, started a load of laundry, climbed in his truck, and did the only thing he could do. He drove to the closest movie theater and bought a single ticket to see the movie he had avoided until now.

"One for *Unlocked*, please."

He found a seat near the back, and since it was the first showing of the day, the auditorium wasn't half full. The previews took forever, but finally, alone in the darkness, he had what he wanted. Two hours of Bailey Flanigan ... her heart and kindness, her love for family and God and life. The movie amazed him, not only the tender storyline and powerful message, but the reality that Bailey was a gifted actress, able to convey her heart and soul on the silver screen.

Not that he was surprised.

He soaked in all of it, and as the closing scene came to an end, as the credits rolled and the theater began to empty, he could only be grateful he hadn't opened up too much to Cheyenne. Because he knew one thing after spending two hours with Bailey here in an Indianapolis theater, even if she was — in reality — light years away.

Bailey Flanigan owned his heart. And like his time in Iraq, one way or another his feelings for Bailey would last as long as he lived.

Seventeen

Jenny and the boys were cleaning up after dinner, and all she could think as she looked around the kitchen was the obvious — this was how it was going to be with Bailey gone.

"Where'd Bailey go?" Jim had gone in the office to take a phone call.

"She's outside on the front porch!" Ricky sank his hands elbow-deep in sudsy water and grinned in Jim's direction. "Meaning she got out of the dishes again."

"Meaning she's probably texting someone." Shawn cleared three glasses from the stove area and set them in the sink next to Jenny. "Right, Dad? When girls sit out on the front porch it's never because they just want fresh air, right?"

Jenny laughed to herself. Shawn had asked questions since they adopted him from Haiti.

"Well," Jim picked up a stack of dirty plates and followed Shawn to the sink. "It can mean that."

"Yeah, because why else would she go outside right after dinner?" Justin shrugged. He wasn't one to jump to conclusions, but he clearly liked where this conversation was going. "I mean, maybe she's texting Matt Keagan. That would be cool, right? Matt Keagan and Bailey?"

"Last week it was Bailey and Brandon Paul." Jim gave the boys a goofy grin, as if to tell them not to take any of Bailey's friendships too seriously. "If Bailey falls in love, I'm sure we'll be the first to know."

"That won't happen any time soon." BJ was the quietest in the group. When he spoke, his approach was matter-of-fact and straightforward. He dragged a soapy washcloth over the kitchen counter and shrugged one shoulder. "She loves Cody Coleman. You all know that."

For a long beat an awkward silence came over them, and Jenny was convinced as she had been a number of times before that Cody's absence hurt the boys more than they talked about.

"Yeah, well," Connor entered the room with an armload of dirty placemats. "If he loved her, he would call."

"Right." Justin gave Connor a determined, loyal sort of look. "He obviously doesn't care."

Jenny didn't add to the conversation. She hurt for how the boys had to process Cody's absence. When he was at war, the missing him was different. He had no choice but to be gone. But this time ... Cody moving away without saying goodbye. The way he'd cut ties and moved on. It was hurtful. All of it.

"Anyway." Ricky stuck out his chest, and like his brothers it was obvious he would defend Bailey to the end. "I like Matt."

"I think he's seeing someone else. So let's talk about something else." Jenny smiled at her boys, stepped back from the sink, and dried her hands. "Okay, Connor ... your turn."

Connor did as he was told, but his eyes danced more than usual. "Guess what I found out?"

"Don't tell me ..." Jim grabbed a towel and began drying the counter. "The 300-pound offensive lineman at Bloomington High is transferring to Clear Creek?"

Laughter came from all the boys and Connor pumped his fist in the air a few times. "As the quarterback I have to say ... that *would* be great news."

"Ahhh, yes." Jim chuckled. "We live in hope."

"Anyway," Jenny enjoyed this and, in light of Bailey's looming

move, she appreciated times like these more than ever. "Connor, you were saying..."

"I was saying..." He shook the water and soap from his hands and turned to the others. "I found out *American Idol*'s auditioning in Indianapolis this summer!"

"And..." Jim froze, his hand mid-circle as he dried the stove. "You mean you're trying out?"

Connor waited until he had the attention of everyone. Then when he couldn't seem to hold the answer in a moment longer, he raised both hands in the air. "Yes! I'm going to audition."

A round of cheers and celebratory jumps and slaps on the back followed. "You can do this, Connor. I know you can do it." Ricky seemed ready to go into vocal coach mode. "We need to do a little work, but you can do it."

Connor explained that if he made it past the first few rounds the weekend of auditions, he would be invited to audition in front of the celebrity judges. "But not until mid-December, Dad, and only for a weekend." His tone was serious, as if he'd thought the timing out along with everything else. "So don't worry... nothing will get in the way of football."

The boys were still talking about *American Idol* when the doorbell rang. Jenny left them in the kitchen and headed down the hall to the foyer. She opened the door to find Roberta Johnson, her next-door neighbor. The woman was holding a plate of what looked like brownies. "Roberta!" The laughter in the background was louder than before. "Come in. If we can hear ourselves above the uproar."

Roberta was pretty, a late-forties leukemia survivor with a strong faith and a keen sense of God's presence at work in everyday situations. "Don't apologize for that." She pointed down the hall toward the sound of their laughter. "Life is too short, Jenny." She snapped her fingers. "You blink and they're gone." That was true for Roberta's five kids — all of whom were in college or headed there.

Jenny crossed her arms and felt a sad smile tug at her lips. "You're right about that."

"Hmmm." Roberta frowned, her eyes shaded with a knowing. "Bailey?"

"Yes." Jenny tried not to think about it … tried to live in her left brain most of the time, where they had much to do before Bailey was ready to move. But in this moment tears gathered in her eyes. "She leaves in two weeks."

"Oh, honey." Roberta set the brownies down on the floor and took Jenny's hands. "You'll be okay." She smiled, willing a certain strength with her eyes. "You'll cry and feel like your world is falling apart. You'll miss her with every heartbeat." Roberta nodded. "But you'll be okay."

Jenny didn't see this coming, the visit from Roberta and the emotion it would stir within her. But life was tenuous — Roberta was proof of that. As a cancer survivor, she had no guarantee about tomorrow. But then, none of them did. "She's … she's ready." A sound that was part-laugh, part-cry came from her. "I guess … I'm not sure I am."

"You never will be." Roberta squeezed her hands gently, and then released them as she picked up the brownies again. "These are for you." She peered beyond Jenny to the kitchen. "Rumor is you have a very special visitor tonight … Matt Keagan?"

Jenny tried to imagine how Roberta had learned that Matt Keagan was there for dinner. But she laughed instead. "That was last week. But the kids love your brownies." Jenny took the tray. "This will be great."

"So … I missed him?" She grinned like a kid. Then she pulled a copy of *Sports Illustrated* from her purse. Matt was on the cover. "Okay, well the next time he's here … my son would love an autograph."

Moments like this didn't bother Jenny. Especially from a great friend like Roberta. She was generous to a fault, always arranging neighborhood drives for special charities involving soldiers or orphaned children. She volunteered her time at homeless shelters and raised her children to be the same sort of Christians. Jenny took the magazine. "I'm sure he'll be by again in the next few month. I'll ask him to sign it."

"It won't be a problem?" Worry flashed in Roberta's eyes. "I really hate to ask, I mean . . . it's not like me, but I thought it would just tickle my son."

"Really." Jenny put her hand on her friend's shoulder. "It's fine. Matt's great about things like this. In fact, Jim has a few official balls upstairs in the closet. I'll get Matt to sign one for your next orphanage benefit."

Roberta gasped. "Oh, Jenny . . . that would be perfect!"

They talked for another few minutes, and Roberta mentioned her family's upcoming mission trip to Chimbote, Peru. "You really should come. It'd get your mind off missing Bailey."

Jenny struggled with the way that sounded, but she nodded anyway. "Yes," she pictured her family headed off to a Peruvian mission trip without Bailey. The ache in her heart doubled. "That'd be nice. I'll talk to Jim, for sure."

Roberta left and Jenny took the brownies and the *Sports Illustrated* back to the kitchen where the boys were finishing up the cleaning. This time they were talking about the smell in the locker room, and whether a small woodland creature had crawled in and died in one of the equipment closets or whether certain sectors of the defense simply needed to stop eating double burritos for lunch.

Laughter rang through the kitchen, just as the boys noticed that she had walked into the room. Connor raised his hand toward the others. "Okay . . . Mom's here. Enough."

A quick look around the room and Jenny saw the giggles and

embarrassment on the boys' faces. "You heard us, huh, Mom?" Ricky tried to contain his laughter, but it escaped in a happy outburst. "Plus, guys, it doesn't matter. Mom knows how we are."

"All too well." Jenny laughed, and plugged her nose so they'd see she wasn't too girly to join in the locker room humor. At least not vicariously.

The sight of their mother plugging her nose in the kitchen moments after the story about the defense was enough to put all the boys over the edge. Their laughter grew until they were falling against the kitchen counter or bent over trying to catch their breath. Jenny took in the moment, the way it was so different from the tender-hearted memories of sitting on the front porch swing or sharing a Starbucks that marked her time with Bailey. This was fun too. Boy humor ... all of her young men in one place, lighthearted enough to laugh at silly things. Jenny was grateful that she enjoyed these times. Because this was a snapshot of her days ahead.

Her life without Bailey.

BAILEY WALKED TO THE FRONT PORCH SWING and sat down, setting it in motion with her feet. She was back on Facebook lately, using it the way she'd used it before — as a way to reach out to her friends, encourage them, and help them draw closer to Jesus. And once in a while to check up on Cody Coleman — just in case maybe he started up his Facebook account again, the one that hadn't been active since his high school days.

She pulled out her phone and used the Facebook app to check her page. She commented on a few of the posts by distant friends. One was from an Indiana University girl Bailey had met at Campus Crusade meetings last semester. "Bailey," the girl wrote on her wall, "haven't seen any pictures of you and Cody lately ... what's happening?"

A frustrated pang of anxiety rippled across her heart as she typed her response. "Not much ... how've you been?"

She tapped the search line, spelled out Cody's name, and then hit enter. Immediately a list of names came up — but none of them were her Cody. The swing rocked gently, and the wind settled down some. A quick switch of screens and she called up her text window. She could write a text and in five seconds he could know she was thinking of him. She poised her fingers over the miniature keyboard and began typing. Why not text him? She could tell him hello, right? There was no harm in that. Her fingers moved faster.

Hey, stranger. Thinking of you ...

But just as she was about to hit the send button, her mother's words flashed in her mind. *Next time that boy pursues you, he better do it like a dying man looking for water in a desert.* She stared at the unsent text and the pain in her soul became a legitimate anger. The sort of anger that could fester and root itself into her heart, where she might have it always if she wasn't careful. She closed her eyes, ordering her emotions under control. As she did, her phone vibrated, signaling a text coming in.

If this was Cody then maybe ... maybe God was trying to tell her that he hadn't moved on. That on nights like this, even after a great day, he still thought about her the way she thought about him. She opened her eyes and raced over the text.

Thinking about you, Bailey girl ... not letting NY stop me. Just so you know.

The text was from Brandon, and though a part of her was disappointed, his words lifted her spirits and made her smile. What was she supposed to do with Brandon? He wasn't leaving, he'd made that clear. His last phone call was a week ago, before he set off for some island location to work on his current movie. "I saw it in your eyes, Bailey. You care for me. If you'd let yourself fall ... I think you could love me."

"Brandon,... you're crazy. This is all we'd ever have. A phone call every week or so." She had to be honest. "We prayed about God shutting the door, and He did."

"Maybe not." Brandon's answer was quick. "Maybe this is just a closed window, and now we're supposed to work on finding the real door."

He made her laugh, and that phone call was no exception. The truth was, his call had made her head spin, and her heartbeat didn't feel normal the rest of the night. He hadn't had cell reception since then — until now, anyway. She typed back her response.

You found a cell tower in the jungle? Or you're back in LA.

His response came lightning fast: *LA. Missing you.*

Bailey allowed a weak laugh to slip. Was God really allowing her life to be this complicated? *What am I supposed to do with him, Lord? Brandon Paul? Really? Should I take him seriously?* She thought about the craziness of his life, the paparazzi, and magazine covers, and twenty-four-seven scrutiny.

Miss you, too ... The stars in Bloomington right now remind me of our night on your balcony.

Bailey hesitated, re-read the text, and then in a rush she hit send. It was true ... she did miss him. Again, his response was immediate: *Everything reminds me of that night. Can I visit you tomorrow?*

Bailey laughed out loud. Was he serious? He would fly to see her just like that? Without a plan or a few weeks' notice? The answer was an obvious yes. Brandon could afford to be impulsive. She tapped out her reply. *Umm ... I'm packing ... getting ready to leave.*

She stared at their conversation and looked again at his texts. Half a minute later, another message flashed on her screen: *Perfect. I'll help you pack. I'm good at it.*

This time Bailey's heart danced. What was she doing? She'd show these texts to her mom later. Maybe she'd help shed light on the situation. The dilemma she felt lately with the guys in her life was a distraction — the way she missed Cody but still felt a growing attraction to Brandon. She needed to go through everything in her room and pack her things, and once she arrived in New York, she needed to finish her semester online and rehearse for the biggest role of her life.

How could she even consider maintaining a regular friendship with Brandon, let alone daydream about whether Cody ever thought about her? Her fingers flew across her phone's keyboard. *Sure, Brandon ... stop by. It's not like you're in the middle of shooting a movie or anything.*

Almost immediately he responded. *You think I'm kidding. I'm hurt.*

No ... really. Come. I'll be waiting. She laughed, but not as hard as before. She didn't want to tease him if he was perfectly serious. That was one of the problems with texts. There was no way to get the tone.

Okay. The minute I have a break, I'll surprise you. Don't say this can't work, Bailey ... I'll show you.

Ahhh ... Brandon, you make me smile. She thought of her dad's famous line, and she tapped out the letters. *I'll leave the light on, okay?*

She stared at the text as she sent it. Why was she doing this? Even if they found a way to make their cities and schedules work, she'd have to live his public life. And what about Cody? His name reminded her of the months of frustration and hurt, the anger she felt earlier because he hadn't texted or called. And that could only mean he wasn't thinking of her.

For me? Brandon's text came flying in. *You'd leave the light on for me? Bailey ... you just made my night. And why is it I can still see your eyes looking into mine that night?*

"You know just what to say," she whispered the words. Then

she responded as quickly as he had. *I can see yours, too ... I have no idea what that means ... but just so you know, I still can.*

Or maybe they were Cody's eyes she could see — even in a moment like this. The sudden thought interrupted her good time with Brandon and made her angry with herself. *Dear God ... Cody doesn't care ... Help me move on, please ... I need You.*

I am enough for you, daughter ... Fill your heart with me.

The answer came swift and certain, filling her heart with the soft whisper of truth. He was all she needed — not the heartache of Cody ... or even the thrill of possibility with Brandon Paul.

The crazy thing was that in all her life, she hadn't thought she'd reach a point where she would beg God to help her forget about Cody Coleman. She sorted through her text conversations, found Cody's name, and deleted the message she was going to send him ten minutes ago. She would follow her mother's advice.

So where did that leave things with Brandon? What if he really jumped on a plane and came here to help her pack? She giggled at the thought as she stood and walked inside. Darkness had fallen, and she wanted to talk to her mom.

Not because of Cody this time, but because of Brandon Paul — which had to mean something. Brandon was fun and adventurous, and his new faith seemed stronger all the time. So why not allow herself to consider the idea? As she shut the front door, she did the one thing she had to do before the night got too late. The thing she had promised she would do ...

She flicked the porch light on.

Eighteen

FROM HIS PLACE IN THE DUGOUT, LANDON BLAKE COULD SEE the packed stands. Not that there were many rows in the bleachers — but what was there was full to capacity. Cole's Yankees were undefeated, and at this point in the season with half the games already played, people from the community were coming out and cheering them on.

"Dad," Cole was fitting his catcher's gear on his chest, "You're feeling good, right?"

Landon had been using his inhaler, taking the medication. But still there were moments when the dust kicked up from the infield and he'd cough a couple times. He hadn't noticed it himself, but this afternoon was probably one of those times. Landon patted Cole on the back. "I'm fine, buddy. Just fine."

There were two outs, and with the game tied, they were putting Cole behind the plate. He was as good pitching as he was catching, but this team was known for stealing bases.

"I love catching, by the way," Cole grinned as he snapped the last buckle in place. He put one shin protector on and began working with the other. "Those guys won't get past me."

"Terminator. Right, Big C?" Avery Schmidt gave Cole a few pats on his head. "Actually we're the terminator team. Me at short, and you at catch."

"And me on the mound," Thomas joined in, and then Mitchell, all of them agreeing that the combination about to take the field would inevitably stop the other team from scoring in the final three innings.

"I love the confidence," Landon grinned. "But let's let our game do the talking." He was about to pull the kids together and go over the lineup, when his pager went off. He checked the message and gritted his teeth. A house fire. He was on call, so he'd have to leave now. "What is it, Dad? Is it a fire?"

"It is," he winked at Cole. "I'll try to be back for the last inning, okay?"

"Sure." The worry in Cole's eyes was something new. The boy had loved the sense of adventure that came with Landon's job. But today he only stared at Landon, his lips parted. "Be safe."

"Of course." Landon gave Cole a side hug and nodded to his assistant coach, Kevin. "I'll be back."

Kevin was perfectly capable. The man had more coaching experience than Landon, but his work kept him away from the early games. "Go on." Kevin grabbed the clipboard from the chain-link fence. "We'll be waiting."

Landon found Ashley in the stands, sitting with her sisters — Kari, Brooke, and Erin — and their families. It was one of those rare days when most of the family managed to be there. Ash's dad and Elaine sat on the highest row, and even as Landon explained the situation to Ashley, he could feel John Baxter's nervous eyes on him.

"Do you have your inhaler?" Ashley's tone had a quiet panic in it. "Baby, check. You can't go into a fire without it. The doctor told you."

"I know." He pulled the plastic device from his pants pocket. "I've got it."

"Okay." She knit her brow together, stood, and gave him a quick hug. "Be careful. I love you, Landon ... I'll be praying."

"I love you too." He smiled at her, caring for her with everything in him. "Me, too."

With that, he ran to the waiting fire engine and drove off. His partner was already in the passenger seat — content to watch the game from the rig as long as they were on call. Now they flew into action, racing to the fire as quickly as they could. The fire was downtown, and as they pulled around the corner they saw two trucks had already responded. But even with that the dwelling was fully engulfed.

Working with precision, they parked as close as they could, donned their masks and gloves and gear, and ran to the command post out front. "We still have two people trapped inside," the lieutenant yelled above the sound of flames and water hoses. "Three have been rescued, but we can't find the two. It's an older couple — husband and wife."

Bloomington didn't have many fires this serious — with people trapped inside a burning house. But suddenly he remembered the time a decade ago when it was a child lost in a fire like this. Landon refused to give up as he went through the house that day, and he found the boy unconscious. He buddy-breathed with him until he blacked out … and it was in the aftermath of that fire that he first realized Ashley Baxter had feelings for him.

The memory passed as quickly as it came. He couldn't black out this time. His lungs couldn't afford it. He hurried in, his partner at his side. Already fighting their way through the burning building were four other firefighters, the first responders. They could communicate from within their gear, but the noise around them was deafening — oppressive, same as the heat. In a burn this fully involved, Landon and his partner had just one choice: stay together. That way there would at least be one person to know where the other one was if something terrible happened — a collapsed beam, a broken floor board, a fallen wall.

Command had told them to head to the back of the house. The upstairs had been checked, same with the bedrooms on the right side. Already, the first two teams were back outside, getting oxygen and water before they might make another attempt at finding the victims. Landon peered through the bright orange wall of fire and looked for an opening, any opening. *Dear Lord ... they're in here somewhere. Please ... help us find them. This is why You asked me to fight fires, Father ...*

I am with you, my son ...

Landon felt the certain calm of the truth of God. The Lord was with him. He would not fight this fire alone. Landon used his axe to sweep debris out of the way as they headed back, deeper into the burning house. Within a minute they found the woman. She was collapsed on the floor in a doorway, unmoving. Together, Landon and his partner picked her up and moved her quickly outside. No telling if she was still alive, but once they had her safely on the lawn, paramedics took over.

"You okay, Blake ... you're coughing." The lieutenant in charge grabbed Landon's shoulder and stared at him. "Don't go back in if you're coughing."

Landon hadn't even noticed. He lifted his mask, reached for his inhaler, and took two quick puffs. After fifteen seconds, he exhaled and nodded. "I'm fine. I'm going back in."

The look from his lieutenant told him that at this stage in the fire, there might not be any point. But their job was to save lives, not to stop and count the cost. He'd done that the day he'd agreed to fight fires for the city of Bloomington. His partner was ready, and again the two of them positioned their headgear and masks and hurried back into the burning house. The fire was at its peak now, consuming everything in its wake. Landon ran as quickly as he could, trudging over fallen beams and pushing his way past piles of burning embers. The heat pressed in against his skin and he could barely see his own feet.

Another scan of the place, and at first it looked like maybe command was wrong ... maybe the old man had gotten out earlier and in the chaos people had missed him. But just when they

might've turned around and given up, Landon saw a leg sticking out from a doorway down the hall from where the woman was found. He signaled to his partner, but even as he did he felt something strange in his lungs ... a burning or tightness that hadn't been there before. He fought through, working so that the two of them lifted the man and carried him back through the burning house, out onto the lawn where his wife was receiving CPR.

With every step, Landon became more sure that something was seriously wrong. *God ... I can't breathe ... can't ... draw a breath.* A sense of panic welled in him as they set the man down. He had thought often lately about what could happen, what the problem in his lungs might be. Sometimes at night when Ashley was already asleep, he considered the very strong reality that he might have a serious lung disease. A fatal lung disease. He wasn't worried about himself. He loved God, and when he walked the bridge of death, it would be to a place called eternity. Landon was certain.

He tried to draw in one breath ... one single breath. But again his lungs wouldn't work. Wouldn't allow even a little air into his body. In a rush, he ripped his helmet off and slowly fell to his knees, desperately trying to calm his airways, grabbing for his inhaler. But the doctor had warned him about this: an inhaler could only work if a person could draw a breath. Now, though, with the smoke and heat, Landon couldn't suck back a single bit of the medication.

People were shouting all around him, screaming for help and running toward him. *It's okay,* he told himself. *Everything's going to be okay.* Now, just like at night when Ashley was sleeping, he wasn't concerned with his own life or how come his lungs were failing him ... or even if this were the end. After all, he fought fires because this was the work God wanted him to do. His last thought ... the last flicker of consciousness left in his body was devoted to one single uncertainty. Not about himself, but about his wife.

What would happen to his precious Ashley?

Because if this were the end ... if he never got to hold Cole and Devin and Janessa again, then he would wait for them in heaven, where they would share forever. In time they would all be okay. But what about his wife ...

Ashley ... Ashley, baby. God, help her ... Don't let me die, Father. Please ...

It was his final cry, his final prayer. Because if he knew her at all, he knew this. After all they'd been through, if he didn't survive this fire, he was fairly certain the news wouldn't only devastate Ashley.

It might destroy her.

ASHLEY HADN'T MOVED FROM LANDON'S BEDSIDE since she got there, three hours ago. Since then Landon had been hooked to machines, on life support — pure oxygen being pumped into his weakened lungs. The rest of the family was in the waiting room, and at times one or two of them had come in to offer support and pray for Landon.

But for now it was just the two of them — where they began — here in a hospital room with Landon fighting for his life. She had prayed, of course ... but only in short bursts. For the most part, she couldn't move. Couldn't stop looking at him or watching his chest rise and fall, willing him to breathe on his own, to find the strength to grab hold of life and stay here. With her.

"Landon,..." she barely recognized her voice, strained and high pitched. Filled with terror. "Stay with me, baby ... stay. Please, God, let him stay."

Some people talked about times like this, when life was on the line and a sudden rush of awareness came like a tidal wave. Things

that should've been said, love that could've been expressed, memories they could've made. But that awareness was not part of this moment. Ashley had no regrets when it came to loving Landon Blake. Every day she gave to him all she had, the same way he gave to her. They seized every moment, made the most of every situation. They had loved like their next breath depended on it, and so that wasn't the problem.

Ashley touched her fingers lightly to Landon's rugged face. She was vaguely aware of tears streaming down her cheeks, but she made no attempt to stop them. No loud sobs or cries came from her, because she couldn't focus on anything but Landon. He needed all of her, every bit of her attention. Otherwise how could she will the life back into him?

No, the problem now wasn't all the regrets she'd have if he didn't get up from this hospital bed, if the machines couldn't get his lungs working and he never woke up. The problem was if he didn't make it, she didn't want to either. Already heaven had her mother and her infant daughter — the girl who would've been Janessa's older sister. But if God took Landon too?

Ashley refused to let herself think about it. "You're okay, baby ... breathe ... come on, Landon. Breathe, sweetheart."

A sound came from behind her, but it took a minute before Ashley realized the doctor was calling her name. She turned, but only for a moment. If she looked away from Landon for too long he might not be there when she looked back. The doctor was saying something, but his voice changed and it became Landon's.

I'll never love anyone like I love you, Ashley ... the way I've always loved you ...

And suddenly she wasn't sitting here at Landon's bedside begging God to let him live. She was a young single mother, painting outside in front of her family's home, painting and missing Landon and longing for him ... And like the wind someone was touching her hair, the side of her face, and she turned and it was him. Landon. Come home from New York and Ground Zero, his mission accomplished. And he was taking her in his arms and telling her how much he loved her, promising he would never leave her again, never be apart from her ...

The scene changed and she was standing by Irvel's graveside. Irvel who had only loved Hank all the days of her life. Irvel who, for the last seven years at Sunset Hills Adult Care Home where Ashley worked, believed only that Hank was fishing. Not that he was dead, but just gone with the guys ... for the afternoon. Irvel, whose love added to the picture of love Ashley's parents had given her when she was growing up.

She was there at the cemetery again, and Irvel's funeral had just ended, and like so many other times Landon was walking up alongside her, putting his arm around her. "Has anyone told you ... you have the most beautiful hair?" It was the question Irvel always asked her, never remembering that she had already asked it. And there was Landon, knowing just what to say and how to remind her that life would go on, and that Irvel's love and wisdom would continue to live, because it would live in her.

And there was Landon, sitting in the dugout helping Cole with his catcher's gear and even from the bleachers, even in the middle of a screaming loud baseball game, she had heard his pager go off, and she had known ... absolutely known that this was the one fire he shouldn't respond to.

But he had responded.

And now ...

"Ashley."

The doctor. She had forgotten about the doctor. Again she turned, keeping her shoulder to Landon, her arm alongside his. "Yes?"

Her father entered the room then, and without saying a word he pulled up a chair and moved it right next to her. If only her mom were here. Because this was a time when a girl should have

her mother. When all the world was falling apart and the sky was upside down and nothing made sense. This was when she needed her mom the most, right?

"Ashley." This time her father was talking to her. "Sweetheart, Dr. Jacobs needs to talk to you. It's about Landon's lungs."

Landon's lungs? The lungs that breathed life into the only man she'd ever loved? Was she ready to hear about Landon's lungs? She shook her head slowly and then faster.

"Ashley?"

It was the doctor again.

Ashley closed her eyes. The thing with her and Landon was, they needed each other. If he couldn't breathe, then she couldn't either. Because when he inhaled, she felt life. That's how it had been since the last time she sat at his bedside after a fire nearly killed him ten years ago. She blinked her eyes open and studied his face, the peacefulness of his closed eyes. "Breathe, baby ... I'm here ... breathe."

"Ashley."

She turned and looked at her father. Something in his tone snapped her from the blur of memories and fear and shock. Complete and utter shock. She became suddenly aware of her surroundings and what was happening. The reason she was there.

"I'm sorry ..." She looked at the doctor, still standing a few feet away. He was holding a manila folder. Landon's chart, most likely. The chart with the bad news. *Stay in the moment, Ashley. Listen to the man. Dear God give me the strength to listen to the man.* "Doctor Jacobs, forgive me ... I can't ..."

Her father put his arm around her and held her close, holding her up so she wouldn't fall to the floor.

"Don't apologize." Dr. Jacobs took a step closer. "We ran additional tests on your husband when he was admitted, and I'm afraid ..." his voice trailed off as he opened the manila folder.

"When I look at his records, the tests that have been done ... I can only conclude that your husband does, indeed, have the lung disease we feared. All signs point to polymyositis."

Polymyositis ... polymyositis ...

The word screeched at her, stripping away her composure and her strength and her heart's ability to carry out a normal beat. "That ... that's the disease we talked about?" She looked at her dad, begging him to tell her she was wrong, that this was a different sort of a disease ... an illness, maybe. Something he could take antibiotics for and be fine in a few weeks.

But her father nodded. "Yes, sweetheart. It's that disease."

What had the doctor said last time Landon had an appointment? That people with polymyositis wound up on oxygen full-time, and that ... that they needed a lung transplant if they were going to live? Was that it? Her mind was in that instant very clear. How could this be happening? She put her head in her hands and tried to block out the doctor's words, willing the clock to turn back two minutes to a time when the word *polymyositis* had never been read from the diagnosis in Landon's chart.

Her father rubbed her back, whispering soothing things about God's peace ... His plan ... His presence ...

Somewhere over the course of the next few minutes, Dr. Jacob left and Kari brought Cole and Devin into the hospital room. Janessa was in Kari's arms, her thumb in her mouth, her eyes wide. Ashley wanted to get up and go to her children, but instead they came to her. Cole was still in his New York Yankees uniform, dirt still smudged on his cheek from the game. He put both arms around Ashley and held her, hugging her, his eyes focused on Landon.

Devin reached up and took hold of the hospital bed railing and peered through the cracks at his father. *This can't be happening. It can't be ...* Ashley closed her eyes and tried to convince herself it was all a dream, a terrible nightmare. She would wake up, and they'd be in bed, and it would be Thursday morning ...

time for school. But when she blinked her eyes open, Devin was still looking through the bars of the bed, and Cole was still holding her, and Kari was still standing helplessly a few feet away, Janessa on her hip.

"Is Daddy going to die?" Devin was the only one willing to put their terrifying fears into words.

The response came from her father, who had positioned himself on the other side of Ashley. She leaned into him more as he spoke. "Jesus is with your dad, Devin ... he'll be just fine. It's our job to keep praying."

And then ... in the way they'd been taught since they were born, Cole and Devin linked hands with Kari and Ashley and Ashley's father, and they prayed for Landon, that God would breathe life into him, and that he would wake up from his coma, and that very soon he would be well enough to come home.

But even as they prayed, Ashley couldn't help but think about the only word that screamed through her mind, the one Dr. Jacob had talked about earlier.

Polymyositis.

Because no matter what miracle God might do to get Landon through this night and out of bed and back home where he belonged, this was only the beginning. The disease that had caused Landon's lungs to shut down was aggressive and sure ... fatal in every case without a lung transplant. The very idea was nauseating to Ashley, sickening. Landon was the picture of health: tall and built and bullet-proof. Until today. The devastating reality was only just beginning to take root in her mind, and it was enough to destroy her. If not for her kids, her father, her God — who was with her — Ashley wasn't sure how her heart would keep beating.

Landon was sick. He was fighting for his life, and beyond that he had a deadly lung disease. How was that even possible? She clung to her father, her sister, and her kids. *I can't do this, God. I can't ... please, change this. Take it away ...*

My grace is sufficient for you, my daughter. I will never leave you nor forsake you.

Jesus, no. Ashley sobbed out loud, right in the middle of her father's prayer ... railing against the reality, refusing it. *Please, God ... take it away.* Fresh tears spilled onto Ashley's cheeks and again she leaned into her father's shoulder so she wouldn't collapse. The reality was something she could only gape at in horror, like a grotesque monster that had stepped into the room to devour her. She closed her eyes, her breathing faster than before. Too fast. She drowned out the sound of the prayer and her children crying and the machines beeping in the spaces around them.

Instead she was back on the baseball field and the sun was shining and Cole's team was going to win ... they were definitely going to win ... and Landon was coaching the boys and Devin and Janessa were beside her ... her family all around. And no one had yet labeled Landon with any disease, and he was laughing with the boys, and she was thinking the same thing she always thought when she was with him.

Despite all the ways she'd messed up in life, she must've somehow gained God's favor anyway.

Because Landon Blake loved her.

Nineteen

CODY HAD TO SEE HER, HAD TO GET IN HIS CAR AND GO FIND Bailey, or he wouldn't survive the weekend. He balanced his roommate's guitar on his knee and played the first few notes of his new favorite song, "Walk by Faith." It had been around for awhile, but Cody didn't care. It spoke straight to his heart and gave him a reason to look forward to tomorrow.

"I will walk by faith ... even when I cannot see ..."

The song was by Jeremy Camp, and Cody was learning another of his too. A song called "Give Me Jesus." Both songs filled in the lonely spaces when he wasn't sure he could go another day without at least talking to her, finding real closure for the empty months that were proof of how poorly he'd handled their talk in January.

Cody strummed a few notes and stared at a framed photo of Bailey and him. The two of them had gotten drenched in Lake Monroe, and on the way out, with the football tucked under Bailey's arm, her dad had snapped the picture. It stood like a beacon of light, a reminder to Cody of all he'd walked away from, all he might never find again. Especially after what had happened this morning.

For the first time since his flashbacks started, earlier today he had gone to a Christian counselor. The guy was nice, patient with him — and kind enough to take him on a Saturday. But the man kept focusing on Cody's mind-set when he was in captivity. What kept him alive, what gave him a reason to go on, what motivated him to plan an escape, and risk his life and the lives of the other men, so that they could fully and finally be free.

"For many people the reason might be a deep love for their country, or a competitive nature that refuses to be beaten — even in a life and death situation," the counselor's voice was calm, soothing. Cody felt like he was acting out a scene in a movie. "Of course for others it's family back home, a wife ... children. And many times it's a combination."

He went on to explain that when a soldier faces post-traumatic stress disorder, oftentimes the motivation for escape, the thing the soldier lived for during the most horrific times of his life, was now in jeopardy.

It wasn't what Cody wanted to hear. He wanted the guy to walk him through those awful days and remind him that he was here, he had survived. Yes, he had been seriously injured, and he would bear the scars all the days of his life, but the ordeal was behind him. Somehow, if he heard that from a professional, Cody figured he could walk out of the counselor's office whole and ready to face tomorrow. The nightmares, the flashbacks would stay behind him, and he never would have to worry about becoming Coach Oliver somewhere down the road.

But instead the man looked at him, his expression open and mildly curious. "Can you identify what that might be, Cody? The thing that motivated you to stay alive, the thing that pushed you to escape during your time as a prisoner of war?"

Could he identify his motivation? She was as close to him as his own heartbeat. "Yes, sir. I can."

The man waited and then gave a slow, patient nod. "That's fine. We can talk about specifics at our next session. The point is, do you feel that motivation is now in danger of no longer being a part of your life? Like maybe you risked everything to escape only to find out that the motivation is no longer valid?"

Cody stared at the man. "Do you mean is she still in my life?"

"Okay." Another nod. "Let's say it that way. Is she still in your life, Cody?"

He clenched his jaw, fought back a sudden freight train of anger at himself and the situation. "No." Was that why he was here? Because he'd been a fool and let her go? "She's ... she hasn't been in my life for several months now."

"Hmmm." The man's slight smile was sympathetic, as if maybe even untrained Cody might see the connection now. "And when did your flashbacks begin?"

Cody was glad he wasn't paying for this session. The school had set it up, and so this first appointment was free. "They began back in January." He massaged his temples with his thumb and forefinger. "Around ... the same time we said goodbye."

"Okay, then." The man slid to the edge of his seat. "You've told me about the dreams, the details. What happened back in Iraq." He stood and held out his hand. "I think we're getting somewhere as to the motivation. Very often people think the traumatic event is the problem, when in reality it can be a secondary trigger, something that causes us to rewrite a terrible time in our past and find that the danger or trauma no longer has meaning in our lives, because our motivation has been removed."

"Right." Cody shook the man's hand. "Meaning next time we'll talk about what happened in the last three months. Why she's gone?"

"At least for part of the time." The man's eyes were warm, and he clearly had a kind heart.

But Cody was pretty sure this was his last session — for now anyway. How could he come spend an hour with this guy, when the bottom line was so obvious? He didn't need time with a counselor, at least not at this point. He needed Bailey. He had driven back home, and for nearly an hour he had picked up his roommate's guitar and played around with a few chords.

Never in all his life had Cody played guitar or piano ... and he'd never been interested in singing. But on lonely nights here in the apartment near the Indianapolis campus of IU, there were times when Cody wanted any connection he could find to Bailey. And since she played the guitar, he figured maybe he would learn to play too. His roommate had taught him a few chords, and now he could sing a few basic praise songs.

He strummed his thumb over the strings and hummed the song again. "I will walk by faith ... even when I cannot see ..." The words were like his anthem. A song about the broken road of life, and how in the end he had to believe that even the brokenness was somehow preparing God's will for his life. He checked the time on his phone. Just after ten o'clock. If he left now, he could be at Bailey's house by eleven. She would be home helping with the chores, the way the Flanigan kids always did Saturday mornings. Unless the boys had a scrimmage. His own team had a scrimmage next Saturday. It was that time of the year.

The guitar was nice, but it wasn't a replacement for what he needed to do. Cody set it down, stood, and stared again at the photo. Why was he putting himself through this? No, they might not be meant for each other. And yes, Bailey might've moved on by now. At the very least she would be upset with him. He knew her that well. But if he didn't go to her, he would never know, never tell her how sorry he was for his silence. Never put a final goodbye to their years together.

Suddenly, with an intensity that he'd only known a couple times in his life, he grabbed his keys and wallet and headed hard toward the front door. He was about to open it, when there was the sound of a few light knocks. He stopped, and for a few seconds he was unable to breathe or move or respond. Was it her? Had Bailey figured out where he lived and found a way to come to him?

He opened the door, and almost called out her name. But standing there on his step wasn't Bailey. It was Cheyenne. Her

dark hair was ironed straight and it fell right to her shoulders. Her brown eyes held a depth and sorrow he hadn't seen before. "Can ... can I come in?"

"Of course." Cody jumped back. His heart slammed around inside him, because how was he supposed to handle this situation? He was on his way out the door to see Bailey, and now this? "Come on ... follow me."

She stepped inside, and Cody hugged her a little longer than he intended. She smelled wonderful, like cinnamon and vanilla mixed. He closed the door behind her and led her into the living room. It was small — only a worn-out leather sofa, a beat-up chair, a coffee table, and a smallish TV. Perfect for a couple of college guys. "Here." He pointed to the sofa. "Sit down." He had no idea what could've brought her here without a phone call or a plan. Cody had never even given her his address.

He took the spot beside her, though he left room. Something about her cried out to him, made him wonder if they were building more between them than friendship. Her eyes and her expression were vulnerable and tender, and a part of Cody knew he could fall for this girl if he let himself. Even if he could be ten minutes closer to Bloomington by now.

"I'm sorry for coming without calling first. Tara gave me your address." She put her hands on her knees and seemed to struggle for the right words. "I ... got word this morning. Kassie ... she spiked a fever a few days ago, and the infection ... it tore through her little body." Tears filled Cheyenne's eyes. She covered her face with her hand and a few quiet sobs broke through.

Cody slid closer, his heart racing faster than before. "Is ... she sicker?"

Cheyenne lowered her hand and looked at him.

She didn't have to say anything, because Cody knew ... he knew that look because it was the same look he'd seen in the eyes of a soldier delivering the worst news a mother could ever hear.

"Chey,… tell me." He took her hand in his, soothing his thumb over her soft skin. "What happened?"

Again she looked at him, her eyes marked by fear and doubt and sorrow deeper than the ocean. "She died, Cody … They couldn't save her."

He took her in his arms, wishing he could do anything to take away her pain. "I'm sorry … Chey, I'm so sorry."

"I thought …" two sobs shook her slight body, "God could hear us … when we prayed."

Cody closed his eyes and held her tighter than before. Wasn't that the question he'd asked himself over and over again? If God could hear them, why had he been captured in Iraq, and how come he'd lost so much during his time at war? If God answered the prayers of His people, how could Cody's mother be back in prison, and why would some homicidal drug dealer make death threats that would finally push Cody forever away from the only girl he'd ever loved? If God answered prayer … then why didn't Cheyenne's fiancé Art make it back home?

"Why, Cody … how come God let this happen?" She might as well have said why did God let it happen *again*. Because that was her tone.

Cody could do nothing but hold her and run his hand across her back, soothing her pain and letting her know he was here, he cared. There were simply no easy answers, and that was fine. Like Pastor Mark from Bloomington once said, "If we could figure out God's plan, then He wouldn't be God." But right now that wasn't what Cheyenne needed to hear. She didn't need answers … she needed a friend.

For a long time they stayed that way: Cody holding her and Cheyenne sobbing her heart out, devastated at the loss of little Kassie. After a while Cody found a box of tissues and handed them to her. This time he sat on the sofa again, but much closer than before. When her nose and cheeks were dry, she sat back, emotionally drained. "She was doing so well."

"Did you go there ... by the hospital?"

She shook her head. "No ... I told her grandpa I'd come by his house later today." She exhaled long and slow, as if she hadn't done so since she started crying. "I mean really, Cody ... why would God need that little girl now? Her family loves her so much. Don't you think they need her more than God does?"

Cody searched her eyes, her heart. "Like you and Art?"

Another layer of tears appeared in her eyes, and she blinked, her chin trembling. "Yes ... like me and Art." She took another tissue from the box and pressed it to her eyes. "I ... took down his things. Put them in a box." She shook her head, and a flash of anger mixed in with the sadness in her expression. "But it didn't help, Cody ... I still know that he should be here ... with me."

"He should." Again Cody had no answers. "I tried, Chey ... I would've saved him if I could have." This was a conversation he never thought he'd have with her. But from the first time he met her, a part of him wanted to say this. Just so she'd know. "Art was one of the guys from my division. One of the guys sent in to rescue us."

She nodded, and he wondered if maybe she already knew these details. "He was a hero. They told me that."

"He was ... no regard for his own safety." Cody closed his eyes and he could see the first burst of daylight, the first few seconds after he'd been released from captivity, when he had no choice but to run through a hail of bullets toward freedom. He blinked and found Cheyenne's eyes again. "I saw him lying there, Chey ... He and the others set us free. And Art ... he was the first to rush the compound where we were being held. His death ... it was a distraction that allowed the others to free us. He was absolutely a hero."

Tears fell onto her cheeks and she bit her lip, as if she were bracing herself against the pain of the terrible truth. "Do you ... remember him? How he was at war?"

"Of course." Cody took her hand again. "Art was bigger than life ... always smiling, always laughing. No problem too big to handle." Cody's smile couldn't take full form under the weight of his own heartache. "He was Tara's son."

"So you think about him?" For some reason this seemed to lighten Cheyenne's burden, help her find a point of focus again.

"I think about him ... about the last time I saw him." Cody studied her face, her eyes. He hadn't told this to anyone but the counselor. "I think about the way it felt to be crammed in a prison cell, and how I watched men die on either side of me as we were set free." Cody shivered a little. "I have flashbacks, Chey. I saw a counselor about it this morning."

She leaned closer, shock written into her eyes and face. "Cody,... why didn't you tell me?"

"It's my problem." He appreciated her kindness, but he would never have told her about this until now. He stared at nothing in particular. "I guess ... it's like a weakness. I should be stronger. Nothing about the past should be haunting me now."

For a while she only looked at him, and the care and concern in her eyes was so great Cody wondered why he'd waited so long to talk to her. Of course she understood. She was engaged to a soldier, after all. "Everything about war haunts the people who've been there." Her half smile was proof she was going to be okay. "Didn't anyone ever tell you that, Cody?"

"I guess. But it's been a while now. Close to three years." He gritted his teeth and shook his head, frustrated. His eyes met hers again. "The counselor said a lot of times it's not the flashbacks that are the problem. They're a sign that something else is wrong." He hesitated. He hadn't told her about Bailey. There had been no reason before today, but now ... if he was going to be any sort of longtime friend, Cheyenne needed to know. "He asked me about

my motivation, what kept me alive when I was in captivity, what
kept me fighting to come home again."

Cheyenne's smile warmed her eyes this time. "I was Art's
motivation." She angled her head and looked off. "The Army
insisted I get counseling when he was killed, and that's what we
determined after ten sessions. I was Art's motivation. He was
fighting and surviving and living each day as carefully as he could
so that he'd get home for me." Her smile let up. "Having perfect
motivation doesn't guarantee a perfect ending. One of the first
rules I learned at counseling."

"No ... it doesn't."

Slowly a curiosity seemed to come over Cheyenne, and with it
a knowing. That if she followed this thought line the answers might
not be what she wanted to hear. "You're thinking about it ... so tell
me." Her voice softened. "What was your motivation, Cody?"

For a long time he wasn't sure he would answer her. At least
not specifically. It was enough to explain that friends and family were what drove him to find a way back home — whatever
the cost. But he liked Cheyenne ... he did. And he couldn't have
a friendship with her, let alone whatever the future might hold,
unless starting here he could be honest.

She was still waiting, searching his face, trying to see past the
walls he so easily kept in place. He sighed and the sound added to
the weight of the subject. "Her name is Bailey Flanigan. She's a few
years younger than me ... lives with her family in Bloomington."

Cody watched the walls go up in Cheyenne's eyes. He was
sorry ... she'd been through enough today without this hurting her too. But they'd never actually established that they had a
thing for each other. Anyway, he couldn't turn back now, and her
expression told him she didn't want him to stop at this point in
the story. "Bailey." She said the name, watching Cody for his reaction. Nothing about Cheyenne's tone or expression said that she
was angry or jealous or frustrated. Rather, there was a knowing,

as if this was the missing piece she hadn't quite understood about him. "Do you ... still see her?"

"No." He moved to the edge of the sofa and folded his hands. How could he explain Bailey in a single conversation? "It's complicated. She ... we parted ways in January."

"January?" She must've figured out that they'd met before that. "I guess ... I didn't know you had a girlfriend back then?"

A sad laugh rattled Cody's hurting heart. "She was never my girlfriend. Back in high school, I lived with her family. We became close ... like best friends."

"Meaning," her smile didn't quite reach her eyes, "you didn't mean to, but you fell in love with her."

Cody managed the hint of a smile. "Something like that."

Again they shared a quiet moment between them, this one more tense than before. Because Cheyenne was clearly surprised by the revelation of Bailey ... surprised and maybe a little hurt. Which could only mean the obvious: She was starting to have feelings for Cody, the same way he was starting to have feelings for her. She sat up straighter, more composed than before. "So ... what did the counselor suggest?"

"I guess just that maybe I need to figure out what's happening with her ... with the source of my motivation."

"With Bailey." Her tone wasn't accusatory and it wasn't a question. Again Chey seemed to erect walls that hadn't been there before. Cody turned, facing her. "I was on my way to see her when you got here."

This time Cheyenne looked awkward, startled even. She checked her watch and then stood, her smile polite. "I'm sorry, Cody. I didn't mean to change your plans. I just ... I live down the block and ... I called Tara. She though it'd be okay." She shook her head. "I should've called."

He stood and put his hands on her shoulders. "No, Chey, don't be sorry." He willed her to see that she was wrong. That he was grateful she'd come. "I want to be that kind of friend for you ... where you can come by anytime and talk about anything."

Cheyenne opened her mouth like she might say something, refute him in some way, but then he took half a step closer to her and pulled her into a hug, the sort of embrace the two of them had never shared together.

"I never ... should've listened to Tara." She was crying again, Cody could feel her body trembling against his. "She told me God saved you ... for me." She leaned back and met his eyes again. "Isn't that crazy?" She dabbed at her eyes with one hand, and kept hold of him with the other. "Here you are in love with someone else."

The realization of what she'd just said hit him with a force that made him hold tighter to her for fear that his trembling legs would give out. Did she really mean what it seemed like she meant? That she had listened to Tara and now she had feelings that strong for him? Did she believe Tara was right ... that God had spared him so that Art's fiancé wouldn't be alone in life? "Tara said that?" His voice was low and shaky. "About us?"

"Yes." She sniffed and shook her head quickly. "I didn't want to believe it for the longest time." Her face was so pretty — even with tear stains on her cheeks. Faith and love emanated from everything she said and did.

Cody was suddenly very aware of himself, his feelings, the way his body felt pressed against hers. Without meaning to, he brought his hand up and cradled the back of her head. Was this what he'd been fighting with Cheyenne all this time, feelings for a girl as rare as April snow? She wasn't Bailey. But she was genuine and loving, and in some ways she was as broken as he was. "Chey, what are you saying?"

She shook her head. "I can't ... It doesn't matter." She started to push away, but he held her gently and almost immediately she gave up the fight. Then with her face inches from his she looked in his eyes, searching for answers. "I can't let myself fall for you, Cody Coleman ... because you have *her*."

He could kiss her. And in that single instant, kissing her was the one thing he was certain he wanted to do. She was so close he could feel her breath against his face, smell her perfume as it filled his senses. Yes, he could kiss her and maybe ... finally ... he could get Bailey Flanigan out of his system. Cheyenne understood war better than Bailey ever would, so what if Tara was right? What if God had spared him for the purpose of finding love and a lifetime with Cheyenne?

She seemed to know what he was thinking, because she didn't say anything, but she stayed in his arms, their faces closer than before ... still closer. Cody brought his other hand up, so that he held her face in his hands and the feelings from a few seconds ago doubled. He could kiss her and give in to the aching loneliness that had consumed him for so long, and maybe here ... now, he would find something with Cheyenne that would be real and lasting. Something better than what he'd felt for ...

Bailey.

Her name hit him like cold water, and he stepped back just enough to find his composure again. "Chey, ..." He allowed two breaths ... three. "I care about you. And maybe ..." He saw that the walls around her heart were down again. "Maybe Tara is right. Maybe we're supposed to be together and we're only just now figuring that out." He was still shaking with the desire that had come so quickly over him. But as quickly as it had come, his longing for Cheyenne had been replaced with a certainty about Bailey. He ran his hand softly along Cheyenne's face and he backed up another step. "But ... I have to figure things out first."

No bitterness hid in her smile. Just an openhearted understanding wrapped in a thin veil of hurt. "You mean ... you need to go find her. Your Bailey."

"Yes." He hugged her again, but the intensity from a minute

ago was gone. "I'm sorry about Kassie ... I really am." He paused, not sure what else to say. "Please tell her grandfather I'll pray for his family."

"I will." This time Cheyenne stepped back. She picked her purse up off the floor and slid it over her shoulder. "Thanks, Cody. For listening." They walked to his door together, and she turned to him one last time. "I'd like to be your friend ... no matter what happens with her."

"Yes." He touched the side of her face once more. "I'd like that, too." He was grateful for her attitude, glad she didn't say that because of Bailey, she was never going to talk to him again.

As she left, as she drove away, Cody felt himself relax. He had dodged a big mistake there, and he could only thank God for watching out for him. If he would've kissed Cheyenne here ... now, when there was no relationship between them ... how could he look Bailey in the eyes and tell her how much he missed her? Tell her that he still cared and try to explain the reason he'd sent her away last January? No, if he kissed Cheyenne now he wouldn't be headed to Bloomington today. He'd be struggling to stop and knowing that if this was how he could act after three months away from Bailey, then he must never involve her heart in his life again.

But he hadn't kissed her.

And leaning against his door frame he looked up at the cloudy sky and thanked God. Thanked Him for sparing both of them the confusion that would come after kissing ... and the way they could never go back to the pure friendship they'd had before. *You're with me, God ... I can feel Your presence ... thank You, Father.*

It didn't occur to him until he was in his truck and already on the highway headed west that the truth was something slightly different. Yes, God had spared him from making a hasty decision, and maybe hurting himself and Cheyenne in the process. But Cody was still confused — no question about that. His confusion baffled him and frightened him and made him doubt everything he had ever known to be true about himself and his feelings for Bailey Flanigan. Because even as he drove to find her, even as he imagined what he'd say and how she'd respond ... even as he worked to keep his nerves calm when every mile brought him closer to her ... even then only one scent filled his clothing and his senses.

Cinnamon and vanilla.

Twenty

BAILEY REACHED TO THE BACK OF HER LOWER DESK DRAWER, amazed at the junk she'd managed to cram inside it. This Saturday she had set aside the whole morning and most of the afternoon to go through her things, figure out what needed to be tossed or given away, and what needed to make the trip with her to New York. Her dad was at practice with the Colts and her mom was getting the boys started with their homework, and then she'd be up to help.

She was playing Taylor Swift for the occasion ... especially the song that spoke most to her right now. A song called "Never Grow Up." The idea that someday soon she'd be in a different state, a new city ... a new home without her family nearby was sometimes more than Bailey could take. She could give in to tears at any time if she thought about all she was going to miss.

But right now she didn't have time to cry. She only had a week before she moved, and her room was a disaster. Not only that, but she still had no housing lined up. The uncertainties were enough to make her stay awake at night, and sometimes Bailey would lie in bed staring at the ceiling, tossing from one side to the other wondering if she were crazy to take the job.

Mornings were better. A breeze drifted through her open window. She would be fine. God would work out the housing, because He had opened this door, after all. If she needed to stay in a hotel at first, her parents had said she could do that. They'd help with the costs until Bailey was making a paycheck.

Dear Lord ... how am I supposed to go through all this?

She blew at a wisp of her hair and doubled her efforts to clean her room. All around her were stacks of her belongings. Clothing she'd give away to the church's Closet Essentials ministry, and old shoes that had long since seen their last day. One box held books she'd collected over the years and another held devotions and notebooks full of her thoughts on love and various Bible verses. She still wasn't sure exactly what she was taking to New York City. She'd been on the phone with one of *Hairspray*'s assistant producers, and he'd assured her he was looking for housing. But until he found something, she wasn't even sure how much space she'd have.

"You want to walk to work, right?" he'd asked her that morning. "No tunnels or subways?"

"If possible." She and her mom had talked about what would be safest, and they'd decided that living with someone in the city made the most sense. Fewer places where she'd have to stand and wait by herself every day of the week. Bailey thanked the man for working on the situation.

"I do have something that might work," he sounded lost in thought, and she could hear him turning pages of a document. "It looks like three of the dancers share a flat not far from the theater. They're looking for a fourth person to share costs with."

Bailey had ten questions immediately, but she only asked one. "Would I have my own bedroom?"

The man paused and a jaded laugh sounded across the phone line. "I don't know anyone with their own bedroom. With those girls it'd be more like a cold spot on the floor. They don't share their beds with broads," he snickered. "If you know what I mean."

She figured he meant the girls were straight. But his comment brought up another concern. If the girls shared their beds at all, the situation wasn't okay with Bailey. Her mom and dad would rent her a place by herself and hire a bodyguard to get her to and

from work each night if that's what it took. "Let's forget about that setup," Bailey kept her voice kind. The man meant well. "I really would like my own room. And I don't have to live with dancers. It can be a family ... a couple ... that sort of thing."

"Oh, right," the man chuckled. "I forgot. You're the girl with money and connections."

The comment hit Bailey like a slap in the face. Especially in light of the comments from some of the dancers at the audition. Like she hadn't really earned her place on the cast. She wasn't sure what to say to the man, but he didn't seem to notice her hesitation.

He began rattling off boroughs almost like he was talking to himself. "Anyway, I'll keep looking."

Now Bailey was surrounded by boxes and piles of her things, and still she didn't know where she was going to live. Her entire family was praying about the situation ... and her dad had taken the prayer to a new level last night. She smiled as his words ran again in her mind. "Father, we trust You with Bailey ... and we believe You're working out her housing situation even at this moment. But we ask for more than a safe place to live, Lord. We ask that You place Bailey in a home where she can learn from the people she's living with ... and they can learn from her."

Bailey loved the idea, and even now her father's words helped her dismiss the comment by the assistant producer about her money and connections. Instead she focused on the very real possibility that this next season in life might not only be about learning how to work on Broadway and how to live in the city, but learning from the people around her. She looked at the chaos that made up her room. Every picture, every scrap of paper ... all of it meant something. And now it was time to sort through it and take what mattered most. As sad as today would be at times, in light of her dad's prayer she was beyond thrilled for what lay ahead.

She pushed her hand to the back of the desk drawer again, and this time she pulled out a journal. An old one she must've hidden here years ago. Bailey squinted at the cover, trying to remember how long ago she'd written in this book. It was faded pink and white, with butterflies fluttering across the top corner. Across the middle it read, "For I know the plans I have for you . . . to give you a hope and a future. Jeremiah 29:11."

Bailey smiled and ran her thumb over the worn cover. The Scripture was her favorite, the one her parents had taught her when she was very young. The one she still clung to when life didn't make sense. She opened the book and her eyes fell on a random entry somewhere near the middle.

Dear Lord . . . thank You so much for saving Cody. For getting his attention and helping him see how much he needs You. He's changed, God. I can see it. When we talk, he's so nice to me. And he told me not to ever settle for a guy like Bryan Smythe, because I'm worth so much more than how Bryan treats me.

I don't know, God. When Cody talks to me like that I sometimes feel like I'm falling for him . . . like You saved him for me, Lord. I mean, I know I have to grow up a little and we have a lot of life ahead. But I catch him looking at me sometimes, and even though we're friends, I think he cares for me more than that. Like I'm more than Coach Flanigan's daughter.

Bailey's heart melted as she read the words, as they filled her heart and reminded her of the way she'd felt back then. Cody had been so careful. He lived with them, and at first he had so many troubles she never would've considered that he might be the guy for her. He almost drank himself to death at one point, but God saved him.

She had written this journal entry some time after he was released from the hospital. Because almost immediately he had started alcohol awareness classes, and he and Bailey's dad had begun a Bible study. She closed the journal and tried to remember how she felt, so young and unsure of herself. Cody had been very aware, certain never to say or do anything that might be misconstrued as flirtatious or suggestive. He treated her with the utmost respect, and he always had.

So much so that when he joined the Army after high school and left for the war, Bailey wasn't sure if he saw her as anything more than a friend. Then, when he returned — wounded after his escape from captivity — he kept his distance. Even told her she should date Tim Reed. How was she supposed to think he had feelings for her when that's how he had acted?

Still ... she believed. Every time they were together, any time they talked or shared a walk back from their Campus Crusade meetings, Bailey was certain she saw something more in his eyes. But it wasn't until last Fourth of July that finally he opened up about how he felt. By then she'd broken up with Tim, and with all her heart she believed she and Cody would never be apart again.

But she won the part opposite Brandon Paul in *Unlocked*, and Cody became busy. Almost like he didn't want to be part of her life if she were going to be in the limelight. His distance troubled her and angered her, and finally — when the movie wrapped and after Christmas break — Bailey went to Indianapolis and found out what had happened. His mother had been arrested for drug use again.

This was Cody's constant demon, the reason he never thought he was good enough to date her. Because he was the son of a drug addict. It was the reason he had lived with them in the first place, because Cassie Coleman was in prison through most of Cody's high school days.

Something else must've happened too. But Bailey had never figured it out. Because she had told him a dozen times that she didn't care what decisions his mother made. They could visit her together, pray for her together. Cody loved her like no one ever would — Bailey believed that. So then why — the last time they were together on her parents' porch last November — did he imply things were over? That he had to move on?

She thumbed through the journal again, but no answers jumped out. Either way, she would save the book. Maybe someday alone in New York she could pull it out and read it again. Maybe it would help her understand how she had fallen so completely in love with him, and why she wasn't able to let him go.

Downstairs the doorbell rang through the house, but Bailey didn't get up. Probably Mrs. Johnson from next door or one of the neighborhood boys looking for a pick-up game of basketball. One of them would get it. She tucked the old journal safely in a box of must-keep items and dug through her desk drawer again.

Old math papers, history notes ... a long lost science book. She pulled out everything left in the drawer and spread it on the floor in front of her. "Trash ... trash ... trash ..." she muttered. It felt good to scrunch up the papers that had once taken so much time and toss them in the black garbage bag a few feet away. "Now Mr. Science book, you're another story. I should probably have Connor take you back to school where someone else can have fun with you."

"Hmmm. Looks like I'm just in time."

She gasped.

It couldn't be. But it sounded like the voice was ... Bailey whipped around and, yes, there he was at the open bedroom door: Brandon Paul, looking like he did on the balcony overlooking the beach. He held his hands out, grinning in a way that made her realize how much she'd missed him. "Surprise!"

Suddenly she was on her feet rushing to him, the two of them coming together in a hug that almost knocked him down and left both of them laughing. "What in the world?" She felt the heat in her cheeks, but she didn't care. He had really done it. He had flown to Indiana and now he was here, right in the middle of her messy room.

"I told you I'd come help." His grin lit up his whole face as he held onto her, still hugging her. "Your mom said to tell you she'd be right up." He kissed her cheek and then stepped back, surveying the room. "She said you needed all the help you can get, and wow …" He raised his brow at the piles of belongings strewn across the floor. "I guess she's right."

"She is." Bailey let her shoulders sink as she studied the space around them. "It's terrible in here."

"What color's the carpet, anyway?"

A hand towel lay across the edge of her bed and she grabbed it, flicking at him. "Stop." She laughed at the situation, the hours she still had ahead of her. "It's not always like this."

"All right then," he made an exaggerated move of rolling up his sleeves. "Where do I begin?"

The truth was, he couldn't do much. She had to go through every item, since only she could decide whether it was something she should keep, move to New York, or get rid of. "You know … I'm not sure there's anything you can really do."

"I bet there is." He looked around and scratched his head, still being overly dramatic about the job they needed to do. "How about I wait until your mom's here. Maybe she'll know some way we can work together. Teamwork, right? Isn't that what your dad's always telling his players?"

An idea hit, just as she was about to agree with him. "We could take the trash out."

"Yes, perfect." He nodded, his brow raised again. "That would at least give us a place to stand."

They both laughed, and she pointed out the bigger of the two trash bags. Brandon picked up that one, and she took the other. As they headed downstairs, even while they were still laughing, a tenderness stirred within her. He had really done this, and at a time when he was finishing up a movie. Break or no break, it was a tremendous thing to fly from LA to Indianapolis and drive to Bloomington — all so he could help her pack.

Downstairs they talked to her mom and brothers for a few minutes. Her mom and the boys had been in on the surprise. "Brandon wanted to make sure you'd be here." Her mom was working with Justin on his algebra.

"So you've known for a few days or what?" Bailey shot laughing eyes at Brandon and then back at her mom. "Did he set the whole thing up last week?"

"Oh, no." Her mom shared a look with the boys. "He set it up an hour ago. That's the first we knew about it."

Brandon shrugged, his look all innocent teasing. "It seemed like a good day to help pack."

"I love that!" Ricky's exuberance added to the joy of the moment. "Just get on a plane and go wherever you want." He looked at their mother. "I want to be like that when I'm older."

"Sure, buddy." She peered over her shoulder at him. "Anytime you want to hop a plane to help someone clean their room, I'm all for it."

Bailey led Brandon outside to the place on the side of the house where they kept the family's trash cans. The connection they'd shared in Los Angeles was still there, still making her dizzy enough to wonder at what point she should start taking her feelings seriously. No matter how crazy his life might be.

He lifted his bag over his head, and the action showed off the definition in his shoulders. Brandon wasn't quite six feet tall, but he was fit and his face was one girls around the whole world clamored to see. Bailey stayed close behind him, watching him, trying to take stock of her feelings.

As he reached the side of the house, he held the trash bag with one hand and lifted the lid of the oversized bin with the other. He easily dumped the contents into the bin and then did

the same with her bag. Then he wadded them both up. "You still want to use these?"

"Yes." She winced. "I have a feeling there's still more trash up there."

He laughed. "You think? We could use heavy equipment for a day and still come up with more." His laugh filled the air around them. Brandon loved to laugh. It was one of the things that drew her to him from the beginning — the fact that he laughed easily.

They walked around the corner and up onto the porch that ran along the front of the house. Halfway to the front door he set the bags down and turned to her. "Do you know how amazing this feels? Being here with you?"

"It feels perfect." She caught his hands in her own and squeezed them, the way friends sometimes did. "And it feels crazy all at the same time."

His laughter quieted and he looked into her eyes for a long moment. "I missed you, Bailey. I don't know …" He breathed in sharply through his nose and turned toward their vast front yard. He seemed to take in the trees that lined the driveway and the pretty bushes flowering along the edges of their seven acres. Maybe even the fact that there were no cameramen running up to snap their pictures. "I'm not sure I can go back."

"When do you leave?" She hadn't wanted to ask because she knew the answer — he couldn't stay long. Not when he was in the middle of filming a movie.

"Tomorrow morning." He narrowed his eyes, as if he were trying to see to the deepest places in her soul. "But I need a week at least. Maybe two." He hesitated and put one of his hands on her shoulder. "Maybe a whole lot longer than that." His voice fell to a whisper. "Let me stay, Bailey … I don't want to say goodbye again."

"Hmmm …" A part of her wanted to believe him. As if he could walk away from Hollywood and she could walk away from

Broadway, and they might find a simple, satisfying life here in Bloomington. She could forget about Cody Coleman and together they could pretend the rest of the world didn't exist.

But the idea brought with it a sad reality check. "Ahh, Brandon . . . come on." She looked around for a few seconds and then turned her eyes back to his. "This would never be enough for you." She put her arm around his neck, careful not to stand too close to him. "I love this . . . being with you. But it's not the answer. You flying out on a whim to help me pack. Moments like this . . ." She tilted her head, hoping he could see her sincerity. "They would be rare . . . the world wants too much of you, Brandon."

"Here's the thing," he put his other arm around her and still maintained the space between them. They probably looked like a middle school couple slow-dancing in the gym. "No matter what you say, I've thought it through." His eyes shone, and this time there was no question he wasn't teasing. He was serious. The way he'd been serious on his balcony a few weeks ago. "The next year . . . yes, it'll be busy." He came closer, and his eyes told her he wanted to kiss her. But instead he brushed his cheek against hers the way he'd done before.

"Very busy."

"Okay, very busy." He put his hand alongside her face. "But it's just a year, Bailey. Who knows what'll happen after that? You only have a year-long contract, right?"

It was something she didn't think about very often. Most of the time a year felt like forever, but the truth was something he had clearly thought through. A year from now she might move back to Bloomington or maybe even to Hollywood. "They've mentioned a second year."

"Mentioned it." He nodded, his experience with the entertainment industry written into his expression. "There's no guarantee in a mention."

Something about his tone, the look in his eyes made her

laugh ... and once she started, she couldn't quickly regain her composure. "Do you hear yourself?"

"Hear myself?" He sounded wounded, but he was back to teasing. The ground where they both felt most comfortable. "Am I stuttering? Or maybe my voice is cracking?" He massaged his throat and made a funny face. Then he touched the tip of his nose to hers. "Of course I can hear myself. If I weren't making sense you wouldn't have all that nervous laughter."

She was about to tell him the conversation was over. They had nothing to talk about, since everything about their futures was so uncertain. Besides, they needed to get in and figure out her room. But before she could say anything, a pickup truck pulled into her driveway. In as much time as it took her to turn and look, she knew it was Cody's. She would know his truck anywhere.

"What?" Brandon followed her gaze and turned so that he had just one arm around her waist. "Who is it?"

He was almost up to the circle in front of the house before Bailey realized how this must look. Brandon and her, together on the porch, their arms around each other. He was close enough now that she could see his face, his eyes ... the guy she could never quite get out of her mind. And he could see her too ... the way he'd caught her and Brandon together.

"Hold on." She pulled away from Brandon and jumped lightly off the two-foot high porch and onto the grass below. But even as she ran toward him, Cody pulled away. He didn't peel out or race down the driveway, but he definitely wasn't going to stop. She knew him better than that. Fifteen yards from the house, she stopped and watched him go. She could still see his eyes in the rearview mirror, and she thought about running inside, finding her phone, and calling him.

But Brandon was here, and Cody hadn't talked to her since January. Four months ago. She could feel Brandon walking up beside her, feel his curiosity and maybe even a little alarm. "Bailey?"

She turned and looked at him, and then back at the pickup truck disappearing over the hill headed out of her neighborhood. "I'm sorry ... it's just ..." She turned back to him. She was breathing harder than before, and no amount of acting could hide the pain she felt in her eyes. "I haven't seen him ..."

Brandon came closer, and again he framed her face with his hand, searching her eyes. "Was that him? Was it Cody?"

"Yes." She hung her head, her emotions wildly conflicting. How could she enjoy the feel of Brandon's hand against her face and still feel like she was betraying Cody for doing so? She lifted her eyes. "He didn't call."

"Hmmm." Brandon was quiet. "Seems to be a trend today."

She smiled, but she couldn't laugh, couldn't shake the image of Cody driving away again. "I'm sorry ... I didn't mean to run off."

"But you did." His eyes told her he wasn't angry or slighted by her action. But he was aware of what it meant — no question about that. "So the truth, Miss Bailey, isn't so much that our crazy lives are taking us in different directions." He ran his thumb over her cheekbone, his eyes full of a longing that seemed deeper than before. "The problem is Cody." He backed up a step and took her hands in his. "Right?"

With everything in her she wanted to tell him he was wrong, that she was over Cody because he hadn't cared enough to hold onto her in the first place ... that no matter what happened tomorrow, she wasn't about to let Cody Coleman impact her decisions one way or another. But she couldn't lie to Brandon. Not now ... not ever.

"That's okay ... you don't have to say anything." His sad smile was tinged with a fresh determination. "If he's what I'm up against, I'm ready for the challenge." He looked over his shoulder

at the empty road, and then back at her. "I'll show you, Bailey ... he doesn't love you like I do."

His words stirred across her already tender heart. Until now, Brandon hadn't talked about love ... not like this. And she certainly wasn't ready to respond by telling him she felt the same way.

"Come on," he nodded toward the front door, his confidence firmly back in place. "Let's get back to work. Otherwise you'll never get to New York." His tone was tender, aware that this was a difficult situation for Bailey. But he also wasn't going to let her wallow in the moment. This was supposed to be a happy day, and he was clearly going to see that she found her way back to happy again.

She hugged him close, resting her head on his shoulder and begging God to clear up the confusion in her heart. "Okay." She smiled at him, and he took hold of her hand. Together they walked back to the house, quiet ... but without the sense of awkwardness that Cody's brief visit had brought to their time together.

No matter how badly she wanted to go after Cody, get him back here where they might talk and figure out why he had stayed away for so long, she couldn't. This day belonged to Brandon. Maybe if they went inside and got back to work in her room ... maybe if her mom joined them and they set their minds on the task ahead, they would find the laughter and magic from a few minutes ago. Or at the very least if they went back inside she might be able to shake the image locked in her mind.

The image of Cody Coleman's eyes in the rearview mirror.

Twenty-One

THE BAXTER FAMILY TOOK TURNS HOLDING VIGIL IN THE WAIT-
ing room at the Bloomington Hospital — but Ashley never left.
Not since Landon was brought in five days ago. Ashley had
asked her extended family to keep the situation quiet ... so they
wouldn't have a host of visitors. Landon was fighting for his life,
after all. The newspaper had reported the death of the old man,
the one Landon found in the fire just before his near fatal asthma
attack. They had referred to the fact that one firefighter had been
seriously injured, but they didn't follow up with a name or other
details. Ashley remained grateful for that.

She couldn't imagine how she'd feel if the paper printed the
truth — that Landon was still in a coma, still not able to breathe
on his own.

The Baxters were so well known in Bloomington that if word
got out about how serious Landon's situation really was, they
would have a waiting room full of dear friends around the clock.
And while it would've been nice to have hundreds of people
praying for him, for now it was enough to have the Baxter family
involved. At least that's how Ashley felt today.

The doctor had been in earlier this morning, and for the first
time since Landon's hospitalization, the news wasn't entirely bad.
"His lungs are making progress ... healing from the attack."

"So maybe ..." She stood, the news so good she couldn't stay
seated. "Maybe it isn't polymyositis?"

Dr. Jacobs' enthusiasm faded. "Ashley, the diagnosis is sepa-

rate from the asthma attack ... separate from the smoke damage. He has to get past this crisis before we can talk about the lung disease. If he ..." he stopped himself and stared at the ground for a second before finding Ashley's eyes again. "When he comes out of this ... he'll still be very sick. You need to keep that in mind."

Ashley didn't want to keep it in mind. She was going crazy sitting in this hospital room, begging God to bring Landon back, desperate for him to open his eyes and look at her ... breathless for him to smile at her and tell her what she wanted to know more than anything in the world. That he was okay. That no matter what the tests showed, his lungs were fine.

The room was quiet. Cole, Devin, and Janessa had been in half an hour ago, but now Kari had taken them home to her house. She and her husband, Ryan, were taking care of all three kids until Landon woke up. And he would wake up. Ashley stared at the clock on the wall. A little before nine in the evening. The kids planned to go to school tomorrow, and then Kari would bring them over around three, when they got out. During the day, her dad would come by the way he'd done every afternoon since the fire.

But for now she was alone with Landon ... the way she wanted to be. Only when they were alone could she utter her most intense prayers, the ones that she was sure God would hear. She stared at the man she loved, at the steady, uniform way his chest rose and fell. At first watching him breathe like that had been a comfort — because at least he was breathing. But now every breath, every movement of his chest made her cringe. Because there was nothing natural about it. The movement was mechanical, the result of a machine breathing air into him.

"Breathe, baby ... I'm here." She stood over his bed, brushing her fingers against his face, his shoulder. Along the length of his arms. "Feel me, Landon ... I'm here, baby. Breathe." She let her hand settle on his bicep, on the muscle that still bore the signs of health and life. Landon had always been strong, but more so now. Since his diagnosis. He had no guarantee what his health might become, so he spent more time than usual in the gym ... lifting weights, doing pushups. Anything to keep his strength.

She loved being in his arms, and even now it took all her willpower not to climb into bed beside him and drape his motionless arms around her body. Landon's arms that so easily could lift their children and heave a fire hose into a burning house. The arms that had hauled a man from the flames of a fully engulfed dwelling just in case he might have a chance to live.

From what she'd heard today, Dr. Jacobs said it looked like the man's wife wasn't going to make it either. They'd been in their nineties — high school sweethearts married nearly seventy years and living with their granddaughter. Everyone else in the house had made it out. She stared at her husband, at his face and his closed eyes. Even asleep he looked kind and willing to help. No matter what disease was attacking his lungs, Landon would've done it all again. He would've spent those months at Ground Zero searching for the body of his firefighter friend Jalen ... and he would've gone into the burning house looking for the old man.

It was how Landon was wired.

She closed her eyes, her hand tighter around his arm than before. *Dear Lord ... I know You are here ... and I know You hear me.* She hesitated, and for a few seconds she could remember herself praying this same sort of prayer for her dying mother. And her infant daughter. God didn't always answer prayers the way she wanted Him to, but He was always near when a person prayed. No matter how difficult the road ahead, Ashley believed that.

Still ... there was a limit to how much a person could take, right? Wasn't that why God said His people wouldn't have to fight the battles of life? *Take up your positions and see the deliverance the Lord will give you.* The verse was from 2 Chronicles 20:17, words Ashley had memorized in the past few days. Yes, God would fight for her ... and she need only take up her position and watch Him win the battle. But right now everything seemed at a stand still.

Father ... I want to trust You, I want to lean on You with every passing minute. But please, Lord ... let Landon breathe on his own. I'm not sure how much more of this I can take. Breathe life into him so that he doesn't need these machines, Father ... Thank You. Even though I don't see the answer, I thank You.

She opened her eyes and sat back down. As she did she slid her hand through the bars on the hospital bed and held onto Landon's forearm. "I'm still here, Landon ... I'll be here until you wake up."

Her Bible sat on the bedside next to him, and Ashley decided to read. This was what she loved about her time alone here. She could memorize Scripture, pray whenever she wanted, and talk to Landon. Almost like they were alone in their room back home and he were only sleeping now. She opened the Bible to the chapter in 2 Chronicles. No matter how many times she read about the battle God's people were in, and how He delivered them, the story never grew old. For only as the Israelites began to sing and praise the Lord did the enemy begin to fall.

As she read, the door opened and Cole slipped inside. His eyes were wide, as if he expected Ashley to be upset with him for returning to the hospital room. "Honey ... why are you here?" The kids were supposed to be getting ready for bed with Kari and Ryan. Ashley had no idea any of them were still here. "I thought you already left."

"Grandpa said he'd take me over there later." He came closer, his eyes on Landon. "I know you said it's quiet time now. But ... I thought if I sat on the other side of him. Maybe he might wake up if he had two of us here."

Ashley set the Bible down on the nightstand again and held out her arms to him. "Come here, Cole."

He went to her, and she stood to hug him. He was almost taller than her now, her grown-up little boy. "Thank you, buddy."

"Yeah." He stepped back. "And I didn't want you to be alone for so long."

He walked around the bed and took the chair on the other side. "Is he any better?"

Cole asked this all the time, and always Ashley hated her answer. But there was no way around it. She sighed and gave Cole her most optimistic smile. "I can't tell. But Dr. Jacobs said his lungs are doing more of the work on their own. Remember? From earlier?"

"Yes." Cole reached through the bars of the bed and took hold of his dad's other hand. For a long time he looked at Landon, clearly deep in thought. She could read the Bible later. For now she wanted to hold onto this image, the picture of Cole sitting next to Landon, probably praying for him, begging God for a miracle. "He's my real dad. Right, Mom? I mean, just because he wasn't there when I was born ..."

Ashley's heart felt like it might rip in half. She stood and went to the other side of the bed. With her hand on Cole's shoulder, she stared at Landon and searched for the right words for their son. "He's definitely your real dad."

"Yeah, because one of the guys on the baseball team was talking about his step-dad and he said that since he wasn't his biological dad, he wasn't really his dad." Cole looked back at her, squinting to keep the tears in his eyes from falling onto his cheeks. "So I just wanted to make sure ... you know? That Dad was my real dad."

This wasn't a time for lessons on biology and DNA. Cole simply needed reassuring. "Yes, this is different than a step-dad situation. You never had a real dad until Landon came along." She didn't mention that Landon might've been his biological dad, too, if only she hadn't been so stubborn in the years after high school.

Anyway, life didn't work like that. Cole was who he was because of his biological father—a married artist from Paris, who had died several years back of AIDS. Details Cole certainly didn't need to know now ... maybe ever.

"Remember my bracelet?" Cole looked at her. "The one I wore a few years ago. It said PUSH — Pray Until Something Happens."

"I remember." Ashley's heart was full for the way she loved this boy ... the way she had always loved him. "Whatever happened to it?"

"I found it last night in my sock drawer." He held up his arm and pushed his sweatshirt back. Sure enough the green rubbery bracelet was back on his arm, where he'd worn it for nearly a year back when he was nine or ten. "That's how it is now. We have to pray until something happens."

He looked at Landon, and then up at her. "You can sit down, Mom. It's okay. Read the Bible if you want. I'll keep praying."

This was Cole trying to be the man of the family, looking out for her and letting her know that he would stand sentry in prayer — so that she wasn't alone, so that she didn't have to carry this burden by herself. It was further proof of how Cole was growing up, how very much like Landon he was becoming.

She bent down and kissed his cheek. "Thanks, buddy." Once she was back in her chair, she took the Bible onto her lap. But she still didn't open it. The sight of her son and her husband together was one she couldn't break herself away from. After a few minutes, Cole began to pat Landon's hand, his forearm. And as he did he began to sing a song they'd sung in church lately ... it was by Chris Tomlin, Ashley was pretty sure.

Cole wasn't the most gifted singer, but when he reached the chorus, she had never heard a more beautiful song in all her life. "Our God is greater ... our God is stronger ... God you are higher than any other ..." His voice wasn't overly loud, but it filled the room with the peace of the Holy Spirit. Ashley slid her chair closer to the bed and held onto the scene before her.

Every word of the song Cole knew by heart — further proof of his new interest in worship songs. It sang of God being Healer and having a most awesome power, and Cole sang it for all he was worth. Ashley remembered what he'd said a month ago, how worshipping God in song was his favorite part of church. "When we're all standing and singing," he'd told her, "it's like Jesus is right there with us."

The same could be said now. *Dear Lord ... listen to that boy. Please, Father ... Let Landon hear him too. Please let him find enough strength in his lungs to wake up ... to breathe on his own without the machines. Please, God. We are at Your mercy ...*

"Our God is greater ... our God is stronger ... God you are higher than any other ..."

Cole was on his second round of singing the same song when Ashley saw something move ... something near the pillow. She was on her feet almost instantly, and across from her Cole stopped his song mid-note. "What was that?"

"I'm not sure." She stared at Landon's face, searching it for any sign of movement. "I thought I saw something ... like maybe he moved."

"Me too." Cole stood, studying Landon. "Dad, ... can you hear us?"

Then, as if he'd only been taking a nap and not unconscious since Tuesday, Landon slowly blinked and peered at Cole. First at Cole.

Ashley gasped and brought her fingers to her lips. *Dear God. Thank You ... thank You for this miracle ... thank You.*

"Hi, Dad." Cole's tears spilled onto his cheeks, but a smile stretched across his face. "Can you hear me?"

Landon ran his tongue over his lower lip and swallowed a few times. The tube in his mouth made it impossible for him to say much, but even so he managed a slight smile at Cole and he mouthed the words, "I heard ... you sing."

"Landon!" Her tears came harder than Cole's, but they were mixed with a giddy sort of laughter. He was back! Landon had come out of his coma! This was the miracle they were praying for, and now she couldn't break herself away to call his doctor. "Baby, I'm here."

He couldn't turn his head easily — too long laying here in one position. But as he heard her voice, he strained to see her. And when their eyes met, his teared up. "I ... I couldn't breathe." Every word was distorted by the tubing, and she figured it might not be wise for him to get too active.

"I know, baby ... we've been praying for you. All of us." Without taking her eyes from his, she reached for his call button and pressed it. "We all believed you would wake up. And here you are!"

"Yeah, Dad. It's been like five days." Cole laughed, but the sound was marked by the cry in his voice. "That's the longest nap ever."

Landon sent a quick smile in Cole's direction, but then he returned his gaze to Ashley. His eyes said everything his body couldn't say — not yet anyway. They told her that he hadn't wanted to die, and that with everything in him he had fought for this chance, this moment to be here with her. Alive with her. A single tear spilled out of the corner of his eye and rolled down his cheek onto his pillow. He tried to move, tried to reach up and touch her face. But there were too many wires connected to his arms, and he let his hand fall back to the bed.

"Can I help you?" It was the voice of the nurse, coming through the tinny speaker on the emergency call button.

"Yes." Ashley laughed and again the sound came out more as a cry. "My husband is awake. Can you please tell Dr. Jacobs. Someone needs to come in right away."

"Question ..." Landon looked from Ashley to Cole. "Who won ... the game?"

Both Cole and Ashley laughed out loud. "Dad, really? You even need to ask?" Cole put his hands on his hips, his chin high. "Your championship Yankees, of course."

He was clearly weak, and there was no way to tell what lay ahead. But Landon managed to give a thumbs-up to Cole just as Dr. Jacobs walked into the room. "Look at this," the doctor announced. "You're awake!"

"It was my singing." Cole put his hand on Landon's shoulder. His eyes were dry now, the joy in his face too great for tears at this point. "I was singing to him and he woke up."

Not until later, when the doctor had checked Landon's lung function enough to take him off the respirator, and even long after Cole had gone to Kari's with his grandpa, and Ashley was alone once more with Landon, did she process all that had happened that night, the way God had worked a miracle in their midst. Landon was tired—something the doctor said was to be expected. His road to recovery was still ongoing—and even then there was the next battle. The one with polymyositis. But for now one very strong truth kept her company as she watched Landon sleep—finally free of the machines and wires. Everything but his IV bag.

Like in the days of 2 Chronicles, the battle had been won not when Ashley fretted over Landon or when she cried out for help or tried to figure out what she could do to save him. Rather the battle for Landon's life was won while she merely took up her position at her husband's bedside, and in the most simple way of all.

While Cole was singing.

LANDON HAD BEEN OUT OF THE HOSPITAL for two days, long enough that the doctor had cleared him to be at this evening's

baseball game. It was the last Wednesday in April, the last game in regular season. After eight years of batting practice and fielding practice and car washes to raise money for his team ... after coming to this field several days a week every spring, it had come to this.

Cole's very last Little League game.

From here they would move to another field. Some of the kids would play in the Amateur Athletic Union league and others would choose the more established Metro team. But this, their time together on this field, where they'd grown up from T-ball ... after tonight this stage of their lives would be over.

Her dad and Elaine, her sisters, Luke, and their families — everyone had made it out for the occasion. Everyone except Dayne and Katie who were in Los Angeles working on a movie this month. Ashley looked around and she was hit by a realization. The kids were blissfully unaware of the lasts at hand, at the way the clock was stealing today a little too quickly. Of course they were unaware. Kids didn't grasp the significance of the moment. But her siblings did. Cole was the oldest of the grandchildren, but their turns were coming. The last swimming lesson. Last soccer game. Last ballet recital. Kids didn't stay that way ... it was the hardest thing about being a parent. And moments like this they could only soak it in ... hold onto every inning, the way the sun streaked through the distant trees and splashed light across the ball field, the crack of the bat, and the chatter from the dugout.

They belonged here today. Cole belonged here. But only for another handful of innings.

"Come on, Coley!" Devin was on his feet beside her. "Hit it outta the park, baby!"

Beside her on the other side, Ashley's father chuckled. "That one's going to be a handful, I have a feeling about him."

"Me too." Ashley positioned Janessa in her lap and pointed to the batter's box. "Watch Cole, Nessa … it's his turn."

Landon was in the dugout, where he wanted to be. He had his inhaler with him, but so far Dr. Jacobs had him on enough steroids that he didn't struggle to breathe. He only coughed every so often — and not like before his steroid treatment started. She watched him now, standing just outside the dugout, flashing hand signals to Cole. "That-away, Cole. Level swing … Just make contact, buddy. You got this."

From the dugout, Cole's teammates cheered him on, clinging to the chain link fence. "Come on, Big C!" Thomas bellowed at Cole.

"Yeah, come on Cole. You got this."

The kids didn't know the extent of Landon's injuries, or the severity of his time in the hospital. No one did, really. They'd managed to keep it quiet, which was what Landon wanted. Whatever the future held, they would deal with it soon. Landon had more tests in a week, and a consultation about next steps.

Already Dr. Jacobs had ordered him off work. Depending on what the last few tests showed, Landon may have fought his last fire. Something neither of them had discussed yet. Landon wanted to focus on the baseball season for now. "I feel fine," he told her on the way to the park. "I'll be back to work in a few weeks." He smiled at her, his hand on the wheel. "I'm not ready to think about the other options."

Ashley was pretty sure she'd never be ready. And for now there was no need to think about it. She looked over the shoulder of the woman in front of her. Christine was the scorekeeper, and a quick glance told Ashley what she should've already known. It was the fifth inning, top of the order. Two outs. The team they were playing was tough, but the Yankees were up one run with three runners on base.

"You see what's happening, right?" Kari leaned in from

behind. "This is probably Cole's last at-bat. One more inning and they can put this one away."

Ashley stared at her son, and uttered the sort of prayer she often said when he was up to bat, or pitching, or before he took the field. *Dear Lord ... I know wins and losses aren't the most important thing. But right now, I pray You would bless Cole beyond anything we could ask or imagine. Not for him, Father ... but to show the world what a bright light can come from a boy just twelve years old — even here in the midst of a baseball game.*

The first pitch came whizzing over the plate a little high, and Cole let it go.

"*Steeeerrrrike!*" The umpire pointed at the plate, indicating that the ball had been thrown perfectly.

Ashley raised one eyebrow, but she didn't say anything. Strikes were in the eyes of the umpire. *Anyway, Lord ... thank You. No matter what happens with Cole right now, thank You for letting him play baseball. For letting Landon coach him. I'll never forget this, Father.*

She remembered Cole's first basketball game six years ago, and how she had caught herself getting a little too involved, too enthusiastic. She'd tempered her courtside behavior since then, because what did it really matter how the ref called a game or whether a pitch really was a strike or not? What mattered was this ... her family gathered around to watch, celebrating the spirit of the game and the kids who played it.

"Come on, Big C. You got this one." Avery joined Thomas at the fence. "This is your pitch, buddy ..."

Landon stood beside them. "Nice and even. Eye on the ball, Cole." He clapped a few times, his sign of encouragement for Cole. "Here we go ..."

The pitch flew from the mound, and this time Cole swung and missed. Two strikes. The next two pitches were in the dirt, and a third went over his head. Full count. And suddenly Ashley felt knots in her stomach. This was it ... this was really it. She glanced at her sister Brooke to make sure she was videotaping. She was. Her eyes found Cole again, and she did everything in her power to memorize the moment. Cole at bat on this field they'd come to love ... the field they'd played at with these same kids year after year after year.

"I can see it, Cole ... this one's yours." That was it, all Landon said.

In a flash, the ball left the pitcher's hand and raced toward home plate. As if the play were happening in slow motion, Cole took what looked like the perfect cut at the ball, his swing level and full, his hips turning at just the right time and then —

CRACK!

The bat connected and the ball was gone ... it was gone as soon as he hit it, and everyone in both sets of stands knew it. People jumped to their feet and the Yankees dugout burst into shouts and hoots and hollers. And sure enough, the ball sailed over the fence and into the distant field where a couple of young boys — T-ball boys — ran after it.

"Homerun!" The team shouted in celebration.

All around her people were cheering and shouting Cole's name. "That's a grand slam, baby! Grand slam for the Yankees!"

Above the other sounds, Ashley heard the one voice that was only in the mix because God had worked a miracle that week. The voice of Landon. "Way to go, son! That-a-boy ... way to go!" Landon led the team out of the dugout and onto the field toward home base as Cole followed the other base runners around first and second and kept running.

"Cole running!" Janessa pointed at her brother.

"Yes, baby. Cole's running all the way around!"

"Homerun!" Devin jumped up and down on the bleacher beside her. "My brother hit a homerun!"

Ashley brought her hands to her face and watched, watched

every stride and the way Cole's smile stretched beneath his batting helmet. The way his cleats kicked up the dust with each step and the joy with which he stepped on each base as he ran. She didn't dare blink or look away or do anything but hold onto the moment. Past second base Cole pointed one finger to heaven — his way of thanking God, like he'd done the two other times he'd hit a homerun this season.

The entire team gathered at home plate, and Cole rounded third and headed toward them. Again he pointed up, and then he pointed at them, his teammates, the players he'd grown up with at this ballpark. All of them were there ... Thomas and Avery and Mitchell ... Nick and Michael and Derek and Eric. Kids who had learned the game together. Kids who had won and lost together, and who would now have to learn how to say goodbye together.

How to leave this Little League field and move on.

Cole's sandlot boys.

As soon as he touched home base, the boys surrounded him, slapping his back and holding his hand in the air, pumping their fists and celebrating the win. The game wasn't over, but fifteen minutes later, when Avery made the last out catching a pop-up at short-stop, it was. The Yankees had won ... and as Ashley stood and cheered with the other parents, she didn't mind the tears that streamed down her face. There was no telling what lay ahead for Landon. For their family. But tonight ... on a warm spring Wednesday at the end of April, Cole had won his last Little League game.

Sometime after the last out, the T-ball boy who had found Cole's homerun ball ran it over to him, his eyes big as he looked up to Cole. It was easy to read the admiration in his face, and Ashley listened from her place in the bleachers. "Here, Cole ... you were great tonight!"

"Thanks, bud." Cole took the ball and gave the boy a high five. Then without hesitating, he walked over to Landon and tapped him on the arm. Ashley knew what he was about to do, but his actions brought tears to her eyes anyway. Cole hugged his father for a long while. He said something to Landon, probably thanking him for coaching the season, and for being the best dad ever. The sort of thing Cole often said. Then he handed Landon his home-run ball. And after another hug, he ran off with his teammates.

Landon must've felt her watching, because he looked straight at her and held up the ball. Even from across the field, Ashley could see Landon's eyes glistening. Because how many little boys had the chance to end their Little League career with a grand slam homerun? And because how wonderful it was that Landon was Cole's father ... and that he was here ... alive for a game like this.

He tucked the ball in his pocket and returned to the boys — all of whom were forming a group so that the team photographer could snap pictures. Capturing the moment for the record books. Like the other parents, Ashley stayed while the league commissioner awarded the Yankees their first-place medals. And while the boys cleaned trash from the dugout. And as the dads joined Landon on the field raking down the dirt infield for the next game ... the next team. Ashley watched all of it, watched while the boys hugged each other, all laughter and loud voices ... replaying the highlights and Cole's homerun again and again and again. No tears for these boys, not tonight.

It wouldn't hit them until later — when they were home and sorting through their photos and trophies — what had just happened. That their time together was over. But maybe that was better. Because it allowed Ashley and the other parents to stand here, mesmerized ... watching their boys in their Yankees uniforms collecting bats and working as a team this one last time. Until every last one of them gathered his gear bag and headed off with his parents. Until these Yankees faded from view and the field stood empty of Cole's sandlot boys.

For now and all time.

Twenty-Two

BAILEY'S BEDROOM FLOOR WAS ALMOST PERFECTLY CLEAR. Brandon had helped a lot, as it turned out. Sorting through her things and organizing clothes into one corner of the room, school work and books in another, and memories — as he called them — in another.

It was early Wednesday afternoon, which meant she was leaving in four days.

She and her mom would fly out together, and her mom would stay most of the week to help her get situated and to assess the safety of her neighborhood and the walk she would have to take to the theater each day. Together they would take four suitcases, packed to overflowing. Until yesterday they weren't sure if Bailey would have to live in a hotel for the first few weeks, but finally, around six last night, the production assistant called with good news.

"We found the perfect place," his New York accent was thick, but Bailey understood every word. She held her breath waiting for the details. "It's an older couple with an apartment three blocks down from the theater. He used to be a producer, and now he's an investor. He and his wife take in dancers from out of town ... with a couple restrictions."

Bailey was thrilled. She grabbed a piece of paper and a pen. "Go ahead."

The man went on to explain that the couple wouldn't tolerate drinking or smoking. "And here's the one that usually makes them a tougher placement option," he hesitated. "No guys in your room."

A quiet ripple of laughter slipped from Bailey's lips before she could stop herself.

"Hmmm ... so that's a no, I take it then."

"Wait." Bailey laughed again. "Sorry. No ... I mean, it's a yes. It sounds perfect."

"No pets, either." He was clearly reading from a list.

"Fine. I don't have pets." Her family did, and she would miss them ... their four cats and two dogs. But she wouldn't have considered bringing a pet to New York City. Bailey checked her notepad. She didn't have any notes jotted down yet except one — the word *perfect*. "Is that it? What's the rent?"

"Cheap. Just two hundred dollars a month." He paused. "And it comes furnished. How's that sound?"

"Like a dream." Bailey was amazed, too baffled to believe the situation was as good as it sounded. "What's the catch?"

"None." It was his turn to chuckle. "Usually the dancers have one of those vices, you know ... smoking or drinking. And if not, then they sure don't want any parent-figure telling them they can't bring guys into their bedroom. Last Broadway dancer to stay at the Owens house was three years ago."

Bailey thanked the man, and he gave her the other details. The couple's names, their address and phone numbers. He assured Bailey they'd be expecting her and her mother Sunday afternoon. They even had theater tickets to *Mary Poppins* and wanted to know if the two of them might want them — since they'd be out to dinner with friends that evening.

The phone call ended and Bailey rushed to tell her mom and dad. None of them could imagine a better scenario, and after she'd shared all the details, her dad did what they always tried to do when God had clearly answered one of their prayers. He put his

arms around their shoulders, bowed his head, and prayed — the
sort of moment she would miss like crazy once she was gone.

And she would be gone far too soon.

She checked the time on her watch — not quite two o'clock.
Shopping could be done once she got to New York, but she and
her mom wanted to make a trip to Target for a few last minute
hair and makeup items — the things she wasn't sure she'd find easily in Manhattan. "You in here?" Her mom sounded sad. It wasn't
something anyone else would've noticed. But Bailey was that
close to her — and she was sure. Her tone wasn't what it would
usually be on a sunny spring Saturday morning.

"Yep." Bailey poked her head out of her bathroom door.
"Tackling the drawers in here."

"Wow." Her mom joined her, leaning against the bathroom
counter. "Your room will be cleaner than it ever was when you
lived here."

"I know." Bailey smiled. She stopped for a moment and looked
behind her at her clean floor and neatly made bed. Every drawer
and inch of her closet had been gone through and organized. She
faced her mom again. "I feel like I sorted through my childhood
and said goodbye to half of it."

"Me too." Her mom's eyes were filled with yesterday. "I can
still see you in my arms, the day we brought you home." She
laughed, but it came out sounding something like a cry. "The
nurse walked with us out to our little blue Honda, and we had to
work to figure out how to buckle you in."

"That must've been crazy … I mean, babies don't come with
a manual."

"Exactly." She shook her head, the memory still dancing in
her eyes. "I remember the nurse sort of made a face like, 'Good
luck,'" her mom sighed, and folded her arms in front of her. "Your
dad and I climbed in the car, and before he started the engine he
looked at me and hesitated. Then he said, 'I have no idea how to

do this, do you?' Well ... after I laughed for a minute, I had to agree. I had no idea, either."

Bailey loved this, when her mom remembered back to when Bailey was a little girl. "It's weird, because I can't remember any of that. But for you ... watching me leave. All of that probably feels like it just happened."

"Like it was last week." She smiled, but a tear slid down her cheek. She laughed at herself, unable to stop the tears that followed. "I'm sorry, honey. I promised myself I wouldn't do this."

"Ahh, Mom." Bailey went to her and they hugged for a long time. "I'll be back. You know that."

"Of course." She sniffed, trying desperately to keep the moment light. "It just won't be ..." She waved at the room behind them. "It won't be the same." She wiped her eyes and lightly she touched Bailey's hair, her cheek. "I was up with you at three a.m., wondering what I was doing wrong and why you wouldn't stop crying ... and I sat on the floor, telling myself I would never find a way to potty train a one-year-old ... and we worked through geometry problems on the dining room table until I thought the semester would last forever."

"Or at least three years." Bailey gave her mom a nervous smile. "I'm sorry about that. I never was very good with math."

"But the point is ..." another tear slid onto her cheek, "I thought those stages would last forever. I mean, I knew better." She laughed again, fighting what seemed like an endless well of missing. "Everyone told me, 'Hold onto every minute ... it won't be like this forever,' and I would smile and nod and think, 'she'll never sleep through the night.'" She reached for Bailey's hand. "And now ... just like that you're all grown up and leaving."

"I remember feeling like high school was a lifetime away."

"Exactly ..." Her mom stepped back and dabbed at her eyes once more. "I guess it's just ... being in your room and seeing it

all cleaned." She glanced at Bailey's bedroom again. "Reminds me that we don't have much time left."

Something about her mother's words struck a nerve, and Bailey could feel her expression change. She didn't have long at all, and what about Cody? He didn't even know she was moving. She and her mom walked back into her room and they sat on the sofa near her window, turned in, facing each other. Her mom still had hold of her hand. Bailey pushed thoughts of Cody from her mind. "That was nice of Brandon ... flying out to help me."

"It was." Her mom seemed grateful for the distraction, anything but talking about how soon Bailey would be gone. "Has he called?"

"He texts me every day. But no ... we haven't talked."

Her mom was quiet for a long moment. "He's very nice, Bailey." Her mom sniffed, a thoughtfulness in her tone. "So much different from when we first met him. I don't know ..."

Bailey smiled, but she understood what her mom meant. "He won't let up, that's for sure. The way he talks about us ... his feelings for me. It used to be more like he was teasing. But now ..." She shrugged slowly. "Now I have to really think about the two of us ... whether it could ever work."

"You don't have to, honey."

"No, I didn't mean it like that. I mean ... I love being with him, and I can see it, the two of us ... it's complicated, I guess."

Her mom watched her, waiting for a long time before she spoke. "Why do I have the feeling you weren't thinking about Brandon when you first switched subjects?"

"Hmmm ... yes." She smiled and released her mom's hand. Leaning the other direction she reached for the framed picture of Cody and her. "I see this every day, and I can't believe he hasn't contacted me." She set the picture back down. "You said there wasn't much time left ... and I thought how crazy it is ... Cody doesn't even know I'm moving."

The hesitation that followed made it feel like her mom knew more than she had said. "Dad talked to Ryan Taylor an hour ago ... I guess he found out Cody's the new varsity coach at Lyle High. That's one of the reasons I came up here."

"What?" This was the first news they'd heard about him since January. Bailey's mind raced. "Where's Lyle?"

"It's a small school northeast of Indianapolis toward the Ohio border."

"That far?" Bailey felt her eyes widen. She returned the photograph to the end table. "So that's like what, three hours from here?"

"Your dad and I looked it up on the map. It's more like two hours ... maybe a little less."

Bailey didn't want to acknowledge the hurt in her heart, but there was no getting around it. "He's coaching in another city? And he didn't call?"

"He did try stopping by ..." Her mom winced, as if she hated to bring up Cody's recent attempt to reach out to her.

Like a hundred times before, Bailey could see his eyes again, looking at her in his rearview mirror as he pulled away. "You're right. He did ... maybe because he's basically changed everything about his life in the last four months."

"Coach Taylor said the position came about quickly. And Cody's still living in Indianapolis, taking classes at night and commuting to the school every day. He teaches PE too."

Bailey's mind raced and she felt dizzy, so much that she wondered if she might fall off the couch. They had known everything about Cody for years. Now ... to think he'd moved on to a fulltime career and a head-coaching job without telling them ... it was one more bit of proof, right? "He really doesn't want anything to do with us." She lifted her eyes to her mom's. "I mean, how else can we read that?"

This time her mom had no answer. She looked down for a

few seconds and shook her head. "Your dad and I just got through saying the same thing." Her tone found a level of hope again. "We did decide that we'll invite him for dinner sometime. After you're gone."

Bailey wanted to ask why they would wait until then, but she understood. The feelings she and Cody had shared not so long ago complicated the relationship between him and her family. "I wish you and I could go see him … so I could tell him goodbye."

"Bailey …" She didn't need to say anything. Her expression — though kind — said it all.

"I know," she breathed in, trying to put him out of her mind, "like a dying man in the desert." She smiled, but that didn't stop the fresh pain these new details brought. Why would he start a new life out there and not text her … not call her parents? Did he really think stopping by her house one time was all the attempt he needed to make? She stood and picked up a list off the end of her bed. "Want to run errands with me?" The ache in her heart wasn't going away any time soon, but she needed to get things done.

"Target?"

"Yes, and I still need to stop by Walgreens for those prints." She had picked out a bunch of pictures from her family's photo library, and she and her mom had ordered prints online. Some of them would go on Bailey's wall in her new room, and the rest would go in an album.

She guessed the photos would become the favorite part of her new living space.

"Sounds good." Her mom stood and headed toward the door. "Meet downstairs in five?"

"Perfect." Bailey waited until she was gone before returning to the picture of Cody and her. How could she leave Indianapolis without talking to him? Without at least telling him that she was moving and letting him know how she felt — that she didn't want him running off the other day and that he should've called. Or at least texted. Suddenly, without giving the matter any real thought, she picked up her phone, found his number, and dialed it. Her heart pounded as she dropped to the end of her bed and waited.

One ring ... two ...

She could do this, right? He had been a part of her life since she was a freshman in high school. Telling him she was moving was the least she could do.

Three rings ... four. His voice came on the line telling her to leave a message, and for a few seconds she let him talk, let the recording play out. The sound of his voice felt that good against the rough edges of her heart. But at the last second she didn't know what to say, didn't know how to bridge the span of time with a simple voicemail. She hung up, and a plan began to form in her mind.

She and her mom could make their couple stops and still have time to drive to Indianapolis. Maybe even to Lyle. The boys were staying late at school, and Dad could pick them up later. Besides, she and her mom would enjoy the adventure, right? One of their last before Bailey moved. They could use the GPS to find Lyle High, and surprise him ... show up at his practice so he would know how much they cared. Forget the dying man in the desert business. Cody had been her friend before any other feelings complicated matters. Bailey smiled at the idea, and just like that her heart felt lighter than it had all week. She was going to see Cody! She grinned as she ran down the stairs.

Now she only had to convince her mother.

Twenty-Three

DARK CLOUDS GATHERED OVERHEAD AS CODY WALKED OUT TO the Lyle practice field. He was running later than usual, stopped by a parent who had dropped by during his last PE class to talk. The man had been full of compliments, telling Cody that years had passed since anyone had cared about the football players at Lyle.

"You'll have 'em whipped into shape in no time," the man wore a flannel and Wranglers, and he could barely talk for the wad of tobacco stuffed behind his lower lip. Cody was pretty sure the guy owned the feed store at the end of town. After just a few months already he could put a face to nearly every shop along Main Street — mostly because the Lyle men had started coming out to watch spring practice.

A buzz was in the air. Coach Oliver was gone and hope lived for the Buckaroo football program.

As Cody reached the field he did a quick count. Twenty-seven men along the outer fence — many of them with the look and limp of retirees — all out to watch today's scrimmage. The townspeople weren't the only ones who had taken notice of the change in the football program. Talk around school had brought another two dozen players to the spring practices. Every day the bond between them grew, and gradually Cody was learning their stories.

DeMetri lived alone with his mother in tenement housing on the outskirts of town. Last week the player confided in Cody that sometimes his mother got in a little trouble. Cody didn't push for specifics, but that conversation was coming. He wondered if DeMetri had any idea how closely Cody could relate to his situation.

There was Marcos Brown — a six-foot-five lineman whose highest grade was a D in music. His father was in prison, and his mother had died of the flu three years ago. Marcos lived with his cousin's family and spent every day after school working his uncle's farm. Homework was considered a sign of weakness.

Arnie Hurley was the team's quarterback, a good kid with average grades. But talk was that Arnie spent most nights at his girlfriend's house. Her bedroom window was an easy access, and her parents didn't care what the girl did in her spare time. As long as the guy sneaking in was quarterback of the football team.

Two of the offensive line were rumored to be alcoholics — drinking so much on the weekends that more than once Cody had seen burst blood vessels in their eyes Monday at practice.

The kids weren't all bad — just an average mix of high school boys searching for significance and scared to death about what to do after graduation. More of that in a small town, Cody had learned since he'd been here. College wasn't a given for these kids, and sometimes they couldn't see past Friday night.

There were a few guys who had started praying with DeMetri. LeSean Peters, Andrew King, Josh Corothers. Guys who could smell change in the air and weren't willing to settle for defeat or mediocrity. Corothers was president of the school's Christian club. Cody planned to learn a lot more about his players between now and summer. Already he was working out the details of taking the boys to camp. Like everyone else in town, he wanted a winning season this fall.

But more than that he wanted players who were winners at life. He was almost to the end zone, where most of the guys were

already stretching and coming together, when two of the men approached him.

"Howdy, Coach," the bigger of the two stepped up first and shook Cody's hand. "If you don't mind, me and Verne here would like a minute of your time."

Verne nodded, polite the way Lyle prided itself on being. But his smile seemed forced.

Cody was about to explain that he couldn't talk. Practice was already running later than he wanted, but the man didn't wait for his answer. "Anyway, thing is our boys are the running backs. Talk is a few new boys came out this past week and they might look to take the starting positions."

Was this really happening? When it wasn't even May yet? Cody stopped and squinted at the men. "I don't have a starting lineup yet, gentlemen. Let's talk about it then." He thanked them and walked away. As he did he heard the big guy mutter something about Cody being too young to make a lineup, let alone coach it to a winning season.

This was something he hadn't expected — the way parents talked. Maybe he would have a big barbecue here at the school before summer. Let everyone know that he was ready for the challenge ahead, and welcome them to share their thoughts whenever they wanted. He was certainly open to suggestions. Just not manipulation.

"All right," he yelled over the din of conversation among the townsmen on the adjacent sideline. "Bring it in. This is a big day, men."

The scrimmage would stage his top offense against his second team defense for a series of ten plays. Then he would switch and give his best defense a shot at the second-string offense. He would've liked to have the top teams go against each other, but six of the guys played both ways, so that wouldn't be possible.

"This is about plays and play-breakers, gentlemen." He

looked at each of the guys, one at a time. "No contact. If you're touched, you're down." He explained the rules of two-hand touch and then held up his clipboard. "If I call your name, you're first team offense." He glanced at the dads on the sidelines and looked right at the bigger guy. "This is the lineup for today only." He turned back to the players. "Don't gripe about where you think you should be. Let your play do the talking, men. You're winners. All of you."

Cody was halfway through the list, reading the names and second-guessing whether he'd found the right mix of players for each team when from two blocks down came the sound of tires screeching loud and long and then a blood-curdling, deafening crash.

"Dear God ... what happened?" One of the older men cried out, and everyone stopped and turned toward the sound.

The screech of glass and twisted metal still rang in the air, and Cody felt his face go white, his knees weak. Whatever had just happened, the sound was as horrific as anything Cody had ever heard. In a rush, the townsmen hurried from the field and rushed down the street toward the sound of the crash.

Cody did a quick count of his players. They were all there, each man. But the victim might've been a teacher leaving school or a parent coming to watch practice or any of the other Lyle residents — all of whom were connected somehow. Cody needed to know, needed to assure the boys that everything was okay and they could carry on with practice.

"DeMetri," his voice rose above the murmuring among the players. "Lead the guys in the first three stretching drills." He set his clipboard down and took off at a run. "I'll be back."

It was crazy, really ... his almost desperate need to go to the crash and see who was hurt, how the wounded might be connected to Lyle High. Cody's heart pounded in time with his feet as he passed the older men and made it one block, then two. Cars were stopped and already sirens were blaring through town. He tugged on his baseball cap, shading his eyes as he strained to see beyond the gathering crowd, beyond the commotion.

Only then did he catch a glimpse of something that made him stop cold. The tangled wreck had come to a stop twenty yards from the intersection. A delivery truck and ... and ... He couldn't feel his hands or his feet, but he had to keep running, had to reach the scene of the accident, because the other car ... the other car was as familiar to him as his name.

"No," he whispered out loud as he ran. "Please, God ... no." He passed people pouring out of their houses and parking their cars in the middle of the road to look in on the mangled vehicles. "Please, God ..."

But the closer Cody came to the scene, the more certain he became. The truck must've run a stop sign, because it had crashed square into the side of a yellow Volkswagen.

The same exact type Cheyenne drove.

Emergency vehicles were racing up to the intersection, and paramedics were flying from their vehicles, sprinting toward the wreck. As Cody ran up, people were lined two and three deep along the street, their hands to their mouths. Two guys from the hardware store across the street were pulling on the door of the yellow VW. "Over here," one of them shouted. "We can't reach her."

Her.

Cody stopped running, and everything around him went into a horrifying slow motion. The man had said *her*, which could only mean ... *Not Cheyenne, please, Lord* ... if it was her, then she was coming to watch his scrimmage. She hadn't called, but then she usually didn't. Just showed up, proud of him and ready to support him.

He had to move, had to make his way to her car door, but as he did the scene changed and he wasn't in Lyle, but in a sandstorm outside Basra and bullets were flying everywhere and beside him

... right beside him his buddy was saying, "We gotta get out of here ... run for — " and before he could finish his sentence a bullet hit the guy square in the face.

"No!" Cody screamed, but he wasn't sure any longer if he was screaming here or in the flashback, and he was dropping to his knees next to his buddy and trying to find the pieces of his face, grabbing at sand and flesh and wanting desperately to put the guy back together, and someone was pulling on his arm, pulling him up off the ground.

Cody blinked, his breathing hard, his fists clenched, and suddenly he was looking into the eyes of a businessman, a banker maybe. A guy with a white shirt and tie. "You're the new football coach, right? Cody Coleman?"

Fear and embarrassment collided in his mind, and he scrambled to his feet. What was he doing on the ground? The flashbacks again ... he couldn't escape them. "I ... I must've tripped." He dusted off his jeans and stared back at the wreck. "I think ... I might ... I might know the girl in that car."

"I'm sorry." The banker stepped back, helpless.

Cody moved into the street, closer to the mangled yellow bug. The truck had hit her passenger side, but at this point it was hard to make out any part of the car. More sirens sounded in the distance, and police and a fire truck arrived on the scene. "Get the jaws," someone yelled. "She's trapped. Hurry up ... we're losing her."

Losing her ... Losing the driver of the yellow bug? Were they losing Cheyenne? Cody kept walking, fighting back the feeling of sand against his skin and the baking sweat of the sun on his back. *No*, he told himself. *I'm not in Iraq ... God, please, keep me in the moment. If it's her ... God, please ... don't let her die.*

"Excuse me," a paramedic stopped him. "You'll have to stand back. We're bringing machinery in here."

"But I think I — " Cody didn't finish his sentence. He couldn't

finish it. Because at that moment he saw what used to be the back window of the Volkswagen lying in pieces on the road. And the piece Cody couldn't take his eyes off had a simple bumper sticker that read Indiana University Nursing Program. The same sticker Cody had stared at the other day for half an hour as he followed Cheyenne to the hospital outside Indianapolis. So there was no doubt now, the woman trapped in the car was Cheyenne.

He wanted to fight his way past the paramedics until he was at her side, because maybe they'd missed something. He'd fought his way through battles worse than this, so there might be a way to get the car door off without using the jaws of life, right? He could rip the metal apart with his bare hands if he had to. Anything to reach her, to hold her and beg her to hang on.

But people were staring at him, and the paramedic needed to get back to work. So Cody did the only thing he could do. He stepped back to the curb, moved past the gawking bystanders and the banker, and he found a quiet doorway. Then he dropped to his knees and began to pray. As he did, as he prayed believing that somehow Cheyenne would live through this nightmare, he promised God that he would do whatever he could to help her. Behind him he could hear the machine being moved in, the wretched sounds of the jaws of life as it set to work to free Cheyenne from the wreckage.

Was Tara right, Lord? Did You save me back in Iraq so that I'd be here now for Cheyenne? The possibility was so real it consumed him. *Please, God ... Let her live.* He cared about her more than he had allowed himself to believe. She was one of the sweetest girls he'd ever met ... he knew that now. She had to live ... he hadn't had time to tell her how he felt, to let her know how much he valued her friendship.

The machines roared to life, filling the air with deafening sounds of metal on metal. "Watch her head," someone shouted.

Please, God ... Keep her alive.

As he tried not to listen to the voices shouting about CPR and blood loss and the victim's spinal cord, he became absolutely convinced of one thing. If Cheyenne lived through this, he would be at her side when she woke up.

And every step of the way after that.

Twenty-Four

ONE BUSY DAY HAD BLENDED INTO ANOTHER, AND BAILEY STILL hadn't made it out to Lyle High to see Cody. But all of that would change this morning. With every passing hour her determination to see him had grown. She had pulled together a shoebox full of items she'd found when she cleaned her room. Things that belonged to him ... items that would remind him of his past with her. She could hardly wait to hit the road.

Her mother knew she was seeing Cody this morning, and she'd offered to go along. But today was another scrimmage for the boys at Clear Creek High, and their mom was in charge of the team's sub sandwich lunch. Bailey planned to head out to Indianapolis as soon as possible. That way she could be back before kickoff for the late afternoon scrimmage.

It was ten o'clock and already she'd been up for three hours, gathering the items for the box, showering, and getting dressed. Now she was finally ready to head out, but she wanted to check the box first ... make sure she wasn't forgetting anything. She sat on the edge of her sofa and sorted through the contents.

There was a small stuffed Tigger — a carnival prize she'd won for Cody at the Indianapolis state fair a few summers ago. Her whole family had gone, and Cody had come with them. They'd teased each other about whether he would win something for her first or the other way around. At first neither of them won a thing, but then they sat side by side and played the squirt gun contest, each of them aiming a stream of water through the mouth of a clown. When the balloons burst, out of all ten contestants, she and Cody tied.

He gave her a stuffed Winnie the Pooh, and she gave him the Tigger. Her prize sat on the shelf next to the picture of Cody and her. But his had somehow wound up in a box of mementos and memories she'd pushed to the back of her closet years ago. It was one of the things she'd found while cleaning her room.

The same was true for the broken pair of sunglasses at the back of one of her bookshelves. Last Fourth of July at Lake Monroe, when everything about life and love had seemed too perfect for anything to ruin it, Cody had run down the beach a stretch to catch a pass from Justin. But as he snagged the football, his sunglasses fell to the shore, and at almost the same instant Ricky landed square on them — snapping them in two.

Cody had picked up the identical pieces, laughing like crazy. "You couldn't do that again if you tried."

Ricky ran up, his face a mask of guilt. "Cody ... I didn't mean to ... I didn't see them until I stepped on them and — "

"It's okay ... no big deal." Cody had given Ricky a kind pat on the back. "I bought 'em at a gas station." Then, still laughing, he ran the pieces over to Bailey. As he did, he took one half of the broken glasses and slipped it over his ear. He looked beyond goofy as he handed her the other half. "Here. Quick ... put this on."

Bailey had been laughing since Ricky's ill-fated move. She took the other half and slid it over her ear. "How do I look?"

"Perfect." Cody stood straight, mustering up his most official expression. "Now ... if we ever don't see eye-to-eye, we'll pull these out. That should solve the problem." They both burst into another round of giggles and chuckles, and after a few seconds, they fell to the sand in laughter, the broken glasses hanging off both their faces.

Bailey let the memory fade as she ran her fingers over the broken sunglasses. She kept the other half. Just because. The box

also held a friendship ring Bailey had given him her junior year of high school. She'd bought it at the Bible bookstore in Blooming-ton, and at the time she'd told him he didn't have to wear it. "It's more the meaning of it that counts," she'd told him. "I've never had a friend like you, Cody."

But the amazing thing was he *had* worn it. He wore it every day through half that year until somehow, somewhere along the way he must've left it in the kitchen or on a bathroom counter. Maybe before playing basketball with the boys. Rings could get caught on the rim — especially if a guy dunked. So maybe that was it. Either way, the ring had wound up in her room, shoved to the back of her top desk drawer and mixed in with an assortment of broken pencils and dried up markers and pens. The ring had a Bible verse engraved on the outside — the verse Cody loved most. *Philippians 4:13 — I can do all things through Christ who gives me strength.*

She'd found a few of his paperbacks and a handful of old *Sports Illustrated* magazines that he'd set aside downstairs. They were in the box too. The last thing she'd done was thumb through a number of her journal entries. Most of them were private, and they would remain so. But once in a while she'd used her journal to write Cody a letter, some musings about whether they would ever be more than friends, or some private bit of encouragement for him.

If she was going to find him and tell him goodbye before she moved to New York, then she wanted him to remember every-thing about her. Not just the past year, or the way he had felt compelled to run when his mother was put back in prison. But all of it ... the bond they'd shared as far back as her early high school days. So she'd copied a handful of entries, folded the pages, and laid them on top.

It was all there — everything she wanted to give him. She placed the lid on the box, and checked her look in the mirror once more. She wore a pale blue turtleneck and new jeans. Her long hair fell in curls alongside her face and down her back. No big deal, she told herself. She should look nice, right? It was her last full day in Bloomington.

The house was empty as she took the box to her car and set out for Indianapolis. Her first stop was the prison ... because she wanted to tell Cody's mom goodbye, and because she had no idea how to find him, otherwise. Bailey focused on the highway ahead, glad the roads were empty this morning. The week had been crazy enough without having to fight city traffic today.

She stared at the road ahead of her and thought about how much her life had changed since January. The part in *Hairspray*, her move to New York City, and of course her deepening friendship with Brandon Paul. Every day she felt her doubts about dating Brandon erode a little more. Life was too short to worry about paparazzi and magazine covers and Hollywood starlets. Brandon was worth a little inconvenience — especially after he'd taken the trip to Indiana to help her pack.

His charm left her dizzy at times, and there were long moments when she'd catch herself thinking about him, wishing for the next time when they might be together. Already Brandon had plans to fly to New York and take her to dinner. Sometime in the next two weeks, as long as his schedule of retakes allowed it. "And we're going to do that love story together someday ... I'll make sure of it." He had told her that yesterday when he called.

"We'll see ..." she had laughed lightly at the idea. From what she heard, it could be years before Brandon's agent would let him make that movie.

"Bailey," Brandon's voice softened, and even across the phone lines she felt the impact of her name on his lips. "I'm not talking about a movie. I'm talking about us."

Bailey tightened her grip on the wheel. Clouds gathered in the distance and she hoped it wouldn't rain. Her dad planned to barbecue tonight, and all of them wanted to eat outside on the back patio. Bailey's last dinner at home.

She pulled into the prison parking lot just as her phone vibrated. Once her car was parked, she glanced at the message window and saw it was a text from Brandon. She smiled, and a part of her heart warmed at the sight of his name.

No doubt, Brandon's attention was an unexpected blessing in this season of her life. Without him, she would've thought about Cody every day ... wondering about him, staying angry at him. Instead, she no longer allowed herself to believe Cody would come back, that he would change his mind and want her in his life again. She missed him, yes. The way she would always miss him. But Brandon had shown her something she desperately needed to know.

Cody wasn't the only guy who could turn her head.

Bailey locked the car and crossed the prison parking lot. A pang of guilt hit her, because the last time she was here she had promised herself she'd visit Cassie Coleman every weekend. Or at least once a month. Instead she hadn't been back since that day in January. The last time she'd seen Cody.

She walked up the stairs and through the front doors where it took thirty minutes while the guards notified Cody's mother that she had a visitor. Finally Bailey was led through a familiar series of hallways and doors to a room where Cody's mother sat waiting for her at a round table. She smiled through teary eyes as Bailey walked up, and for a brief moment she stood, and they shared a hug — an awkward moment since Mrs. Coleman wore handcuffs.

They both sat down, and for a few seconds Cody's mom stared at her hands, chained in front of her. "I've ... I've been praying for you, Bailey." She lifted her eyes, and the familiar shame was still there. "Every day I've prayed."

"Thank you." Bailey had never been close to the woman,

mostly because they'd only been together in person a handful of times. "I'm sorry it's been so long ..."

"That's okay." She was quick to dismiss the idea that Bailey should've been by sooner. "Bloomington's a long way from here."

New York was farther ... Bailey took a deep breath and explained why she was here, how she was moving away, but she had a box of Cody's things and she wanted to see him today. If that was possible. "We haven't talked." Bailey felt the same sadness in her heart. She still couldn't believe Cody had let this much time pass.

"He told me ... he came by one afternoon." She raised her eyes to Bailey's. "You ... you have someone else now, is that right?"

She was talking about Brandon Paul ... Bailey smiled, not sure what to say about him. "I have a friend, yes. He was over when Cody came by last time." She thought about dismissing Brandon, telling Cody's mother that he meant nothing to her. But that was no longer true, so she left it at that. "What about Cody ... is he seeing anyone?"

It was the question she had dreaded, but she needed to know the truth, needed the complete picture if she was going to find him later today. Mrs. Coleman sighed and fidgeted for a long while before she looked up again. "Yes ... Cody has a friend."

The words hit like so many rocks, pelting her soul and making her wonder if this wasn't some kind of nightmare. Cody loved only her, right? So how could he have moved on so quickly? But as soon as the question filled her mind, an obvious train of thoughts followed. She had Brandon Paul, a friend who had replaced the everydayness of Cody. So how could she be upset? She nodded ... ignoring the sting of tears in her eyes. "Are ... are they serious?"

"I'm not sure, really ..." Mrs. Coleman looked nervous. "The girl ... she was in a terrible car accident a few days ago. Cody's with her right now — at the hospital in town." Another long sigh from Cody's mother. "She was on her way to surprise him this

past Wednesday ... to watch his football team. But she was hit by a truck before ... before she reached the school."

On Wednesday? The accident happened then? That was the day Bailey had wanted her mom to drive with her out to his school, only their errands had taken too long and they hadn't gone. But if they had ... they might've been there when this ... Bailey dismissed the thoughts. "How badly is she hurt?"

"Bad." Cody's mother shook her head, her eyes dark with concern. "She hasn't woken up, but ... they used that machine to get her out of the car and now," she shrugged, her eyes welling up again. "Her brain ... her back ... they're not sure how bad it is."

Bailey had no idea what to do with the information. Cody had found someone else, and now she was severely injured. Even at this moment he was sitting at her bedside. "Do you think he'd mind ... if I stopped by?"

A look of deep apology came over Mrs. Coleman, and she slid her cuffed hands across the table toward Bailey. "He has always loved you, Bailey."

She covered the woman's fingers with her own. "I've always loved him."

"Then go to him." She sniffed, struggling to keep her composure. "Take him whatever it is that belongs to him, and tell him goodbye. He would want that ... I'm sure."

They talked for a few more minutes — about the Bible study Cody's mom was doing with a group of fellow inmates, and about how God continued to speak to her. "I actually enjoy being here." Her smile was weak, but sincere. "Because for the first time, God truly has my attention."

Their visit drew to an end and Bailey hugged her once more. She wrote down the name of the hospital where the girl was a patient, and before she left she asked Mrs. Coleman just one more question. "What's the girl's name? I'll probably need that."

"Cheyenne." Mrs. Coleman's eyes held Bailey's, as if she didn't want Bailey to walk out of their lives now or any time in the future. "Her name is Cheyenne."

As soon as Bailey heard the name, she felt her knees give way ever so slightly. Cheyenne? The former fiancée of Cody's buddy, Art Collins? That's who he was seeing now? She stuffed her questions in the basement of her heart, thanked Cody's mom again, and walked back to her car. Along the way she remembered how Cody had sworn he wasn't interested in her. She'd been invited to a dinner thrown by Art's mom in Indianapolis. And once Cody had accidentally sent Bailey a text he'd intended for Cheyenne. But he had promised her he didn't see her as anything more than a friend — the grieving former love of one of his closest friends from Iraq.

Either way, she could hardly be mad. The girl was fighting for her life by the sounds of it. Bailey would simply go to the hospital, bring the box up to the girl's room, and ask for a few minutes with Cody in the hallway. Then she'd do once and for all what she should have done last January.

She'd end things with Cody Coleman for good.

Twenty-Five

THE WHIR OF MACHINES WAS REASSURING ONLY BECAUSE IT reminded Cody that Cheyenne was alive. For now, anyway. He sat in a chair beside her bed, and across from him, Tara Collins sat in the other one. They had kept vigil next to her since she'd been brought in — Tara around the clock, since she had sick time she could use from work. As for Cody, other than school and football hours, he was here.

This morning's practice let out early so he could hurry back, sit by her side. He'd only been here a few minutes when the doctor appeared at the door. He knocked lightly and stepped inside. "Hello." He had been by a few times, so the man was familiar. He knew that Tara and Cody were the only family Cheyenne had.

"What's the latest?" Tara was on her feet, her arms crossed. Worry deepened the lines on her forehead as she waited. "Is she coming out of it?"

"Now remember, we don't want her to wake up just yet." The doctor seemed nervous, like there was something big he wasn't ready to tell them. "Her brain is still swollen ... so it's very important that she lays still until we see most of that cleared up." He talked about the possibilities, the way he had every time he'd stopped by. Cheyenne had a possible brain injury and her spinal cord had been damaged enough that she might have partial paralysis. Beyond that there was the possibility that her lacerated liver might quit working, sending her into immediate shock and perhaps death.

The possibilities.

Cody took a deep breath and held it for a few seconds. As he released it, he looked at Cheyenne. Her face was full, still battered from the effects of the crash. The fact that she was still alive was a miracle — they'd been told that a number of times. But still he believed. "She's in there," he turned to the doctor. "She can hear us when we talk to her. I think her brain's going to be fine."

"It may be." He nodded, quick to agree. "We'll keep monitoring her. I've scheduled another CAT scan for mid-afternoon today."

With that the man moved on. Another ICU patient, another life interrupted just down the hall. Cody watched the man go, grateful this wasn't his job — working around tragedy every day of the week. If it were, his flashbacks from Iraq would never go away. He turned to Tara. "What do you think?"

She looked at Cheyenne. "Do you hear him, baby girl? He wants to know what I think." Tara stroked Cheyenne's thin hand and leaned over the bedrail a bit. "But you already know, don't you? I think you're going to hurry up and get better so you can get out of this hospital bed and back to school. Where you belong."

Cody smiled. Even here in the face of disaster, Tara had a faith that defied logic. God was with them ... Cheyenne would be fine.

"Art would want you to fight, Chey. So you keep fighting." Tara looked pointedly at Cody. "And what do you think, Mr. Cody?"

"I agree." He nodded and stood, looking down at his friend. "Cheyenne's going to come out of this, and we'll cheer her on when she does."

"Exactly." She fell quiet for a few minutes, and that's when Cody knew the truth. Because Tara was never quiet. Her silence now could only mean one thing — that deep down she was worried. Maybe far more than she let on."

"You have feelings for her, don't you?" Tara let five minutes pass before she sat back in her chair and directed the question at Cody.

With Tara, there was really only one right way to answer the question. Especially in light of how much she cared for Cheyenne. "Of course." Cody stared at the beautiful girl in the hospital bed. "She's one of the kindest girls I know."

Tara squinted, trying to see to a place in Cody's soul that had always been off limits. "So what is it ... what holds you back?"

"Maybe it's Art." Cody sighed, too tired to find a way to turn the conversation back to something safer. "She was in love with him, after all." He hesitated. "Maybe she still is."

"That's horseradish and you know it." Tara waved a frustrated hand in his direction. "Art's happier than ever up in heaven with the good Lord. Last thing he'd want is Chey living down here all alone without him." She crossed her arms again. "Chey's moved on ... I know that."

Cody remembered that Cheyenne had boxed up Art's things ... so maybe Tara was right. Which meant what? That the hold-up was his? He kept his eyes on Cheyenne, so Tara couldn't see through him, to the real reason why he hadn't allowed himself to feel more than friendship for her. "It's complicated, Tara." He met her eyes briefly. "Life can be very complicated."

He was about to explain that he'd had a life too, before he met Cheyenne. But before he could say anything there was a sound at the door. Cody turned and in an instant his heart fell to his shoes. He stood, and her name was the slightest whisper on his lips. "Bailey ..."

Tara followed his stare, but Cody was barely aware of anyone but the girl standing at the doorway. The girl who still took his breath with a single look. He stood and slowly he walked to her. For a long time they stared at each other, their eyes remembering everything the way it had been between them. Then he hugged her — a quick embrace that felt unnatural. Like their bodies had forgotten there was ever anything between them. "How ... how did you find me?"

She held a shoebox in one hand, and with the other she brushed a section of her long hair back from her face. With a quick look at the girl in the bed, she met Cody's gaze. "I visited your mom today." She paused, her eyes locked on his, but all he could see there was the concern she must've felt for Cheyenne. Beyond that her heart was no longer available to him the way it had been when they first saw each other. "She told me what happened ... and where you were."

They couldn't have this conversation here. Cody looked back at Tara and found her watching them, one eyebrow raised. He had never explained Bailey to Tara, and now he chided himself for the fact. Either way, he would have to tell her later. For now he needed to talk to Bailey. He motioned for her to follow him into the room, and she did. "Tara, this is Bailey ... she's a ... a longtime friend of mine." *Longtime friend* ... the words felt like glass on his tongue. How had Bailey gone from being the girl of his dreams to a longtime friend? He let the moment pass as he looked back at Bailey. "This is Tara, my buddy Art's mother."

The two said hello to each other, and then Tara nodded at the door. "Go ahead, Cody. Go talk. I'll be here."

"Okay." He could've hugged her. But instead he nodded. "I won't be long."

"Take your time." Again she raised her brow, but her tone was kind like always. Even so her expression let Cody know without a doubt they'd talk about this later. She smiled, as if she remembered she hadn't smiled once since Bailey walked in the room. Again she waved them toward the door. "Go ... go on. Looks like you two have lots to catch up on."

Bailey thanked Tara, and Cody led the way out of the room and down the hall. "There's a private waiting area at the end of the

hall." Cody had sat there a few times since Cheyenne's accident. When he needed a quiet place to pray so he wouldn't go crazy with worry for her.

Once they were inside, Cody faced her, his eyes searching hers. "You're here . . . I can't believe you're here."

Like before, she refused him her eyes. She looked at the box in her hands, but when she turned to him, she caught his eyes only briefly. "I'm moving to New York."

"What?" Cody felt the ground beneath him shift, like the carpeted floor was no longer sturdy enough to hold him. "When?"

"Tomorrow." Guilt was written across her face, and again she looked briefly away. Down at her feet this time. "I won a part in the show *Hairspray*. I'll be living and working on Broadway." Her tone held none of the thrill that must've been a tremendous part of her recent days. Like she was merely conveying a dry set of stats to a casual acquaintance. As if she intended only a few minutes' conversation before she'd be on her way. "We start rehearsals in a few weeks." She looked at him again, but still with the coolness of a stranger. "Here." She held up the box. "I brought you this. Things I found when I was packing."

He took the box and opened it. But after only a few seconds, he knew he couldn't do this, couldn't sort through the box and look at things that had once held great meaning for the two of them. Not while she seemed to be pretending they'd never been close at all. He set the shoebox and the lid on the nearby vinyl sofa and turned to her. "Bailey, . . . look at me."

She did, but only with the greatest reluctance. "This doesn't have to take long . . . it's okay, Cody." She narrowed her eyes, refusing to linger anywhere near his. "She needs you."

Understanding dawned on him. So that was it . . . Bailey was upset about Cheyenne. "She does." He hesitated. "But what about you, Bailey?" For the first time since she'd arrived, he let his tone show a little of the hurt he'd felt in the last few weeks. "Did you and Brandon Paul already say your goodbyes?"

An exaggerated exhale sounded on her lips and she crossed her arms. "I don't want to fight. That's not why I came."

"Then why?" He took a step closer and tried to take her hand. But she folded her arms just as he was about to touch her. His hurt and frustration doubled. "Bailey, don't do this."

"It's too late." She looked uncomfortable, like she didn't want to draw out this moment more than she absolutely had to.

"You don't think that. Otherwise you would've mailed the box."

She leaned back against the door and looked away, at an ocean landscape that hung on the sidewall. "I didn't want to mail it." Gradually, like ice melting on an April day, the stonewall she'd brought in with her, the one around her heart, began to crumble. "I wanted to see you."

"Bailey,..." He touched her arm, just the lightest brush of his fingers against her skin. "Come here. Please."

She held her ground, brought her fingers to her face and hung her head. "I never ... I never wanted it to end like this." Once more her eyes met his, but not long enough for him to read her. "You told me you'd be my friend ... that you'd try. But ..." She lowered her hand, defeated. For the first time since she'd shown up, tears flooded her eyes. "You haven't called, Cody ... you haven't tried."

How could he tell her that he never planned to call? That his mother's boyfriend was a gun-wielding drug dealer, and back then if she'd shown up somewhere with Cody, they both could've been killed. Now she was dating Brandon Paul ... he'd seen proof of that himself. The whole situation was a mess. "I told you ... our worlds are different."

"And I told you it didn't matter." Her voice rose and she let out a loud breath, clearly trying to compose herself. "All this time, Cody? Really? That's all I mattered to you?"

Cody hadn't expected this, couldn't have seen it coming. "I figured you were busy ... the movie and the premiere and Brand—"

"No! Stop it!" This time she didn't try to quiet her voice. She walked straight up to him, her eyes blazing anger. "I told you, Cody. We stood there outside that prison in the snow and I told you I loved you." Saying the words again, even repeating them for the sake of the story, seemed to break her. Her anger remained, but now her heartache was obvious. Tears fell onto her cheeks and her voice was softer, pinched with everything she must've felt these past four months. "I've never said that to anyone but you."

The realization of what he'd done to her, how his silence had hurt her since January hit him full force. He had intended to let her go, planned on staying away from her for her sake. But he hadn't told her that. He closed his eyes and hung his head, and for a long while he rubbed the back of his neck. When he lifted his head, she was looking at him, and when their eyes met the walls were gone completely. "I'm sorry."

"Why?" She wasn't pretending anymore, but she was still very upset. "You told me you loved me too, so how come ... how come I didn't hear from you?" She spun around and walked to the door and for a few seconds it looked like she might leave without a goodbye. But instead she whipped around and came back to him. "Did you think I wouldn't miss you?" Her eyes blazed and he couldn't see where her pain ended and her fury began. "I told God I'd be patient, I'd wait for Him to work in your heart ... so you would know you were all I ever needed. But no!" She was crying harder now, and she wiped her cheeks lightly with the back of her hands. "I just ..." She threw her hands in the air and let them fall to her sides. "I don't get it, Cody. I can't understand."

He hadn't said much, and the more she shared her heart the less he had to say. He could remind her again that she had Brandon, but there was no point now. The damage was done ... they'd both moved on to some extent. He came to her, touched her arm once more, and this time his fingers found hers. "I still love you, Bailey ... I do." He took hold of her hand and for this one last time she let him.

"Don't play with my heart." She whispered the words, and her eyes looked deep into his, past this moment to that long ago place where they had first connected. "Never mind about Brandon ... you know how I feel, Cody. Please." She tightened her fingers around his.

"You're right." His words were quiet, like flags of surrender. "I thought you were better off without me and ... maybe I was wrong." He couldn't take his eyes off her, couldn't help but wonder what might've happened if it hadn't been for the drug dealer's threats or his mom's latest arrest. Or if he wouldn't have cared about all that.

Bailey groaned and wiped her eyes again. She seemed to have found at least some of her composure. She withdrew her hand and crossed her arms. "This meeting ... it wasn't supposed to go like this." She waved her hand toward the waiting room door. "I didn't know about ... about Cheyenne. Not until I talked to your mom."

She didn't ask, but Cody felt the need to clear things up where Cheyenne was concerned. "We're friends, Bailey ... nothing more."

For a long few seconds, she only looked at him. Right at him. Then she looked off again and shrugged one shoulder, a sad sort of shrug. "You're here aren't you?"

"Bailey ..."

"I'm not saying you shouldn't be. That's fine." Sincerity rang in her tone, because she cared about the tragedy at hand. Bailey was nothing if not deeply caring. "I'm very ... very sorry about the accident."

He couldn't think of anything to say, anything that would

make the strain between them lessen. But there was a question he needed to ask ... just so he'd know where her heart was. "You and Brandon ... is that ... is it serious?"

For a few seconds she said nothing, just looked up at him, the way only she could do. "Not yet." She was only inches from him, but she looked closed off again. "It could be, I guess. We're ... we're talking." She nodded to the door again. "And Cheyenne ... you have to be here for her."

He could do nothing but agree on that point. "I am." Never mind that Cheyenne might never wake up, or if she did she might never be the same. That wasn't the point.

"Anyway ... I need to go. I have to get back home."

Panic welled inside him. She couldn't leave yet ... she'd just gotten here. And now things felt worse between them — like they were dating other people and maybe this might be the last time they saw each other. Even if none of that was true, it felt that way. "What about the box ... can I look at it ... do you have a minute?"

"I don't." She was already pulling away. She glanced a few times at the door. "I have to go, Cody."

He felt more defeated than at any time in his life. "Can I ask you something?" She waited, and he took her silence as a yes. "How did you think this was going to go? You coming here?"

The hurt in her eyes was so great he felt it as a physical blow. "I didn't know about Cheyenne."

"But you have Brandon ..." Again, he didn't want to argue with her, but the truth remained. "So tell me, Bailey ..." he kept his tone kind, his voice softer than before. He reached for her hands and like before she didn't pull away. "Tell me. How did you picture it?"

Seconds passed and he could almost read her eyes. But not like before. "I don't know." Her anger was gone, and in its place a resignation. Their time was coming to a close. The only thing left to say was goodbye.

He took a chance, mainly because he didn't have more than a minute or so. Without asking her or doubting himself or the wisdom in whether he should leave her this way, he drew her slowly to himself. "Please, Bailey ... let me hold you." He whispered the words against her face, her hair.

And this last time she came to him. She eased her arms around his waist and he wrapped his around her shoulders. Whatever ways she had wanted to keep her distance during this visit, she was no longer able. It was the only redeeming aspect of her visit so far. "No matter how things look ..." he breathed against her hair, his words quiet, straight from his heart to hers. "I'm sorry. I didn't know ... how much it mattered to you."

"How much *you* mattered." She pressed her head against his chest, the way she'd done the last time they were together in January. "I won't forget you ..."

Cody wasn't sure how long they stayed like that, but neither of them said anything. What could they say? There were no promises to make, no pronouncements of friendship or future visits. She was moving to New York. Their time for friendship had passed. But here ... in a brightly lit hospital waiting room, Cody held onto her as long as she would stay in his arms.

She must've felt the same way, because minutes passed and still she held him. When she finally pulled back, her eyes were the same ones he'd loved since she was a senior in high school. "Goodbye, Cody." Her voice was barely loud enough to hear. She smiled, ignoring the new tears in her eyes. "You know how to reach me."

He wanted to kiss her, wanted to put his hands alongside her face and show her how much he still cared — how much he would always care. But she deserved better than a rushed kiss in her hour of goodbye. Instead he slowly stepped back, his eyes never leaving hers. "Knock 'em dead on Broadway, Bailey. I know you will."

"Thanks." Her smile was as familiar as his own heartbeat.

"By the way ... you were amazing in *Unlocked*."

"You saw it?" She had one hand on the door already.

He hesitated, hoping she could see in his face everything he couldn't say. "Of course I saw it. I loved it."

"Well ... thanks." Her smile died. "I've got to go."

"Bailey, ... please." He wasn't sure what he wanted her to do. Clearly she had to go, but the idea of watching her walk away now was more than he could bear.

"Goodbye, Cody." She came to him in a rush then, and hugged him one last time. As she did, her body trembled against his, the emotions too much for them. This time when she pulled back, she said nothing. Just looked straight at him for a long moment, and then opened the door and walked out.

Cody stared at the place where she'd just stood. Maybe he should run after her ... tell her how wrong he'd been. They could make things work, no matter what his past held, because what did it matter, anyway? No one would ever love her the way he did. But he couldn't bring himself to make a move.

Not here. Not in this season of their lives. She was grown up — leaving Indiana, heading off to New York where she needed to make her way in life. Down the road, he would find her again ... look her up and see if Brandon was still in the picture or if by some miracle of God she still loved a football player she'd watched grow up ... a guy who had come back from the war for her alone.

Cody smiled, despite the aching emptiness in his heart. Whether she knew it or not, Bailey had left him with more than whatever was in the shoebox. She'd left him this: In their final minute together she had held back nothing. Her eyes had told him everything he had only guessed at since January. The look was something he would hold onto forever, a memory that would never dim. Because no matter what she thought about Brandon, or how much time had passed, or how hurt she was about

Cheyenne, the truth was clear in her eyes. As clear as the water in Lake Monroe. Her eyes told him that she hadn't only loved him back then. She loved him now.

The way she just might love him forever.

Twenty-Six

THE FEEL OF CODY'S ARMS AROUND HER STAYED WITH BAILEY ON the drive home and through the barbecue with her family, and long into the night. They hadn't cleared anything up, really. He had no explanation for why he hadn't called, and there were complications now that hadn't been there before. His friendship with Cheyenne, and hers with Brandon Paul.

But all of that paled to how it felt simply to be with him.

His question haunted her — how had she expected their time together to go? Once she knew that Cody was holding vigil at the hospital with Cheyenne, she certainly couldn't have expected it to be a reunion ... or a rekindling. But she'd gone anyway, walked into a situation that was in some ways a guaranteed heartache.

She understood the answer better now, after a night's sleep. She wanted something like a scene from a movie. He would tell her he had no interest in Cheyenne and she would say the same about Brandon. They would hug and hold onto each other, and promise each other that they'd never say goodbye again — no matter how far apart they might live for a year or two.

But the thing about movies was this: People paid money to watch scenes like that on a big screen, because they never played out that way in person.

No matter what they might've said to each other, the truth wasn't going anywhere. He had feelings for Cheyenne — even if he couldn't quite define them. And it was the same for her and Brandon. Otherwise she wouldn't feel giddy every time he texted her. Whatever separate roads their hearts had set out on, they each needed to finish the journey ... see where it took them.

And maybe somewhere down the road, they'd find each other again.

It was Sunday morning and her family was headed back from church. Home to load up her suitcases and say their final good-byes. She stared out the window of her parents' Suburban and recognized the quiet around her. As if no one wanted to state the obvious — that this might be their last day together as a family for a very long time. Their last day of a childhood that had been beyond amazing. The sort of childhood other people only dream about.

From the backseat there was no joking or teasing, no casual conversation about the practices in the coming week or who was taking who in the draft or what homework assignments loomed. She heard the slightest sniffling and she turned to see Ricky, sitting in the middle of the backseat between Justin and Shawn. Ricky's face was red with quiet tears ... Ricky who had struggled with his own health a few years back, and who was always the one quick with a joke or an opinion.

He caught her looking at him, and he smiled ... even as his face scrunched up with another stream of tears. He shook his head, as if to say he couldn't talk, couldn't say anything. Not here with everyone all around. She returned the smile and glanced at Shawn, and then Justin. They weren't crying, but they each made eye contact with her and held it for a few seconds.

She sat between Connor and BJ, and it was clear the youngest of her Haitian brothers was feeling this goodbye like everyone else, because he only stared out the window. Connor reached for her hand and squeezed it. No words were ever needed with Connor. He had been her best friend as far back as she could remember. Saying goodbye to him would be hardest of all.

They parked and climbed out of the car, and her dad was the first to speak. "I'll load the suitcases."

"Thanks." Bailey and her mom had taken care of every detail. There was nothing left to do but say goodbye. She checked her purse, making sure she had her wallet and her cell phone. "You've got the boarding passes, right mom?"

"I do." Her mother was struggling, same as all of them. "We should probably get on the road."

The boys had homework — even if they didn't talk about it — so only her dad and Connor were riding with them to the airport. As Justin and Shawn helped with the last two suitcases, everyone gathered alongside the Suburban, and their dad cleared his throat. He hadn't talked about how hard this was for him — watching his only daughter leave home. But the sorrow in his eyes said it all. "Let's hold hands." He looked at her, his smile assuring her that no matter how difficult this was, he was happy for her.

Slowly the boys joined hands, all of them delaying the goodbye that was coming. When they were in a tight circle, shoulder to shoulder, their father began. "Lord, you're in this move Bailey is making, and we thank you for that. She's leaving, yes ... but she's not leaving alone."

This time the sniffles came from several of the boys. Bailey could hear it, but she didn't want to look. Otherwise she might change her mind and stay here — where she was loved and where danger and uncertainty didn't lurk around every corner.

Her dad continued. "She's not leaving alone because you go with her." There was a catch in his voice. "And we see proof of that with the way you arranged her housing. Thank you for this couple — the Owens. And we pray Bailey will learn much living with them." He hesitated, and clearly he was fighting back tears, fighting to keep control.

The sound of his sadness sent Bailey over the edge, and the

tears came. They came in streams down her face, and she did nothing to stop them while her father kept praying.

"You gave us Bailey twenty-one years ago and you trusted us to raise her. Now ... now we trust you to take her from here. Please, God ... keep her safe. Keep her eyes on you. And bring us back together again someday soon." He sniffed once. "In Jesus' name, amen."

Bailey opened her eyes and looked at her brothers. All of them were crying except Connor — who was standing awkwardly by the car door. His turn was coming ... an hour from now at the Indianapolis Airport. Bailey could barely see for her tears, but she smiled at the boys. "I'll miss you. All of you."

They nodded, and Justin wiped his fist across his cheek. He made a sound that was more laugh than cry. "Just get it over with, Bailey ... I can't do this."

"Me, either." She appreciated his honesty and the light moment it provided for all of them. He was standing closest to her, so she went to him first. "Bye, Justin ... text me, okay?"

He nodded. Then he put his muscled arm around her and held her like he'd never done before. Like he would've done anything to keep this moment from happening. "I love you," he whispered.

"I love you, too." She made her way to BJ, and though their goodbye wasn't as emotional, she had a feeling he would cry himself to sleep that night. He had told her yesterday after dinner that their family would never be the same with her gone. That was all she'd needed to hear from him.

Shawn promised to Skype with her, and like with the other boys, they exchanged *I love you*'s. Ricky was last — her little brother. At six foot, he was all legs and puppy dog eyes, his big feet giving him the appearance of a human *L*. But inside he was still the boy who had undergone heart surgery as an infant, and who was maybe the most tenderhearted of the Flanigan boys ever since. He threw his arms around her neck and held on.

"Buddy ... we need to get going." Their dad's voice was kind.

Ricky nodded, but he was crying too hard to talk. As he pulled back, he mouthed the words, "I love you so much."

"I love you, Ricky." Bailey's tears were making her T-shirt wet, but she didn't care. In some ways, saying goodbye to Ricky was harder in its own unique way. He was only thirteen. Depending on where life took her from here, he could spend the rest of his growing up years without his sister living under the same roof. It was the way of life, but it broke Bailey's heart all the same.

Finally, it was time to go. Bailey would be back, of course. There would be breaks in the schedule, and anything could happen on Broadway. Producers closed shows all the time. But that didn't change the significance of the moment.

As they drove down the driveway, Bailey looked back once more at her brothers, all of them lined up, waving at her. A million memories flashed in her mind, times she would take with her always. All the mornings waking up in her room, and the laughter around the breakfast and dinner table ... every football game on TV or family game night ... all of it was behind her now.

She watched them until her dad turned the corner, and the house and her childhood faded from view.

The drive went too quickly, and along the way Connor shared his iPod with her, playing songs they both loved and making her laugh the way he always had. As if this were only a trip to pick up their aunt from Texas or a drive to her father's training facility. But all too soon they were at the airport, and they were forced into a final round of goodbyes.

Her dad went first. He hugged her and stroked the back of her head. "You'll always be my little girl, Bailey." He didn't try to hold back his tears this time. They filled his eyes and fell onto his rugged face. "A part of me wants to beg you not to go." He blinked, struggling to see her. "But I can't do that. You're ready." He brushed away her tears with his thumb. "No matter how hard this is, you're ready." He hugged her again. "Be the brightest light on Broadway, sweetheart." He took a step back, and he put his hand over his heart. Like she was taking a piece of him with her. "I'll leave the light on, okay?"

"Okay." She watched him hug her mother goodbye, and the two of them talked about the details. When they would arrive, and how she would be sure to call him when they got there safely.

Bailey turned to Connor. He had laughed with her right until the moment they pulled up at the airport drop-off. And even now … his hands tucked in his pockets … Connor didn't cry. He held his arms out to her and pulled her close.

This was the hardest part of all — the fact that she wouldn't have Connor there. And suddenly in a rush the finality of the goodbye, the transition between all they'd known growing up together and the uncertainties of tomorrow loomed like the greatest hurt she'd ever felt. Sobs wracked her body and she clung to him, as if by holding on she might find a way to turn back the clock. Even for one more day.

"I can't … believe … you're so strong." She was getting tears on his sweatshirt, but neither of them cared. He didn't answer her, so she wiped at her tears and looked up at him. Only then did she see how difficult this was for Connor too. He was crying as hard as any of them. Maybe harder.

He kissed her cheek and took a step back. His eyes told her that he loved her and he wanted to go with her, and he couldn't imagine finishing up his last two years of high school without her. Couldn't imagine the long Friday nights without swapping movie lines or watching the latest funny video on YouTube.

But he only smiled at her through his tears and nodded at her. Nodded as if to say she was doing the right thing. She'd found her dream, and she needed to follow it. He raised his hand and waved

once, his eyes so like hers. Then he climbed into the passenger seat of the Suburban and brought his fist to his face. Their dad was already at the wheel, and with Connor's door shut, the two of them drove off.

Bailey waved until they were gone, and then she fell into her mom's arms and the two of them stayed that way nearly a minute, until they were composed enough to head inside and check in. Then and through the security line, and even as they took their seats on the plane, she and her mom said very little. Their goodbye was still days off, and for now both of them were too sad to talk about the significance of this moment.

The way it marked the end of her growing up years.

She took the window seat, and her mom sat in the middle. They leaned on each other, and when she saw tears on her mom's cheeks, Bailey held her hand until the sadness passed. It was like her mother had told her yesterday: Everyone in her family was happy for her — thrilled, even. She was going to do what she was born to do.

But that didn't make it easier to say goodbye.

Bailey looked out the window as the plane took off and headed east. Her mom leaned back, her eyes closed ... emotionally drained from all the leaving. But Bailey couldn't sleep. Eventually her cheeks dried, and her skin felt tight from so many tears. Her nose was still stuffy, but a realization dawned on her.

It's really happening ... Dear God, You've opened this door and now it's my time to walk through it. How great You are, Father ... to trust me with this chance.

I am with you always, Daughter ... No matter how far.

The voice spread peace through her heart and soul, and made her smile. Yes, she would miss her family. There would no doubt be nights when she cried herself to sleep like BJ was bound to do. But that didn't change the fact that this coming time in New York was a gift from God. Bailey breathed in slowly and looked out the window again. As she exhaled, she thought about the guys in her life.

Brandon Paul ... and Cody, of course.

Always Cody.

She had no idea what would happen with them, or who would follow after her once she reached New York City. No idea who she would love in the years to come. But she knew this much — God had great plans for her life. Jeremiah 29:11 promised her that. And, even more, she could rest in the fact that God was in control. He would soothe her heart when she missed her family, and He would help her give her heart to the right guy ... all in His perfect timing. For now, He would give her the ability and stamina to start rehearsals for *Hairspray* and do the one thing her father had asked of her.

Be the brightest light on Broadway.

Bailey felt the excitement rising within her, and suddenly — more than the missing and sadness and saying goodbye, she was consumed by a single thought.

She couldn't wait for the adventure to begin.

Read an excerpt from the next book
in the Bailey Flanigan Series: *Learning*. Coming soon!

Learning

TWENTY-FOUR HOURS HAD PASSED SINCE BAILEY STOPPED BY the hospital to tell Cody goodbye. A full day of wondering and remembering and missing Bailey more than he could put into words. But none of that changed the reality of his situation. He was sitting bedside with Cheyenne, praying for her and pleading with God to save her life.

The machines around her whirred and beeped and reminded him that she was still alive. But everything was tenuous ... her condition, her prognosis. Her future. Cody shifted in the chair and looked around. It was a new hospital, and the room had a sofa sleeper against one wall. Tara had gone home for the night, but Cody had stayed. Someone had to be here if she woke up. When she woke up.

Cody had brought his guitar — something he hoped might make a difference in bringing Cheyenne around. He wasn't very good, and he still knew only a couple songs. But they were songs that spoke of God's faithfulness, His mercy and grace. If Cheyenne could hear ... if any part of her was still connected to the world around them, then these songs would help. Cody was sure. Besides, he had told her that he was playing the guitar a little. They'd texted about it the day before her accident. Cody still had the texts.

So that means you'll play for me one of these days, right?

He'd laughed at the time, and his response hadn't promised anything. *I better practice first.*

Don't practice. Just play the way you play. All music is beautiful, Cody.

It was that last line ... *all music is beautiful* ... that convinced him to bring his guitar to the hospital. He'd had time to rush home after her crash and bring a few things to the hospital. He'd gone home since then to change clothes and shower, to prepare for work and coaching. But otherwise he was here. Last night — after Bailey's goodbye — he even slept here.

Because if he went home with the box of things Bailey gave him, if he looked through the box and remembered every good and wonderful thing about being with Bailey, he might never come back. Why be here when Cheyenne woke up if he didn't have feelings for her, if he wasn't going to be here through her recovery and maybe afterwards? But the truth was something he was still grabbing hold of. Once again, Bailey was dating someone else — this time Hollywood's most popular actor. He couldn't compete with Brandon Paul ... he wouldn't try.

Instead he kept reminding himself what Tara had told him, Tara who had once a long time ago dreamed about having Cheyenne as a daughter-in-law. *Maybe God saved you from Iraq for Cheyenne ... have you thought about it?* Cody stared at the beautiful girl in the bed, at her peaceful expression and the way her body lay so perfectly still. Maybe Tara was right. It was all he could think about, and so he hadn't gone home last night. He'd stayed right here beside Cheyenne, sleeping when he needed to, and otherwise praying.

Cody stood and stretched. Tara would be coming soon. She had called and told him that after church she would be by for a few hours. This ordeal had to be so hard on her. She'd lost her son, and now the young woman who would've married him was

fighting for her life. The room was quiet other than the sound of the machines. Cody walked to the place a few feet away where his guitar stood and he picked it up.

If she wanted to hear him play, he would play. And never mind that he wasn't all that good. He sat down at her bedside again and found the right chords. The song was an old one, something he'd heard in chapel every now and then while he was serving overseas. The music filled the room, and Cody was surprised. It didn't sound half bad. "Great is thy faithfulness ... Oh, God my Father ... there is no shadow of turning with thee ..."

The doctor had explained that when Cheyenne woke up she might not remember him. She could have amnesia or any number of brain injury symptoms. Her list of damaged body parts was long and frightening. The impact of the truck hitting her broadside as it ran the red light had slammed her head against the inside door frame. The swelling in her brain had stopped, but there was no way to tell just how damaged her cognitive functions might be.

In addition, she'd received a laceration across her liver and internal bleeding. Emergency surgery her first day in the hospital had stopped that and stabilized her, but there was no telling exactly what the long-term damage to her organs might be. She had also broken her lower right leg, broken her ankle, and fractured her wrist. She would likely need surgery to repair the broken leg, and possibly surgery on her back as well.

Cody kept singing. There was something stripped down and raw about the hymn, its message painfully honest. No matter what a person might go through, God was faithful. He was merciful and loving ... and His abundance was new again every morning. Like he'd once heard Bailey's father, Jim Flanigan, say: "We can have as much of God as we want."

Cody needed a lot of Him right now. He closed his eyes and

his song filled the room. "All I have needed, thy hand hath provided ... great is thy faithfulness, Lord, unto me."

He finished that last line and was just about to head into the chorus when Cheyenne moved. Not a lot or with any sound, but her fingers flexed, and then her arm shifted a few inches on the blanket. Cody breathed sharply and set his guitar down at his side. "Cheyenne ... It's Cody. Can you hear me?"

Again she moved, and this time she winced. Cody sat up straighter, his heart thudding hard inside him. If she could feel pain ... if she could respond like that, then she had to be better off than they thought, right? "Cheyenne ... I'm here."

She breathed in deeper than before, deeper than she'd breathed since she'd been in here. She was responding to his voice! She had to be. Slowly, like someone coming out of a winter-long trance, Cheyenne tried to blink, tried three times before her eyes opened just the slightest.

Cody looked over his shoulder at the door to her hospital room. Should he call for the nurse ... tell them what was happening? He looked back at Cheyenne and decided to wait. Better to put his full attention on her right now and not worry about what the doctors would say, what tests they might want to run now that she was showing signs of consciousness. At least for the first few minutes.

More blinking, more movement — and again she made an expression that showed how much pain she was in. "Cheyenne ... I'm here." He stood and leaned over the bed, touching her healthy hand with the lightest sensation. "It's Cody ... can you hear me?"

Cheyenne turned her head so slowly it was almost hard to tell she was moving at all. But she did move, and this time she blinked a little faster than before and her eyes remained open. As they did, she looked right at him and their eyes held. Cody hadn't known her very long, but he knew her well enough to be absolutely sure about this — Cheyenne remembered him. Her eyes searched his, and she seemed to have a hundred things to say.

"Can you talk, Chey?" He didn't want to push her, but he was desperate to know exactly how much of her might come back ... her mind, her intelligence, her kindness ... her love for God and people.

She moved her mouth a few times and then closed her eyes, clearly exhausted.

"Don't work too hard. It's okay. You don't have to say anything. As long as you can understand me."

Again she opened her eyes and looked straight at him, and in a way that was unmistakable, she nodded. Yes ... she could hear him. She understood. Another blink and the slightest sound came from her throat.

"Are you trying to talk?"

She nodded again.

"It's okay ... You can talk later. You're very tired ... don't overdo it." Once more he wondered if he should call for the nurse. But she looked a little more uncomfortable than before, so he let her have this moment. He soothed his hand gently over her dark hair. "Does it hurt ... are you in pain?" His voice was soft, his tone quiet so she wouldn't feel startled.

A sigh came from her and she nodded again. But then the corners of her mouth lifted just a little and a hint of the familiar sparkle danced in her eyes. Almost as if to say, Of course it hurts. But none of that mattered as long as she was alive.

Still, again she opened her mouth, and this time in a scratchy whisper she began to speak. "Cody ..."

She knew his name!

A fierce sense of protection and caring came over him. This precious girl had been through so much, so many seasons of heartache. How could she face the days ahead without someone who looked out for her, who understood and appreciated her?

He ran his thumb over her brow. "I'm here for you ... I'll stay no matter what."

Peace filled in the pained lines on her forehead and she nodded, more slowly this time. Her eyes looked deep into his soul, to the places that might've doubted the wisdom of being here. "Please ... stay."

"I will." Cody felt the commitment to the outer edges of his heart. He put his hand alongside her face, speaking close to her, directly to her lonely soul. "You have my word, Chey ... I'm not going anywhere."

(To be Continued — June 2011)

READER LETTER

Dear Reader Friends,

When I wrote about Bailey Flanigan for the first time — years ago in the Firstborn series — I never dreamed that one day she would have her own story, her own set of books. Her own series. As most of you know, the character of Bailey Flanigan was inspired by my daughter, Kelsey. In real life there is no Cody Coleman, no Brandon Paul. But the way Kelsey lives for God, her passion for her family, for God's Word, and for His truth are a mainstay in her real life story — the way they are with the fictional character of Bailey.

In addition, Kelsey is the oldest of six kids — the others all boys, three of whom were adopted from Haiti. When I write about Jenny and Jim Flanigan, I am — for the most part — writing about my family. Kelsey and I have the relationship that Bailey and Jenny share: an open communication that has allowed Kelsey to trust me with any conversation, any decision, any heartbreak. I have had the privilege of raising this one-in-a-million girl, and the very great responsibility of seeking God's wisdom in helping shape her into the young woman she is today.

And so, along the years — through five Firstborn books, and four Sunrise series books, and especially during the four books in the Above the Line series — as I watched Kelsey (and Bailey) develop a love for musical theater and a longing for the dreams God has placed in her heart, I could feel the time coming when the character of Bailey would need her own story.

But here's the part I didn't see coming.

As the time drew closer to write the first book in the Bailey

Flanigan Series, Kelsey announced that she wanted to attend university in California — fifteen hundred miles from our home in the Pacific Northwest. That meant that while I was outlining *Leaving*, I was helping Kelsey pack her things, helping her get ready to leave home. (Talk about an intense time of research.)

I remember sitting on my porch one day, feeling like all of life was about to change. I felt heavy with the hurt of actually reaching this season: the season of goodbye. But I also knew that I couldn't end a book called *Leaving* with only sadness. See, there is a joy in knowing that our kids are ready to leave home and become who God made them to be. No matter how sad, it's right that they grow and become ... and yes, sometimes even that they leave.

The story of Bailey has many twists and turns ahead — believe me. The books to come will be *Learning, Longing,* and finally, *Loving.* And I think you'll be amazed at where God takes this fictitious girl in the books ahead. Here's a funny, fictional fact. The books in the Bailey Flanigan Series will release over the next eighteen months. But during that same time, we'll follow Bailey through three years of life.

Ahh, the marvels of storytelling.

Anyway, thanks for joining me on Bailey Flanigan's journey. And, yes, the journey of one more ride with the Baxter Family. Some of you might have seen Landon's lung issues coming. I have to admit, I saw it ... even though I didn't want to write about it. Only God could've given me the strength to take Ashley and Landon through yet another trial. But even with that there is much ahead.

As always, I look forward to your feedback. Take a minute and find me on Facebook. I'm there at least once a day — hanging out with you in my virtual living room, praying for you, and answering as many questions as possible. I have Latte Time, where I'll take a half hour or so, pour all of you a virtual latte, and take questions. We have a blast together, so if you're not on my Facebook fan/friend page, please join me. The group of friends there grows every day, and each of you is very special to me.

You can also visit my website at *www.KarenKingsbury.com.* There you can find my contact information and my guestbook. You could even join the Baxter Family Club — a special set of benefits for those of you who read all my books, pretty much as soon as they hit the shelves! (Just one way I can show how much I care.) Remember, if you post something on Facebook or my website it might help another reader. So please stop by. In addition, I love to hear how God is using these books in your life. He gets all the credit, and He always will. He puts a story in my heart, but He has your face in mind. Only He could do that.

Also on Facebook or my website you can check out my upcoming events and get to know other readers. You can hear about movies being made of my books and become part of a community that agrees there is life-changing power in something as simple as a story. And you can post prayer requests on my website or read those already posted and pray for those in need. If you'd like, you may send in a photo of your loved one serving our country, or let us know of a fallen soldier we can honor on our Fallen Heroes page.

When you're finished with this book, pass it on to someone else. By doing so, you will automatically enter my "Shared a Book" contest. Email me at *contest@KarenKingsbury.com* and tell me the first name of the person you shared with, and you'll be entered to win a summer day with my family. In addition, everyone signed up for my monthly newsletter is automatically entered into an ongoing once-a-month drawing for a free, signed copy of my latest novel.

There are also links on my website that will help you with matters important to many of you: faith and family, adoption, and ways to reach out to others. Of course, on my site you can also find out a little more about me, my faith, my family, and the wonderful world of Life-Changing Fiction™.

Another way to stay in touch is to follow me on Twitter. I give away books all the time, and I'd love to see you there!

Finally, if you gave your life over to God during the reading of this book, or if you found your way back to a faith you'd let grow cold, send me a letter at *Office@KarenKingsbury.com* and write *New Life* in the subject line. I encourage you to connect with a Bible-believing church in your area, and start reading the Bible every day. But if you can't afford one and don't already have one, write *Bible* in the subject line. Tell me how God used this book to change your life, and then include your address in your email. My wonderful publisher Zondervan has supplied me with free paperback copies of the New Testament, so that if you are financially unable to find a Bible any other way, I can send you one. I'll pay for shipping.

One last thing. I've started a program where I will donate a book to any high school or middle school librarian who makes a request. Check out my website for details.

Again, thanks for journeying with me through the pages of this book. I can't wait to hear your feedback on *Leaving*! Oh, and look for Bailey Flanigan's Book No. 2: *Learning* in stores this June. Until then my friends, keep your eyes on the cross.

And don't forget to leave the lights on.

In His light and love,
Karen Kingsbury

www.KarenKingsbury.com

DISCUSSION QUESTIONS

1. What emotions does the word *leaving* stir in your heart? Explain.

2. Do you know anyone who's planning to leave soon? Tell whether they are leaving home or the area or a job ... Tell about that person and what you have observed in this, their season of leaving.

3. What did you learn about leaving by reading this book?

4. Has anything in this story changed the way you view the idea of leaving? Explain.

5. Talk about a special memory you had while growing up.

6. Who from your childhood made the most impact on you? Why?

7. There is a cost to pursuing dreams. What dreams did you have when you were growing up?

8. What sacrifice did you make to accomplish your dreams? Talk about that.

9. Tell about someone you know who sacrificed for their dreams. What were the results of that sacrifice?

10. What have you left along the journey of life? Was leaving that place or person the right choice? Why or why not?

11. If you're new to the Baxter family, you may not know about Ashley and Landon. But from what you do know, what are your thoughts about the love this married couple shares?

12. Do you know anyone whose life was touched by the tragedy of 9 – 11? Explain.

13. Explain Bailey's attitude toward fame. Do you think her attitude is healthy? Why or why not?

14. Brandon is a new Christian in Hollywood. Why do you think it is difficult for Christians to maintain their faith while living in the limelight?

15. What do you think of our nation's fascination with celebrity? How is it a distraction to God's will for us?

Unlocked

A Love Story

Karen Kingsbury,
New York Times *Bestselling Author*

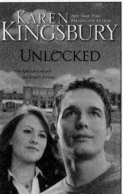

Before You Take a Stand ...
You've Got to Take a Chance.

Holden Harris is an eighteen-year-old locked
in a prison of autism. Despite his quiet ways and quirky behaviors, Holden is very happy and socially normal — on the inside, in a private world all his own. In reality, he is bullied at school by kids who only see that he is very different.

Ella Reynolds is part of the "in" crowd. Star of the high school drama production, her life seems perfect. When she catches Holden listening to her rehearse for the school play, she is drawn to him ... the way he is drawn to the music. Then, Ella makes a dramatic discovery — she and Holden were best friends as children.

Frustrated by the way Holden is bullied, and horrified at the indifference of her peers, Ella decides to take a stand against the most privileged and popular kids at school. Including her boyfriend, Jake.

Ella believes miracles can happen in the unlikeliest places, and that just maybe an entire community might celebrate from the sidelines. But will Holden's praying mother and the efforts of Ella and a cast of theater kids be enough to unlock the prison that contains Holden?

This time, friendship, faith, and the power of a song must be strong enough to open the doors to the miracle Holden needs.

Available in stores and online!

ABOVE THE LINE SERIES

The Above the Line Series follows two dedicated Hollywood producers as they seek to transform the culture through the power of film.

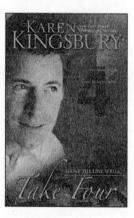

Available in stores and online!

One Tuesday Morning

Karen Kingsbury

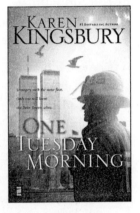

The last thing Jake Bryan knew was the roar of the World Trade Center collapsing on top of him and his fellow firefighters. The man in the hospital bed remembers nothing. Not rushing with his teammates up the stairway of the South Tower to help trapped victims. Not being blasted from the building. And not the woman sitting by his bedside who says she is his wife.

Jamie Bryan will do anything to help her beloved husband regain his memory. But that means helping Jake rediscover the one thing Jamie has never shared with him: his deep faith in God.

Beyond Tuesday Morning

Karen Kingsbury

Winner of the Silver Medallion Book Award

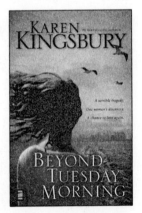

Determined to find meaning in her grief three years after the terrorist attacks on New York City, FDNY widow Jamie Bryan pours her life into volunteer work at a small memorial chapel across from where the Twin Towers once stood. There, unsure and feeling somehow guilty, Jamie opens herself to the possibility of love again.

But in the face of a staggering revelation, only the persistence of a tenacious man, the questions from Jamie's curious young daughter, and the words from her dead husband's journal can move Jamie beyond one Tuesday morning ... toward life.

Shades of Blue

Karen Kingsbury,
New York Times *Bestselling Author*

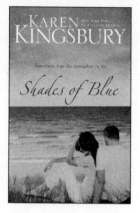

A fairy-tale future. A Checkered past. A decision awaits.

Brad Cutler, twenty-eight, is a rising star at his New York ad agency, about to marry the girl of his dreams. Anyone would agree he has it all — a great career, a beautiful and loving fiancée, and a fairy-tale life ahead of him ... when memories of a high school girlfriend begin to torment him. Lost innocence and one very difficult choice flood his conscience, and he is no longer sure what the future will bring except for this: He must go back to the shores of Holden Beach in search of his first love, and a forgiveness neither of them has ever known.

Three people must work through the repercussions of a decision made long ago before any of them can look toward a new future.

Available in stores and online!

Even Now

Karen Kingsbury

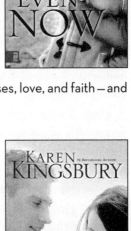

Sometimes hope for the future is found in the ashes of yesterday.

A young woman seeking answers to her heart's deepest questions. A man and woman driven apart by lies and years of separation ... who have never forgotten each other.

With hallmark tenderness and power, Karen Kingsbury weaves a tapestry of lives, losses, love, and faith—and the miracle of resurrection.

Ever After

Karen Kingsbury

2007 Christian Book of the Year

Two couples torn apart—one by war between countries, and one by a war within.

In this moving sequel to *Even Now*, Emily Anderson, now twenty, meets the man who changes everything for her: Army reservist Justin Baker. Their tender relationship, founded on a mutual faith in God and nurtured by their trust and love for each other, proves to be a shining inspiration to everyone they know, especially Emily's reunited birth parents.

But Lauren and Shane still struggle to move past their opposing beliefs about war, politics, and faith. When tragedy strikes, can they set aside their opposing views so that love—God's love—might win, no matter how great the odds?

Available in stores and online!

Between Sundays

Karen Kingsbury,
New York Times *Bestselling Author*

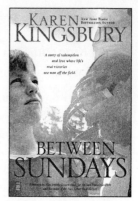

Aaron Hill has it all—athletic good looks and the many privileges of a star quarterback. His Sundays are spent playing NFL football in front of a televised audience of millions. But Aaron's about to receive an unexpected handoff, one that will give him a whole new view of his self-centered life.

Derrick Anderson is a family man who volunteers his time with foster kids while sustaining a long career as a pro football player. But now he's looking for a miracle. He must act as team mentor while still striving for the one thing that matters most this season—keeping a promise he made years ago.

Megan Gunn works two jobs and spends her spare time helping at the youth center. Much of what she does, she does for the one boy for whom she is everything—a foster child whose dying mother left him in Megan's care. Now she wants to adopt him, but one obstacle stands in the way. Her foster son, Cory, is convinced that 49ers quarterback Aaron Hill is his father.

Two men and the game they love. A woman with a heart for the lonely and lost, and a boy who believes the impossible. Thrown together in a season of self-discovery, they're about to learn lessons in character and grace, love and sacrifice.

Because in the end, life isn't defined by what takes place on the first day of the week, but how we live it between Sundays.

Available in stores and online!

Oceans Apart

Karen Kingsbury,
New York Times *Bestselling Author*

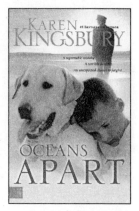

A riveting story of secret sin and the healing power of forgiveness.

Airline pilot Connor Evans and his wife, Michele, seem to be the perfect couple living what looks like a perfect life. Then a plane goes down in the Pacific Ocean. One of the casualties is Kiahna Siefert, a flight attendant Connor knew well. Too well. Kiahna's will is very clear: before her seven-year-old son, Max, can be turned over to the state, he must spend the summer with the father he's never met, the father who doesn't know he exists: Connor Evans.

Now will the presence of one lonely child and the truth he represents destroy Connor's family? Or is it possible that healing and hope might come in the shape of a seven-year-old boy?

Available in stores and online!

ZONDERVAN®
.com

Share Your Thoughts

With the Author: Your comments will be forwarded to the author when you send them to *zauthor@zondervan.com*.

With Zondervan: Submit your review of this book by writing to *zreview@zondervan.com*.

Free Online Resources at
www.zondervan.com

Zondervan AuthorTracker: Be notified whenever your favorite authors publish new books, go on tour, or post an update about what's happening in their lives at www.zondervan.com/authortracker.

Daily Bible Verses and Devotions: Enrich your life with daily Bible verses or devotions that help you start every morning focused on God. Visit www.zondervan.com/newsletters.

Free Email Publications: Sign up for newsletters on Christian living, academic resources, church ministry, fiction, children's resources, and more. Visit www.zondervan.com/newsletters.

Zondervan Bible Search: Find and compare Bible passages in a variety of translations at www.zondervanbiblesearch.com.

Other Benefits: Register yourself to receive online benefits like coupons and special offers, or to participate in research.

ZONDERVAN®

ZONDERVAN.com/
AUTHORTRACKER
follow your favorite authors